SCALES OF INJUSTICE

A Corruption Universe Novel

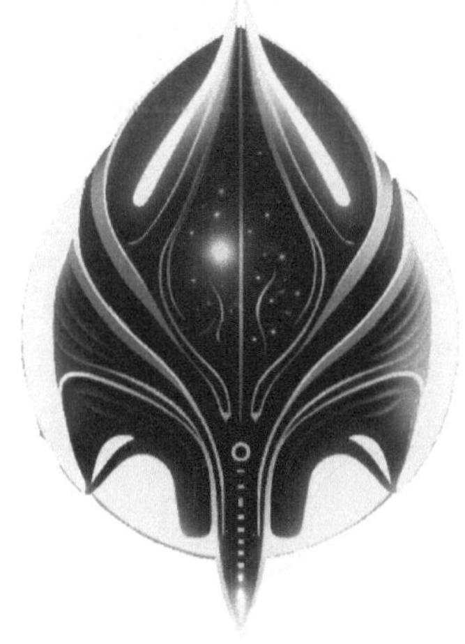

By J.F. Posthumus

Three Ravens Publishing
Chickamauga, GA USA

Table of Contents

Dedication

Dedicated to my eldest son, Chris Wagner.
Who answered all my questions and gave advice and
suggestions.

Ar scáth a chéile a mhaireann na daoine

'til Valhalla, son.

Special Thanks

This story, this series, the entire universe... It belongs to first responders and military vets.

This universe would not, could not, exist without them. The Injustice universe and K'lais in particular were built to show a place where lessons learned about what they deal with, the cracks they witness in the system, and even our society are actually appreciated and acted upon with the same dedication these people show in their callings of duty.

This is for them. These people see the worst humanity has to offer. And they still choose to help.

In duty, we prosper.

Chapter One

Violetta Cq'linns checked the clock built into the interface she held. She quickened her stride, concerned she was going to be late for her meeting with Police Chief Ylvran Me'addn. Her shift at the department had ended over an hour ago, but she hadn't bothered to go home and change. Her home was in the opposite direction of his, and she wanted to be close by. The evidence she had to show him couldn't wait a minute past the time he'd specified.

Only now it looked like she was going to be late after all. She had stopped at an eatery for what she'd hoped was a quick meal. Normally a bowl of che'tck was easy to fix: just slice the fruit and cook it. And for those of mixed heritage like Violetta, toss in some green figs and other Earth ingredients and the result was a simple, delicious meal that any but the most stuck-up native K'laisians would enjoy.

Except tonight must've been training day for "the new guy" because it took forever. Violetta had sat and sat and farking *sat*. As if the news she was bringing to the chief wasn't bad enough, she had this to deal with, too?

Only when she was ready to get up and leave did the bowl finally arrive, steaming hot and smelling so *damned* good! It had felt like a crime to wolf it down without a chance to savor it, but what choice did she have?

She'd left the eatery a few minutes later and wanted to run, but she'd forced herself to move at a quick walk. Not being of pure heritage meant she already stood out from the majority of beings in the city. Her eyes were bronze instead of the gleaming silver or gold. Her hair was dark auburn, often mistaken for black. Completely native

K'laisians had black hair if they had gold eyes, so at a distance she seemed to be a full native. There was no mistaking her for the silver haired, silver eyed, and starkly pale natives that made up the other group of K'laisians.

Out of habit, Violetta looked over her outfit. Once she made sure that her gear was in place, ready for use, and no wrinkles marred the material, she increased her pace to a trot.

She'd built a reputation of professionalism, from the way she dealt with the public to her thoroughness and impartiality during criminal investigations, to the way she dressed. As a result, when she'd come across evidence of corruption within the police service, Chief Me'addn had taken her seriously. He was known as a just being, one who didn't care if those he interacted with were humans, natives, or of mixed heritage.

He'd also known Violetta's father, and he'd welcomed her into the police service in part because of that connection.

Her interface beeped as she reached Chief Me'addn's apartment building. It was a meeting reminder, letting her know she had two minutes to spare. She tucked the interface into her pocket and held up her left hand to the security scanner next to the door.

The system scanned her hand and eyes. Her name appeared on the screen, along with her rank and designation as an officer with homicide of the 42nd District. Once she heard the click of the scan ending, she waited for the Chief to speak to her via intercom.

Instead, the door opened and swung in. She stepped inside and watched the door close behind her. She found the nearest lift and rode it to the fifth floor. When she reached the chief's residence, the security system had already identified her and the door opened even before she reached it. A quick glance around the front room revealed sparse furniture, reading interfaces, but none for video. Recessed lighting showed two doorways leading out. One was lit.

Violetta headed for the lit doorway.

This was a study, workspace, or both. A large military grade screen took up most of the back wall. A small desk with another interface and stacks of data cards. The chair for the desk was laying on the ground.

So was a body.

Violetta ran to the being sprawled on the floor, and began scanning to identify whom it was. Although the sinking in her stomach made her think she already knew.

"Stop where you are! Don't move!"

Violetta looked up from Me'addn's body. She swallowed hard, her eyes zeroing in on the weapon pointed at her. The pistol wasn't wavering in Detective Ziph Rc'dollph's grip. The hard set of his jaw and determined gleam in his eyes spoke louder than his words.

"Don't make me shoot you, Cq'linns," he added when she didn't move.

Bullshit, she thought, using an Earther phrase she'd picked up from her father.

She knew better. Ziph may have been a fellow police officer, but it didn't change the fact he had never liked her and would love the chance to shoot her. It would solve a lot of his problems.

His, and his handlers. Ziph was as crooked as they got.

"Don't do something you'll regret later," Violetta said. "Ylvran was an old family friend. He has more cameras recording everything here than you'd believe."

She didn't know if it was true, but Ziph's eyes flickered around the posh penthouse room. She stood slowly, her hands outstretched, away from her side. No need to push him into squeezing the trigger. Not when she still had a chance of escaping this… setup? It couldn't be anything other than that.

"Your daddy's dead. His name ain't going to save you this time," Ziph snarled. "Can't say I'd regret seeing you there beside the Chief." He paused, and Violetta realized he was listening to someone on a comm-link. He smiled, then raised his pistol. "You were caught in the act. Tried to shoot me and I had to protect myself."

Violetta threw her hands forward, joined at the palms. One hand pointed up, the other downward. A shield made of pure energy shimmered to life the instant Ziph fired his pistol. The shot ricocheted off the shield, pinging loudly in the otherwise-silent room. If she were a pure-blood K'laisian she'd be capable of so much more, but this would have to do.

More energy blasts pinged off her shield as she dove to the side, pulling a volt grenade as she rolled behind the sofa. She yanked the pin, counted off a second, then lobbed the grenade straight at Ziph. It landed at his feet and went off an instant later, before he had a chance to react.

A field of blue and silver sprang from the device, sending electrical charges through Ziph, and disrupting his own weapon. The man's body vibrated and jittered as the electricity shot through him. He screeched, the weapon falling from his hand, unable to grip it as his fingers clenched and loosened with the jolts. It wouldn't affect him for long.

Violetta didn't waste a single second. She rushed him, her shield still active. She'd spent every day since her fifth birthday training for just this moment. She struck him full-force with her shield, bowling him over onto the floor. She continued forward, kicking off what she thought was his groin as she sprang over his prone body.

Despite his armor, Ziph screamed like a little girl and bent in half. She glanced over her shoulder as she raced from the room to see him cradling his crotch while gasping out orders to someone unseen.

Damn it.

Someone had set her up, and they had done a damn good job of it. How in the hox had they known she was going to see the chief tonight?

Fark. Fark. Fark!

Pulling her comm-link from a pocket, she slipped it into her ear. "Frequency 777. Dial Issik. Code Blackguard."

Please, Issik, answer, she thought as she raced down the emergency stairs until she reached the main floor.

The hallway was empty. Instead of going right towards the front entrance, she turned left. The maintenance entrance would be a better option. She doubted anyone would know she'd learned all the ways in and out of a building she'd never been in before, but she was nothing if not thorough.

Always plan for the unexpected. It was a motto Violetta lived by. She'd planned ahead by giving Issik a scrambling device that had once been used by her father. The other had been attached to her own communicator. Military grade, only those with a high enough clearance would be able to decode their conversations.

She'd planned for that, but she hadn't planned for someone murdering the Chief of Police.

This could not only be a stumbling block, it could be her death.

The call finally connected.

"What the ever-loving-fark is going on?" she hissed at Issik Ha'kksworth, her partner with K'lais Police Department.

"Where the hox are you?" he snapped in return.

"A side door to the Chief of Police's apartment." One without an alarm. She opened it and peeked out.

"You need to get out of there fast!"

Not seeing anyone, she slipped out the door and crept her way along the side of the building. Thankfully it was night and clouds were growing thick in the sky. Thunder rumbled. "No shat," Violetta retorted. "What do you think I'm trying to do?"

Perfect, she thought, looking up. *No moon. No stars. Only possible lightning. Oh, and rain. Someone needs to hire new weather forecasters.*

"You need to ditch the comm-link and go underground, Violetta."

Hox. It must be serious for him to call me by my actual name, she thought. Issik never called her 'Violetta'. Usually he called her "Violence" or Vi. Or by her surname.

"What do you suggest, Issik?" Violetta asked, shaking away the old memories.

Staying in the shadows of the building's topiary, she watched as the police cruisers began pulling into the front of the building. They hadn't started moving towards the back, so she continued that way. There was an alley across from the apartment. Her steps quickened as she neared the back of the building. She looked around before racing across the road and into the alley.

She didn't stop there, though. She needed more distance between her and that apartment. It wouldn't take long for an All-Points Bulletin to be sent out. Everyone in her precinct knew what she looked like and it wouldn't take long for her photo to be shared throughout the city. And once the news got hold of it, there'd be nowhere she could hide without fear of recognition.

Issik growled. "You won't like it."

"Too bad for me," she retorted. "Tell me."

"You've got to contact Zane Morelli."

Violetta stopped dead in her tracks. Her eyes shot to the side as her brows furrowed. "Insane Morelli? The 'mob boss'? Are you crazy?"

Issik snorted. "Look. He's the only one in this city who will hear you out and not turn you in. Or put two in your head and throw you in the trash."

Violetta grunted.

"Good. I've got your attention. Tell him I sent you."

"What the fark? Why would he know you, Issik?" She paused, then asked, "How would *you* know *him*?"

"I'm often in communication with Morelli. Have been since I started working here," he replied. "Knew his predecessor."

Damn. He'd been on the force for at least a decade. Maybe longer. He'd always said he was content being a sergeant. Now she knew why.

"You never thought to tell me any of this?"

"Is now the time to have this discussion?"

"How do I find him?" she grudgingly asked, moving again.

A large frigid raindrop splattered on the top of her head. Another fell on her shoulder. The sky opened up as Issik told her how to locate one of Morelli's businesses.

Thankfully, the diner Issik suggested wasn't far from the apartment she'd just left.

All she had to do was get there without being seen.

"Talk to you later, my friend," she said. "You're going to have a lot of questions to answer."

"Just survive long enough to ask them. And remember: *A chi dai il dito si prende anche il braccio*," Issik said. "Be safe."

"Ciao."

Without waiting for another word, Violetta removed the scrambler from her comm-link before dropping said comm to the ground. She destroyed it with her heel, ensuring there was no way to track her. The rain battered down on her as she trotted through the darkness.

With luck, she'd be able to get to the diner before anyone spotted her. After taking the first step, she remembered that her interface could be traced. The handheld device was standard issue from the police service. Cursing under her breath about how the department budgeters were going to hate her, Violetta dropped the device to the street. It took several stomps of her foot to break the interface into uselessness.

Issik's words, a warning, bounced around her head. She couldn't believe she was turning to the biggest criminal in the city for help, but she had no other choice. Not if she wanted to survive. She'd just have to remember Issik's words and keep them close to heart:

"Give them a finger, they'll take an arm."

Chapter Two

The journey took her an hour. Several of the police hovercraft all-environment vehicles, or HAVs, had converged on the Chief's place for a good four blocks, so she'd had to take the extra long way around. That had included crossing a few rooftops and abandoned yards where city cameras were fewer.

Rizzo's was an old diner. A hole-in-the-wall eatery she almost missed. Cocooned between two buildings that vanished into the stormy night sky, it was just wide enough for a door and small sign. There were no robotic door keepers, no blinking scanners demanding identification. Violetta pushed on the door and a bell sounded. She looked up. There was an actual, antique-style bell rattling above the door.

Talk about old school charm. Most of the bars and eateries she frequented were sleek with chrome and steel. Robots gave numbers to tables and orders were placed by interfaces. Robots brought your order to you, unless you went to the fancier establishments that could afford warm- or cold-blooded waitstaff.

This diner was different. The woman behind the counter wore a simple black top with a white apron over it. Dark blonde hair was pulled back into a short ponytail. Embroidered in white, the diner's name could barely be seen around the apron top. The name tag said Betty.

Booths lined the right side of the eatery and a bar stretched along the left near the door, curling around to the side. A door could be seen behind Betty. The bar stools were spaced evenly and secured to the floor. There was a small cubby hole in the back and towards the left, blocked from view by a dividing wall.

Shrugging, Violetta swiped her dripping hair from her face and stood with her body facing the door, close enough to see anyone coming through it, but not so close she'd be spotted from the street.

"What can I get you?" Betty asked.

Lines around the woman's hazel eyes and mouth shifted into appearance as she spoke and Violetta reassessed the woman's age from early twenties to mid-thirties.

Taking another moment to ensure the diner was empty, Violetta answered the question. "I'm Violetta Cq'linns." She paused. "Issik Ha'kksworth sent me to ask for Zane Morelli. I need to see him."

Betty's eyes narrowed. "Cq'linns, you say."

Violetta nodded.

Betty's lips twisted. "Ha'kksworth's partner."

Violetta nodded again.

"There's a price to pay if you wanna see Signore Morelli."

Violetta felt the blood rush from her face. "I… I don't have a lot on me."

"Oh, honey. You misunderstand what's required."

The grimace-like expression on the woman's face melted into a look of sympathy. It was almost kind. Betty held her hand out to Violetta. It seemed an innocent enough offer. Cautiously, Violetta placed her left hand in Betty's outstretched fingers.

With astounding strength and speed, the woman yanked Violetta sideways across the bar. Jerking her arm back around Violetta's back, Betty pinned her to the fake linoleum counter-top.

"What the hox?" Violetta demanded.

She tried getting leverage to push against the weight on her back. Betty shoved down harder, knocking Violetta's breath from her chest. She went limp, lifting her right hand in supplication. Betty let off some of the pressure and Violetta could at least breathe again.

Betty chuckled. "Your old man was something, but he didn't know everything. Not sure if he's rolling over in his grave or beaming in pride right now."

"Leave Dad out of this," Violetta snarled. "What do you want?"

There was a distinct click of a switchblade and Violetta began struggling again. Fear and panic raced through her. Was this it? Did Issik sell her out? Was this woman going to kill her for being a cop not on the take?

"Stop that."

Betty shoved her weight against Violetta's back. Air whooshed out of Violetta's chest again and she slumped against the counter top. The knife dug into her elbow, and what little air she had left escaped in a strangled yelp.

"They don't tell y'all about this gift. The military don't use 'em, especially for those who go off-planet. Too tricky. Too dangerous for anyone to know what those phantoms are doin'."

The knife dug deeper as Betty talked. Violetta gritted her teeth but remained silent. Talking wasn't going to change what was happening. Pleading or bargaining would just make everything worse. Instead, Violetta concentrated on what Betty was doing to her.

"The police, though?" Betty continued. "They like to keep tabs on their people. Bet they told you this was some shot. What did they tell you it was? A vaccine?"

A vaccine. In the elbow.

A memory sprang to life.

She'd just finished her final physical and body scan at the academy. Still in the sterile hospital uniform, a healer and two medics had appeared from nowhere with a syringe. She hadn't seen any of them before, either at the academy hospital or the clinic. Hell, she'd never spotted them anywhere on the academy's grounds.

The shot to the elbow had seemed strange, but they'd claimed it was less painful to take it there than the neck. Her elbow had hurt like hox and felt weird for days afterward. They'd claimed it was a vaccine to help protect her against the diseases she'd encounter on the street.

There was a whoosh of spray and cold liquid hit her open, bleeding elbow. It effectively shattered the memory and jerked her back to the present. Violetta gave a short squawk at the additional pain. She twisted her head around and saw a small canister being shoved back to a shelf under the counter. Mequrokrome. Healed injuries almost immediately, but hurt like hox.

"Wasn't that stuff outlawed years ago?" Violetta demanded.

Betty smirked and shoved Violetta back to the formerly-vacated seat. Instead of answering her question, Betty held up a small black chip with thin gold lines between her thumb and forefinger.

"Quite the little present, isn't it?"

A man about Violetta's height walked up to the counter, holding his hand out. Betty dropped the chip into his waiting fingers. Without asking, he grabbed Violetta's arm and yanked her jacket free. Instead of arguing, she shrugged out of the coat and let him take it. She had no idea where or when he had arrived, and it made her nervous.

The stranger nodded and departed the diner, vanishing into the rainy night.

Betty looked up at one of the lamps hanging from the ceiling. The light dimmed then grew brighter again. She looked to Violetta and nodded towards the back of the diner. "Back door. That way and to the left."

Violetta slid from the stool, rubbing her still-aching elbow. She gave a nod and made her way past the booths. There was a small hallway with three doors to the left. The doors on each side had generic "men" and "women" signs on them, indicating they were restrooms. The third door, straight ahead, said 'employees only' and nothing more.

No time to waste, Violetta thought. She pushed on the swinging door to find a small landing platform and stairs. Small pale yellow motion lights lit the narrow staircase. There was no indication of where she was going or when the steps would end. She did notice the tiny cameras imbedded into the ceiling and walls. There were also tiny holes lining the steps on each side.

Traps, maybe? It would make sense. Keep any unwanted intruder from nosing around where they didn't belong.

Whatever they were for, it didn't involve her. Violetta continued down the steps hoping that somewhere she could find an end to the horror her day had become.

She rubbed her elbow. "Least that bitch could've done was offer me something to eat," she muttered, and hoped the cameras had microphones to pick up her complaint. "The service at this diner stinks."

Chapter Three

After what seemed like forever, the stairs ended into a foyer-like area. A human guard stood in front of a door wearing a black suit. The dark suit could easily hide a body's physique, but Violetta had been taught by one of the best.

This man was in top physical shape. He had wide shoulders and his stance was of someone capable and willing to fight. Honey brown hair was cut short in the style the humans preferred while in the military. He didn't wear a tie, another indicator he was no stranger to physical altercations. Violetta suspected he was armed from the way he stood and the shift of his jacket as he moved towards her.

Without having to be told, she stood with her arms to the side, away from her body. She caught a faint whiff of sage and wood as he removed her service weapon, tucking it into his waistband. Whatever cologne he was wearing, it smelled pleasant.

It was all she could do to not roll her eyes at him. If she hadn't used her gun yet, she wasn't going to. Although, she suspected it was standard procedure when anyone was in the same room as Morelli.

When he stood back up, his blue eyes met hers. There was no challenge or any other emotion she could detect. He backed smoothly to the door and pressed a thumb against the plate just below the doorknob. There was a soft click as the door unlocked. The guard nodded to her and she stepped through the door.

A large human male sat behind what looked like an old wooden desk. Violetta thought the desk might have been an ancient Earth design from history vids she had seen in Orientation with Other Species classes. The man had slicked-back black hair and was dressed in a cream colored button-up shirt, looking to be in his mid-forties. He leaned towards her, but his concentration was upon the miniature wood model on the desk.

It was an antique watership of some design she wasn't familiar with, although she knew enough to recognize the bow, stern, sails, and masts. He was applying colors to the model, meticulous in his focus as he used a small implement to change the wood of the mast to a deeper brown. His wide jaw clenched and released frequently, making light reflect off the dark stubble around his chin and broad nose. His dark eyes were narrowed, but Violetta felt confident they were a shade of gray.

A single chair sat opposite of him. Aside from the desk, chair, and one cabinet, the office was otherwise empty.

Violetta stood still, her fingers curled lightly as she watched the man who had to be Don Zane 'Insane' Morelli. His complete attention was on his hobby. She could only guess that he knew she was there, but she was reluctant to say anything. Or move closer. Or sit. Or do anything other than wait to be acknowledged.

This was often a psychological thing. To see if she would fidget or be goaded into breaking the uneasy silence. Violetta had never understood why people did this to her, but she'd learned to play the game.

More silence passed. He didn't look up, but after several minutes he waved his implement at the empty chair.

"Sit down, officer. Tell me what you need."

His voice was pleasant, but measured. Violetta couldn't pick up any emotion from it.

She gave a nod, even though she didn't think he'd seen the gesture. It was an old habit learned from her father. She sat gingerly, not taking her eyes off the man across from her. Swallowing hard, she took a moment to gather her thoughts.

"I need your help," she said bluntly.

His eyes flicked up to her and the corner of his thin lips rose slightly.

Inwardly, she cursed. Obviously she needed his help. Why else would she be there?

"A dirty cop by the name of Ziph Rc'dollph was part of a setup to finger me as the murderer. I suspect he and his accomplices found out I was going to the Chief about their corrupt activities. I can't go to the DA until I can clear my name."

"Whose murder are you referring to?" Morelli asked. "I need you to be concise if anything is going to be done for you."

Hox. She was babbling already. Not a good way to prove herself to anyone. "Sorry. Chief of Police, Ylvran Me'addn. I'd managed to get some proof that Rc'dollph and at least two others are corrupt in my precinct. Ylvran was willing to hear me out, because I'm Vrehn's Cq'linns' daughter. The two of them are—*were* old friends." And now they were together again.

She paused. It hurt like hox to continually hold back her emotions, but she'd find time to mourn later. Yet another lesson she'd learned well: how to shove your feelings down until the danger was gone. Those in command rarely had the luxury of allowing their emotions to show. It was even rarer for an emotion to rule their decisions.

That way led to a path of danger and possible destruction of not only the commander, but his crew and even his ship. Vrehn Cq'linns had taught her how to do it, even if she didn't use it until after graduating.

If Morelli noticed her hesitation, he gave no indication. She continued. "Chief Me'addn was dead when I got there. Rc'dollph appeared at the same time I was checking for a pulse."

"Are you presuming Rc'dollph's guilt because of his arrival so soon after yours?" Morelli asked. "He may have been tipped off by someone and simply carried through."

"As much as I'd like for him to be the triggerman, I have nothing tangible to corroborate it." Violetta didn't hide the fact she disliked that admission. Morelli didn't seem like the kind of person you hid anything from, not if you wanted his help.

Morelli continued to work on the model seacraft. After a moment, he asked, "What do you need?"

"I need to remain off-grid. Gathering evidence will take time, so I'm not talking about a day or two, unfortunately."

"Why not just contact the military, turn in the evidence you have, and allow them to resolve your problem?"

"The military doesn't step into local police matters unless, and until, it involves national security." Was Morelli testing her? This was a fact every K'laisian knew, but perhaps not all humans were aware of the inner workings of how the different Services worked. "They would accept the evidence, then turn me and it over to the local police department. Placing me in the one position I can't allow myself to be in."

The lips rose a little further and Violetta realized it really had been a test. But why? To see how clearly she was thinking? Or to see if she'd attempt to garner special treatment?

Not that she'd expect such. Those who her father had been closest to weren't in this district.

"So you need me to keep you hidden, despite your intent to go out into the streets. That's not a small request." Morelli placed the small tool into a tiny metal cylinder, before applying a different color onto one side of the craft. "I do not tolerate foolishness or my gifts being squandered."

"Putting myself or another being in jeopardy is not how I intend to proceed.".

"Intent is meaningless. Your actions are what will determine what help or hindrance you receive from me." His tone was the slightest bit colder than before.

Violetta shifted in her seat. "My actions will prove my intent, and determination."

"Your youth is showing."

Violetta clenched her jaw. She wanted to punch him, or Challenge him to a Duel. But neither would help her, so she remained silent.

He continued after several heartbeats. "I need to know what I'm investing in. Excessive energy and stubborn rage are cheap. Both can be found in the hungry kids that constantly walk the streets."

She shifted in her seat again. "Rc'dollph and his cohorts are dirty and need to be brought to justice, but I can't go to the district attorney until I can prove I didn't kill the chief of police."

Morelli's expression didn't change.

"If you're asking what my aspirations are," Violetta continued, "that's different. I'm certain you're aware my mother was human and died after giving birth to me. I want to go up in the ranks. I want to show that just because someone is only half native K'laisian, they shouldn't be dismissed. Those of mixed heritage can be as important and useful to the world as those who are full-blooded."

Her tone at the end had been sharper than she'd wanted. The words had been thrown at her and others who were half-bloods for as long as she could remember. Her father had taught her to rise above them, but that hadn't stopped her from pummeling the bullies who used it to hurt others. It was how she'd earned the nickname "Violence".

Morelli stopped painting. He took a long breath, sat back, and fixed his eyes on her. "Finally, I get to see the person across from me. Having faith in one's underlings and associates' opinions is good, but nothing replaces seeing the true personality of someone."

"I... I- what?" Violetta stammered.

"I don't grant an audience with everyone who requests one," he explained. "For that matter, you only suspect you're speaking with Zane Morelli. I could be a double to make sure the Don stays safe while you are observed for possible threats."

There was a long, deep silence as those words hung in the air. Finally, the man smiled. It added a boyishness that hadn't been there earlier. "Pleased to meet you, Violetta, even under the circumstances. I am Zane Morelli, and I'd like to help you, as I can."

Violetta's brain pieced it all together. "The other people are all checkpoints. A being has to clear them before they can proceed."

Morelli nodded. "And everything is recorded, as is custom for your world. So before you judge anyone in my employ or any who is associated with me, remember that as of now, you are one of them. You have asked me for help, and that has been recorded for posterity."

"Understood."

"Now that I'm beginning to get the shape of who you really are, we need to be transparent about our dealings," Morelli said. "I'll begin by explaining your situation from my side. You are a police officer, and of mixed heritage. You have no recourse in your chosen profession or the people within it, and so you have come to me. This means going beyond what is considered acceptable by many, including those within your job. I and my resources are prepared to do whatever it takes to get the results you need. By mostly legal means, we hope; however, what I will eventually expect from you in return is for you to go exactly as far as was needed to aid you, and no further."

Violetta chewed her lip. A very human behavior, but one she'd never been able to break. "To be perfectly clear, you're saying if you kill someone, you expect me to do the same at some point."

Morelli smiled, but it was charming rather than wolfish. "We try to adhere to the K'laisian way. Death in defense of self and others, and the honor of The Duel. Those who kill for the thrill of killing are ill and need to be treated, even put to death to protect society. I will not expect you to act in a way that is not natural to you."

"Oh." The word escaped her lips. Violetta took a moment to consider what he was saying. "I thought... the history of your organization implied to me that the Earth theology of 'an eye for an eye' was the primary discipline."

"It had been, under many leaders. We grew beyond it."

As Violetta searched for where to take the discussion, Morelli leaned back and continued speaking. "Humans can learn to look beyond their own childish, greedy wants.

When that happens, you'll find us to be remarkably adaptive and sympathetic. This planet of yours? Our organization found what is called 'a kindred spirit' in the natives and the society they built. I usually value things as you do. There are always exceptions, naturally. But I try to phase out such to ensure consistency."

"What will I owe you in return for your help?" Violetta asked.

Issik had been right. Her current situation sucked. She disliked being indebted to Morelli even more, but she also had no choice if she wanted to survive. With luck, she wouldn't be too deeply in debt to this man and his organization.

She still didn't understand how he'd earned the moniker "Insane". He appeared as sane and rational as most K'laisians. She couldn't say all, since beings like Ziph existed.

"That will depend entirely on what we have to do to help you," Morelli replied. He seemed relaxed. "The deal is I will help you as much as I can, and your recompense will not compromise you. As is the way of your people."

He put out his hand. "Do we have an accord?"

Violetta looked at his hand for a moment until she recalled the human tradition. A shaking of hands to seal an agreement. Considering this being's reputation? This was all going way too smoothly. Was he going to snatch her hand, chop off a finger or three and call that a down payment? Would that be enough to satisfy a being who had done much worse to dozens of people? He'd said no compromise as was the way of K'laisians, but how did she trust that his notion of being compromised in any way matched what she'd been raised with?

The question that loomed over all of that was quite simple. What choice did she really have? She had chosen service in the police over following her father's path in the military, so there couldn't be any reliable help in that quarter. Without Morelli, her only other option was to try to survive on her own.

She grasped his hand. His grip was firm and his skin cool.

As he released her hand, she wondered what she had just gotten herself into. Was this agreement going to be on the up-and-up? Or was he going to show up one day demanding something that would jeopardize everything she believed in and had worked to gain?

It was too late to renege and she needed his help. Only time would tell if his man would eventually spell her doom.

"The first step is getting you to a safe house," Morelli said. "Until you can move about securely, and with a plan to put in motion, the primary objective is sanctuary."

He opened a desk drawer, revealing a low tech tablet with three physical buttons. He pushed the leftmost button, and the tablet's screen lit up with a green glow. He pushed the drawer closed.

Ten seconds later, another person entered the room from far behind Don Morelli's desk. Violetta had not identified an exit until the door opened. The being was a tall K'laisian male wearing a tailored human suit of dark gray fabric. He bowed to the don before gesturing for Violetta to follow him. His silver hair braided away from his face, silver eyes, and pale complexion marked him as a native.

Violetta stood, nodded to the don, and followed the K'laisian. He glided through the hallways with the grace only a pureblood could manage. They passed several doors as she followed him. Her sense of direction and memory was good, but there were too many twists and turns for her to figure out how to backtrack to the room they'd departed.

The man stopped at a door and removed a long trench coat from a hook. He handed it to her and she put it on. He removed a second, larger coat for himself. After shrugging into it, he opened the door.

Thunder roared right on the tail of flashing lightning. Rain poured down in sheets. Violetta could see a HAV waiting for them a few yards from the doorway. Her eyes widened as she stared at the older hovercraft. At least two decades past its prime, it appeared to be in great condition. Not enough to stand out, but enough for someone to have pride in their antique ride.

Ducking her head, Violetta ran for the car. Her escort followed behind her. She hurried to the passenger side where the door slid open just as she reached it. The pair climbed into the HAV at the same time, the doors sliding shut simultaneously. Violetta shivered, despite the fact the coat kept most of the rain off her.

Pressing his thumb to the panel, her escort started the HAV. He flipped a couple switches and warmth flooded over her. His silver eyes met hers. She gave him a grateful smile and settled into the seat. The windows of the HAV were tinted and the nighttime thunderstorm helped to keep her in the shadows. It didn't hurt that her escort took alleys and streets that kept them away from the well-lit main roadways and strips.

Fifteen minutes later, the HAV stopped in front of a three-story building in the poorer part of the city. The building looked like a burned-out drug house that had been boarded up. Complete with a bum huddled near the door, his body mostly under the eave of the building's front.

It fit in perfectly with the rest of the grime-covered buildings, the trash-strewn sidewalks, and the questionable denizens that lived in this area. This was the part of District 42 where Duels were fought openly and daily, drugs could be bought, and anything illegal could be found.

Violetta knew the police in this precinct wore heavy-armor and always traveled in pairs or small groups.

It wasn't surprising that Morelli sent her here.

Her escort got out and Violetta followed, realizing that her weapon had not been returned to her. Not yet, anyway. She felt naked without her sidearm. Moving closer to her escort, she forced herself to trust this man, who had been sent by Zane Morelli.

Once again, the brief wonder of why he was called "Insane" flashed through her mind. She'd have to ask Issik at some point. Certainly he would know, considering he worked for the don. Which was something else they'd have to discuss at a later time.

Hopefully there would be a later time.

Her escort stepped past the bum, who barely glanced up at them. Violetta caught a glimpse of shiny silver as the bum shifted. Instead of pausing to investigate further, she followed her escort through the door.

The last time she'd seen something like that, they had been an undercover military serviceman. She highly doubted this person was a member of their military, though she couldn't dismiss the possibility.

She followed in silence as her escort led her into what was obviously a lift.

Puzzled, she kept her questions to herself. Pushing for answers wouldn't help her. It could do the exact opposite.

The lift was shockingly smooth. Violetta had expected a lot of rattling and for rust to start flaking from the ceiling.

Instead, the interior was clean, despite the appearance of rust, and there was no sound or shaking. Someone had spent a lot of time and effort ensuring this lift appeared questionable from the outside. A smile pulled at her face and she looked at her feet. The more she saw, the more she realized how clever Morelli was and she couldn't help but respect him for it.

Within seconds, the lift stopped and the doors slid open. She followed her escort into the room, blinking in the bright light. Nearly running into his back, she stepped to the side, then stared in unblinking shock.

The room was incredible. Chandeliers hung from the ceiling, crystals sparkling and twinkling as they hung from the metal. She had no clue how they had been converted from electricity to the solar power her world used. If her father hadn't kept one of the ancient Earth antiques in his home, she would have been clueless as to what they were.

The walls weren't the usual sleek silver she was accustomed to, but rather finely polished wood. The furniture was a mixture of old Earth-style chairs and sofas and the typical sleek K'laisian styles that conformed to whoever and whatever sat in them.

Everything was a delicate balance of human and K'laisian. Against a far wall was a bar filled with decanters and glasses of every type. A male stood at the bar, his back to them. He was looking down at something on the polished countertop, but Violetta couldn't see what it was.

Fixating on him, to keep from being overwhelmed by the difference between the luxury on the inside and gritty exterior of the building, she realized there was something familiar about him. She couldn't keep the puzzled frown from her face as she tipped her head to the side. Did she know him?

"Our guest has arrived," her escort said. It was the first time he'd spoken.

Violetta tensed. She hated having someone at her back, but she wasn't going to move. Another power play.

The other man's head bowed once. He turned and Violetta's heart skipped a beat. Her jaw dropped.

"Malik?" she asked.

"Violence?" Malik said at the same time. He seemed pleased to see her, but not particularly surprised.

They stared at each other. Butterflies fluttered about her stomach in the extended silence. Malik, Violetta realized, had changed for the better. His straight black hair fell in a single perfect sheet, unlike her own dark auburn hair. She had to work at keeping it as straight as a pure blood K'laisian. It also always became curly when wet, much like the hair her mother had. Even the color was identical to her mom's hair.

His bronze eyes stared at her, his lips curved up into a slight smile. Nervously, she tucked her hair behind her pointed ears. She knew she appeared bedraggled and horrible, soaked from the storm, and wearing a borrowed coat.

"So, you two know each other?" the escort asked.

"Yeah, we do," Malik replied, his eyes never leaving hers. They drifted from the top of her soaked head to her toes before returning to her face. His smile grew. "We went to high school together. Though I haven't seen her since..." He trailed off, sorrow filling his eyes.

"Dad's funeral service," Violetta said quietly.

"He was a great guy, even if he didn't like me much."

Violetta chuckled despite the severity of her current predicament. Memories of her father and their childhood brought some relief to the stressful situation.

"Dad didn't like how much trouble I got into while around you. He wanted me to find my own way before I 'settled down.'" Her smile faded. "I guess now I know why you didn't stay in touch."

Malik tipped his head from the left to the right, the K'laisian equivalent of a shrug. It was something Violetta had to be mindful of in her day-to-day. Failure to know the natural movements of K'laisians had led to many a Challenge and Duel.

Like K'laisian natives, he was slender, but Violetta knew it was deceptive. She had seen him throw a classmate across a room, and Malik didn't look like he'd let himself go over the years.

Malik looked at the escort. "I've got this. You can go."

The escort glanced at Violetta, then to Malik. He gave a slight nod, turned, and left, leaving them alone. Violetta tried to smile, but unease at the reminder of her ignoring him made her feel guilty. She didn't even know the escort's name, though she assumed that was intentional.

"Come on, I'll show you to your room," Malik said. "Or would you like a drink first?"

She shook her head. "No, no drink, not right now. Maybe later once I've processed everything that's happened."

And seeing you again, she added silently. *Talk about a blast from the past.*

Nodding, he turned and crossed the room, his steps silent on the hardwood floor. Violetta followed after, torn between amusement and surprise. When she'd known him in high school, he hadn't been able to do that.

Guess we've both changed over the years.

Moving without sound came naturally to natives of their world. Those of mixed heritage often discovered they could do it as well or with great difficulty. Her father had taught her from the moment she could walk. Drilled it into her, really. Malik had always been envious. Now it appeared he'd mastered the art.

He opened a door that revealed a short hallway. There were four doors with a table against the end of the corridor. A vase filled with native flowers sat on the table below a painting of what she believed to be a city from Earth. There were no canals with small boats on K'lais. She followed him to the first door on their right, which he opened for her.

The room within was lavish. The bed was a large monstrosity. She stepped in and the lights came on. A soft yellow light revealed the rest of the room, which was filled with antiques she would expect to find in a museum. A nightstand sat on the left side of the bed, with a smaller vase of flowers perched on top. A large wardrobe filled a corner of the room opposite a desk and chair.

She couldn't see anything new in the room. Turning to Malik, she found him standing in the doorway watching her.

"The bathroom is through there," he said, pointing to the door across from him.

Opening the door, she discovered an equally luxurious bathroom, complete with a tub she had only seen on history tapes. It was a pearly white ceramic with clawed feet.

"I'm sure you will want to wash up and change into some fresh clothes. You should be able to find something in the wardrobe." Without waiting for an answer, he stepped back and touched a console. The door slid shut without a sound.

When there wasn't the familiar click of a lock, she walked over and tried the door. It opened, but Malik had already vanished into another room. Shrugging, she closed the door. Malik was right: she needed a shower and clean clothes.

With the door closed, and Malik nowhere near, she sank against it and slid to the floor. Pulling her knees up, she hid her face against them, eyes closed. Her body shook, even though tears didn't come.

Everything she'd worked for was gone if she couldn't clear her name. Someone, somehow, had decided she should be pinned for the chief's murder. It wouldn't be difficult to stage the scene or hide the murder weapon used. And Ziph had been determined that she die.

Chief Me'addn's body flashed through her mind. She hadn't been particularly close to him, but she'd respected him. He was the kind of officer she aspired to be: honorable, capable, and accepting of all good citizens who lived in his district, despite their social status or bloodlines. And he'd been such a good friend with her father. Another living connection to her father was gone, the link snapped.

The thought of her father was sobering. He'd taught her to compartmentalize, prioritize, not let anything happening be so distracting that she couldn't act.

He had been one of the best battle strategists K'lais had seen. He'd commanded a battlecruiser and only when he was threatened with a promotion to admiral had he retired. The stars had been in his blood, and if he couldn't be among them, he'd chosen being planetside with his only child. He had still received the promotion at his retirement party.

What would her father say if he were able to see her huddled on the floor? What would he have done?

Violetta knew what he would say. He would tell her to pick herself up and start strategizing. To not let the *t'iachs* gain the upper hand. To not let them win. Her father had never backed down from a fight. No matter the odds, he met his opponents head-on.

Now, she had to do the same.

Drawing a deep breath, she let it out slowly as she stood. Lifting her head, she strode to the bathroom. She would not dishonor her father by doing anything less than meeting this obstacle head-on.

The world's motto may have been "To serve is to prosper" but her father's had always been "Survive, no matter the price." And she'd be *ka'deshed* if she didn't follow that motto and hold it close.

Chapter Four

Just over an hour later, Violetta emerged from her room. The wardrobe had been well-stocked with everything from daytime wear to wispy nighties and even lingerie. All of it in her size. Someone had been paying close attention and had done a fast shopping trip.

She'd chosen light, loose-fitting pants and a tunic in the style preferred by K'laisian natives. Her now-dry, mostly straight hair was braided away from her face in typical K'laisian style, hiding any sign of waves. It also revealed her pointed ears. Unless someone knew only those of mixed heritage had bronze eyes, she could easily pass for a full-blooded native. If she chose to wear contacts to turn her eyes gold, she'd pass without effort.

Her father had raised her to be K'laisian, though he honored her mother by teaching Violetta about her human heritage. Despite her father's efforts, she'd learned more about humans and their habits from Malik's father and family than her own.

Malik, standing behind the bar, paused from whatever he was doing with a handheld tablet. He tapped the screen before placing it on the counter in front of him. It was dark, indicating he'd turned it off.

They stood there for a few moments, staring at each other. The butterflies returned, and she squashed them down. She wasn't a high school kid anymore. She'd never been nervous around him before, so why start now? There were more important problems to deal with than wondering what his response would be after so many years of no contact.

Malik's eyes kept darting over her. Slowly, a smile curved his lips as he gestured to the bar stools across from him.

She sighed. Who was she kidding? This was Malik Addelia. No matter what had happened in the past five years, he was still Malik. She couldn't change the fact she still trusted him. As it had been throughout their school years, he was here. Helping her when she needed it the most. Maybe it was stupid, but she just couldn't bring herself to distrust him.

She crossed the room and settled onto the bar stool across from him. She forced herself to relax, though it took considerable effort to keep from falling into the defenses she'd spent five years building around herself.

Violetta crossed her arms on the bar's ceramic counter. "About that drink…"

"Whatever the lady wants." Malik gestured to the various decanters.

Leaning forward, Violetta studied him. "Bet you don't remember my favorite."

Within seconds, Malik gathered Earth gin, boraberry juice fresh from the farmland neighboring the district, and a glass. Just as he was about to pour the gin, he stopped.

"Almost forgot how it starts," he admitted.

Malik went back to the decanters and tall metal cylinders. He opened each of the cylinders. In the last one he found what he sought. One hand grabbed the tongs sitting nearby. With them, he took out a single sphere of dry ice, over two inches in diameter. He placed that in the large bottomed cup that he'd been prepared to pour the gin into.

Once the circle of sub zero liquid sat on the bottom, Malik poured a measure of gin, topped off with an equal measure of the boraberry juice. The chemical reaction and expelled energy of the liquids surrounding the dry ice increased and the thick vapor bubbled over the cup's rim.

He brought the concoction over and placed it before her.

"Maybe I still do," he said.

Her fingers brushed his as she accepted the glass. An unconscious act that made it feel like the butterflies in her stomach had morphed into bats. She dropped her eyes to the bubbling drink, refusing to jerk her hand away. No matter how tempting it was to do so. This had to be some crazy reaction to being in a fight-or-flight situation. Or perhaps it was something from being half-human?

She didn't regret their past, but it was definitely creating a problem she hadn't expected.

"It does appear that you do," she said in a voice far calmer than she felt. She lifted the glass to her lips and took a sip. "Delicious. Just like I remember."

"How long has it been since you had one?"

"Not since you made me one the night after Dad's service," she admitted, glancing away.

Warmth crept across her cheeks. What a night that had been, too. She couldn't even think of the drink without remembering the night, so she avoided them whenever she went out with Issik. Or anyone else, for that matter. Not that there had been many others.

"Thanks for being there for me. For helping me now."

"In service, we prosper." Malik spoke the K'laisian motto in their native tongue.

He smiled, trying to appear relaxed. Violetta could see the minute details that gave away his nervousness and pent up energy. His eyes couldn't stay still, they darted all around her face. His body was tense in places where he could have been at ease.

He broke the brief silence as she remained silent.

"You're gazing right through to my inner self, aren't you?" His voice was mildly exasperated, but he did relax the slightest bit. "As always. Fine, I'm nervous about being this close to you. I remember the night after the service quite well. I'm worried about making some foolish gesture that will wreck any fond memories you may have."

Violetta hid her amusement by taking another sip of her beverage. The smile was still there when she sat the glass back on the counter. "I don't think there's anything you could do that would ruin those memories."

"Even though you find me employed by the Earthers' most infamous syndicate?" He chuckled. "I wasn't that good!"

"We'll have to disagree on the latter." She turned the glass on the bar, watching as the fog bubbled over the edges. "I suspected you'd start working for the... syndicate, since your father was a part of it. I know you've never been brought in for anything and have a clean record." She looked up at him and shrugged. "All things considered, can I really complain? Or object? Considering where I am and the fact I'm currently considered more of a criminal than you?"

"Not even the don, who has little faith in anyone, thinks you've done anything other than your job. However..." Malik winced. "How secure is the data you found? Do we need to have soldiers and enforcers get to your dad's, I mean, your place, right now or sooner?"

"It's safe. In fact, I have a copy here with me. The original is at home on Dad's secure, off-net console." Violetta smiled. "The department won't be able to get within two blocks of my place without the military knowing and meeting them at the door, weapons in hand. As for Dad's console, it's DNA-activated and completely off all subnets. Even if they could get a finger on the interface, it would explode and leave only a cube behind. Only those with the top-most security would be able to read it. I doubt anyone would come out of that intact."

"Your dad was very demanding about his security. Not surprised that you kept the tradition." Malik relaxed. "The data is currently safe, then. That's all I need to know. Admittedly, I would have thought the military would have reclaimed his console. He was pretty high in rank when he retired."

"Promoted to admiral at his retirement party," she admitted. "I had to acquire clearance and pass an in-depth psych eval from the military to keep it." She took a longer pull from the glass. "It wasn't hard, since I've had to keep a certain level of clearance for as long as I can remember. I was also given a choice: I could go into the military, possibly end up going off-planet, or go to the police academy and become an officer if I wanted to retain his console. I did the latter, since I didn't want to chance going off-planet. There was a good bit of complaining from my, um, recruiter about it."

"You never mentioned that before." Malik spoke slowly, drawing each word out.

"You know every K'laisian must retain clearance of certain levels while a family member, especially a parent, is in the military. That hasn't changed." Violetta sighed and met his eyes. "So why would I *need* to mention it? I always knew I would choose this path to follow. I'd already been planning on entering the police academy, so it was merely a formality in declaring my intent. Getting the security clearance needed was a technicality and only necessary because of everything Dad kept off the subnets."

She shrugged, trying to keep the irritation from her voice. She needed his help and an argument wouldn't help her. "He taught me on that ancient interface. I could have let the military take it, but..."

"It's one of the few connections to him you still have," Malik finished for her.

She nodded. "I would have done anything to keep it. With the console, came the apartment. It's in the military housing district, otherwise I wouldn't be able to keep it, despite my clearance."

Malik placed a hand over hers. Sadness lurked in his eyes. "He'd be proud of you. You know that, right?"

She nodded, not trusting herself to say anything. The pain of his death was still too fresh.

"Good." He squeezed her hand, then let go. "You'll get through this and come out on top."

She nodded again and he chuckled. "You haven't changed at all, Violence. Still in the thick of everything. Speaking of which, how did you get involved in this mess?"

"I seem to remember you saying something similar several years ago," Violetta teased. She grew somber as she continued. "Last week the interface for half my area went down. An upgrade went awry and we were forced to find other interfaces to use. I was allowed to use Lieutenant Cancio's. Supposedly, it was because I had the clearance. Now I'm wondering if that was merely an excuse for me to use it. I filled out my paperwork and I went to delete the trash bin, as is my habit. I was in a hurry and I accidentally opened it instead. That's when I noticed there was a folder with a large amount of vidclips."

"Let me guess, curiosity got the best of you?" Malik interjected, a knowing smirk on his face.

"It's almost as though you know me," Violetta joked. "I opened the file and discovered vids of a fellow sergeant, my lieutenant, the captain, and a lot of others, doing every illegal thing you can imagine." She paused and took a pull of the drink. "I had to do something, so I opened Cancio's drawer and grabbed a drive that would hold the contents of the entire folder. I didn't think he'd notice a missing chip, considering how cluttered his drawer was, but I guess I was wrong. I copied everything over and left. Didn't delete the trash for once."

"Maybe that's what tipped them off. You did something different," Malik suggested. "Where does your dad's old friend, the Chief of Police come in?"

"After I got home, I used Dad's interface to make a backup copy using a card only military-grade interfaces can read. I knew I had to contact someone higher than the captain, someone who wasn't on any of the vids. Chief Me'addn was the only person I could think of. Using Ylvran's personal number Dad kept in his files, I called him. He said he'd talk to me at his place today. He wanted to see the evidence, so I took the backup chip with me."

"Why didn't you contact any of your dad's friends in the military?"

"Most of them aren't planetside. The ones who are would've told me to go to Chief Me'addn. Chain of Command and all that."

"That makes sense, I guess. Vrehn was loved, but I doubt they'd alter their typical procedures for one being. Not without a good reason."

Violetta nodded. "Exactly. To do otherwise would allow for others to demand the same treatment. K'laisians aren't so different from humans in that factor."

"Or other races," Malik added. "So, what happened when you got there?"

"The door opened for me and I found Ylvran on the floor. I suspect he'd been shot, considering the amount of blood. Ziph Rc'dollph came in as I checked for a pulse." Violetta stared into her glass. "There wasn't one either, damn it."

"How well did you know him?"

"I met him a couple times, but he was a great man to work under," she replied. "He was well liked and respected."

Malik nodded, but didn't say anything. He wasn't doing anything to make her think badly of him. As like in their childhood, he listened and considered his words before replying. A cool head versus her quick temper.

Just another day in the life with her best friend.

"I need to figure out how to clear my name," she stated needlessly. "Ziph wants me dead, and I imagine Lieutenant Cancio and Captain Monroe do, as well. With me gone, all their problems go away."

"There's nothing you can do tonight," Malik stated firmly. "The entire police service will be out searching for you before too long." He paused. "Did you use your service weapon?"

"No." Violetta shook her head. "I used my Gift and a grenade to get past Ziph."

"Good. That's good," Malik murmured. He narrowed his eyes as he studied her. "Can I trust you to remain here without needing to lock the doors and windows?"

Violetta glowered at him. Perhaps the trust only went one way. "Obviously. Without knowing what's being planned against me, I can't counter it. Right now I'm on the defensive. And I'll have to stay there until we know their plan."

"You sound like your father."

"I'm his daughter."

"So you are." Amusement sparkled in his eyes.

"Don't forget it," she said primly. At his raised brow, she felt warmth flooding her face. Time to change the topic. "So, um, what have you been doing these past years?"

"Are you asking what I've been doing socially? Or do you want to know why I have this job?"

Now that is a dangerous question, Violetta thought, refusing to meet his eyes.

She truly didn't want to know if he'd found a mate. She'd given up the ability to ask when she didn't contact him after their night together. "I wouldn't want to pry into your personal life, so let's go with the latter."

"That's a fun tale. I went into the military, figured to be off-planet within a year. After Initiation Academy, like everyone, I took the aptitude exams. I was scored as a healer, of all things!" He chuckled. "Of course I had to follow the results and that path, otherwise I'd have had to pay for my training to be an off-planet specialist. Two years into my training I was a competent but unsettled student. The rules of conduct made sense, the healing procedures as well, but nothing else did to me."

"I didn't know you stayed in the military."

Everyone had to serve at least a year, if they didn't attend the police academy. Both began on the first day of the fourth month after high school concluded for the year. She never expected to hear he had hoped to leave their planet. She tried to not cringe at the thought. Guess that's what she deserved for not staying in touch with him.

"Oh, there's more." Malik smiled. "One weekend, I was invited to a party by a fellow student who'd become a friend. The party was run by Zane Morelli, who had only been on the planet for a year. My friend was a soldier for his syndicate. Don Morelli was very interested in me, a half-breed with no innate abilities to the energies of our planet, but very adept at understanding how our people thought and lived."

"So you started working for him. When did you quit the military?"

"You may find this terrible, but I finished my third year in the Service, still attending instruction, while working the dark hours for the don."

"When did you sleep?" she asked.

He laughed. "Usually during instruction!"

"That's just so bad," Violetta said, trying to not laugh. "I'll bet you retained everything from instruction, too!"

"Quite a bit, probably not all." He gave her a more typical K'laisian wink, tipping his head to the right for a brief moment. "But by the end of that year, I felt more purpose doing my consulting and protection work in the syndicate than what I could eventually do as a healer. I'd done my required year in the military service, so I left and never regretted it."

"I'll bet those lessons have come in handy, though," Violetta said thoughtfully. "I'm not surprised you tested high for healing. You've always been adept at that sort of thing." She paused a second before adding with a straight face, "Of course, I also know you have talented hands."

Malik opened his mouth and raised one finger. He stopped moving, looked at the finger, and his skin went dark. He put his hand down out of sight.

"It was mostly healing of the mind," he murmured.

"Is that what it's called these days?"

"I need a drink. You really enjoy making this awkward."

"It's only fair," Violetta replied cheerfully. "You've been wound up far too tight the moment you saw me. About time I get through that shell you're wearing."

"Truth and testament, I cannot deny." Malik walked back to the decanters and began fixing himself a drink. "At least you haven't changed, and made quick work about making me grovel in my anxiety."

"You've never groveled," Violetta replied. "Grumbled, yes. Growled, definitely. But I've never known you to grovel."

Malik shook his head, chuckling. He didn't turn from fixing his drink, though.

She continued, her tone serious. "I'm glad you're the one helping me. I wouldn't be able to trust anyone else as much." He turned to say something and she held a hand up. "Before you argue that I don't know you, that's true. But I do know you've made certain everything you've done is legal. Or have kept anything illegal hidden. I need that, and I trust the man I knew."

"Very well. I accept your faith in me and thank you," he said. "You'll come out alive on the other end of this situation. I vow it."

She smiled. "I'm going to hold you to that. I don't know exactly what you do for Morelli, and I'm not going to ask. All I can promise is to do as you require, and follow your lead in resolving this mess."

"That would make this arrangement run more efficiently than most I've dealt with. But, I insist, if you see or sense anything that you think I have missed? Tell me."

Violetta lifted a single dark brow. "I doubt I'd be able to keep from it. I've investigated a lot of murders, but this is the first time I've had to prove someone's innocence. All the avenues I typically use are gone, so I'm at a bit of a loss. Issik sent me to Morelli. Morelli sent me to you. I may ask questions, but it will be because this is a whole new situation. I don't even think Dad could have prepared me for this situation."

"Your father taught us both to prepare for any situation. Asking intelligent questions was part of that. If you don't ask questions, I'll wonder why. You always questioned everything."

Opening her mouth, she snapped it shut and bit her lip, a pang of guilt running through her. "Okay, I can't argue that. And because you said that, I have to ask: what have you been doing socially?"

"I don't have a social life, or a reason to have one, not really. Most of what I do and am seen doing is work related." Malik opened his mouth to say more, stopped, and shrugged. "I find few people that I want to spend time with."

"I'm surprised," Violetta replied, taking a sip of her drink. "You always enjoyed social events in school." She laughed a little. "Not that I'm anyone to talk. I just find it hard to believe you've been alone for the past five years."

"Alone?" he said. "Perhaps I can have company when I want it. As I said, most people I meet aren't the type to spend long hours with."

She glanced at him sharply, uncertain of what to say to such a statement. A yawn solved that problem for her. "As much as I'm enjoying talking with you, if I don't go to bed now, I'll probably fall asleep here."

Malik finished making his drink. The concoction was a bubbling, green mixture in a small glass. He clicked the edge of his glass against hers, tossed back the drink, and placed the empty glass on the bar. Tossing back the last of her drink, she slid the glass towards him. He caught it with ease.

"Sleep well, Vi," he said. "I'll see you at breakfast."

She stood and stretched. "See you in the morning."

With a final smile, she left him standing behind the bar. The drink had helped her relax, as did talking to him. She wondered briefly if Morelli knew about their past together, and decided it was possible. Her father's funeral had drawn a large crowd. From people who knew him to people who knew *of* him. He was part of the group that spearheaded the interactions with humans, and their subsequent integration with K'lais. Though it wasn't the only event that had propelled him into K'laisian history. Just one of many.

Shrugging it off, she slipped beneath the covers of her bed and closed her eyes. If Morelli had known, she wasn't going to complain. Seeing Malik gave her faith that she would come out on top of this problem.

Chapter Five

The following morning, Violetta awoke at the same time she normally did, despite the fact it wasn't a normal day. Violetta had fallen asleep with more ease than she would have believed possible. Yes, she'd made a deal with a career criminal whose reputation had started with him going into a rage, beating four classmates over who got the last sip of a drink in the school yard. Further, one of the most prevalent people from her past was working for him. But the latter surprise had some comfort to it, as ridiculous as that seemed in the moment.

One did not become a healer without passing multiple psych evals. And those evals did not stop after the assignment was earned. She doubted Malik could have changed so drastically in the past two years since his time in the Service. It was a being's steadfast, solid psychology that allowed beings to remain in the K'laisian military as a healer. Even humans weren't immune or exempt from the rigid military standards.

She dressed in a snug-fitting tunic and leggings, the earth-tone fabrics soft against her skin. As she pulled on her boots, she double-checked the pocket she'd cut between the outer- and inner layers. The holcrom card was still there.

Made of lightweight, transparent fiberglass, holcrom cards had once been the preferred method of transporting data off-net. The card fit easily in the palm of her hand, so tucking it into her boot, a method her father had taught her as a young girl, had been easy. Now, chips were the preferred method, since they held more data and their sizes were color coded. They were also hardier, though Violetta had put her holcrom card through a lot and it had held up to everything. Including being stepped on once by accident.

Patting her boot, she met Malik at the bar where a buffet of take-out containers awaited her. The biodegradable containers were filled with everything from fresh fruit to bacon and breakfast sandwiches. Bacon was a favorite of humans that natives had quickly developed a taste for. The smell of coffee wafted from a tall cup to the side. She spotted several containers of what appeared to be juice behind Malik, in front of the decanters of alcohol.

"You thought of everything," Violetta stated, drawing closer to the food. "No sweets, though? I'm disappointed."

Malik smirked as he reached behind him and produced a tray of donuts, desserts, and even native ahvara pastries made with local berries and drizzled in ro'shii nectar.

Narrowing her eyes slightly at Malik, she took one of the ahvara pastries. His smirk stayed in place as he slid the cup of coffee to her.

"Pay up," a familiar voice said from behind her.

Violetta turned, the treat halfway to her mouth. "Issik?"

Issik smiled, and bowed slightly. Her partner wore the same style of clothing as always. A button-up shirt, long coat, and light-weight pants, all in dark tones. His straight silver hair, tucked behind his elegantly tipped ears, fell around his shoulders in a sleek sheet. Not a stray hair anywhere. His silver eyes danced with mischief, despite the severity of the situation.

"Told you she'd go with those," Issik stated, nodding to the ahvara pastry. "Good to see you in one piece, Cq'linns."

"They've been her favorite since childhood," Malik commented. "Vrehn taught us both how to make them."

"Not wrong." Placing the pastry on the counter, Violetta gave Malik a sharp look before crossing the room to her partner. "How—? When—?" She stopped just shy of him, her eyes narrowing. "Just what do you do for Morelli?"

"I'm an informant," Issik replied nonchalantly. "I tell him what I see in the poorer areas of the city so he can help those areas. He tells me things to look for."

"Nothing to do with your position in homicide?"

Issik shook his head. It was one of the few gestures that K'laisians shared with humans. "No, Vi. Nothing like that."

Tipping her head to the side, she gave a slight nod. Did she really have a right to object? She had no proof he was doing anything illegal and she had not seen him in any of the vidclips.

She stepped forward and embraced the older man. He hummed a little, the K'laisian version of a chuckle as he hugged her back. "I'm glad you're alright," he murmured.

"I could've done without Betty's knife in my elbow." She broke the embrace and studied Issik. "Don't you also have a tracer?"

"Oh, that." Issik waved dismissively. "Ever since I started working for Morelli, his hacker has been rerouting the tracer so it always appears I'm somewhere else when I need it. Usually it shows me at home."

"Huh. That explains a few things," Violetta said, returning to the bar and her pastry. "We're going to have to have a long talk when this is all done."

"I'll make sure to have a few ales on hand," Issik joked.

Violetta nodded and bit into the pastry. Glancing at Malik, she noticed he hadn't moved and was wearing his "shell" again. Some things never changed. There would be plenty of time to figure out what had made him wear it later.

"What brought you here?" she asked, after swallowing her mouthful of pastry. "It couldn't be just to see I'm okay and in one piece."

"Is this the part where I say 'Nothing is easy with you, is it, Cq'linns?' Too bad, because I'm not," Issik replied. "I thought you'd want to know what details have come out about the case against you."

"He kept the details from everyone except the don," Malik interjected. "Insisted on telling you personally. Maybe he does care."

Glancing sharply at Malik, Violetta studied her old friend. He avoided her eyes, watching Issik instead.

"I never said no one cared," she muttered. She raised her voice. "What do you have, Issik?"

"Someone has been working for months, waiting for you to step into a trap. The Police Subnet Datasource has your pistol firing the shot that killed Chief Me'addn. The data feed registered your weapon's discharge as being in the Chief's home, approximately four meters from him. I... I don't know how that could be faked."

Violetta's mouth dropped open. She had been naively expecting someone to eventually check the weapon registration and see that her service pistol had not been fired for over two days. She was certain the murder would have been framed using more mundane methods.

Every pistol, rifle, cannon, and grenade on the planet that was given or sold to military, police, or civilians was built by the military armories and registered through the Military Subnet Datasource. Since they fired energy projectiles, every round fired created data. The triggered weapons would feed data of owner, location, and time to the Datasource.

The intent was to keep everyone accountable for their use of a projectile-firing weapon. Police and military would end their work days by signing off on daily reports that detailed any shots fired or grenades used. For target practice, everyone went to military-run ranges. The weapons were temporarily fixed with a chip that altered the type of energy the weapon fired and registered them as "practice shots". Each weapon could be deactivated remotely when a crime or violation occurred.

Issik's eyes never left hers. "A different partner would suggest you turn yourself in and hand over your sidearm for testing. Since I work both sides, I'm advising you to find a method to prove your own innocence. Someone went to a lot of trouble to pin this on you. They're waiting for your sidearm to complete the frame-up."

"They'd lie and say it was my gun and no one would question them." It left a bitter taste in Violetta's mouth. She looked at the pastry and put it on the bar, no longer wanting the tasty treat.

"Not in time to save your scrawny butt, in any event."

"For the millionth time: my butt isn't scrawny." It was a running joke between them, except this time it didn't make her smile.

"Really? Have you looked at it lately?" Issik completed the joke's routine.

Violetta still didn't smile, but she appreciated her partner's attempt.

Malik cleared his throat, and Violetta could have sworn Issik was smirking. Was Issik goading Malik? No, that was impossible. Right? Why would he goad Malik?

"Your service pistol has been delivered to Nualith Ln'ann," Malik said.

"The munitions expert?" Violetta furrowed her brow. The name was vaguely familiar.

"Who?" Issik asked.

"That's the one," Malik said, ignoring Issik. A smile tugged at his lips. "Nualith was the primary designer for the software that tests weapons to determine when they were last fired. It's more than simply looking it up in the Database. Her program goes into the innards of the weapon and sorts through all the bits and pieces inside it. The software can narrow the time down to as much as the last three minutes of a weapon's use, the exact distance, and more."

"She was in the military, not the police," Violetta added. "She retired shortly before Dad did. He took me to her celebration party. He respected her greatly. The last I heard, she was tweaking her software to determine if weapons could be hacked. I don't know if that's still in development or if she finished the project."

"She's not on the don's payroll, so anything she finds will go without question," Malik stated. "Apparently she thought highly of your father, too. She told our, ah, agent, that she'd inspect the weapon. She wouldn't falsify anything, but she would keep silent on whose weapon it was and why she was testing it."

"Good. Did she give an ETA on when she'll have the results?" Issik asked.

"A day or two. She said she'd give it priority, but the tests take time."

"In order for it to be a definite answer, she'd have to run the tests more than once and get the same answer each time," Violetta added. "It was one of the things that irritated Dad when time was a factor."

Malik snorted. "Irritated? You really know how to understate things."

"Don't make me come over that bar."

Malik's smile broadened. He held his hands out in mock-challenge. "I'm not going anywhere."

"You two can Duel this out later, Violence," Issik said. "For now, can we concentrate on the fact you're a wanted criminal and how best to rectify that problem?"

Malik's eyes narrowed, the smile fading. Issik lifted his chin in turn. Violetta glanced between the two men. If she didn't know better, she'd swear there was some sort of competition going on. There was no way Malik could possibly be jealous of her. Was there? She knew for certain Issik wasn't romantically interested in her. He treated her more like a little sister than a potential mate. He'd never once attempted to Match her with anyone. A fact she'd been eternally thankful for since she'd had zero interest in anyone. Aside from Malik.

"What else do you have for us?" Malik asked, still staring at Issik.

A smirk crossed Issik's face. "The captain and acting Chief of Police are arguing with the district attorney about getting permission to search your place. The DA is claiming the whole thing is preposterous. Cancio and Rc'dollph are practically foaming at the mouth about not being able to enter your place. Apparently no one knew the military was watching your home closely." He raised a single brow. "Any idea why that is?"

Violetta shrugged. "I haven't the faintest idea why the military would be watching my father's home that I now occupy. How would I know that I was being watched?"

"Right. And you aren't one of the most observant people I know," Issik retorted. "Be careful out there, Violetta. Everyone local with a badge is searching for you. They're paying close attention to your favorite places, and especially your home."

"I'll keep her safe, Ha'kksworth," Malik stated. "You'd better be going. Don't want anyone to get suspicious or anything."

Issik chuckled. "I'm sure you will, Addelia." He turned to Violetta. "I'll talk to you later. Don't do anything foolish. Well, more foolish than normal."

"Very funny, Issik." She crossed to her partner and gave him another hug. "Thanks for everything."

"I'm glad I can be of service." Without warning, Issik kissed her on the forehead. "Be safe. Be wise."

He walked from the room, leaving Violetta to stare after him in bewilderment. Issik had never, ever kissed her. Not on the head, not on the cheek, not even on the hand. Not anywhere. Ever.

Why the fark had he done that?

The silence that accompanied Issik's departure grew thick. Violetta searched her mind for something to say.

"So, that's, umm, your work partner." Malik spoke slowly and carefully. "How much time do you two spend outside of work? I'm told he's the reason you got an easy pass to see Morelli."

"He's more like a drinking buddy than anything," Violetta insisted, hoping to get some reaction from him. Still baffled, and feeling as though she needed to explain, she continued. "I have zero social life. None. He makes certain I have someone to talk to and decompress from the job. That's it. Honest. He hasn't even been to my place."

Malik raised his head slightly. "Oh, that's fine. Not my place to ask. Wait, no social life? That sounds familiar."

He tilted his head to the right for a brief moment. Earthers who spent any time on the planet had to learn that the gesture was the native equivalent of a winking eye. Or else they could find themselves being mocked or mistake humor for a challenge to a Dual.

"Why do you think I chose homicide? Less pressure to socialize."

Malik gave her a cock-eyed smile, one right out of their childhood.

"What about you?" she asked, hoping for a better answer than the one she received the previous night. "You said you weren't alone. And I remember you never lacked for invitations to summer concerts and plays at the amphitheater."

Thinking back on those fun summer events, she found herself longing for that time of her life. Those had been simpler days, filled with cold treats, warm nights, and laughter. Violetta refused to dwell on the implications of those thoughts. They led down a narrow, rocky path. One she didn't want to walk alone.

"What little socializing I do can be categorized as work related," Malik admitted. "There are plenty of events that I have to be at to protect and monitor clients. Sometimes I get a little extra attention from them. Most of the time I don't bother."

A small smile flashed on Violetta's face. "I'm sure you grab attention from the ladies, even when you don't mean or want to."

"Attention can be nice, but it's never the kind that lasts. You never lacked for attention, either. Does Issik scare the would-be suitors away? Or are you still doing it?"

"I've perfected my technique." She refused to meet his gaze. "None that I've met have interested me, and thankfully Issik's never tried to Match me with anyone."

Matching one person with another, in the hopes an interest or spark would occur, was common in their society. Often it was friends or family who tried matching the being with someone who was compatible. Or if an interest was noticed with someone in particular, a match would occur.

Humans called them "blind dates," a confusing term to Violetta.

"You never did go for just anyone with a pretty face or sweet words," Malik teased.

Violetta was relieved to hear him joking with her. She preferred him being comfortable and at ease instead of constantly wearing a shell. It helped her to relax a bit in the aftermath of the previous evening's horrors. *Perhaps that was an intentional move on someone's part*, her mind pondered.

"My apologies," Malik said, "I've gotten us away from the issue at hand."

"Yes, I suppose you did." Violetta had enjoyed the conversation, but it was time to get to work. "Where shall we begin today?"

"You tell me what you want, um, need. Yes, need," fumbled Malik. "I make it happen."

Well, if he was going to ask, she was going to take advantage of it. Eventually she'd figure out what just happened, and she'd tease him about it later. For now, she needed to focus on clearing her name.

She pulled the holcrom from her boot and held it up. "I need an interface that can read this. Once I have the information on it, I can make a report to present to the DA."

Malik peered at the holcrom for a few moments. He nodded.

"I know just where to find what you need."

Chapter Six

It was no surprise to Violetta that Malik took his job seriously. He knew the city well. Better than during their childhood. Though he didn't break any traffic laws, he kept the HAV out of the eyes of the police searching for her. That took considerable skill, considering the large-scale manhunt for her.

She remained silent, allowing him to focus on driving. After some time, they arrived at a large, factory-sized building on the outskirts of the business district. She was surprised by the location, but grateful for the reduced police presence in this area.

They exited the HAV and approached the front entrance. There were no signs anywhere, so she wasn't entirely certain where they were or who owned the building. The door buzzed as it opened, and they entered the main foyer. The receptionist was a pretty human with brilliant red hair, green eyes, and freckles splattered across her nose and cheeks. Violetta suspected she was in her mid to late twenties, around five feet with a trim physique. She smiled at Malik before giving Violetta a second look.

"A moment, please, while I contact Nualith," the receptionist said, her eyes not leaving Violetta's face.

"You sure this is a good idea?" Violetta murmured to Malik.

Malik slid an arm around her waist, pulling her closer. He leaned down, his lips next to her ears. "Nualith knows we're coming. She has complete control over her people. You'll be safe."

A shiver ran down Violetta's spine. She had to force herself to keep from inhaling sharply. He was too close and it brought back memories she did not need to be reminded of at the moment. It would be a complication neither of them needed. Not to mention, she didn't even know if he still felt the same towards her.

His lips brushed against the point of her ear, a sensitive place on any K'laisian native. Most beings of mixed heritage also were incredibly sensitive there, regardless of the shape of their ears. She couldn't stop the shiver it caused.

She glanced at him sharply and saw a twinkle in his eyes. Maybe he hadn't forgotten their night together, either.

Not that she could say anything. Not in the middle of a lobby with a receptionist watching them with a neutral expression and amused eyes. Giving him a curious look, Violetta remained silent and turned her attention to the lobby.

It was a standard lobby with bare furnishing, a couple tables with two handheld interfaces each, and the large desk where the receptionist sat. A frame on the right wall displayed two-dimensional photos and vidclips of products and employees. A holograph shelf was against the opposite wall, displaying three-dimensional videos and products.

Two doors were positioned behind the front desk and there were hallways to both sides with doors at the end of each. One of those opened and a native woman stepped through. She wore a white lab coat over a snug-fitting light tan tunic and matching leggings. Gold eyes danced with delight as she saw Malik.

"A pleasure, as always, Malik." Tucking her black hair behind her pointed ears, she turned to Violetta and bowed at the waist. "It has been many years, bures'a Violetta, daughter of Vrehn, but it is a delight to greet you again."

The formal greeting surprised Violetta. She stepped away from Malik, bowing at the waist in return. "The honor is mine, Bures'a Nualith. May you and your family fair well and prosper in service."

The title of bures'a and bures'o, for males, was a title of respect. The bow hadn't surprised Violetta as much as the fact Nualith had used an older form of distinction.

Never before had Violetta been referred to as "Daughter of Vrehn". It was the oldest method of greeting the child of a distinguished being. It meant the child was due great honor and distinction equal to the being's name mentioned. The phrase was reserved for those who had done great service for their world, and typically only used by military personnel and their families.

A way to memorialize the being so their name would never be forgotten, all the while bringing honor to the descendent.

"Please, join me in my office." Nualith gestured towards their left and began walking in that direction. "Do you desire a refreshment? We have a variety of options."

"Thank you, Bures'a, but I'm fine," Violetta said, glancing at Malik in confusion.

"The offer is appreciated, but no," Malik added, giving Violetta a slight human shrug.

At least, Violetta thought, she wasn't the only one confused by Nualith's words.

Nualith gave a K'laisian nod by lifting her head before lowering it as she pressed her hand against the door panel.

The door slid open, revealing a mid-sized office. A large frame filled one wall, separated into various slideshows. A desk divided the office in half. Three conforming chairs were positioned on one side of the desk, while a conforming office chair sat on the opposite side of the desk. Several large interfaces were positioned on the desk, along with a countertop touchscreen.

Nualith spoke a word in their native language, and the interface screens went black.

There were a few small electronic items scattered about the desk, but the office was otherwise void of decor.

"Please, have a seat." Nualith gestured a hand towards the chairs. "I knew your father well, Violetta. We worked together often and he spoke highly of you. As such, I don't doubt that my tests will prove your innocence. Tell me how I may assist you."

"I need an interface that can read a holcrom." Violetta extracted it from her boot and showed it to Nualith. "It's rather old tech and requires a military grade interface."

Nualith laughed. It was a light, beautiful sound. "I won't ask how you came into possession of such a thing, though I have my suspicions. You're as crafty as your father. I've got just the interface you need." She tipped her head to the right side, a sly smile on her face. "They may be old, but those holcroms come in handy, don't they?"

"They do indeed," Violetta replied. "Thank you for your help."

"I could do no less for Vrehn's daughter," Nualith replied. "Come. I'll take you to the interface."

Several minutes later, Violetta and Malik were staring at a room the exact opposite of Nualith's clean and Spartan office. This room was filled with old interfaces, cables, and peripherals, all packed and stacked haphazardly. Violetta was afraid a single sneeze would bring it all crashing down.

Nualith navigated the mess with ease, leaving Malik and Violetta to follow cautiously. The other woman cleared off two chairs, piled with cables, and a small area on a desk. She tapped the screen, then pressed her hand against the front edge of the interface. It glowed a silvery blue as it powered up, casting its light on the broken cases and cracked peripherals surrounding it. Nualith slid a reader from beside the interface screen.

"I'll be in the room connected to this one, when you're done." Nualith opened a drawer that was surprisingly neat and withdrew another, newer, handheld interface. "This isn't connected to the subnet. Anything you input into this will be stored directly onto a brown chip."

She then gave the handheld interface to Malik and left the room, a pleased look on her face.

Violetta turned to Malik.

"That was interesting."

"Indeed." He pointed to the interface. "Shall we?"

Violetta sat in one of the chairs and was surprised to find it very comfortable. She could only figure that this entire room was either a ruse to keep this particular interface off the subnet, or the woman was crazy. Considering how intelligent Nualith was said to be, Violetta leaned towards the former. Either way, the woman was a hoarder of epic proportions to have kept everything in this room.

Anyone else would have allowed the items to be recycled and repurposed.

Placing the holcrom onto the reader, the interface displayed the data Violetta had saved from her lieutenant's interface. Leaning back in the chair, she gave Nualith's ancient interface a few moments to load everything. Once it was ready, she picked it up.

"What's the plan?" Malik asked.

"I'm going to document everything possible. Then investigate it to the best of my abilities. The only way I'm going to get out of this is to make certain I have a solid case to present to the DA. Hopefully there's something on a 'clip explaining how they did it."

Malik nodded. "I'll do what I can to help."

"I know you will."

As she played vidclip after vidclip, she made concise detailed notes about what she viewed along with the timestamps. She kept her focus on her own department, although she found videos of other departments. The corruption ran deeper than she thought, but that would be for the DA to sort out.

Going through all the files, searching for those involving her fellow homicide officers was a tedious, time-consuming process. She clicked yet another and stretched, stopping in mid-motion as she recognized the location.

In the corner of her eye, she saw Malik lean forward. He must've noticed her sudden shift in behavior. She kept her focus on the vidclip.

The street corner was familiar, a popular intersection in the business district. She had discovered a pastry shop near that very corner while working her second homicide investigation. It had become one of her favorite places for sweets. As a man stepped into view at the street corner, she realized this wasn't just in the same area of her second case. This *was* her second case.

The man standing there was the murder victim.

Another person stepped from the shadows, to the side of the man in the center of the video.

Violetta froze.

"Ziph?" she murmured aloud.

Her fellow sergeant lifted a weapon and aimed it at the man. The man turned and gestured to Ziph. A moment later, the man dropped to the ground, blood flowing around his now-lifeless body.

Violetta paused the vidclip and backed it up a few seconds. A clear image of the weapon came into view. She touched the interface with her fingers and enlarged the image until it filled the screen.

The weapon was not one she recognized. Larger than the usual service sidearm, it was blocky with sharp edges. It lacked the smooth curves of the weapons built by the military.

She'd seen firearms built by humans, the type they preferred to use. Her mother's friends had shown her theirs during her childhood when they visited her father. She'd even shot some a few times. Their weapons hadn't looked like this odd mix of human and K'laisian technology.

Violetta pointed at the pistol. "What is that?"

"I have no clue. I've never seen anything like it." Malik paused. "Want to tell me what we just saw?"

"Do you remember that murder a few years ago on Disom Corner? Where Er'ver, Omeqi, and Caernshys meet? A K'laisian was accused of driving up and shooting the victim. Suler Sg'tonn was found guilty of premeditated murder and executed." After Malik nodded, she continued. "That was the second homicide I worked. Something seemed odd about all of it, but I never could say what bothered me. I guess this explains it. Ziph set it all up."

The same way he set me up.

"But didn't the report say Sg'tonn's registered weapon was used at the crime scene? That he and the victim, Bethala Fw'ntees, had a huge argument the day before at one of the stores?" Malik asked. It was Violetta's turn to nod. "That isn't the guy's weapon, though."

Violetta shook her head. "It wasn't the one entered into evidence. Do you think Nualith might have an idea on what the hox is going on?"

"Maybe. Let's go ask."

Violetta took a screenclip of the weapon with the interface, then removed the holcrom from the reader. After tucking it into her boot, she followed Malik to the next room. Nualith was speaking with a K'laisian in a labcoat. Upon noticing them, the K'laisian excused herself and left.

Nualith turned in her seat. "You two look rather grim."

"Have you ever seen anything like this before?" Violetta held up the interface with the screenclip.

Nualith studied the image for a long moment. "No, I haven't. Where's this from?"

"Do you remember the Fw'ntees murder? Suler Sg'tonn was convicted and executed for it."

"Yes, I do." Nualith's eyes darted over the image. "If I remember correctly, this was not the weapon used."

"No, it was one of standard design. The Database placed Sg'tonn and his weapon at the scene of the crime, but the vidclip that image came from says otherwise."

"I knew it!" Nualith jumped to her feet. "I knew it was possible to do this! It's why I've been working on the software update. To show if a weapon was hacked or reprogrammed. I told the division supervisors that someone would figure out how to do this! This!" She waved the interface. "This is the proof I've been needing!"

"Could you perhaps explain what it is we're seeing?" Malik asked.

There was an edge to his tone and Violetta nudged him sharply in the ribs.

"Oh, right. Sorry." Nualith took a deep breath and sat down. "The only way to do this is to duplicate another weapon and program this one—" she tapped the picture, "—to replicate the other weapon's signal and frequency."

Violetta and Malik shared a look. Nualith must have noticed, because she added, "Put simply, the murder weapon had been cloned."

Violetta stared at Nualith. There was something familiar about what she had just said. She closed her eyes and took a step back, trying to remember. She could hear her father's voice and it finally came to her.

She opened her eyes, and squeezed Malik's arm. "I've got to get to my apartment. I've got to get to Dad's files! I remember him talking about someone, some 'idiot' is how he put it, who wanted to clone military weapons. He advised the person to drop it and included it in one of his reports. I know he would have made a note about it in his personal files."

"Now that you mention it, I remember your father mentioning that to me years ago," Nualith said. "We discussed it before a meeting. It inspired me to start planning the software upgrade to discover weapons that had been tampered with. I suspected someone would one day think of it, but I didn't realize someone had already come up with the idea and had approached Vrehn."

"It was one of the few times Dad ever said so many negative things about a single human. He grumbled about it for days. No wonder I remembered it," she added quietly.

Amusement flashed across Nualith's face. "Knowing Vrehn and his temper, I'd be surprised if you hadn't remembered it."

Malik looked between Nualith and Violetta. He sighed heavily. "I hope you know how to get into your place."

Violetta smiled. "I have an idea."

"Good luck, and stay safe." Nualith handed the interface back to Violetta. "The test results should be complete by tomorrow. The rare use of your weapon has been an immense assistance in the testing."

"There has been a rare need for it in my job so far. For which I am thankful." Violetta accepted the interface, a smile on her face. "Thank you, bures'a Nualith. May you also be safe, be well."

"Thank you for your assistance," Malik said.

Nualith bowed. "To serve is to prosper."

They returned the bow and Nualith led them back to the front entrance. They bid her farewell before returning to the HAV, with Malik driving once again.

After a few minutes, Violetta frowned. "This isn't the way to my apartment."

"We're not going to your apartment until tonight."

"You brought me here," she argued.

Malik glowered at her. "This did not require going near the area where practically the entire police precinct is searching for you. Your apartment may be near the military base, and it may be used by mostly retired career military servicemen, but you have to go through the busiest part of the city to get to it. Not to mention, there will be officers watching for you to return to your home."

Violetta sighed and crossed her arms over her chest. Everything he said rang true, even if she didn't like it. "Fine. What do you suggest we do until then?"

"We return to the safe house. By the time we return, it should be time for lunch. I don't know about you, but I'm hungry."

"Maybe a little," she grudgingly admitted.

By the time they arrived at the safe house, Violetta had to admit she was more than 'a little' hungry. As they entered the lift, she glanced at her companion. "Thank you."

"For what?" he asked, clearly startled.

"For making the right call, regarding waiting until tonight. Going now would be reckless and foolish. So, thank you."

"Just doing my job."

She smiled, a bit smug. "I'll bet you don't rationalize with every person you're hired to protect."

"How do you know I don't?"

"Because I know you. I know how stubborn you can be, remember?"

"Maybe I changed."

"Maybe you're being stubborn now."

He grinned. "Guess you'll just have to figure it out on your own."

"Is that a Challenge, Malik Addelia?"

"Take it however you want, Violence," he retorted as the lift stopped. "I-" he stopped mid-sentence as the lift doors opened.

There was someone else there. A human with sandy blond hair stood with his back to the lift, but Violetta saw his face in the mirror behind the bar. She took in his blue eyes and clean-shaven face, which revealed a scar going from his right ear to his cheek.

"What the fark is he doing here?" Malik said softly.

"Is he a rival of your don's?" Violetta asked.

"No, but I'm not Malik's favorite person, either," the stranger interjected in a loud voice.

"Maybe you should tell me why I'm cursed with your presence, Tagliani," Malik said behind a grim smile.

"I'm here to remind you that you're on the job, flashy Dan. You are protection, not on a blind date with your school sweetheart."

Malik bristled. "Nothing's happened to her. She's safe and intact. Which puts me higher on the success charts than you usually are, Tagliani."

Tagliani smiled. It did not improve his looks. The smile was too wide, with too many sparkling white teeth and narrowed eyes. Lines creased his forehead and cheeks, as though the effort was stretching his face to hereto unforeseen extremes.

"Wouldn't want to spoil your public record, now, would we?" Tagliani said.

"I dunno," Malik began imitating Tagliani's distinct accent. "Maybe I should just kill ya right here and have less to worry about."

"And embarrass yourself in the attempt? In front of your lady friend? I know you won't take that chance."

"Is this person important to the don's day-to-day business?" Violetta interjected, moving closer to Tagliani.

She had no clue what their argument was about, but that had never stopped her before now. In fact, it reminded her of their childhood.

"He's what humans call 'an enforcer.' Not high on the food chain, as they like to say," Malik explained.

"Oh," Violetta said. *Perfect.* She punched Tagliani in the nose before declaring, "I feel threatened by him."

Tagliani bent forward, pinching his nose to slow the bleeding. Crimson red flowed between his fingers.

"We cannot have that," Malik said, and drove his knee into the human's groin.

Tagliani grunted, and fell to his knees, clutching his groin.

"They never seem to think to wear protection," Malik observed.

"That's a weakness of theirs?"

Most K'laisians wore protection to protect that area of their bodies.

"In the males, mostly. Shall we leave him here?"

Violetta gave a single nod. Together, she and Malik punched both sides of Tagliani's face. When his blue eyes rolled up until only the whites could be seen, they each grabbed an arm and dragged him behind the bar.

"Someone will eventually show up looking for him. Unless he wakes up before then, while we're gone, and stumbles his way out," Malik commented.

"That was actually a lot of fun. Just like old times." She gestured towards the containers of take-out on the countertop. "Do you think it's safe to eat?"

"Absolutely."

As they began opening containers and dividing up the food, Violetta said, "I'll be a good girl, and at least try to behave."

"Since when do you behave?" Malik teased.

"I can behave. Sometimes," she replied with not a little indignation. When he laughed, she nudged him with her shoulder. "I'll even pick a safe… well, safe-ish topic."

"Like what?"

"Like: how is your family?"

She took a bite of her pasta as she waited for him to respond.

"My family is doing well. My sisters are too busy being protective of their children to worry about me, but I do see them at least once a month." He stabbed at a salad with his fork as he continued. "My parents finally retired, having passed on the bakery to my youngest sister. Of course, since my father worked for the Don, and the bakery was a means to keep things legitimate, she took that on as well. Syra has two sons, who help at the bakery when not at school."

Finishing her bite, Violetta turned her eyes to the pasta, lest he realize her little secret.

"Keaty stayed in the military, she is a captain now. On the other side of the world most of the time. Her daughter is well known for her sculpting, even though she is still in studies. And Yndi has five children, her mate is a supervisor for the hospital in the 43rd District. They come visit the most often, because I can make sure they have private boxes at events. So I have some use left to the family," he joked, before eating what was on his fork.

"At least you don't have to worry about your parents nagging you for a mate and children. Or even trying to Match you with someone," Violetta said, trying to not sound envious. "I imagine your parents are enjoying their retirement."

"Oh, yes. My parents spend most of the solar year visiting and traveling between our respective homes. They converted one of those first generation HAVs. You know the ones, they were just smaller than military tanks with better accommodations. They park outside our homes, stay for months, then go see our planet's wonders before coming 'back to port' at the next sibling's home. I'm due to have them in another six weeks."

He paused long enough to eat some of his salad. Violetta remained quiet, allowing him time and giving him space.

"As for mate and children, I fear they don't want to dare ask until they see me with someone they can tolerate or consider more suitable than a passing distraction." He smiled slightly. "Mom believed we could find our own mates without Matching us. Instead, she just bluntly tells us if she approves or not. Da is a little more subtle, but not by much."

"I haven't seen your parents in years," Violetta mused, sadly. She stared at the pasta on her fork. "They always treated me well. Your mother was the closest I ever had to one of my own, aside from my grandmother, of course. Your father, I think, found me amusing."

"He found you endearing. Come by and see them? I can provide you with my address and private contact info. They have asked if I see you in the city. I am confident they would be delighted to catch up with you in person."

"I would love that," she replied. "As long as it won't cause problems for you." He paused in another bite of his salad, a brow raised. She explained, "I doubt I fall under the 'questionable female' category. At least, not if they are asking you about me."

"It won't be a problem. I vow it," Malik reassured her. Laughter filled his eyes, as he added, "Though, my sisters may decide to interrogate you."

She giggled. So far, he hadn't realized she was keeping something from him. Yet.

"That'll be an interesting change. About what, though?"

"What you've been doing. How you've been. Why you haven't visited. Or messaged. Or visited the bakery." He paused, and tipped his head to the side. "Though, Syra will probably start sending baskets of treats to your department. She's very much like Mom when it comes to being motherly."

"I could absolutely see her doing that," Violetta commented.

"So, what is it you aren't telling me?" Malik asked, his eyes narrowing on her.

Clearing her throat, she tried to keep the laughter from her voice. Though it was becoming increasingly difficult.

"I visit Syra's shop often. Any time Issik and I visit the Master of the Dead for information on a homicide, we stop by her business," Violetta admitted. She wasn't entirely successful at keeping the smile from her face. "She's only asked if I've seen you. And I answer that I haven't. Though, I suspect she'll be absolutely thrilled when she finds out you've been helping me. And I'll be seeing you more often after this is finished."

Malik stared at her, his eyes blinking. In a pure blood native, it was a sign of complete surprise or shock. Then he started laughing.

"I'm going to have to talk to my littlest sister after this is finished," he joked. "I would never have thought she'd be keeping your visits a secret from me."

A comfortable silence descended upon them as they returned to eating their meals. Malik went behind the bar and vanished, before reappearing with two bottles of flavored carbonated beverages. "Sweet or dark?"

"Oh, is that kaerik root?" Violetta asked eagerly. Malik nodded and she held her hand out. "I'll take the kaerik root."

He flipped the lid off with a practiced move before handing it to her. He did the same to his melvelas flower-flavored beverage. "How have your grandparents been? Are they still Council members?"

"Still." Violetta sighed. "Every so often they hint at the idea of grandchildren."

"I'm sorry," Malik said. She could tell he was being genuine, too. He returned to his seat beside her. "How often do you see them?"

"I visit them every few weeks. Though we video-chat frequently. I'm certain they'll be visiting after this is resolved."

"What do you think they'll say if they find out I'm helping you?" Malik asked, choosing his words carefully.

Violetta chuckled a little. "Probably the same your parents will be asking. And your sisters. I believe they always thought we would end up together."

"They aren't going to frighten you off?" he teased. "What if they try to Match us?"

"From visiting you?" Violetta chuckled. Her heart was telling her there were still feelings for him, but her brain was telling her to consider everything. To remember now was a bad time to consider anything other than what was happening to her. After everything was resolved, then she could figure out her feelings. She hoped. "No. If you can handle their teasing, then I can handle it as well. And so what if they do? It would be interesting to see what they try."

"But you want us kept secret from your grandparents," he stated, a sly twinkle in his eyes.

"Unless you want a public announcement that we're a couple," she replied dryly. "Yes."

Something flickered over his face and she couldn't decipher it. At least he wasn't concerned about her grandparents, who tended to be very traditional beings. They had loved her human mother and embraced many human traditions because of her human half. Bigotry, racism, and xenophobia were not words that could ever be attributed to her paternal grandparents.

"Maybe we should decide after this is resolved," Malik suggested, his tone teasing. "That way if they try to Match us up, it won't be so problematic."

"Would probably be for the best," she agreed.

In silent, mutual agreement, they delved back into their food. The silence between them was companionable and warm.

Chapter Seven

Waiting until nightfall was one of the hardest things Violetta had ever done. Malik had tried his best to keep her mind off what was to come, but it was impossible. Every scenario possible ran through her head and she spent every minute thinking about the possibilities. Scenarios and counter scenarios. Trying to not dwell on the 'what if's' that plagued her.

Now with the moon rising into the darkened sky, Malik drove her to her apartment. The HAV he drove this time had two back seats with a window that could be partially opened. She sat in the back, hidden by tinted windows and the front seat. That worked perfectly for her, since she wasn't planning on getting out of the car at the front of her building.

Near the entrance was what appeared to be a homeless man, sitting on the ground with canvas bags and clothes piled around him. Filthy black hair fell to just below his shoulders, and his clothes were wrinkled and as dirty as the rest of him. He was so disheveled it was difficult to tell if he was human or native. Only his bronze eyes gave away his mixed heritage.

Those of pure-blood had either gold or silver eyes. Never bronze. Not even if someone with silver eyes and gold eyes had a child. The child's eyes would always be one color or the other.

Those with silver hair and pale skin always had silver eyes. Those with dark skin and black hair always had gold eyes. Such was the biology and genetics of K'laisians.

Violetta grinned as Malik stopped in front of the homeless man.

"Are you sure about this?" Malik asked, eyeing the man warily.

"Yep."

Shaking his head, Malik pressed the button for the front window to slide down. "Got a match, my friend?"

The man shoved himself to a standing position and shuffled back and forth. His body shook with jittery energy, reminding Violetta of someone who was taking an illicit drug of some sort.

"I use a lighter," the man replied. His voice was roughened and gravely, as though he smoked several packs of something a day.

"Better still," Malik replied.

The man shuffled forward, his eyes darting around as he moved. Violetta forced herself to remain hidden in the back, able to watch using the reflection in the windows. As much as she wanted to pop up, she had to stay out of sight. He would see her soon enough.

Once the man was up near the side of the car, Violetta spoke. "How's it been, Faulkner?" The 'homeless bum' started. Violetta rose slightly from the back seat and waved, a grin on her face. "Miss me?"

"What the hox is this?" the man, Faulkner, demanded.

"It's called saving her ass," Malik retorted. He glanced back at Violetta, his eyes narrowing. "Want to clue me in on the joke?"

"Faulkner is part of the detail that guards my father's apartment. Dad's interface holds a lot of classified documents. They make certain no one unauthorized touches it."

"Including you?"

Faulkner chuckled. "Nah, she's got clearance." He studied Malik, then smirked. "Going to punish her later for not telling you she's got a detail watching her place?"

Malik glowered at the man. Violetta decided it best to break up the little party before someone said or did something stupid. Like issue a Challenge to a Duel.

"I need to talk to Captain Ae'staa," Violetta said. "Where is she?"

"She's coming down. You shoulda warned us you were going to get accused of killing the chief. Would've been nice," Faulkner joked. "It's been hopping with your cop buds trying to get into your place. So far they don't have the needed paperwork."

"Where's the joy in that?" she retorted. "Got to keep you guys on your toes."

Faulkner snickered as a tall, svelte native woman in a business suit of subdued colors came out the front door. He adopted his 'homeless bum' demeanor. Nodding jerkily, he turned and shuffled his way back to his spot at the door. The woman shot a disgusted look towards the 'bum' but didn't deviate from her path to the car. Opening the door, she slid into the front seat, as though Malik had arrived specifically for her.

Captain Inarayi Ae'staa was the perfect epitome of a successful native businesswoman. Her dark hair was braided into a tight chignon. A necklace of strung bepril pearls wrapped around her neck, their pale blue colors contrasting with her darker skin. Violetta knew this persona was all an act. Ae'staa was a woman who could be deadly.

The moment the door was shut and the window up, Malik drove away. "Where am I going?"

"Just drive. Nowhere specific. Just keep going so Violetta can explain what the ever-loving-fark is going on," Ae'staa demanded. A hard edge to her tone sharpened her words.

The woman was furious.

"I didn't do it," Violetta began.

Ae'staa cut her off. "We know that. What really happened in that room?"

Violetta blinked. She hadn't expected that answer. "I got to Chief Me'addn's building, the door opened for me, so I figured he was expecting me. His apartment door was unlocked and slid open when I neared. I went in and he was lying in a pool of his own blood. Ziph Rc'dollph showed up and tried to kill me. I never once fired my weapon. I used a grenade instead."

Ae'staa gave a curt nod. "Good thing you didn't fire. Why did you go to see the chief of police?"

"Found out Ziph, Cancio, and Captain Monroe are all corrupt. Along with a bunch of other officers. Doing everything illegal you can think of. I contacted the chief using his personal number I got from Dad's interface." She paused, glancing at Malik's stiff posture. He obviously didn't like any of this, but there really was no other option. "There's more. I need to get into the apartment and use Dad's interface. I need your help to do it."

The captain stiffened visibly. Her words were clipped when she spoke again. "Why do you need to use your father's interface?"

The words 'it better be a good reason' hung in the air.

"Someone has figured out how to clone weapons. I can give evidence that a civilian was framed and executed for a murder they didn't commit. Framed by Ziph Rc'dollph."

Violetta held out the interface Nualith gave them. The photo was enlarged and filled the screen. There was no mistaking Rc'dollph's face or the unusual weapon.

"I have video of him using that weapon to murder a civilian, along with other vidclip footage proving the guilt of other crimes. Dad told me about someone who had approached him about cloning weapons when I was a freshman in high school. I know that name would be on my father's interface. I need that name, Captain."

Captain Ae'staa sighed heavily. Her head was bent and Violetta suspected she was still staring at the interface. "If this is true, you will tell me the name in exchange for my squad's assistance in this task."

"Deal. Get me to Dad's interface, and I'll give you the person's name."

"Why are you so willing to help her?" Malik asked suddenly. He clenched the controls of the HAV so tight his knuckles were white.

"The squad isn't there simply to keep unauthorized people from accessing Vrehn's interface. It's to make sure no one interferes with her." There was amusement in the captain's voice as she continued. "We've been informed of what happened. Helping Violetta isn't interfering with her. It may be interfering with the local police service, but that isn't our problem."

That was news to Violetta, but she remained silent. She'd been under the impression they were there solely because of her father's console and his classified documents. Had that changed? Or had they always been there to keep people from interfering with her?

"How are you going to get her in without having every officer in the city knocking on her door the moment she enters it?" Malik asked.

Instead of answering, Ae'staa said, "Turn here." Malik did as he was told. "Go one block, then turn right. Stop at the corner of the alley to the butcher's shop."

The muscles in Malik's neck and shoulders tightened. Violetta was surprised that he hadn't bent or broken the delicate controls. He did as ordered, though, following the instructions to the letter.

Ae'staa opened the door and grabbed the bag sitting on the corner. She tossed it surreptitiously into the back, where it landed on Violetta's chest, before closing the door.

"Drive."

Malik drove, favoring the darker streets to the well-lit ones.

"You'll need to change into those clothes if you want to get into your apartment," the captain stated.

"Enjoy the show," Violetta muttered as she opened the bag.

The first article of clothing she pulled out was a standard military jumpsuit. Beneath the jumpsuit was a shirt, large jacket, and pants. All of which smelled as though they'd been washed in the cheapest liquor money could buy. There were several marks where ashes had charred the leather of the jacket and the edges showed signs of wear.

Wiggling around in the floorboard of the backseat of the HAV in order to change clothes had her giggling.

"Glad you're having fun back there," Malik grumbled.

"Brings back memories of time spent with Dad," Violetta explained as she pulled the pants up over the military jumpsuit. "Dad made it a game. Now I know why he did it. Wonder how many times he had to do something like this."

"That sounds like something your father would've done," Malik admitted. "Remember when he decided to teach us some hand-to-hand combat?"

"You got your rear handed to you. So did I," Violetta said, before giggling even more. She finished pulling on the jacket over the shirt. "We only ever did manage to hold our own with him."

"Only took us that entire summer to manage that feat," Malik replied. "You dressed?"

"One final piece," she replied. Pulling a wig from the bag, she slid it over her hair before shoving it all under a cap. "How do I look?"

"Horrible," Captain Ae'staa replied. "It'll do. I hope your father gave you acting lessons. Addelia here will have to 'assist' your drunken ass into the building and up to your floor. We'll park in the back. I'll tell you where."

"Yes, ma'am," Malik said, smiling slightly. "Think you're up for it, Violence?"

"I may be able to manage it," she replied with a grin.

More fun memories sprang forth. If her father couldn't be here, then at least she was able to finally use the lessons he'd taught her. Lessons from childhood games that she'd always enjoyed.

Fifteen minutes later, Violetta was pulling off the hat and wig inside her apartment. The soothing sounds of a forest at night filled the room. It put her at ease, despite everything occurring. She walked over to the chair her father had always used, running her hand along an arm. It came from the last ship he'd served on. When the ship had been decommissioned, he had requested the chair and had been granted it. She often curled up in it, reading a book on her handheld interface.

Beside the chair, on a table, a hologram displayed her parents dancing at their wedding. Her mother had been beautiful, and though she had died giving birth to Violetta, there were plenty of stillgraphs and vidclips of her parents in the apartment.

From the corner of her eye, she noticed Malik watching her little ritual. She'd always gone to her father's favorite chair and the hologram every time she entered the apartment. Doing so now gave her normalcy in an otherwise insane time.

The captain cleared her throat.

"We really don't have a lot of time," she said apologetically.

Violetta nodded and headed towards her father's office. Malik gave her a nod.

"You don't have clearance-" Ae'staa began.

"To go into his office," Malik finished for her as he moved to the cabinet that held decanters and a variety of glasses. Opening one door, he removed a tumbler. "I wasn't expecting to. Haven't been allowed since I first started visiting. I didn't think it would change all of a sudden. I'll be here when you ladies finish."

Captain Ae'staa stared at him, even as Violetta opened a door off the main room. "You haven't been here for several years."

"Five years, to be exact," he replied, looking through the various containers.

"Curious," the captain replied. She turned to Violetta. "You don't mind him making himself at home?"

"What? No. He's always welcome here. Dad always liked him. He just didn't like the mischief I found while with him."

Without another word, she entered her father's office. The lights came on automatically, adjusting to her preferred setting. Crossing to the console, she flinched as she pressed her hand against the frame. Anytime she wished to use the interface, a needle extracted a small amount of her blood. It wasn't that painful. More like a mild stinging.

Once the interface analyzed her blood and matched her DNA with the registered users on file, the screen sprang to life. She sat in what had been her father's chair, moving closer to the interface.

Tapping the screen, she navigated to the files listed as his advisory notes. Typing the word 'clone' into the search function, she began going through the files that appeared, searching for the right one.

"You're very adept at using that interface," Captain Ae'staa commented.

"That would be because Dad taught me how to use it," she replied. "He taught me how to use an interface and how to maximize its usefulness."

The captain made a noncommittal noise. "What's the history between you and Addelia?"

"We met in primary school and became best friends. I asked Dad if he could visit and Dad gave his permission. After that we did almost everything together. He had my back throughout school, and I had his." Violetta sighed, a sad smile on her face. "He was my rock when Dad was off-planet on missions. When Dad died, he was there for me. I can't tell you how much I regret not keeping in contact with him when I went to the police academy."

"What happened after your father's murder?"

Violetta bit her lip and unconsciously looked towards her bedroom. "I was stupid and didn't keep in touch. Thought it was better, since we'd be expected to find pure blood natives for mates. I didn't want him to deal with trouble during his year in the Service with being so close to me. After I entered the academy, I had to deal with the bullying and attempts at Matches. Add to it, I thought he was going to do... a different career. So, I didn't contact him."

"Do you still like him?"

That stopped Violetta's every movement. She turned to the captain and saw a gleam in the woman's eyes. A gleam she couldn't decipher.

"I… Yes. I do," she said slowly, admitting what her heart knew aloud. Even if she may not be ready to admit it to anyone else. "Does that change anything?"

"Not really," the captain replied. "He passed the psych evals when he entered the military. He may not have the same level of security clearance you have, but otherwise?" There was amusement shining in the captain's eyes even as she grinned. "We'd be happy to ensure you have another 'blackout' if you decide to invite him over."

"Another 'blackout'?" Violetta asked, almost afraid to ask. "You knew he was here five years ago? And… what happened that night?"

"We've been watching you since before your father's death, Violetta," Captain Ae'staa said gently. "Before his death, we watched while he was off-planet. It became a constant, permanent assignment after his death. So, yes. We were here that night he came over. Does that change things?"

"I didn't realize…" She trailed off, shaking herself mentally. That answered a couple questions and opened up several others.

"Well? Are you going to invite him over?"

"I… I don't know if he even feels that way towards me now. Anymore." Violetta managed to stutter. She didn't think she had been that easy to read. Nor did she want to jump to conclusions about Malik. She still didn't know if he was still sore about her ignoring him for five years. "It's been five years. He may not want to rekindle that relationship. I *did* ignore him for those years. Even if I was an idiot for giving into societal pressure and expectations."

Captain Ae'staa laughed. "Right. Keep thinking that. In the meantime, just remember what I said. And stop worrying about what close-minded fools think." She nodded towards the interface. "Any luck finding that name you're searching for?"

"Not yet, and I think I'm going about this wrong." Violetta leaned back in the chair, staring at the screen. "My father said 'clone gun' to me years ago while writing a report, and it was such an odd thing for him to say. Especially with such… dire overtones in his voice. But I just realized, it's doubtful he would use such a goofy phrase in an official report."

"No, he wouldn't have used that," the captain confirmed. She tilted her head to the side. "This weapon, how does it work?"

"They somehow duplicate another weapon," Violetta replied, glancing at the captain.

"You need another word for duplicate," Ae'staa said. "What about 'replicate'? It's what I would use, if I were to write the report."

"That... that might work," Violetta replied, her fingers flying over the keys.

Within seconds, a short list of reports appeared on the screen. It didn't take long for Violetta to locate the advisory report her father had written. As with everything her father had done, the report was detailed, but to the point.

Everything they needed was in that report. The name, the date, the race of the man who had come up with the idea. Her father had told the man the military was not interested in such a thing and to not continue with the idea. He added that the man should be watched closely, to prevent him from pursuing his idea.

Violetta read the report a second time. "Do you want a copy of this?"

"Please," the captain replied.

Seconds later, she had two copies of the report. Violetta handed one to the captain. "Do you mind if I have a minute to myself?"

Captain Ae'staa squeezed Violetta's shoulder. "Thank you. You've got five minutes."

"Thank you," Violetta said.

She waited until the captain shut the door behind her before navigating her father's files again. Her father hadn't reached his position by leaving things to chance. She knew how her father's mind worked, probably better than anyone else. He kept his own set of dossiers on people. There were files on herself and Malik, though she had never been able to bring herself to look at them. Her mother's was filled with memories, photos, and vidclips, along with reports she'd never read. Her father had loved her mother. That was all she needed to know.

The dossier on Matt Gomez was thin, but it did include an address and other contact information. There was a picture of him from his time in the military. After memorizing the address, she saved the dossier to a small white poker chip that could be read on any interface. That chip was tucked into her boot beside the other holcrom card.

With three minutes left, she opened the file that contained data from her high school days. Photos and vidclips of her, her father, and Malik filled the screen. Blinking back tears, she touched a photo of her father. She missed him terribly and wished he were here to talk to. There were photos of her father's parents, also. They probably were aghast at what was happening, and she couldn't even contact them about it.

Her grandparents were retired military with a life spent in the service. Only retired military personnel of honorable discharge and good standing could become politicians. Same for those in the police service; they had to be of an honorable discharge and go through the highest level of psych evals to ensure they met the same criteria as the military personnel.

Those not of the military or highest positions in the police service had to petition the councils to earn a position. They, too, had to be evaluated to ensure they were not xenophobic, racist, or were afflicted with a variety of mental illnesses and phobias that would hinder, even harm, their world. The being had to show exemplary service to K'lais and the citizens to even attempt to petition the council. It was not an easy task or one most K'laisians desired. The positions fit those retired from the military, for they were ones who had gone offplanet and served for decades while interacting with almost every race in the galaxies.

The political arena had become her grandparents' careers following the military. They served on local city councils and lived busy lives.

When her name was cleared, Violetta vowed to schedule dinner with them as soon as possible.

A knock sounded on the door. She closed out of all the files and turned off the interface. Time to continue working on clearing her name. The sooner that was done, the sooner she could return to her normal life.

This time, she vowed to remain in contact with Malik.

Chapter Eight

Once Violetta and Malik were safely back in their HAV, Malik began driving in a direction Violetta recognized. He was heading towards a park on the outskirts of the city. Her father had taken her there often, teaching her things that most kids would never learn in a school. In fact, she doubted most children had learned the lessons her father had given her. Vrehn Cq'linns had passed his lessons from his service in the military down to her. Most of those survival lessons had taken place in the park.

The park also happened to be a nature preserve protected and patrolled by the military. Certain parts required military identification and clearance. Those areas had been where Violetta had learned from her father. He had informed her the cameras were military property, when she had once commented on the lack of police presence. The local police did not have access to those cameras, which meant there was no local police presence in the preserve. Only military personnel who took their jobs seriously.

Even the homeless would not be found slumbering within the preserve. Let alone doing anything else.

They would be safe there.

He parked the HAV in an empty picnic area. "Why didn't you tell me?"

Well, fark. He wasn't looking at her and from his body posture, Violetta knew he had withdrawn from her again. She sighed. Reaching over, she turned his face until she could meet his eyes.

"I *couldn't* tell you. *I* wasn't told about them."

When he didn't jerk out of her touch, she felt a sliver of hope. She didn't want to lose his friendship. Not when he was probably the only friend she currently had.

"I owe you an explanation," she said, leaning back in the seat.

His eyes were cold and hard as they met hers. "Yes, you do. Starting with now."

Okay, she deserved that. She had to admit it.

"After Dad's murder, you know I had to get clearance to keep his interface." He gave a sharp nod. She continued, her voice soft even as she kept his gaze. "I also began noticing certain people around the apartment. Dad taught me to be observant of everything, so I kept note of them. After a few months, I approached one of them and demanded answers. The person I approached happened to be Captain Ae'staa. She took me aside and explained their detail was classified and on a need-to-know basis. Because I had the clearance to keep Dad's military property, lived in his apartment, and approached them, she was able to tell me everything. Or, as much as she wanted at the time. Captain Ae'staa did not tell me, then, they'd been sent to ensure no one interfered with me."

"So when Issik asked if you knew anything, you couldn't tell him because he didn't have the clearance?" Malik asked. "They didn't tell you to stop… to not contact me?"

"No. No one told me to do that. I was an idiot who was afraid you'd be hazed or harassed by our friendship while in the military. As for the detail? It isn't my place to talk about their presence. As it is, I don't know what clearance you had in the military. I do know that the military will be watching you closer, because you know about them." Violetta bit her lip. "I'm sorry I wasn't able to tell you."

"Apology accepted," Malik said, his body relaxing slightly. "Before I left the military service, my clearance was probably above yours. Mental healers, which is what I was studying to become, hear intimate and secret information from their patients. If I were to treat an admiral or general, I would have to be cleared to hear anything that came out of their mouths."

Which explained Ae'staa's amusement regarding his clearance level. Oddly enough, she found that fact appealing. And it made her question how much Captain Ae'staa and her crew knew about her and Malik. Why weren't they concerned about her and Malik having a relationship, despite what was typically expected?

"Then you'll probably have less to worry about." Her eyes kept drifting to his lips and she suddenly felt like a teenager again. Ridiculous, really. She was an adult. Even if this was a great make-out spot, this was most definitely not the time or place to partake in such activities. "Is that why you brought me here? So if we argued we wouldn't wake anyone? Or create a disturbance?"

"I wanted to have some space between us and the guard squad," Malik said.

"Huh? What guard squad? The one watching Dad's apartment?"

"Yes, them."

"Oh. I thought there was one at your safe house and you were referring to them." After what Captain Ae'staa said, she couldn't help but wonder if they were being watched at the safe house. It wouldn't surprise her in the least. Taking a chance, she caressed his cheek with the tips of her fingers. "Any particular reason?"

"I wanted honest answers and I doubted you could be completely honest with them around." He paused, his brows furrowing. "Why would you think they are at the safe house?"

"Ah," she replied, dropping her hand. Maybe he didn't feel the same towards her, after all. "Because the bum outside it reminded me of Faulkner. His hair was too clean to be an actual bum. Do you have any other questions?"

"He's a lookout for the don," Malik replied with a smile. "And yes, I do have one more. Want to come back here when there isn't all the stressful events?"

Warmth spread from the center of Violetta's stomach outward upon hearing the question. Her heart skipped a beat before pounding against her chest. She met his eyes and smiled.

"I would like that. Not mad at me?" At his confused expression, she explained. "For ignoring you these past years because I was an idiot? For not wanting to think about you being with… well, with someone else."

"No. Though I will be if you do it again."

"Not going to happen. I've learned that lesson and it's a lonely life." Her eyes glinted as she added, "Though if you try it with me, I'll find you and Challenge you."

"I'll remember that."

"I'm sure you will," she replied softly, her fingers caressing the tip of his ear.

The same tender smile she remembered from their night together five years ago formed on his lips. "Perhaps we should go, then, before a repeat of that night happens again tonight."

Well, she was screwed. Regardless of what the future held for them, at least she knew the physical attraction was still there. Somewhere in her head, she heard her father's voice scolding her for allowing her emotions to get the best of her. He'd have had her head if he saw them now.

"We definitely need to be leaving before someone spots us. Maybe change topics, too. Something to distract us," she said, trying to force herself to think straight. She pulled her hand back reluctantly as Malik nodded. "Even if this place is patrolled by the military, that doesn't mean those who aren't dirty won't try to take me out. Even here."

"Do you think they would risk the military's anger? By intruding on military property?" Malik asked. His body language shifted to being far more alert and concerned. As though all other emotions had been flipped off.

"I don't know. I wouldn't put it past Ziph. He's known, at least in the department, to break the rules if he thought it would get him the result he wanted."

"Then we leave," Malik replied simply. "We get the answers you need so you can turn it all over to the DA. Once the results from Nualith come back, you should be free to turn it all in."

"I'm going to need the weapon, Malik. Without it or something solid to prove there is a 'clone' weapon, I've still got nothing."

"So how do we get it?" Malik asked.

"I have the file of who Dad talked about. A human male by the name of Matt Gomez. Here's his picture." She handed him the printout, her fingers lingering on his.

He lifted her hand to his lips, kissing her knuckles before placing it in her lap. It did nothing for her racing pulse or the rise in her temperature.

Malik glanced at the printout then did a double take. "I remember this guy. He was on one of the vidclips you were watching."

"Are you certain?"

Malik peered again at the image. "Yes, although I think he was older."

"Do you think we could go back to Nualith's place and look through the vidclips again?"

"I believe it would be safer to be around other people than alone right now," Malik admitted. He started the HAV and turned it around. He glanced at her as he drove from the nature preserve. "Did you mean what you said about your father earlier?"

"Yes. Dad really did like you. I know there are some factions that don't approve of mixed marriages, let alone the children of those couples having relationships. Dad and his parents thought it was ridiculous. 'Fools stooping to the most idiotic beliefs of humans.' Dad said it wasn't a person's blood that helped the world prosper, it was the person's actions." Violetta chuckled, shaking her head. "Dad liked you. He enjoyed your visits and having you around. If he didn't, he wouldn't have invited you to so many activities. Let alone allowed me to invite you over to begin with. Or when he was offplanet."

Or allowed her to be with him in any capacity. Her father had taught her quickly how to discern if someone was interested in her because of who she was, rather than the 'perks' her father and she enjoyed. If Malik wouldn't have passed the military's approval, he would never have been allowed inside her father's apartment.

"Good to know," Malik said quietly. "I always enjoyed the time spent with him. He encouraged me to sign up for the military. Said I would do well."

"Did he say to go off-world?" The words came out calm, curious, but she felt as though she were staring down the barrel of a cannon.

"No, he didn't," Malik replied, thoughtfully. "Think he knew the path I'd be pushed towards?"

It took every ounce of discipline Violetta possessed to not breathe a heavy sigh of relief. She would have been heartbroken had he given an affirmative answer. "Maybe? Dad was very astute about a lot of things. He always knew who to put in a position where they would serve the best."

"He was at that," Malik murmured.

"You realize we shouldn't have done that," she said quietly. "Letting our emotions rule us, that is."

"No, but I don't regret it." Malik's eyes shifted to her briefly before turning back to the road. "We can't let it happen again until this is over, though."

Violetta nodded and settled against the seat of the car.

The rest of the ride to Nualith's lab was in comfortable silence. There were still a few lights on in the building when they arrived. Nualith met them at the front door, a smirk on her face.

"I figured you two would be back at some point," she said. "Come on. I'll take you to the room again."

Violetta glanced at Malik. He gave a slight shrug.

Once there, Nualith added, "You can let yourselves out. I'll be back in the morning. Let me know if there is anything else I can do for you." With that, she turned and left.

The interface was up and running already. As though someone had given her a heads-up.

"Do you think Captain Ae'staa suggested we would return?" Violetta asked Malik.

"Possible," Malik replied thoughtfully. "Someone certainly did. Whoever it is wants to help you. Otherwise, the police service would be here awaiting us, instead of Nualith."

Violetta nodded as she loaded the holcrom. Once it loaded, she began going through the files again. A slow, boring process, she watched vidclip after vidclip. Malik fell asleep in the chair after the twentieth vidclip. His head rested on his arms that were crossed on the desk. Dark hair fell across his face, giving him a boyish look.

She was debating whether to continue searching or call it a night and return later when she found the vidclip he had mentioned.

Enlarging the vidclip, she kept the sound muted to not wake Malik. This wasn't a vidclip from just any camera. It came from his bodycam. Every officer wore one and the bodycam recorded everything, complete with vital signs. The dataset from the cameras those in the police service wore were not as detailed as those in the military. A fact her father had always been disgusted about because they could easily have been equal.

Violetta had known Lieutenant Cancio was dirty, but she hadn't realized he was so mentally ill as to shoot someone in cold blood. Even if the person didn't die immediately from the injury. There was no mistaking the contents of the vidclip, though.

Matt Gomez approached Cancio. He was older by at least ten years, though there was no mistaking his features. She turned the sound up and listened to the conversation as she replayed the vidclip.

"Why did you call me? I thought I told you to never contact me. We'd contact you," Cancio said.

Gomez seemed on edge, shifting his weight nervously. "Look, I thought you were just going to use the weapon for testing. To see if everything matched up and if the design worked. You know, make sure the signals matched and the data showed up properly."

"We had other plans. Your intentions are not the same as ours," Cancio replied. *"You're getting your due. Just keep doing your job and we'll keep paying you."*

Violetta noticed Cancio's vitals change. His pulse quickened and his blood pressure rose. She knew where this was leading.

"I'll turn it all in. I'm sure someone would be interested in what you pigs are doing," Gomez retorted. His face curled into a snarl. "I'm sure your higher ups would be interested in knowing how dirty you guys are and how it's done when I show them the prototype."

"It'll be hard to do if you're laying in a hospital bed," Cancio replied. There was the unmistakable hum of a weapon firing and Gomez's body dropped. "You won't die. We still need you. But if you force us, we will kill you and find someone else to replace you."

"Asshole," Gomez gasped, clutching his stomach.

Cancio laughed. "Come on. Let's get you to a hospital. We have the perfect place for you."

After the vidclip ended, Violetta stared at the blank screen for several moments. Once she'd processed what she saw, she gently shook Malik's shoulder. He jerked, snapping awake. Sitting up, he looked around before zeroing in on the interface.

"Did you find the vidclip?"

"Yeah. You need to watch it." Tapping the screen, she started the video again.

They watched in silence as the vidclip played. When Cancio shot Gomez, Malik swore softly.

"They've got him holed up somewhere. Let's get back to the safe house. I'll need to contact a few people before we can do anything."

"Sleep first, please," Violetta said. Yawning, she stretched. "You still look cute when you sleep."

Malik made a face. "That's supposed to be my line."

"Been spying on me, Addelia?"

"No," he said, drawing the word out. He stood and held his hands out to her. When she took them, he pulled her up against him. "If I'm going to watch you sleep, it'll be after I wear you out."

Stars help me, she thought, her breath catching in her throat. She swallowed hard, trying to not pant at the vivid memories that sprang to life.

"Maybe we should, ah, go," Violetta said, forcing those thoughts away as she stared into his eyes.

Did he know what he was doing? Was this on purpose? Or was her body betraying her because of her celibate life?

"Before we start something we shouldn't be doing here."

Malik chuckled. He tucked her arm through his and began walking with her to the door.

"As you wish."

Chapter Nine

It was late morning when Violetta finally woke up. She'd collapsed on her bed at the safe house as soon as she entered the room. The adrenaline from the day's ups and downs had worn her out.

Dressing in borrowed clothes once more, she left her room to find Issik and Malik in deep conversation. Neither looked pleased. Both men turned away from the interface they were watching when they noticed her presence.

"You're going to want to sit down," Issik said, not bothering with a greeting. Everything about him was grim.

Malik nodded. "It's bad, Vi."

Crossing the room, she took the proffered interface, ignoring the suggestion to sit. A list of articles filled the screen.

The first read: Local homicide detective suspected of murder!

Daughter of Vrehn Cq'linns suspected of killing Chief of Police Ylvran Me'addn, another announced.

They were all variations of a theme: that she, Violetta Cq'linns, was wanted for the police chief's murder.

Issik reached over and tapped the screen. A newsreel appeared.

A lovely native woman sat behind a news desk. "Now, for news on the death of Police Chief Ylvran Me'addn. Local homicide detective, Sergeant Violetta Cq'linns, daughter of the late Vrehn Cq'linns, is suspected of the murder. The local police force is requesting the assistance of the citizens of K'lais in locating Sergeant Cq'linns. If seen, do not approach. Contact local police and allow them to apprehend." She paused, glancing to her left. "Now, for more from District Attorney Nyzril Lc'sonn."

The video flipped to the district attorney, a native man with silver hair trimmed close to his scalp and brilliant silver eyes. "The evidence surrounding the late police chief is purely circumstantial. We are seeking Lady Cq'linns with the desire to obtain her record of the events surrounding the chief's death. This search for her is needed to learn the truth behind Chief Me'addn's death. She is a respected officer, and deserves to be treated as such."

Malik tapped the screen, pausing the news reel. "The hunt for you is very real. I spoke with Don Morelli. He has set a plan in action to get some heat off us. It will take time, though."

"What's the situation at the precinct?" Violetta asked Issik.

Issik shook his head. "There are only a couple of us who think you're innocent. Most of them think you're guilty. The question of the day is why would anyone go to this much trouble if you weren't guilty." A sigh escaped him as he ran his hands through his hair. "They've started demanding everyone pull double shifts. The military isn't budging on giving extra men for assistance. It's pissing off Captain Monroe to no end."

"Too bad for him that they're sticking to protocol," Violetta said. "What else?"

"That's not enough?" Issik snapped. "If you don't exonerate yourself soon, you might as well be dead. You won't have a job to come back to, let alone be able to rise through the ranks." He paced the room. "You've got to get the evidence together, and get it to higher authorities. Military Overseer, DA, the governor. Someone high up. Someone who won't dismiss anything you bring to them."

"We can't work but so fast," Malik began.

Violetta held her hand up. She didn't need him arguing for her. "He's right, Issik. We know how it was done, and a name to go with it. If the military is refusing to aid the department, it's because someone high up the chain made the decision. Higher than the usual person who handles the calls for assistance. The military is aware of what's going on, that much I can tell you. I don't know why they aren't doing anything to help me or the department. Maybe they can't. Maybe they want to see how I survive this for some crazy reason. It's not like I can just call them up and ask."

She let the words hang in the air, even as she took a breath to continue.

"We'll get the evidence and I'll take it to someone. It's just going to take more than a couple days, since I can't do this in the open."

Issik stared at her. "Something's changed about you." His gaze shifted to Malik. "You're supposed to be protecting her. There are things you don't do when you're guarding someone."

"You questioning my skills, Ha'kksworth? Or what I've been doing?" Malik demanded, taking a step forward.

"Maybe I'm finally being the daughter my father taught me to be," Violetta interjected.

There was a definite threat to Malik's posture and the last thing any of them needed was Challenges being thrown about like candy at the fall solstice celebration.

"I worked hard to get where I am, without people thinking I was simply using Dad's name to achieve my goals. It's time I start heeding his lessons and stop following the rules dictated by societal norms."

"*That* is more like the Violence I knew," Malik said, satisfaction coloring every word. "I'll keep her safe,

Ha'kksworth. I have a vested interest in her welfare, after all. What we do after her name is cleared is no one's business but ours."

"Just get this resolved, and fast," Issik grumbled. "The sooner, the better. For everyone involved."

Turning on his heel, he stomped from the room. Once the door closed behind him, Violetta breathed a heavy sigh.

"This just got exponentially more difficult."

"That goes without saying," Malik replied. It was his turn to study her closely. "Lovely speech you made. Now what do you actually plan on doing?"

"We need to find out where Matt Gomez is located and visit him," Violetta replied. "Captain Ae'staa knows about Matt Gomez, but if Cancio and his pals carted Gomez off, she's going to have a harder time finding him."

"Any ideas? Morelli didn't find anyone with that name in any hospital. Private or otherwise."

"I need breakfast and something to drink. Hard to plan on an empty stomach."

Malik grinned and pointed to the counter. A takeout box and cup sat on the marble top. "For you, Lady."

Kissing him on the cheek, Violetta crossed to the counter and opened the lid. There was an omelet of native vegetables and protein, a pastry, a croissant, and fresh fruit. Her favorite breakfast foods. She took a sip of the beverage and discovered it to be jakka, her favorite blend, too.

Jakka, in her opinion, was far better than the human's coffee. Coffee humans preferred always tasted bitter and burnt to her, no matter how much flavoring they might add to it.

Shaking her head, she dug into the food using the utensils attached to the lid. Malik returned to his usual place behind the bar where he waited in silence.

After several bites, she finally spoke. "They wouldn't have put him in just any hospital. It would be a private one. You have the date from the vidclip of when Gomez was shot. Check all the private hospitals, especially those for retired military personnel. The captain would have access to those hospitals."

She paused long enough to eat a few more bites and washed it down with the jakka.

"He would've been admitted that day, or close to it. Look for someone who needs permanent or long-lasting care. That shot was perfectly placed to keep someone hospitalized for a long period. They would also make certain he remains in the hospital, to keep him under surveillance," she concluded before returning to her food.

"When did you get so smart?" Malik teased, grabbing a drekka berry. He popped it into his mouth. "Want to go over the patient intake lists I've got from all the private hospitals in our district?"

"Were you testing me?" she asked, poking him lightly with her fork. His grin was the only answer she received. It was enough. "Sure. Though I suspect you already have one in mind, along with a name."

"Maybe, but I'd like your opinion on it."

"As you wish." She took another bite, chewed deliberately, then sipped her jakka. "Bring it up on the interface and we can go over it while I eat and you steal my drekka berries. Thief."

Malik laughed and did as bid, pausing long enough to grab another of the berries.

There were two hospitals and a dozen people total that fit the requirements. Of those, four were men, the rest were women. Malik had one person highlighted, but Violetta highlighted one of the female names, also.

"If they're trying to keep him hidden, they wouldn't list him under the same race or even gender," she said, pointing to a native female's name.

"But that hospital is two blocks from where he was shot," he argued.

"All the more reason to have him there. The first place most would look would be on the opposite side of the city. Since the only hospital in between is a public one, easily accessible by everyone, that leaves this one."

He reached over and patted Violetta on the head. "And here I was wondering if all those lessons at the academy, and on the force had dulled your senses. Good to know I wasn't right."

"Do that again and I'll smack you," she grumbled. "Have I passed your tests? Or are there more to come?"

"Oh, you sure I wouldn't like that?" he asked, a twinkle in his eyes. "I test every one of my charges. Things are going to heat up and I need to know you're not going to go stupid on me."

"I promise to not go in with weapons firing," she retorted, stabbing the last of her omelet. "Though, I would need a weapon before I could do that."

"If I believe you need to be armed, I'll arm you," he reassured her. "For now, let's try to get through this without having to shoot anyone, shall we?"

"Hope for the best, plan for everything else," Violetta stated, quoting her father. "I'd prefer something on hand, should anything go awry. Dad taught me how to aim to disarm and incapacitate, not just kill. The Academy was not nearly as thorough as my father's lessons."

Or the lessons taught by her caretakers while her father had been off-planet on his military missions.

A grimace crossed Malik's face. "Is there a reason you're pushing so hard to be armed? Don't trust me to keep you safe?"

"What if we get separated at some point? Or you get injured or lose your weapon? What then?" Violetta countered. "It isn't about not trusting you, it's about expecting the unexpected. If those articles and news reels are any indication, do you want to take the chance? If we're both armed, we stand a higher chance of being prepared should everything go sideways."

"You sound like your father."

"I am his daughter."

They stared at each other for several long minutes. Violetta's gaze never wavering once. This wasn't the first time they'd ever argued. Nor, she suspected, would it be the last.

"We both know the laws of our world, Malik. To kill—to take a life—anywhere but in a Duel is considered the highest crime. Yes, people die even when using non-lethal force. By accidents. Even in those instances, investigations occur, complete with psychological evaluations by Master Healers." She pointed the fork at him. "So if I, of all people, were to use anything other than a non-lethal method? Even as a last resort? I'd be punished quickly and without concern for *my* health. Ziph and his crew already want me dead. I don't need to give everyone else a reason to wish for my death, also. Even by an accident."

"Fine." Malik finally relented, albeit reluctantly. "I'll make certain you're armed. It won't be a legal weapon, so keep that in mind before you fire it. As well as what you just told me. You're already up to your ears in trouble. You don't want to risk drowning from it."

"I'd rather have it and not use it, than need it and not have it." She popped a berry into her mouth. "When do we go to the hospital to talk to our only lead so far?"

"This evening. I'll have to make arrangements for that and to get you a weapon."

"Fair enough," Violetta said, finishing up her breakfast. "I'm sure I can find something to keep me entertained."

"Do you still enjoy reading?" Malik asked. She nodded. "There's a library across from your bedroom. That should keep you entertained. At least until everything has been arranged."

"You certainly know the way to a woman's heart," she teased. She'd been an avid reader during their school years. So much that the librarians allowed her access to more than most of the students. "Thank you."

"I enjoy being of service," he replied, a twinkle in his eyes.

Chapter Ten

Dusk was setting when Malik finally said they could leave to talk to Matt Gomez. The pair changed clothes, Malik grabbed a standard military issue duffle bag, and they set out.

Although the private hospital was less than an hour away by HAV, they arrived after ninety minutes. To lessen the chance of detection, and being tailed, Malik drove through other portions of the city that had less reliable cameras and subspace signals. When they came to the large unmarked parking deck across from the building, Violetta voiced her opinion of the place.

"It looks like a pharmaceutical factory instead of a hospital."

Malik grunted. "You think that's accidental? It's actually both."

"I suppose the hospital sections are more in the center of the complex," Violetta mused. "Looks like about five stories high. Is it on the third floor?"

"It's on the second floor, west wing," Malik replied. "No less than forty beds, so the center of the building wouldn't be large enough to accommodate. Sound reasoning, though."

"Thanks. Did the don put together a packet for you to browse the layout?"

"Nah," Malik said as he opened the boot of the HAV. "I would have shared that. Once our sources identified what building, they instructed me via a briefing."

He opened a duffel with a fingerprint ID lock and removed a small military pistol in a holster and glasses. He offered them to her.

"Infrared glasses, military grade." Violetta observed. "The kind that shows thermal images to the wearer but appear normal to everyone else. When the lights go out, you can see everything. Are we planning to kill the lights?"

"Not plan A, but it's an option."

She nodded and drew the pistol from its holster. "Another military grade item." She sighted the weapon, checked the available energy and options. "Covert pistol used by spec ops, especially off-world. This one looks to be locked on disable. Don't trust me with a lethal setting?"

"It's easier to avoid registering on the sensors and weapons subnet if no lethal force can be used. No matter which grade of security you're trying to avoid."

"I will worry about everything you just said, at another time." She holstered the pistol. "Especially since I have always preferred non-lethal settings."

She opened the hospital-issue jacket and tucked the holstered pistol between her skin and the waistband of the uniform she wore. Someone might notice the heavier material of her pants, which matched the jacket instead of the smock she wore to complete the guise of a military healer.

However, healers were often allowed to dress for their comfort. Comfort did play some part in the flow of a being's energy, and the flow was paramount to the use of the world's energy to heal all manner of wounds. If the being was able to use their Gift in that manner. Even if they didn't have such a Gift, comfort was still important to tending patients.

"Okay, how do I look?" she asked.

Malik looked her over, even walking around her in a circle. His bronze eyes twinkled when he finally answered.

"The weapon is well concealed and the uniform does not give away your gender," he said in a pleased voice.

He removed a small device from the duffel bag. It was circular and less than three centimeters across. He fixed the device to the inside of her jacket collar.

There was a sensation of mild burning on Violetta's skin as the device took effect. She looked at her bare hands and watched as the skin lightened to a gleaming white. Her eyes found Malik, who was smiling.

"You're prettier as yourself, but I think any of the 'clean blood' fanatics would buy you dinner," Malik said.

"As if I'd care what any of those narrow-minded hate mongers think." She paused. "The nanites are that effective?"

"See for yourself." Malik suggested even as he gestured to the reflective surface of the HAV.

Using the mirror of the HAV vehicle, Violetta saw an unfamiliar face. Her skin was the color of pale pearls, and her hair shone silver. Her eyes were polished silver, and her facial features seemed sharper.

"We only have two hours, and that doesn't account for anyone who's Gifts include Sight," Malik warned.

She looked back at him and gasped. He had used a nanite device to alter his appearance as well. The same pale skin, silver hair and eyes that currently hid her identity now graced Malik's features. As he had said to her, Violetta could not see where the changes improved his appearance at all.

"Let's go," she replied.

The ID tags got them through the front entrance. The lobby was decorated in white and silver, right down to furniture and the large semi-circle desk for information and greeting. Violetta felt confident she could blend in to the point of near-invisibility even if there were no other beings around. Nothing in the lobby hinted at medical facilities. Everywhere one looked the pharmaceutical logo was present and boldly displayed.

Two service robots populated the assistance desk.

Consisting of a microbiotic plastic torso and an oval head piece that was mostly screen and microphone to receive data, they moved behind the desk on a track so no matter where someone stood on the other side, the 'bots could move to face them. Every four feet was a screen display, so customers and staff could see results of whatever query they might have for the attending 'bots.

Violetta and Malik avoided the desk and 'bots, opting to go straight to the stairs located to the left. There were personal lift pads as well, but the likelihood of being scanned was greater if they used the lifts.

Once the second floor was reached, Malik took the lead in finding the room possibly occupied by Matt Gomez. Violetta took note of the native beings sitting at interfaces and accounting machines, busily entering and verifying data.

There still was no indication to her of medical facilities here. As they approached the west wing of the floor, there was a subtle change. A pair of double doors was labeled as Emergency Health Services, right down to the gray tentacled mollusk with its wings spread wide, that was the world symbol for healers and medical.

Each room beyond those doors was numbered, but had a tiny version of the symbol as well. The instructions given to Malik had been good. They found room 223 without getting lost or having to double back.

The room was small, compared to the medical standards of K'lais. The bed was less than a meter from the doorway, despite the five monitoring machines standing around it. Since medical beds also served as diagnostic machines, the presence of more than one screen was an indication of a severe condition.

Violetta recognized three of the other machines. The smallest was a respirator, which aided the lungs in breathing and supplied sterile air. A black machine was indicative that the patient had nanites doing work on the patient's body internally, while feeding information and progress reports to the interface screen. Finally, the largest machine was something she had only seen in vidclips and books but not been a witness to. That one came from the Earthers, and its function was to detoxify blood before sending it back into the body.

The single silver unit, with an unlit screen, she had never seen before. A long cable ran from it, disappearing under the bed's cloth covers.

The human occupant of the bed was awake, sitting up, and if either of their experiences with humans were an indication, very angry and afraid. His eyes were opened as wide as possible, so the whites could be seen around the small circles of brown. The circular pupils, which was the only trait both races shared, were small and darted between Malik and Violetta.

Although her experience was likely more limited than Malik's, Violetta wondered if her current partner had ever seen a human look as this one did. Ash colored skin seemed to have slowly melted just a bit. There were sparse patches of hair at the temples and crown, some dark brown but mostly a sickly gray. The body may have been large or lean at one time, but now it seemed to be losing a fight with gravity everywhere. Dark spots mottled the skin of this being's face, scalp, and arms. His lower half and hands were obscured.

"I suppose they finally decided I had no more use, eh?" The voice was strong and defiant, but had a choked quality to it.

"Retired Specialist Gomez?" Violetta asked politely.

"If you're here you know damned well that's who I am. Come on! Let's get this over with," the human demanded.

Malik stepped beside Violetta, and brushed her elbow. She looked at him.

"I know this kind of reaction," Malik said to her before looking at Gomez. "Matt Gomez, we are not here to terminate you. My partner works for this city's police service as a homicide detective. I work for the private sector, but am providing her assistance to find you."

"They haven't killed me yet," Gomez rejoined. "And I'm not responsible for anyone they've murdered! Hell, they have me here as a captive. Haven't even been ordered to do anything for... months? Years? I don't know anymore."

Keeping her hands at her sides, Violetta replied, "We understand that. As witnesses to the video of you being shot by parties unknown, we also are aware that you tried to cease your business with whomever you mean by 'they'. Can you tell me who shot you?"

"Cancio. Lieutenant Asshole Addy Cancio," Gomez said in slow, distinct beats. "Single round went through the liver and one kidney, collapsing a lung along the way. Got patched back together, but by the barest means."

"What do you mean?" Malik interjected. "This isn't medical standard." He gestured towards the room and equipment. "Both our peoples have enough medical knowledge of each other's physiology to easily repair wounds from any handheld weapons. The tech required to do it is decades old and has only improved."

"Yes," said Gomez. "The ability to heal me existed when I was wounded. The decision was made to *not* heal me correctly or completely. Whomever Cancio answers to, decided to keep me alive but unhealthy, dependent on what facilities they would give to stay breathing. The nanites inside me are only programmed for K'lais biology! They're learning, but are denied the data to repair me correctly. So I am stuck with a machine to breathe, a machine to flush my system, do I need to go on?"

"How is that possible?" Violetta murmured to Malik. "Even I know that if a nanite is injected, they aren't programmed the same as those used on the skin."

Malik glanced at her sharply. He probably wasn't aware it had been a discussion with her father when she was a child. The first time she'd needed their use, she'd been full of questions. He had answered all of them, including the first time they'd been used on the first human the K'laisians encountered in person.

He gave a slight lift of his shoulders, indicating he didn't know.

"We are getting ahead of the information needed," Violetta said.

Both men looked at her.

"We have less than two hours," she explained to Gomez. "And we need to know what you have done that inspired members of the public safety's service to treat you thusly."

Gomez frowned, his eyes narrowing at us. "Can you get me out of here and healed up again?"

"It will take more than a day, but yes, we can get you the help you require," Violetta replied.

It wouldn't take more than that to inform Captain Ae'staa of what was occurring. She, in turn, could inform her superiors and get Matt Gomez under military protection. Once under the military's protection, he would be healed.

"Good enough, I guess," Gomez grumbled. "You don't have the time for me to explain all the technicalities and terms, so I'll simplify it for you."

"That would be most beneficial," Malik stated.

"I was approached by Cancio to develop a weapon that could replicate a civilian's registered weapon. I'd mentioned the possibility to my military superiors, and they shut it down fast. Said it wasn't needed or useful and to forget it." Gomez snorted. "Cancio came to me with a big budget and the ability for me to pursue the idea. I went for it, thinking it was to be used for testing. Didn't realize what they were doing until that one guy was killed. Knew then they were up to no good. By then, I'd graduated to replicating their own weapons. Probably what they used to accuse that one police lady."

"Do you have any proof of what you're saying?" Violetta asked, struggling to keep the excitement from her voice. "Without proof, it will be your word, and ours, against their word."

"They took the two I programmed, along with my prototype," Gomez replied, anger clipping the ends of each word. He paused before a sly smile curved his lips. "They did not, however, find my notes. I kept very detailed notes of everything I did. Lessons learned from the years of being a scientist and then working for the military of this world."

"Where can we find these notes so we can present them to the proper people?" Malik asked.

"In my closet is a duffel bag. Bring it to me, and I can give you everything you need to bring down those assholes."

Violetta glanced at Malik, who gave a subtle nod. She crossed to the closet and thumbed the door open. Inside on a shelf was a secure two-toned duffle bag. Silver on the top half, black on the bottom. There was stitching along the bottom, suggesting to Violetta there was more to this bag than met the eyes. She doubted most people would recognize it as a possible hidden area.

She took it to Gomez, placing it close enough for him to unlock the bag.

What she did not expect was for him to press the lock with his pinky finger of his left hand. Or for the seam along the middle of the bag, where the colors met, to open and reveal several pockets.

Clever, she thought, hiding a smile.

Gomez's hand vanished into a smaller pocket, where he pulled out what looked like a hexagonal transparent aluminum card. He held it out to her. After she took it, his hand delved into another pocket and he removed a small notepad and a pencil. He quickly scribbled a random series of numbers and letters onto a sheet, tore it off, and gave it to her.

"That's the key to a storage locker. It's in my sister's name. You'll find it in the warehouse district. Section 8, warehouse 13, locker 269. The notes are on a black data chip. That's the password for the chip," he said.

"Do they know you had that?" Malik asked.

Gomez shook his head. "No. I dropped all the stuff into my little sister's duffle and told her to put it in storage. Then I picked a fight with her. Had a huge blowout, kicked her out. The whole nine-yards. Met up with her later and she said it was done. Then slapped me and walked out of the coffee shop." Gomez snorted. "Cancio made it a point to tell me I was 'all alone' and no one cared what happened to me. Guess the fight worked."

"So they don't even know you have back-up notes?" Malik pressed.

"They can eat shit. I never told 'em I had those notes. Not when I was making those things, and especially not after."

Violetta nodded, tucking the key into a pocket and sealing it shut. "Thank you for your assistance, Specialist Gomez. We will acquire the duffle and your notes, then take it to the proper authorities. They can, in turn, order the proper treatment for your injuries."

Gomez returned the nod, locking the duffle bag once more. Violetta replaced it in the closet, thumbing the doors shut. She turned back to Gomez. The sooner they left, the sooner they could get the data, examine it, and get in touch with someone who could bring an end to everything.

"Thank you for your assistance," she said, giving Gomez a slight bow.

"Yeah, yeah, whatever. Just nail those assholes and get me out of here," he replied. "I'll keep quiet and you two can do what you gotta to make everything happen. Just don't take forever."

Malik and Violetta nodded and departed the room. It took all of Violetta's training to not shiver at what she'd witnessed. Cancio and the others were broken. No one with a well mind would treat another being so horribly and keep them in such a deplorable condition. Ziph, she knew, wouldn't be given the chance of rehabilitation. Depending on what the investigations revealed about the others, they may suffer the same fate as Ziph.

K'lais laws regarding cold blooded murder were hard set, remaining unchanged for centuries. Every being who stepped foot upon their planet was made aware of the laws. Especially those concerning murder, Challenges, and Duels.

There wasn't a being alive who was not aware that any who killed another being in cold blood was sentenced to death. Those who attempted the deed were evaluated thoroughly by multiple healers. If found guilty of wishing to murder in cold blood, they were summarily sentenced to death. Otherwise, they were sent to K'lais' penal colony where they went through extensive treatment, then were reevaluated prior to their release.

The belief of K'laisians was sound: Why murder in cold blood when one could just Challenge another to a lawful Duel? Death was allowed during Duels, though most who Dueled would accept the opponent's surrender. It was not required, though. And you could not refuse a Duel. You could forfeit, but that was it.

Any citizen of K'lais had the right to Challenge another to a Duel. Even children were allowed to partake in non-lethal Duels until they reached mental maturity, which typically occurred between fifteen and sixteen years of age. It was one of the first things taught to every school-age child.

The native people once believed someone could be rehabilitated if found guilty of cold-blooded murder, but too often that person became a repeat offender. The penalty was made law and anyone who had such thoughts was given intense psychiatric care. Anyone who wished to own a projectile weapon had to go through a psychiatric evaluation. They were evaluated bi-yearly in order to continue to possess the weapon. Those in the military and police service were subjected to even more intensive evaluations.

As such, the crime rate was lower and murder in cold blood was almost uncommon, though it did happen. Part of the job of homicide was determining if a death had been from a Duel, natural causes, suicide, an accident, or murder. Those who were homeless were more often to be found dead with no obvious causes, which meant homicide was kept busy.

Turning, the pair departed the floor, once again taking the stairs in silence. Violetta could tell Malik was deep in his own thoughts. She didn't want to even guess at what was going through his mind. She had enough trouble keeping her own from wandering into bleak and nausea-inducing territory.

"So far, so good," Violetta murmured once they departed the hospital through the main doors. "Now all we have to do is make it to the parking deck."

"And through them," Malik amended. That was when the security doors started closing.

Chapter Eleven

As the building doors closed shut, Violetta heard the magnetic locks engage. In another second, heavy plated doors would drop from the inside of the structure, effectively denying entry or exit to anyone.

Two trios of Excessive Force Police came in from the locations that Malik indicated, their tactical jumpsuits and helmets augmented with extra shielding. Each carried the short version of the standard military repeating rifle. Each weapon had a volt-grenade launcher beneath the barrel, meaning there were four of the two inch missiles per officer.

At least they haven't dismissed a non-lethal takedown, Violetta thought.

From ahead of them, a male voice called out.

"Sergeant Detective Violetta Cq'linns." The voice boomed. "For your well-being and the safety of the community, hold your arms out from your sides and prepare to be taken into custody!"

Malik stood still. He was an arm's length away but seemed to be waiting for Violetta's lead. She recognized the voice of the man giving orders, so she answered as if they were at a social function.

"I know the position, Captain Hor'loc. You taught it to me during Academy training. Care to tell me why you're here?"

The darkness of the night swirled directly ahead of Violetta and Malik. The Captain of the EFP had turned off his active camouflage. His face was obscured by the black oval helmet, but she knew his grizzled face and bushy silver eyebrows would be squeezed into a grimace. She could hear it in her former trainer's voice and see it in his body's posture.

"Every shift of this facility's live security includes a Seer, Cq'linns." Hor'loc sounded tired and disappointed. "The one on duty saw right through the disguise you're wearing. Your face is everywhere on the subnet and public broadcasts."

Violetta inwardly cursed. She should have realized this place would have employed the natives whose Gift was seeing through all manner of trickery and deceit.

"I meant you, personally, sir," Violetta replied aloud. Not shifting her posture. "You usually work the daylight shift these days."

"All hands on deck for this insanity, Sergeant," Hor'loc answered. "I'd rather be at a bar, drinking and swapping stories. What farkery is this? Why haven't you turned yourself in so we can investigate your innocence and find the killer?"

Well, at least she knew one other person who believed she was innocent. Not that it would help keep her alive if she were taken into custody.

"If you have to ask, Captain, then the answer should be obvious."

The helmet swung from side to side once. "Not any answer I like, Violetta. Stand down, you and your... whatever he is."

"Oh, my apologies!" Violetta cried. She hoped Malik would forgive her for what she was about to do. "I should have made introductions! Captain, and presumably honorable members of the EFP squad, this is my hostage!"

She punched Malik across the jaw.

He slumped like a defeated boxer. She spun in and gathered his body against hers, turning to face the left trio of officers. Violetta used the movement to unholster the pistol Malik had given her, thankful he'd given in to her insistence. Firing from under Malik's arm, she shot a disabling round of energy at one of the trooper's rifles. Right at the volt-grenade launcher.

As the disrupting energy overloaded and triggered all four of the grenades in the rifle's magazine, several thoughts whipped over Violetta's mind.

She thanked her father for showing her all the equipment used by military, police, and civilians along with the failings of each. She also felt bad for the trio of fellow police who were now writhing in the large field of electrical discharge. Especially the one whose weapon was now useless and had likely damaged his or her hands.

The differences between military, police grade equipment, and the midway weaponry that the special police forces (such as the EFP) used were inevitable. How much endurance said gear could take before permanent harm varied.

Thankfully, Violetta knew the differences and used it to her advantage.

From the lessons given by her father and childhood military caretakers, she knew which angles of fire the remaining trio would probably use to try and take her down. With luck, they hadn't had time to switch their weapons from disable to lethal. She hadn't shot again, so that was at least in her favor, as well as where she'd aimed the weapon.

She also knew how many more members of the EFP would be around this location, posted to take her down. Hopefully using non-lethal charges.

Violetta turned toward the second trio of officers who had raised their rifles at her. She swung Malik's still conscious body before her. The three disabling rounds intended for her struck Malik in the left shoulder blade, neck and right buttock. He slumped against her, this time without trying to fool the others.

"Oh, you owe me for this, Vi," he whispered in pain before he lost the fight with his body.

"Sorry," she whispered back, before charging the three police with Malik's body as both shield and battering ram.

When the impact came, everyone fell to the ground, including Violetta. Her descent was more controlled as she only went to one knee. A shot from Captain Hor'loc's pistol flew over her bent form, hitting the building's front door.

Violetta propelled her body up and ran towards the captain, hands ahead of her, as she fired the borrowed pistol rapidly. Two of the shots struck the center of Hor'loc's protective helmet as she closed the distance between them. She ceased fire when the captain's head had taken enough trauma to make him collapse.

Violetta sprinted past his dropping form and headed away from the parking deck.

There weren't many options available to her. If she wanted to keep from being caught, she had to find a way to hide, which meant losing her fellow officers.

The first thought was to aim for her apartment building. If she could evade the EFP long enough to get there, she could request assistance from the squadron that guarded her home. They knew what she was trying to do, and Captain Ae'staa could step in and keep her out of police custody.

Military trumped all police services at all times. The higher the security clearance, the faster the local police had to stand down.

As Violetta raced down the road, a shot flew above her head, hitting the wall.

Ducking, she sped up, hoping to find cover, or a corner to turn down, before the sniper could fire off another shot. When she didn't find one, and no other shots were fired, she knew something weird was happening.

It never took a sniper that long to fire a second round.

No time to worry about it, she thought as she skidded around a corner.

Moving to the opposite side, she contemplated which alley she could take without getting cornered.

As she neared the first alley, an arm shot out and grabbed her hand, yanking her to the ground inside the alley's opening. Something lightweight fell over her and a finger was pressed against her lips: the universal sign to shut up.

Trying to slow her breathing, and remain calm, she couldn't see anything or anyone. She could hear, though. The unmistakable sound of heavy boots thudded into the alley. There was shuffling, a lot of cursing, followed by whoever it was leaving the alley.

Violetta shifted slightly, moving into a more comfortable position that wouldn't cramp any parts. She forced her breathing to return to normal, though her nerves sang with apprehension. She couldn't see who had saved her. The military, perhaps? Or was it Morelli's people?

Or had another faction joined the fray? An unknown player in the insanity that had become her life. Violetta had no choice but to remain silent and hope whoever had stepped in was friend, not foe.

Seconds turned into minutes. Eventually, though, her rescuer tipped Violetta's chin up with a light touch. Understanding the signal, Violetta stood slowly until the finger left her chin.

Still hidden in near blackness beneath the camouflaged nanite-laden fabric, Violetta waited for her next signal. Whoever the native was concealing them, they were expending a lot of energy. Violetta respected anyone who could successfully conceal two people from so many others. It wasn't a small, insignificant Gift and it took considerable training to do with such success.

The native took Violetta's hand and placed it on their shoulder.

A woman's voice whispered, "Keep your hand on my shoulder. Follow me and don't speak. Not if you want to escape the EFP."

As though I have a choice, Violetta thought darkly.

Tapping the woman's shoulder once, Violetta felt the woman's shoulder shrug in response. It was a universal military signal of agreement from both people involved in such circumstances. Despite the fact Violetta had never entered the military service, her father had taught her the commands soldiers used. They'd used them often instead of words multiple times throughout her childhood.

More life lessons taught as games and turned into normalcy. Violetta doubted anything about her childhood had been typical. She hadn't minded it as a child and minded it even less now, as an adult.

A sensation of warmth and tingling encased her. Violetta recognized the sensations, the woman was using her Gift, one who's manipulated energies were covering Violetta's entire body.

No time to ask questions. Violetta moved with the woman as the latter affected a slow, hunched walk. Such made their trek cumbersome and felt like they would never arrive anywhere. But when members of the EFP hurried past them a few times without so much as a second glance or pause, Vi decided there was no cause to complain. She'd eventually learn who was helping her and why. Until then, she would continue to do as told.

The pair went left between buildings. Half a kilometer away, Violetta could see the dark outline of a parking plaza, one typical of the primary housing blocks on this side of the Nimkelu River. The darkened silhouette of grass and trees were barely visible from a long distance. Two thirds down the distance, the woman quickened her pace, standing straight. Violetta did the same.

At the mouth of the alley's entrance to the plaza, there lurked a group of four vagrants, gathered around a solar log for warmth. As the woman approached them, they stood in defensive postures.

"No one is trailing us, yet! Be swift!" the woman hissed at the group. She came to an abrupt stop. Violetta almost fell over in her abrupt attempt to do the same. The energy dissipated as the woman held out the corner of the material covering Violetta. The closest "vagrant" grabbed the corner and took the woman's place in front of Violetta.

The group of four walked upright and at an easy pace. Instead of going towards the parked vehicles, they led Violetta to the northern end of the plaza.

Being surrounded on all sides and able to move more naturally, Violetta fell into step with this group without trouble. They knew the territory, comfortably maneuvering west from the northern part of the plaza, onto a major street, which Violetta suspected was Dra'as Avenue. The active street was crossed with no attention received from civilians or police.

The cloth had not lightened, but her directional awareness was alive and well. It had helped her all her life.

The older she grew, the more familiar with the city she became, the more accurate it became.

"You doing okay, detective?" the being to her left asked. The voice was feminine, concerned, and authoritative.

"You know who I am?"

"Do you believe we do this kind of thing for just anyone?" The voice sounded amused. "Like we wait around that government issued solar cell, pretending to be cold, in the chance that someone needs our help?"

Violetta had no answer for that. The question was obvious when a moment was taken to think of it. Instead, she decided to answer the first question posed to her.

"I'm doing well. Confused, but well."

The woman chuckled. "Not surprised by that. You'll get your answers soon enough."

This was getting weirder and weirder, especially since Violetta recognized exactly where they were.

Why would they be approaching the Government District? Were they taking her to see the Council of the District they lived in? Or the governor?

Or someone else?

If they knew who she was, they knew exactly the trouble she was in. This could go a variety of ways and Violetta had no method of escape if this went against her. Not yet.

Bide your time. The words came unbidden in her father's voice. *If you're ever in a position where you're outnumbered and out-gunned, bide your time. Learn your foes. Then find a way out that is the least expected. Survive, Violetta. At any cost.*

Who would have thought those discussions while eating dinner or sitting in her father's living room would be needed? Her father had always known her desire to enter the police service. Yet he'd taught her as though she'd be going offworld and eventually taking command of her own battlecruiser. Perhaps he'd always hoped she'd change her mind? Or believed the greater danger lay in their own backyard?

There would be so much meditation later when this was over. And she really needed someone to talk to. To confide in. It had been far too long since she'd been able to talk to someone openly and completely.

She shook her head to clear those thoughts.

When the group veered away from the main doors, and the other connecting doors to the Government Center where business took place, Violetta couldn't help but breathe a sigh of relief.

"Watch your step," said the voice who had originally grabbed her as they entered a side alley between two of the residential buildings where government employees lived.

Violetta then noticed two of the four had moved beside a well-hidden door. Made to look like the rest of the building's exterior, it would be easy to miss, if one didn't know it was there. She followed the other two and her guide through the door and down a set of winding stone steps.

Small blue lights situated at step-level illuminated the path without allowing the light to extend far in any direction. Violetta heard the other two guards move inside, followed by the door closing.

The group paused and the cloth was removed, allowing Violetta to discern her rescuers.

A door opened ahead of her. She followed the woman leading her for less than a dozen paces before they came to a halt.

"Lights, activate," said the woman's voice.

Violetta instinctively closed her eyes, covering them with a hand. When the lights came on, they were dimmed, not causing her retinas to hurt behind the eyelids. Violetta opened her eyes and looked at her surroundings.

Without hesitation, she knew she'd gotten into bigger trouble than the one she'd left. A half dozen beings were in the room, all of them pure blood K'laisians. The woman she'd come with, and another female leaned against the door they'd come through. The others had left them, probably returning to guard the exit. Four males sat at a table. There was no indication that this room was used for food production of any kind.

Which is why the presence of what looked to be at least four dozen knives or similar kitchen cutlery on the table immediately clued her in on the nature of her hosts. Each male was sharpening an implement of some kind. Both women had large cleavers on their belts.

The Moyii Tsaa cartel.

They operated almost exclusively without firearms, and not just because those were closely regulated. The cartel existed before such weapons had developed on K'lais. They were sworn enemies of the Morelli Syndicate, who they considered to be outsiders with no claim to crime on their world. Best guesses by investigators in the police department included that the Moyii Tsaa actually ran a booming legitimate business in kitchen goods and devices. The ability to keep themselves in cutlery of choice was a nice bonus. Ruthless, vicious, and deeply connected to the old ways of the world.

Thousands of dead beings, presumed to be the losers of undeclared Duels, could easily be victims of Moyii Tsaa henchbeings over the years and decades.

And she'd allowed herself to follow one right into a cell of the city's oldest criminal organization. Many curses ran through her head.

"I can't wait to see the kitchen, if you're this well stocked in cutlery!" Violetta said excitedly. She was hoping to cover her nervousness. "I bet you've got all the latest gadgets."

"We can make a four-layer sprizzle cake in half the time as our rivals," a male said dryly.

He put the high-tech blade sharpener he'd been using on an eight inch tumba knife on the table. His black hair was cut down almost to his scalp. His gold eyes looked flatly at Violetta. All of them wore work overalls of a deep brown. Typical of people who worked in food preparation of all levels. However, these clothes were spotless.

"Thank you for coming so peacefully. Fortunately, the more you cooperate, the easier this will be for you," advised the woman Violetta had followed. Her hair was also quite short. Her eyes had a bit of mischief in them, making Violetta wonder if she liked the flat eyes of the male, better.

"Why am I here, then?"

"Since you have no idea where you are, there is little threat to us, Sergeant Detective," a second male replied. This one was nearly identical to Mister Tumba Knife. He carefully tested the edge of the long boning knife held in one hand. He continued. "But we have no interest in your position as a member of the police. You are here to entice a noted member of our hated enemy. We might have thought him a shared enemy not long ago. But since your personal relation with Malik does not include arresting him for the work done for the Morelli Syndicate? You are relabeled as bait."

Oh for the Sea's sake, thought Violetta.

"What if I decide your hospitality is vapid and I prefer to leave?" she quipped.

The sextet of henchbeings laughed. The female at the door spoke up first.

"We have no quarrel with you, at the moment. Once Malik is in our grasp, you will be free. Given an escort to wherever in the city you wish to go. Is that really so bad compared to the situation we liberated you from?"

Violetta bit back the impulsive answer that first sprang into her mind.

"No, so I suppose your hospitality must be marked higher than my earlier thought," Violetta allowed. "How shall I keep from boredom? Little doubt stays in my mind that you would all pass the time by telling me details of your operations."

"That would require planning your death immediately after Malik is ours. Which we have stated is not our intent," said the woman who'd brought Violetta here.

"Fairly spoken," Violetta stated.

"Unfortunately," interjected Boning Knife, "while we have no plan to eliminate you, we must distress you physically. To make certain that Malik is inspired to come quickly to your aid. You understand, don't you?"

Violetta had studied files on the techniques of the Moyii Tsaa. Mutilations by blade of every kind and severity- including extremities chopped into tiny bits and fed to victims- had been reported.

"Do you expect me to defend myself? What if I Challenged one of you, instead?"

"We would be disappointed if you did not attempt to defend yourself! And you may Challenge any one of us. You do realize that each of us would Challenge you in turn, should you claim victory from the first one!" exclaimed Door Woman.

"At least I would not be bored," retorted Violetta. She let one heartbeat strike before adding, "Presumably."

This direct insult had some of the desired effect. All of the males immediately became visibly angry. Three stood, and all of them had frowning faces with furrowed brows.

Violetta was struck from behind, hit at the base of her skull by a sturdy narrow object. Likely the hilt of the cleaver possessed by the woman at the door. Violetta's mind reasoned that was who had come up behind her to strike the blow, even as her legs and vision became unreliable. The floor felt quite unyielding when her body landed on it.

"Did you know that insult was punishable by death, long before the Challenge became a part of our society?" one of the women asked her. Violetta fought to make sense of the blurry figures moving above her. The voice continued. "If we did not have such specific use for you, it would be within our claim to hack you to pieces for such affrontary."

"I say we cut her pretty, insulting face for the vidclip we will send Malik. I swear to stop at that sliceable throat of hers," declared a male voice.

The blurry images now had shiny blobs attached to them. Violetta fought to clear her vision, sure that the henchbeings had brought up their individual choices of blades and were preparing to use them on her.

"Perhaps," allowed another male voice.

She could not get to her feet. Could not make out what was about to happen. The only resistance her body would allow her was to raise a single, shaking hand in a futile gesture. There was mocking laughter at her attempt.

One of the males spoke in a mocking tone. "Look! She's so reliant on firearms that her hand is curled as if she's holding one! May the Sea take me, one of us may be shot!"

More laughter. The blurred bodies and shiny blobs came closer. Violetta tried to scream in defiance of them all.

The blurry body that her hand was "aimed" at seemed to lurch forward, and then go out of her limited vision. Movement, cries of anger, and wet sounds suddenly filled her ears. The twang, reminiscent of an over-tuned string, was sharp against the other sounds. Less and less blurred images appeared in her failing sight. Footsteps were followed by hands under her neck, bringing her head off of the floor. The cool jet of air from a hypo brushed against her neck.

Her vision cleared moments later. The sextet of Moyii Tsaa lay all around her, bleeding against the floor. People in black biosuits and visored helms were kneeling and withdrawing bladed weapons connected to lengths of cord or large flechettes from fatal wounds in the henchbeings. Violetta's restored eyesight caught the badge of the military on each of the living beings' chests.

"Come along, Violetta, Daughter of Vrehn. We've come to keep you safe," said the soldier closest to Violetta.

. . .

The group of eight soldiers led the way back the way she'd originally entered. The leader of this group was Commander Rezra Al'erryn, a native woman with bronze skin and dark hair in rows of braids pulled back into a bun. The one who had applied the hypo spray and helped her to stand was a human woman with equally dark features and eyes. The three men were a mixture of native and human. The other three women were also pure blood K'laisians. A diverse group working together as a single fluid unit.

What K'lais was supposed to be like, in Violetta's opinion.

This time, Violetta could see where she was going as well as the bodies of the Moyii Tsaa who had not remained in the room. The military had far more leeway when it came to killing than even the police service. Even then, they had used methods that did not require firearms. The use of bladed weapons had been to prevent alerting the world-wide detection net of firearm use. The very system that was being used against Violetta, her mind bitterly recalled.

Despite that bit, this event was a stark reminder that the military was not just for appearances. They could, and would use deadly force when it was needed. Against the Moyii Tsaa, Violetta didn't doubt that it would have been needed.

Not a single one of her rescuers would be accused of murder. The rules and laws dictating anyone in the military were far different from the standard laws civilians and the police service were required to follow. As the humans often said, the military was at the top of K'lais' food chain.

Closing her eyes to protect them against the brightness contradicting the darkness outside, Violetta stepped into the alley once again. Even through her closed lids, she could see the strobing lights from official police service HAVs.

When she opened her eyes, she found she was in the center of a military formation. Two soldiers walked in front of her, two at her sides, and two behind her. She suspected there were even more than that hidden in the shadows. The nanites would keep them effectively hidden.

"We'll take it from here," Captain Monroe's voice broke through the night air.

The soldiers ahead of her stopped. Violetta couldn't see past them, but she knew Monroe blocked their way. Doubtless he was in his usual button-down shirt of some bright color beneath a casual business jacket. Dark trousers typically completed his 'suit'. The only oddity would be the military-style boots he preferred over dress shoes.

"We'll take it from here," Monroe repeated. "Stand down."

"No," Commander Al'erryn said.

"Violetta Cq'linns is wanted in the murder of Chief of Police Ylvran Me'addn."

"Stand down, officer," the woman stated. "We have orders to deliver Lady Cq'linns to the base, and we're doing just that."

"Captain-" Monroe began.

"That's *Commander* Rezra Al'erryn to you," the native interrupted, amusement coloring her words. She took a step forward. The native human beside her slid into position directly in front of Violetta. "*Captain* Monroe."

Ouch, Violetta thought, lowering her head slightly, biting back a smile. A commander outranked a captain by leaps and bounds. Being military only added distance between Monroe and Al'erryn's ranks and positions.

"Commander, we have orders to bring Cq'linns in," Monroe reiterated.

"You have your orders. We have ours. You won't be taking Lady Cq'linns in today." Commander Al'erryn's tone grew colder, harder. "Stand down, or we will arrest you for impeding our duty. I'm certain the 42nd District Police Service can make a request for Lady Cq'linns to be handed over when they petition for your release."

Monroe moved stiffly to the right. Commander Al'erryn remained between him and the unit. She snapped a command to move forward in their native language.

As a single group, everyone moved towards the military-marked armored HAV that had been surrounded by police service HAVs and personnel. More soldiers appeared from the shadows and ordered the police service officers to move their vehicles.

Violetta glanced at Monroe. Fury filled his every feature, from his clenched fists to his glaring eyes. She could feel that glare burning into her back, even as she slid into the armored military HAV. The human woman with the dark skin and hair sat against the door, leaving the middle free. Violetta recognized the marks on her uniform that designated the woman as a lieutenant. A driver was already in the front with a partner beside him. Both were males with long straight black hair that covered their ears. She couldn't tell if they were pure K'laisian or of mixed heritage, since she couldn't see their eyes.

The human male and two others remained outside the HAV. The door slid open once more and the commander climbed into the seat beside Violetta. There were two resounding thuds on the side just before the driver began maneuvering the vehicle away from the alley and government center.

"How did you find me?" Violetta asked after they were moving. "Thank you for that, by the way."

Commander Al'erryn remained silent for a few minutes and Violetta had the impression she was listening to an order on a comm. The woman gave a knowing smile at Violetta's slightly raised brow.

"We were advised of who had aided your escape by the unit sent to watch over you and Malik Addelia."

Giving the commander her complete attention, she raised a single brow. "Why you and not the other unit?"

Commander Al'erryn returned Violetta's steady gaze. Approval shone in the woman's gold eyes. "Very good." There was another pause as the woman's brows rose considerably. The look Violetta received was speculative. "We've been watching the Moyii Tsaa in the area for the last several months. That particular cell, to be exact."

Violetta considered the woman's words and their implications. "Why not have the local police service do it?"

A sly smile curved Al'erryn's lips. The natives hummed and the humans chuckled.

"How do you know the local police service isn't already aware of that cell?"

"I don't." Violetta returned the smile. "And even if they did, my current situation makes me question their involvement with said cell."

Al'erryn nodded, as did the human next to her. "When we received word that you were in their not-so-caring hands, we moved in. I'm certain you'll need to be debriefed as to what they wanted."

"That one's an easy answer, though I'm not entirely certain of their reasoning behind it. They wanted Malik."

"They wanted Malik Addelia," Al'erryn repeated slowly.

Violetta gave a single nod.

"Interesting."

"The admiral has cleared our entrance and arrival, Commander," the driver stated. "Seems the police service is rather… unhappy, about not being able to catch the lady."

Shortly after the words were spoken, the HAV pulled through the fence surrounding the military base Violetta hadn't stepped inside for over five years. The last time had been before she graduated.

Before her father had been taken from her and everyone else.

There was nothing Violetta wouldn't give if it meant she could have her father back. To hear his voice. To see his smile. To have him hug her again. To scold her for being an idiot and complete fool.

"Are you well, lady?" Commander Al'erryn asked.

It was then Violetta realized she was alone in the HAV. Everyone else had exited. Shoving her emotions into a mental room and slamming the door shut, she slid from the HAV. Dwelling on the past wouldn't help her now.

"You should be safe here, detective," the lieutenant stated. Her voice was warm and friendly, matching the pleasant smile on her smooth face. "Though, if we don't hurry, someone will be sent to locate us."

"Let's not have that happen, shall we?" the driver said, revealing brilliant white teeth in a broad smile.

Violetta could now see his eyes were hazel, bordering on green and his ears were rounded. She looked around at the rest of the unit who'd escorted her here. She found herself liking the special ops unit, which it had to be, if they were watching the Moyii Tsaa.

"Lead the way, please."

There was a round of chuckling from her escorts.

Commander Al'erryn took point with the same human who had taken point during her rescue. The others fell into a loose formation around her. An easy silence fell over them as they entered the main doors.

J.F. Posthumus

Chapter Twelve

The exterior of K'laisian military bases held their own splendor. They were usually uniform in design, but that did not make them recognized as places of war and conflict preparation. In fact, the first two generations of humans who came to K'lais were convinced the military bases were either worship centers or belonging to financial institutions. What Earthers referred to as "churches" and "banks."

Violetta did not have time to take in the multi-storied exterior, or any of the eight-point spires marking the six primary directions; North, Northeast, Northwest and the corresponding South points. She was well familiar with all those details anyway, along with the plentitude of sea glass allowing for strategic views out but a warped view looking to the interior.

Violetta's favorite detail, since childhood, was the entry halls and passages. The main doors spilled them into the massive entry hall. Dark blue dolomite was used for all walls, as well as the floors on the lowest level. The handrails, stairs, and doors were primarily made of manganese with other metals. The silver gray color of these objects highlighted strongly against the dolomite. The ceilings and floors of all other levels were a honeycomb of manganese and sea glass. The visual was striking, while allowing anyone to look at the level above or below them to see how much traffic and activity existed. Even after decades, she still felt fascination and calm looking through the sea glass.

Nothing had changed over the years.

Violetta followed her security detail through two levels. Finally, they came to a large room with double doors. Commander Al'erryn pressed her hand against the large pad and the doors slid open with barely a whisper.

The three guards in front of Violetta moved to the sides, allowing her to finally see the room in its entirety.

It reminded Violetta of the war room her father had taken her to when she was very young. Maps of the world's districts decorated one wall. A large, highly detailed map of their district filled a wall all by itself. Lastly, a large interface hung from the wall opposite the door. The K'lais military symbol, a shield bearing the body of the elder S'trak dragon, topped with the ancient war helmet of the first K'laisian army, filled the otherwise-blank screen.

Neither the military symbol nor the maps held Violetta's attention for long. Nor did the dozen other military-clad beings in the room who turned towards the door. Some she recognized as being military comrades of her father. None were sitting in the conforming chairs that surrounded the table at the center of the room. Along a far wall, she noticed, was a counter which held a small replicator, a jakka maker, and various fresh foods. Most were standing near the counter or in small clusters on each end.

A man stood among them, his white coat, blue tunic, and light gray pants at odds with the uniforms around him.

Malik.

How angry was he going to be over the stunt she pulled?

"Expecting me to punch you back, Vi?" Malik asked.

Those near him shared amused expressions.

"I'm sorry about that. At least they didn't arrest you for being my accomplice." She gave him a smile. "Not angry?"

"I thought it was brilliant. Right up until you threw my shot-up body onto the small pack of officers," he replied with a morose tone. As Violetta began to frown, he smiled. "That was genius. Glad I could be your distraction. I wouldn't try that with anyone who doesn't know you as well as I do, though."

"I doubt I'll need to worry about that, unless you're planning on ending our, ah, partnership?" Violetta crossed the room to him. "I'm pleased to see you came out okay. Complete with fresh new clothes."

"I can't always dress down to fit next to you," he teased.

Malik turned and manipulated the jakka maker. After a few moments, the beverage streamed out of the machine and into a cup. Malik then handed her the cup as though he did such on a daily basis. In retrospect, he probably had during his time learning to be a healer.

"Oh, ha ha, very funny," Violetta retorted as she accepted the cup of jakka. The smile on her lips only grew bigger despite the words. "I'll remember that."

Malik rubbed the spot where he'd been punched, while arching his back to indicate the sore spots from the shots taken earlier. "Remember it all you want."

Violetta opened her mouth, then shut it very quickly. If she weren't careful, she'd say something that would be anything but appropriate. The last thing she needed, or wanted, was someone to question Malik's ability to do his job. Or what they'd been doing while alone at the safe house.

Instead, she took a pull from the cup, enjoying the pleasant taste of the jakka. He'd even added the right amount of honey to the mix.

"This is all very lovely." Amusement rang in the voice of the man who spoke up. "But perhaps we should turn to the issue at hand?"

A being with an obvious lifetime of military service strode towards them. Hints of a biosuit peeked out in between the slate gray slacks and black shoes, and at the matching gray collar of the formal dress tunic and the skin of his neck. The black and dark silver camouflage was something Violetta recognized, especially since many military personnel wore the suits as though they were outer clothes.

No less than two dozen achievement pins colored the left breast of the tunic. The sleeves bore the quad-stripes of an admiral, along with three sunbursts on his command emblem to indicate the level of his commanding rank. Only admirals were allowed the starbursts. The silver command emblem, an image of the ch'inwi plant surrounded by a circle with their world's motto above it, barely stood out against the slate gray fabric.

In her mind, she could hear a younger version of herself asking her father about the emblem on his uniform. His response had been that the ch'inwi plant was the heartiest thing on K'lais. It grew everywhere, becoming the symbol for K'laisian resilience. Most of the architecture was designed to resemble the plant in some way.

For some inexplicable reason, the K'laisian approaching them reminded her strongly of her father. He had to be a native, with his silver eyes and pointed ears. But in an unusual twist, this male had no hair on his head.

Baldness was all but unheard of among natives, and this man's bright silver eyes left no questions to his heritage. The lack of eyebrows only made Violetta more astonished.

She had to will herself to keep her jaw from hanging open or from staring.

"Admiral It'zarry Mc'narrd, at your service." The man introduced himself. "Pleasure to finally meet the fabled daughter of Admiral Cq'linns." He smiled at her. "I'm not offended by the staring."

Violetta blinked and inwardly cursed herself for being flabbergasted.

"That's a cute trick, calling yourself Admiral Mc'narrd," Malik interjected. Violetta glanced at him sharply. "The being who spearheaded our off-world explorations and negotiations with other races had a thick mane of silver hair. He's also dead."

"At least you paid attention in history lessons during your time in the military," the man said to Malik. "I was declared dead on 2238.4, but here I am."

Still unable to speak or stop staring, Violetta wondered if she could slap herself into action. Her body was as traitorous as everything above her neck, though. Apparently, shock would do that to a person. Admiral Mc'narrd had been one of her father's oldest friends. Seeing the man her father spoke about with warmth and praise standing before her was definitely a shock to her system. A man she'd long thought dead.

Had her father known the truth? Or had he died not knowing one of his closest, most trusted friends was still alive and breathing?

Why does Judge Ta'ba look like Commander Mc'narrd?

The words had been spoken by Violetta as a young girl as she'd watched a newsvid with her father. Her father had studied her for a long time.

Coincidence, he had replied in a bitter tone. Then he'd asked if she wanted to go out for a treat before visiting the nature preserve. It had worked as a distraction.

Now she understood why. Judge Io'siph Ta'ba *was* Admiral It'zarry Mc'narrd.

Her father had to have known, she realized after a couple moments had passed. And she'd been too young to push her father for answers. She'd merely accepted his words, not wanting to cause pain by mentioning someone she thought had died.

"Nearly twenty years ago." Malik rejoined. His shell had returned and this time, Violetta didn't mind it. "Yet you would claim the title and character of one of our greatest beings."

"How does someone who keeps employment with the Earthers' most notorious business model feel such pride in his own planet's accomplishments?" His silver eyes were shrewd and cool as he watched Malik.

"Notorious because it still works, or because of its home history?" asked Malik.

The man laughed.

"Both and more. Much like my own." Closing the distance between them, Mc'narrd placed his left hand on Malik's shoulder. The first part of the traditional greeting between friendly beings of the planet. "Greetings and well met, Malik Addelia."

Malik's eyes narrowed, an expression shared with humans, but he placed his left hand on the man's shoulder. Once both beings nodded, they moved their hands back to their sides.

"I understand your suspicion and applaud you for it. I was declared dead after the betrayal of the Ukraine Xeno-Earthers, and I was badly wounded. The best Earth healers had begun successful replication of our nanites for their own species, albeit on a more primitive basis. My head, neck, and shoulders were badly burned. Our healers were dead, facilities on the ships were all but destroyed. The Earth healers reprogrammed their first generation nanites for zinc-based blood instead of iron-based, and injected me. Their world military and government wanted to keep me alive as much as our own people would have, I was told later by our Military High Command."

Finally Violetta felt she could speak without babbling. It was easier, since the subject of nanites had always fascinated her. "The nanites didn't know how to fix you completely. K'laisian biologies are just different enough for some procedures to work and others to be... guesswork at best."

Mc'narrd nodded. "The nanites actually improved upon our skin. It's denser and heals quicker than what I was born with, although hair follicles were a bit too much for the nanites to understand. They identified them as foreign objects and removed them."

"You probably fit in with the Earthers better at that point," Malik observed. "Bald is a common style among their race."

"It helped that many Earthers in those early days altered their eye color to resemble ours. While I continued to heal and plan, I moved among them with relative ease. Learned a great love for what they call Asian cuisine, and Mexican tequila."

"Why the deception?" Violetta asked.

Mc'narrd turned his silver eyes to her. "Once I became well known, my ability to plot and execute deep military campaigns and missions was compromised. If you are familiar with the history of that era, then you may be aware that my last three years of known activity were mostly ceremonial. Lots of attention and media coverage on any developed planet or moon I visited. While that diverted attention for other campaigns to operate, many failed. I needed to be back where I did the most good."

"There was already a plan in place to put you there," Malik guessed.

"Yes, we waited for an opportunity for me to disappear and be declared dead, so I could return and improve covert operations on and off-world. We didn't expect such an opportunity to almost be my actual death! As the Earthers are fond of saying, however, everything worked out for the best. I do not have to remain hidden on military premises my whole life, and as a result I get a better view of everything."

"Your wife and children did an amazing job mourning you," Violetta commented dryly. "They would have the clearance to know you were still alive. Yet one would never have known at your funeral."

He raised his eyebrows, and she added, "I watched the vidclips after Dad spoke about you the first time."

Sorrow filled Mc'narrd's eyes. "Vrehn Cq'linns was a dear friend. I am sorry I was not able to contact you sooner, but his death did not warrant my approaching you. As for my funeral? Alyssa and my family had not been told yet." His lips curved into a small smile. "Alyssa was not pleased when she was informed. Admiral Ad'dari was not Challenged solely because our son was there to keep her from doing so. But only just."

The amusement of Mc'narrd's statement softened his previous words. Alyssa Zelaya was the first human a K'laisian had interacted with face-to-face. The details of that mission was classified to only the highest in command, but her father had spoken of the pair frequently. And always with warmth and amusement. Mc'narrd had broken many protocols regarding Alyssa, but the end result benefited both worlds, so no punishment had been levied.

Alyssa, Violetta knew, had become as much of a face for Policy Masters and their world as her husband had been for the military. Their eldest child, one of the first children of a human and K'laisian pairing, had risen to the rank of commander and had his own ship. As much a force to be reckoned with as his parents.

"So, why are you here? And why are you able to reveal yourself? Your alias of Judge Ta'ba is also a three-star admiral," Violetta all but demanded, changing topics and gesturing to the room. "I appreciate the rescue, and I thank you for it, but this is beyond what is normal from the military. This is what I would expect if my father were alive." She trailed off, a thought suddenly occurring to her. Her grandparents were retired career military and council members in the 31st District. "Did Dad's parents make a request of some sort?"

"My alias does not have the same position in the military as *I* do. The presence of Admiral Ta'ba would be questioned," Mc'narrd replied, approval in his tone. "As for the rest of your questions? You've been on the Watch List since birth. Your family, alive and past, is a valuable asset to the people. Especially the military and, although some may not recognize it, the police service. We don't need any member of said family being kidnapped, questioned, or detained for anything less than the good of all of K'lais."

She glanced at Malik, whose face was void of expression. His eyes met hers and she saw surprise in their depths. It lasted for only a few short heartbeats, but she felt better knowing he hadn't shut down towards her.

"When you were framed via the use of a cloned weapon," Mc'narrd continued, "that fell into our jurisdiction. The ability to clone weapons from our world has been a concern of mine and your father's for a very long time. Ironic that the responsible parties chose you to implement their new techniques."

There was little Violetta could think of saying in response to that declaration. Wariness and unease swept through her, as well as distrust for the being in front of her. She took a step back.

The admiral must have misinterpreted her intent, because he added, "Since our interests overlapped, it made sense to bring you into the fold on our involvement. No, we aren't going to be your backup every time you go out on the job. We are engaged only as our interests intertwine."

As if that made this whole situation easier to process or puts me at ease, Violetta thought. It does neither.

Obviously Nualith had contacted the military. She'd expected it when the munitions expert had said the military had been approached originally. It also involved the safety and security of the entire world.

Everything else, though? That was different.

The Watch List had been something her father mentioned on rare occasions, but never towards her or their family. He'd never mentioned being on it or anyone in their family being on it. Then or in the past.

The List Mc'narrd referred to was a very short one. Single people could find their way onto the list for the duration of their life, for the service said person provided during their lifetime. For entire generations to be placed upon the list? It wasn't unprecedented as far as Violetta knew. Just very unusual.

Those on it were granted protection from the military. They were watched over and kept safe, even if the being was never aware of it. Those in the being's life whom the military believed to be unsavory or untrustworthy were nudged out of the being's life. If the military believed harm would come from someone going somewhere at a certain time, other options, better options, would become available. Or the trip would encounter problems.

It… was unnerving to know she and her family were on that list. To know she'd been on that list since her birth and would remain there until her death.

On the other side of her situation, if she'd known she could have military assistance with any part of this mess, she'd have approached them first and never thought once of trying to get help from a criminal and his empire.

Past time to change the subject, Violetta decided, refusing to dwell on it.

"Then you're aware of everything I told Captain Ae'staa?"

"Yes, she reported in and was debriefed accordingly." When Violetta didn't say anything, Mc'narrd asked, "Do you have more information on the replicating weapon?"

Sharing a glance with Malik, Violetta nodded. "We located the developer of that weapon. He's currently at Mc'faen's Private Hospital under the name Candace Reedy, a human female. Whoever is in charge of keeping him there and his treatment is doing just enough to keep him alive."

"What do you mean by 'just enough to keep him alive'?" Another of the military personnel present asked.

Violetta turned her attention to the woman, who was a pure blood native with dark olive skin and hair so dark it had purple and blue highlights. Gold eyes were confident and compassionate.

Instead of wearing similar clothes as the admiral, she wore a standard silver biosuit common to most military healers. The emblem on her shoulder was that of a healer. Three lines wrapped around the cuffs of her sleeves. Three starbursts sat above them in easy view, marking her as a Sovereign Healer, the highest ranking a healer could achieve. The three starburst put her at the top of even those beings. Equal to Admiral Mc'narrd's position in the command chain.

Sovereign Healers oversaw the Master Healers and all other medical personnel on K'lais as well as those who went offworld in the military. Until now, Violetta had not met one so high ranking. Thankfully, she was not intimidated by high ranking beings.

"This is Sovereign Healer Zh'oros," Admiral Mc'narrd said, gesturing to the woman who moved to stand beside the admiral.

The healer nodded to each, giving a slight bow as she did so. Violetta and Malik returned the bow.

"He's hooked up to a variety of Earth machines to aid his body," Malik said, stepping forward until his shoulder brushed Violetta. "The nanites are programmed for a native. They have to learn his biology and modify themselves to heal his human body. It's a slow process, and very deliberate."

Mc'narrd smiled, his gaze shifting between Violetta and Malik. The amusement in his eyes didn't fade. If anything, Violetta could have sworn it was growing. Even more frightening was the fact he reminded her a lot of her father.

He gave them similar looks when they'd declared they were going out to a festival or play. The thought tugged on her heart, but she pushed it away. She'd have plenty of time to figure out her confusing emotions later. Though she doubted she'd ever figure out anyone else.

There was going to be so much meditating in her future.

"You're very much like your father, Lady Cq'linns," Admiral Mc'narrd said. "There is more, I suspect."

"Before we get to that, could you explain how they managed such a thing? I thought that if the nanites were injected, they were not programmed for one particular body or another?" Violetta rejoined.

"The nanites used by the military are of a superior grade," Sovereign Healer Zh'oros explained. "Even when injecting them, they need to be programmed towards the race they're being used towards. Because humans vary so greatly, it is still a difficult job if you have not programmed them towards the specific being. It's why healers across our world keep such extensive data on humans, even more so for those of mixed heritage. The variables grow exponentially among those who are not purely one race or another."

Zh'oros paused, giving Violetta time to consider what she said.

"From my instruction, I remember it being mentioned that all nanites for humans are based off the first one they were used on," Malik stated. "So if someone injected a human with K'laisian nanites, they have to fight against what they know about humans, because nanites are always sending and receiving data."

"Very good," Zh'oros said. Her tone turned chiding as she added, "I believe you were just starting to learn about the nanites when you chose to leave the Service."

Glancing at Malik, Violetta saw him glance away as guilt flashed through his eyes. She didn't blame him. Zh'oros sounded like a mother scolding a child with just that slight shift of her tone.

"The nanites are still learning how best to heal humans, and it will be like that for years to come," Zh'oros concluded. Gold eyes met Violetta's gaze. "The first time they were used on a human, it was a risk of immeasurable proportions. No one knew if the nanites would work, or how they would work. The chance she could have died from the nanites was as great, if not greater, than the likelihood they would work and she would survive. None knew what the subsequent consequences of doing such would be."

"And because humans' genetics vary so greatly, the nanites always have to work to learn how best to heal any race other than a K'laisian," Violetta mused.

"Which is why humans, those of mixed heritage, and other races have more frequent wellness visits," Malik added.

"You, too, huh?" Violetta asked him. He gave a slight shrug and nod. "Explains all the blood draws over the years."

There was humming and chuckles from all the beings in the room. Especially Zh'oros.

"We answered your question. Please answer mine," Mc'narrd said, the humanity fading slightly from his face.

"We have a key to a storage unit where Matt Gomez, the developer, has the proof of not only the weapon, but that he created it. The two prototypes were taken by Lieutenant Cancio, but all the notes Gomez made are in the storage unit. Those involved are not aware he has them or their location."

"Do you require a squad to escort you to this proof?" Mc'narrd asked. "Followed by an escort to the District Attorney? Or perhaps the governor?"

"I would, except for one problem." Violetta suspected this was a test, but treated the question as it was spoken.

Mc'narrd lifted his brows and Malik sighed heavily. Violetta glanced sharply at Malik, who shook his head, a look of pure understanding and acceptance on his face.

"I still don't know who killed the Chief," Violetta explained. She turned and paced the length of the table, a behavior shared by humans, K'laisians, and a variety of other races. "We know the how, and possibly even the why. But without the 'who', I can't go to anyone. My name won't be cleared, my reputation restored fully, until I can prove who killed the Chief of Police. Those involved can claim I was as much a part of this plan as they are. I'd have no way of proving them wrong."

"Why do you believe Ylvran Me'addn was killed?" Mc'narrd asked, turning to watch her pace.

"I used my lieutenant's interface and that's where I acquired the proof of their illegal activities. At the time I didn't realize how deep the corruption went, or the extent. I contacted Chief Me'addn and set up a private meeting at his home. The logical reason would be Captain Monroe, Lieutenant Cancio, and Sergeant Rc'dollph found out about the meeting and killed him to prevent him from learning."

"And to set you up for his murder," Malik added. Though his words were bland, there was no mistaking the anger in his eyes. "Do you believe Chief Me'addn was involved?"

She shook her head. "I honestly don't know. I never saw him on any of the vidclips, but that doesn't mean he wasn't aware. Or suspected something was occurring and merely turned a blind eye."

"There is no reason any of them would have knowledge of the military's interest in you," Mc'narrd declared. "We would prefer to keep it that way for the present time, also. The high level of aid you have encountered so far is why I was brought in. Few others could give the command for what has been done to assist you. That began the moment you sought out Captain Ae'staa and informed her of what was occurring."

Violetta blinked. Mc'narrd was perhaps one of the highest ranking individuals in the military. His security clearance was probably the highest possible. He had stated he was involved in special operations, which made sense, all things considered.

"So, what can we do to aid you, Lady Cq'linns?" He paused, the smile turning into a smirk. "Lord Addelia?"

Violetta started, surprised the admiral was using the human's translation for bures'o. Yet, it did make sense, considering he'd been calling her Lady, the translation for bures'a.

Malik snorted. "Please, don't use that title. I've done nothing to earn it."

Mc'narrd narrowed his gaze, making him look even more human. "You have done a great deal to earn that honorable title, Addelia. For one, you've been assisting Violetta and kept her safe. We're also aware of all you have done both during your service within the military and since you left."

Pausing in her pacing, Violetta watched the exchange between the men. She could tell Malik didn't agree, but also wasn't going to argue.

His eyes remained fixed upon hers as he replied, "I will only acquiesce because I cannot argue that I have been helping Violetta, or the fact I will continue to help her."

Violetta couldn't help the warm smile that formed on her lips. Her eyes softened as she stared at him. Dropping her gaze to the floor, she veiled her eyes with her lashes, hopefully before the room full of high ranking military personnel realized how much she valued his words. If she wasn't careful, someone was going to figure out she had more than platonic feelings for him before she was able to clear her name.

"I'm certain you will," Mc'narrd replied, clear amusement in his voice. Her eyes snapped up and there was humor in his silver orbs. "I'm also certain you'll continue to remain in contact with the detective following this series of unfortunate events."

"What a grasp of the obvious you have, sir," Malik rejoined.

A spattering of chuckles and loud humming erupted in the otherwise silent room. Even the healer was humming loudly at the admiral's sour expression. Violetta bit back the laughter, but didn't hide the grin. Malik, as usual, wore a bland expression.

"Now that you've briefed us on all of that, perhaps you can inform us what the Moyii Tsaa desired when they rescued you, Violetta," Mc'narrd said, his eyes shifting to her. "As well as how that was accomplished."

"Ah, that," Violetta said.

Holding the cup of jakka in her hands, she moved until she was leaning against the wall. A better support than if she sat, in her opinion. Settling against the wall, she gave a detailed report of everything that happened from the moment she entered the alley until the military entered the room and rescued her.

Zh'oros, she noticed, frowned when she reported the injury she'd sustained.

"The only thing I learned was they believed I could be used to bait Malik," Violetta concluded. "I don't know why they desired him, or what they planned once they had him, as they put it, in their grasp."

"Commander Al'erryn was informed." It wasn't a question, but a statement from Mc'narrd. Violetta gave a nod, anyway. "I'll speak with her after her debriefing. If we learn why they are interested in you, Addelia, we'll inform you."

Malik gave a nod, his eyes on her. She met his gaze and saw concern in their depths.

"How are you feeling now, Lady?" Zh'oros asked.

"I'm feeling fine, now." She paused, before giving a slight smile. "Aside from the varied emotions I've been feeling during these events."

"After you're examined by Sovereign Healer Zh'oros and cleared, we will send a detachment to watch, at a distance, as you collect the data from the storage unit. After which, you will return to the safe house." Mc'narrd glanced at Zh'oros, who gave a slight nod before continuing. "We'll arrange a pick up from there."

"That isn't going to be a conflict of any sort?" Violetta asked, honestly curious.

Admiral Mc'narrd laughed. It was a very human laugh, which startled Violetta. She expected him to hum, as most K'laisians, yet found it a pleasant sound she enjoyed. Her father had done the same. Perhaps it was because Mc'narrd spent so much time with a human mate? Or was it due to the fact he'd spent so long pretending to be a human?

"Don Morelli provides many services that are not available or possible through other methods. Those methods are all legal. Despite the fact his number of Duels are higher than any other individual's on K'lais, they are always done correctly and follow the laws to the letter." He tipped his head to the sides, giving the K'laisian version of a shrug, instead of a human one.

Violetta found herself liking the admiral. He was an interesting dichotomy of traits and behaviors.

"If those who make the laws do not agree, then they should change the laws. As far as we, the military, are concerned?" Mc'narrd continued. "As long as he continues to follow the laws and provide services to our world, helping everyone regardless of gender or race, he will be watched, but nothing more. He offers services in many sectors that no others have bothered with, a service that helps all our people. Not just one sector or another."

Violetta grinned. "I'm certain the Council members were thrilled with your opinion on the laws."

"They weren't too pleased, to say the least," Mc'narrd confirmed with a grin of his own. "Everything illegal that Don Morelli is suspected of doing has not been proven. Until that happens, we will work with him. Discreetly, of course."

"Of course," Malik muttered. "What do you want from us?"

"We want the proof of that weapon and the names of all those connected to it," Admiral Mc'narrd replied, all humor gone from his face and posture. "Once you have that, we will take care of the rest."

"What about Gomez?" Violetta asked. "What will happen to him?"

"He'll be retrieved from the private hospital and moved to another. One where we can better protect him," Zh'oros stated, her voice calm and emotionless. "We will wait until your situation has reached a suitable resolution, first. We do not wish to 'tip off' anyone involved in the treachery."

Though the healer's words were spoken to Violetta and Malik, Violetta recognized the tone. Gomez had already been argued over, and whoever had won, the healer didn't agree with the reasoning. Probably because a healer's first priority is supposed to be the health and welfare of a patient. Having a patient being mistreated went against every code a healer is taught to follow. Gomez's treatment probably angered her greatly, especially knowing she couldn't do anything for the man yet.

"We appreciate that," Malik said, giving the healer a bow. "And we thank you."

"And after?" Violetta pressed, her gaze not leaving the admiral.

Mc'narrd met her eyes and kept them as he answered her question. "That will be discussed among the admiralty. It will also depend upon the circumstances surrounding why he pursued the creation of the weapon." He paused, then sighed heavily. "He has killed no one. Depending on his intentions behind the weapon, the harshest punishment he will receive is a sentence on P'yka."

P'yka was the moon that orbited their world. It was also where K'lais' sole penitentiary was located. Those who were sent to the penitentiary were rehabilitated or spent time as penance for their crimes.

"Any more questions?" Mc'narrd asked.

Violetta and Malik shared a look before turning back and shaking their heads.

"No," they said at the same time.

"Good. You will be examined prior to leaving the base, Violetta. Afterwards, the team that brought you both here, will be in charge of watching over you. You will be taken to a HAV, which will be used to acquire the data from the storage facility before returning to the safe house." He turned to Violetta. "You both will be issued military weapons. That will prevent any concerns about the local police department tracking either of you. If you require anything else, Commander Al'erryn will handle that, also."

Mc'narrd grasped shoulders with Malik, and then he turned to Violetta. As he placed his hand upon her shoulder, he said, "A pleasure to finally meet you, Lady Cq'linns."

Violetta placed her left hand on his shoulder, a slight smile curving her lips. "It has been an honor, sir."

Chapter Thirteen

"I wouldn't think the biosuit would be that unusual, considering the lingerie you wear," Malik teased.

Violetta's examination had been thorough, complete with the usual blood draw. Also, as was typical, it had taken a couple hours. After which, the military had insisted the pair wait until after sunset to leave. They were delivered to the HAV with far more ease than Violetta had anticipated.

The general agreement was it would be better to wait until dark to find the warehouse and retrieve the duffel bag. They were headed towards the warehouse district now, and Violetta was still shifting uncomfortably in the biosuit she wore beneath her clothing.

The biosuits were standard issue for everyone in the military. Malik, to her annoyance, appeared completely comfortable in his. As though having a complete one-piece snug-fitting suit was part of his typical clothing. Of course, Violetta was aware that he would have worn them during his three years in the military. She just hated the fact he was completely comfortable, and she felt strange having an entire set of clothing under her other clothes.

At least the hooded trench coats didn't feel out of place. Another gift from Mc'narrd, they were designed so the wearer would be invisible to cameras. Due to the built-in nanites, they didn't have to wear additional ones to hide their features. Since Seers weren't common, mostly employed at medical facilities and financial institutes, they weren't overly concerned about being spotted.

"The biosuit is nothing like the lingerie I wear," Violetta replied. "It's not uncomfortable. It's just... strange. I'll get used to it. Eventually." She muttered a few words under her breath in their native language.

Malik chuckled. "Probably by the time you need to return it." He paused, a single brow rose. "They do want the 'suits back, yes?"

"They didn't tell you?" Violetta asked. He shook his head. "They didn't tell me, either. Maybe they want another, better method of tracking me, and now you."

"Possible," Malik agreed.

"Still interested in me?"

"You do know they can hear us?" Malik asked, ignoring the question.

Violetta shrugged. "Nope. The comms are currently turned off." Malik started and she giggled. "That's what I did. These are standard military-issue comms. Dad gave me the override code when I turned eight so we could have private discussions. Either they haven't bothered changing the code, or they're allowing me some privacy."

"Isn't that going to make them suspicious?" he asked.

"Only if I leave them off for more than ten minutes at a time," she replied. "That was Dad's rule, so hopefully it still applies."

Malik nodded. "Makes sense. Plus, they can track us and can tell we're not in danger at the moment."

"Plus, Commander Al'erryn is supposed to be keeping watch, also." She eyed him from the corner of her eyes. "You're avoiding the question. Should I be worried?"

"Being your father's daughter still hasn't put me off," he stated. "This situation changes nothing."

She couldn't help but laugh at the comment. "I'm glad to hear that. I'd have to figure out another method of seduction if you'd said otherwise."

"I'm sorry I said it, now," he teased. "Wouldn't want to miss whatever method you had in mind."

"Oh, nothing nearly as much fun as using you as a shield," she joked. "You know I was never very good at seduction, so it would be rather boring. Dinner out. Maybe a play. Or perhaps dinner at home wearing something very sheer."

Malik didn't reply with words at first. He smiled, eyes narrowed and glinting.

"That would work," he admitted.

"I'll keep that in mind," she murmured, running a finger along the pointed tip of his ear. "Going live, again."

She gave the code to turn the comms back on, and the familiar barely-there hum returned.

"Alright, detective. Now don't do that again," Mc'narrd's voice spoke over the comms. "You and your partner are reading clear all across the interface. Ready whenever you are."

They crossed the Nimkelu River via the single road that went over the powerful water. Dra'as Avenue was the sole connecting road between the east and west sections of the city. Eight lanes wide, with two levels of traffic in each direction, the Avenue was simplistic in appearance but a testament to the technological prowess and considerations of the native people.

Every meter of road that crossed the water was a high density solar panel coupled with a sensor array. Each one collected energy and data constantly. The solar batteries supplied more than enough energy to run all government buildings, military and emergency service utilities, and vehicles.

The data went to room-sized servers that processed the info to maintain traffic at a safe, constant pace. Collisions were exceedingly rare, and any medical issues were flagged instantly. Any vehicle transporting a being with an urgent medical condition was moved to the emergency lane, allowed to accelerate past normal traffic to arrive at a hospital or shut down in a safe place while emergency services were inbound.

Malik piloted the cruiser off of Dra'as Avenue onto the perpendicular stretch that was Ea'ndar Street. On this side of the river, heading south, they traveled through the industrial district. Specialized shops and services rolled past the darkened plex panels that allowed passengers to see outside the vehicle. Once they had turned west onto Ser'ite Highway, only factories and warehouses were visible.

Violetta looked over at Malik, who was sitting up a little straighter than usual. His face showed curiosity, puzzlement, and what she hoped was contentment.

"Are you feeling well about this?"

As his head turned to face her, Malik seemed more puzzled. He must have realized what she was referring to, because he relaxed and smiled before speaking.

"I feel very well. Better than I have for years. As for what we are going to do, I'm confident. But, the expression on my face is more due to how much healthier I'm feeling. Stronger, as though I could run across the river and back just to get my blood pumping faster."

"Forgotten what wearing a biosuit was like?" she suggested.

"No, it's not that. It's as though I'm getting younger and stronger the longer I'm sitting here. A very curious set of sensations."

"Oh!" Violetta exclaimed as she understood. "You've never worn a paramilitary or specialized military biosuit!

You remember that during the time you served, there were nanites available in the suit to do minor medical repairs?"

"Yes," Malik agreed, "Go on."

"You've got your suit from that time, they just upgraded the software and added the specialized nanites. All paramilitary and specialized military biosuits are equipped to keep the beings who wear them in the best physical health."

Malik frowned and his eyes grew wider.

"I don't think I understand what you are implying."

"The nanites don't stay dormant in the suit. These nanites-" she indicated her own suit and his, "-are constantly working. They purify blood, burn excessive fat cells, make sure muscles and tendons get enough blood consistently, and absorb sweat. A long list of assignments to make a body perform at its peak all the time."

"So I'm actually growing stronger?"

"Yes! Your body is being repaired from being lazy, eating or drinking too much of anything, old injuries."

"Thank you for guessing all of my failings," he quipped. "I'm not sure how comfortable I am with nanites working through my entire body, even if the results are this pleasant."

Violetta laughed.

"Close enough," Mc'narrd's voice came through the comms. "What you described, and explained, is true for those who are pure blood K'laisians. Or close enough for the nanites to register them as such. It did not work the same for humans or those of mixed heritages until now." There was a pause before he spoke again. "It's good to know the suits are working as well as they are for you both."

"It's an interesting sensation, certainly," she replied.

It was refreshing being able to talk to someone about her father, again. Something she hadn't realized she'd missed until now.

"Dad said people learn to love it. Most don't want to take the suits off for any length of time. He told me stories of how the off-world troops would come home and take advantage of the suits repairing, as he phrased it, 'their stupidity.' They would drink and eat to severe excess, making the nanites work harder than ever to keep the bodies fit, even while the troops won bets on how much they could eat or drink without passing out, or fight people after consuming enough to have blood poisoning. If they were wearing the biosuits, that is."

Malik joined her second round of laughter.

"Could be fun," he said when they were done laughing. "After we finish this excursion, we'll go to the closest libationary and drink the Earthers onto their backs. Fight the ones who haven't passed out!"

"Malik!"

"Come now! We both know how most of the mercenaries, if not the majority of Earthers who come here, think of us." Malik argued. "Especially the mercs. After they spend too long in their two-legged tanks, or whatever they call them? They grow more arrogant and think they have the same advantages against us outside of their armored war machines. I just think they could use a lesson."

"I agree that some of them are like that…" she began.

"Come on! We're Halfers. They think we're weaker than full blooded natives. They'll never see the lesson coming."

"Hmm." Violetta pondered. "We'd need a third person to place the bets, in order to really clean up the arrogant farkers."

"You will both return to the safe house immediately after completing your mission." Admiral Mc'narrd's voice boomed over the comms. "No side quests for native glory."

"Awwww, Daaaaaaaaaaddd!" Malik wailed in false distress. "We want to go and play!"

Violetta was grateful for her seat restraints. They kept her from falling into the floor of the vehicle due to laughing so hard.

"Muscle up, you're at the location," Mc'narrd rejoined.

"And we were going to ask you to be the third person, sir." Malik pined, winking at Violetta.

"*Focus,*" Mc'narrd barked.

Violetta couldn't stop giggling as she and Malik exited their vehicle.

They were in the middle of the industrial warehouses, close to Crom's Drop Lake. They could smell the water in the breeze that swept in from the lake. The moisture gave life to algae and moss that crept along the sides of the warehouses, giving them a metallic blue, sponge-like appearance. Small dots of iridescent purple blooms gleamed in the moonlight.

The number '13' was written on the main side of the warehouse and main door in a variety of languages, including their native K'laisian and Standard. Violetta nodded to Malik and approached the door. Violetta pulled out the key she'd been given by Gomez, using it to gain entrance.

Together they entered the warehouse.

Like most warehouses set up for personal use, this one had rows upon rows of storage lockers of varying sizes.

Together, Violetta and Malik traversed the warehouse in search of locker 269. They remained silent as they traveled.

Thankfully, it didn't take long to locate the medium-sized unit. Using the key once again, Violetta unlocked the storage unit.

The unit was stuffed with boxes, bags, and containers. Furniture and curiosities filled the two meter by 3 meter unit. Most of it balanced in precarious positions. Violetta and Malik took a step back for fear of something falling out onto them.

"That is a lot of… stuff," Malik said, taking a tentative step forward.

"You're being very kind," Violetta muttered. "And you say I understate things."

Malik snorted.

"Enough chatter, children," Mc'narrd, his voice sharp. "You've got a job to do."

"Was your father like this?" Malik asked in a sotto tone. "I don't remember him being like this."

"Oh, Dad could be very militant sometimes," she replied, searching the unit for the duffel. "Though he had a better sense of humor. Dad would absolutely have been willing to place the bets for us."

"Vrehn Cq'linns would have gone in first, drank them all into oblivion, all the while leaving the biosuit at home," Mc'narrd declared. "Before calling both of you out for being limp plants."

Violetta giggled. "That does sound like Dad. But I think we could've talked him into letting us have some fun, too." She nudged Malik with her hip. "He probably would've considered it our first date."

Malik and Violetta heard a loud snort over the comms. They smiled victoriously at each other.

"I suppose we should find this fabled duffel bag," Malik said, a smirk fixed on his face.

"It's probably hidden somewhere. Hopefully not in the back," Violetta grumbled, despite her grin.

As Malik began looking in the higher spots, she knelt and searched in any hiding places near the floor. After five more minutes, Violetta finally spotted what looked like a duffel bag in a space near the top on their right. Between a couple boxes, it looked as though someone had tossed it and it had sunk down between the containers.

Slowly, carefully as to not dislodge everything around it, she slid the duffel bag from its precarious perch. Only then did she realize it had been specifically placed there. The boxes around it didn't shift in the slightest. She had to give high commendations to the one who designed that physical feat.

Kneeling on the floor, she called to Malik, who came over. He pulled a flashlight from a pocket and shined it on the duffel. Similar in design to the one Gomez had in his hospital room, this one was not a secured duffel bag. Violetta touched the seam and the bag unzipped. She quickly went through the bag, and in the bottom, was the chip Gomez had mentioned.

She held up the black poker chip. "This had better be the one."

"Are there any others?" Malik asked.

She gave the bag a second search, then shook her head. "No. That's the only one I could find, and this isn't a secure bag. Hand me the light."

Malik did as requested, and she quickly went over the duffel bag, holding it close to her face with the light shining on every inch of fabric.

"Nope, nothing showing a seam was opened and sewn shut," she said after going over the bag.

"Is there anything Vrehn didn't teach you?" Malik asked.

Violetta gave him a grin. "Probably plenty. Not like he didn't teach you a few things, too."

"If you two are finished, close up and get out," Mc'narrd said. "The longer you're there, the more likely you'll be spotted."

"Now he sounds like Dad," Violetta said, zipping up the duffel.

Chuckling, Malik took the duffel and replaced it where she had found it. "Yeah. Maybe they went to Parenting School together?"

"Possible," Violetta said. "Shall we?"

Malik nodded. Together, they left the unit and Violetta relocked it. With the chip in hand, the pair exited the warehouse and returned to their vehicle.

Chapter Fourteen

Once they returned to the safe house, Violetta shed the trench coat and tossed it onto the back of the sofa in the main room. She smiled, remembering how her father would chide her for doing that very thing. Malik gave her a knowing look as he produced an interface capable of reading the poker chip.

Sliding onto a bar stool with Malik on the other side, Violetta produced the chip and placed it on the interface. They waited in silence, comms still in their ears and active. Of all the items loaned to them, the comms were the one thing that was very familiar and comfortable to Violetta.

Throughout her entire youth, she'd worn a comm. Either as a way for her father to keep track of her or for easy contact. She'd used it to contact her grandparents. As well as those who watched over her when her father was off-planet and her grandparents weren't available. While many of her fellow cadets at the police academy had to adjust to having something in their ears at all times, it was just another day for her.

Glancing across from her to Malik, she couldn't keep the amusement from her expression at the fact he wasn't bothered by any of it, either. They were so much alike, yet so different.

She had once asked her father what attracted him to her mother. Her father had smiled, leaned back in his chair, and shook his head slightly. He'd said there wasn't a single one thing. Her mother's beauty, her poise, her sharp wit and sharper tongue, and the fact she went nose-to-nose with him shortly after they'd met. He had chuckled and added that she would know when she met her mate.

Her father had loved her mother, so when she'd died in childbirth, her dad had never remarried. As far as Violetta knew, he'd never even dated anyone else. When he was home, his time had been spent with her. Spoiling his only daughter and teaching her everything he knew.

The chime of the interface stopped that chain of thought, bringing her back to the present. She input the password they'd been given. Multiple folders flashed onto the interface's screen. She tapped the folder labeled, not surprising, 'replicator'. File after file filled the screen.

"Gomez wasn't joking when he said he kept detailed notes," Malik murmured. "There's over three dozen files here."

Violetta made a non-committal noise as she scrolled through the files. She tapped a file labeled schematics, her stomach feeling as though it were nothing but one large knot. This was the weapon that was behind her frame-up. Gomez may have made this technology for innocent purposes, but it had been turned into something vile.

The schematics of the replicating weapon loaded.

Malik whistled. She raised her hand, her forefinger curling around her lips and chin, while the rest formed a fist. Drawing a sharp breath, she let it out slowly. The weapon was very real, according to the data.

"What? What is it?" Mc'narrd demanded.

"Don't the 'suits have a camera?" Violetta asked.

"Not those. If it becomes needed, one will be provided. Now answer the question."

Huh. That's unexpected, Violetta thought.

"The schematics here are for civilian pistols, as well as standard-issue police pistols," Malik said in a low tone, replying for them both.

"Gomez was working on a rifle, also," Violetta said, her voice hard. "And he has notes in here for military pistols."

"Military weapons?" Mc'narrd asked. There was a tone in his voice Violetta couldn't discern. It wasn't good, that much she knew for certain.

"Yes," Violetta stated. When Malik looked at her, she pointed to the notations. "Those are public-knowledge stats of older weapons. My grandfather still has one of those pistols. He let me use it a couple times when I was little."

"You sound unhappy, detective," Mc'narrd commented.

"I'm furious." Violetta corrected him. She continued speaking as she navigated back to the main folder, searching for more useful information. "My father tried to put an end to this project. Gomez left the service and shouldn't have been able to continue it, even if he was 'funded' by people in my department."

She paused as she felt a light smack on the head. Looking up, she frowned and swatted Malik on the top of his head. He grinned and returned the swat. The knot in her stomach loosened and she smirked. When she went to swat him on the head again, he moved back, out of her reach.

"I'm going to get you."

He turned slightly, a saucy grin on his lips. "I'm still waiting."

"If you two are done?" Mc'narrd snapped.

"Don't know what you mean, sir," Violetta replied, innocently.

"Are you familiar with the Earther phrase 'get a room'?" Mc'narrd asked in a biting tone.

"With the comms in? Eww! Creepy," she retorted.

Malik snorted. Mc'narrd, however, could be heard grumbling indecipherable things.

"What's that? We couldn't make out what you said," Malik quipped, a grin firmly in place.

"Get. On. With. It." There was no mistaking the irritation in the admiral's voice.

Giggling, Violetta turned back to the interface, tapping on one titled 'funding'. "Let's see what this one is about." She scanned the document, then growled. "Those farkers stole from the Officers Memorial Fund to pay Gomez!"

"No, you can not rend them limb from limb," Malik stated. Fury filled his every feature. "Not unless you let me join you."

"That would be a fun date," Violetta mused, scrolling through the document. "This fits with the timeline Gomez gave us, too."

"Is there a point in reminding you we can hear everything you're saying?" Mc'narrd fumed.

"Oh, we're aware," Violetta stated dismissively. "I'm fairly certain your own people say far worse at times. Unless our people have changed in the years since Dad was serving. Saying something and doing it are two different things."

"Why don't we all work together on a plan to make them repay all they've taken?" Mc'narrd suggested in an overly polite tone.

"If we must," Malik said with a sigh. He gave Violetta a human-style wink. "Want to check to see what that second financial file is?"

She nodded and opened the files. "This is interesting. It's a list of all the deposits. Who they came from, who they went to. By that, I don't mean the fact they came from the Officers' Memorial Fund. Gomez listed the names of those involved in the project. Captain Monroe, Lieutenant Cancio, and Sergeant Rc'dollph. He's made a few notations on when they spoke and how and when each one stated payments would be made, including the amount of each payment."

"There are a lot of files here, Admiral," Malik stated, shifting the interface so he could look through it. "They're detailed notes and kept in an organized fashion. Someone could easily take these notes and further the work, if they so desired."

"That is a frightening thought," Violetta muttered.

"I will need to make a copy of these files, before you use them as evidence," Mc'narrd stated. "We can monitor the subnet for anything using even partial data from the files and end any further development."

"Would you prefer for us to hand this information off to your people?" Violetta asked as Malik opened another file.

"No. You need to witness me making the only copy," Mc'narrd replied.

Malik rolled his eyes and mouthed, *"He can always make copies after you depart."*

Violetta shrugged. She replied in the same manner, *"Obviously. They are the military, after all."* Aloud, she said, "Admiral, my father advised Gomez to end the pursuit of these weapons. Do *you* think there is a use for a weapon that can replicate any other?"

"Yes, it can cause a lot of damage to many people's lives," Mc'narrd stated. "Even though it isn't something we would use, that doesn't mean others wouldn't create it, also. The technology now exists, so we now must find a way to counter it."

"Makes sense," Malik grumbled. He tapped the corner of the screen. Video of the elevator appeared, revealing an unexpected visitor. "We'll keep the chip safe. Violetta's rather adapt at such things. We have a visitor and will have to continue this discussion later."

"What's he doing here?" Violetta asked quietly, closing out all the files before removing the data chip. She leaned down, sliding the chip into her boot beside the other chip.

Malik shrugged.

Mc'narrd's voice interrupted them. "Problem?"

"No. Friend, not foe," Violetta murmured. "Just… hush."

"You just told a three-star admiral to hush," Malik said, biting back laughter.

She nodded. "Yep. I'll probably get in trouble later for it, too."

There was laughter from Mc'narrd. "Not my job to swat your rear, detective." He chuckled again. "I'll just tell your grandparents what you've been doing with Addelia."

Panic set in as Violetta stared at Malik. He gave her a questioning look.

"They wouldn't approve?" he asked.

Violetta shook her head vehemently. "No! The opposite! They'll be planning our celebration feast declaring we're mates before our first date!"

Malik snorted. "We've already had a first date."

"Not helping!"

There was more laughter from the admiral, which was even worse. She suspected he knew it, too.

"What's not helping? Something wrong?" Issik asked as he stepped into the room. The detective looked from Violetta then to Malik, his eyes narrowing. "Something you not doing, Addelia?"

"My, my, detective," Mc'narrd drawled out. "Seems you have a protector."

Great, Violetta thought, feeling warmth creeping into her cheeks. *He's not going to hush at all. Should've known he wouldn't shut up!*

Malik laughed, seemingly at ease with all of it. "I'm doing everything I'm supposed to be doing. Just not everything I'd like to be doing."

And he was determined to not help the situation, also, she added silently, dropping her head into her hands in defeat.

She felt Malik patting her head. Her hand snapped up and grabbed his wrist. Lifting her head, she smirked. He returned the grin, his eyes narrowing as he grabbed her wrist. They grappled for a few moments before both were against the counter, laughing.

Which was much preferable to trying to explain why she was blushing.

"You two are, as the humans put it, stupid for each other," Issik fumed, glowering at them. "You should be taking everything seriously. Yet here you are, flirting with each other like horny high school teenagers!"

"Nah, we've got more decorum than that," Malik retorted.

Violetta glanced over at Issik's furious expression. "I'm fairly certain hand-to-hand combat was never a method used by horny high schoolers."

"You did it," Malik stated.

"I wasn't a normal teenager, either. Dad would never have allowed me to act like a typical teen. Horny or otherwise."

"Enough!" Issik roared.

Admiral Mc'narrd's roaring laughter filled the comms and Violetta wondered if Issik could hear him.

"No wonder you didn't enter the military," Mc'narrd said, when he could finally talk again. "Better for the police force to have to contend with you and your antics."

Violetta couldn't stop herself from snickering.

"You think it's funny?" Issik demanded, storming across the room.

"Actually, I find it very amusing that you would think this is us flirting," Violetta replied, sidestepping the reason she was amused. She turned to Malik. "Told you I'd get you."

"Haven't gotten me yet, Violence," Malik retorted, breaking free from her grip.

He reached for her and she slid back out of his reach. "Next time."

"If you two have finished, we need to talk," Issik snapped. "You two were almost caught. Then the military took you to the base, seemingly under arrest. Or not. It's reported you weren't in cuffs. I don't know how you managed to 'escape', but things have heated up. A tip was called in. Someone claims they spotted you out and about in the warehouse district. Captain Monroe is sending a request in to the krishii handlers."

Violetta's heart hit the floor. She glanced at Malik who suddenly had lost all amusement. Even Admiral Mc'narrd's laughter had stopped.

"I thought that would get your attention. The reasoning behind the request for the krishii is, if you could 'escape' from the military, they'll need the extra force the military refuses to give." He paused long enough to draw a breath. "Approval was also given to search your apartment."

"What?" Violetta screeched.

"It's standard," Mc'narrd said. "We need to keep up appearances, remember?"

She glowered at Issik, since she had no method of glowering at Mc'narrd. Or a way to respond without letting Issik know she had a military comm in her ear.

"I've got video for you to see. Thought you'd find it amusing." He appeared somewhat mollified that they weren't joking around anymore. He handed Malik a red poker chip. "Funny thing. The subpoena stated a 'military escort'. We went there thinking it meant only a couple military guards. Didn't expect a roomful of guards to suddenly appear in the hallway and follow us into your apartment."

Malik loaded the chip and tapped the vidclip the moment it appeared.

The vidclip showed all the guards who watched her apartment surrounding the officers waiting to enter her apartment.

"Of course Ziph and Cancio would be a part of it," she muttered.

"They were not too happy about your military friends," Issik stated. He gave her a sideways look. "You didn't mention you had so many military guards close to you."

Violetta shrugged her shoulders, but didn't say anything. "Isn't it nice how they followed you all into my apartment? Rather lovely of them to spread around the room and watch you all. It appears as though they're protecting my place from everyone."

"Funny, isn't it?" Issik shook his head. "Whatever their reasoning, they followed each of us like shadows."

They watched in silence as the officers moved around the living room, then into her kitchen, then back into the living room. When Issik's body vidclip showed Cancio and Ziph going for her bedroom, Violetta made a disgusted expression.

"Ugh, they went into my room. I'm going to have to pay a company to come in and disinfect the place."

"I'll send someone over for you," Mc'narrd said.

Malik snorted. Violetta glanced at him and suspected he was trying not to laugh. Instead, he commented, "Looks like the same bedroom. Did you change anything?"

"I had to get a new bed."

"Yeah, I guess you would have had to," Malik said thoughtfully. "Looks like it's pretty sturdy, too."

"Why do I suddenly feel a need to punch him in the face, repeatedly?" Issik declared.

"Because you just caught up to where I am," Mc'narrd grumbled, although Issik couldn't hear him.

Violetta snorted laughter, while Malik looked pleased with himself.

The vidclip showed Ziph, Cancio, and three guards standing in the room. The guards appeared ready to shoot anyone who misstepped, a fact that made Violetta feel some comfort. These were people she knew and had developed a sort of friendship with and none of them appeared happy that her privacy had been intruded upon.

When the officers approached her interface, none of them moved. Violetta wasn't worried, because as the vidclip revealed, her interface was clean.

"Interesting how they found nothing on your interface, not even history files showing what was accessed," Issik commented. "How did you manage that?"

"If she told you, she'd have to kill you," Malik quipped.

Issik frowned. "Yet I'll bet she told you."

"He has the clearance," Violetta retorted, smiling all-too-sweetly.

Mc'narrd gave a bark of laughter. "Not too far away from the truth there, detective."

"They're going towards the office," Malik interrupted.

Violetta gave the screen her complete attention. Ziph and Cancio were standing near her father's office talking in tones too quiet for Issik's camera to pick up. Cancio, the higher ranking officer, moved to her father's office door, where he was stopped by Faulkner.

For once, Faulkner wore a spec ops biosuit instead of his usual bum outfit. His hair was clean and shone. There was no trace of his 'bum's' jittery movements. A vast difference between the appearances. Violetta had always appreciated their skills at altering their appearances so drastically.

"*Sorry, officers. You aren't authorized to go into that room,*" Faulkner said.

"*On what grounds?*" Ziph demanded.

"*You don't have sufficient clearance to see the admiral's awards, let alone anything else in that room. You have the rest of this residence to search. Get to it.*"

Cancio stepped forward, trying to stand a bit taller. All the better to look down at Faulkner.

"*That's impeding an investigation, soldier,*" Cancio said. "*You can come in the room with us to protect any sensitive materials or data, but we are going in.*"

Cancio moved to touch the entry pad for the office. His hand was stopped by the sudden appearance of a long, black blade which hovered above his wrist.

"*No offense,* officer, *but if you touch that door in any way, I'm slicing that hand off, shoving it up your ass, and sending you on your merry way,*" Faulkner said in even, measured beats.

Violetta and Malik burst out laughing. Both Ziph and Cancio stared at the guard for several long minutes before backing away from the door.

"Your father's office?" Issik asked. Violetta nodded. "Bet you're allowed in whenever you want. Without an escort."

"Daddy's little girl," Violetta quipped as an answer.

"Right. What about you, Addelia?"

"Never had an interest in going where I wasn't invited." Malik smiled slyly as he added, "Besides, there were more interesting places to go."

Both Issik and Mc'narrd groaned at the same time. Malik and Violetta grinned at each other.

"Do I need to remind you about your duties? What you're *not* supposed to do when guarding someone?" Issik demanded. He didn't seem angry, but Violetta knew he could hide his true emotions easily.

"Maybe I should have sent you both to one of *our* safe houses so you can get it out of your systems," Mc'narrd muttered. "At least then there wouldn't have been a question of proper protection."

"I am properly protected with Malik guarding me," Violetta said, enunciating each word clearly. "Whatever feelings we have for each other will not interfere with the job of finding who killed the chief." She narrowed her eyes at Issik, since she couldn't turn her gaze on Mc'narrd. "And how do you know we aren't saying these things simply to goad *you*? It isn't as though you haven't made it easy to annoy you."

The vidclip ended and Violetta turned her attention back to the men, instead of the interface's screen.

"I hate thinking you would do that, all things considered," Issik grumbled. He gave her a closer examination, looking her over from head to toe carefully. "You seem to be the same Violetta Cq'linns I worked with, but you've become… something. I can't find the right word to describe it."

"Fun? Outgoing?" Malik offered. "Suddenly lacking a large tree growing up her bottom, unlike her cop partner?"

Mc'narrd snorted laughter. Issik, however, wore a sour expression.

"For a former healer, I would have expected a more doctorly explanation, but that works, too," Violetta replied, trying to not laugh. "Perhaps we should return to the problem at hand."

"Which one?" Issik snapped.

Violetta looked at Malik, her brow furrowed in confusion. "There's more than one? I thought there was only the one problem? That being the question of who killed Chief Me'addn?" Malik shrugged his shoulders, and Violetta wondered if he used the human gesture around Issik just to annoy him.

"Well, you're wearing matching jumpsuits. That's new. Should I start to worry?" Issik retorted, nodding towards her clothes.

Malik and Violetta exchanged a glance and chuckled.

"Do you have any vids of the Chief's home? The crime scene? Or any hard prints?" Violetta asked, changing the topic. No need to explain the military biosuits.

Issik reached into his jacket and removed hard copies of the murder scene. He handed them to Violetta, who promptly spread them onto the bar.

"About time you asked me. Thought you might be too busy rehearsing to win Earthers Flashback Party with your dancing partner here," Issik teased.

"Is he always this happy, or should I be ready for him to ask me out?" Malik rejoined, turning his attention to the photos.

"Keep reaching for the stars, pretty boy," said Issik, before he turned to focus on Violetta. "Notice anything in the hard prints? Does anything in particular stand out to you?"

Violetta poured over the prints, carefully examining everything in the photos. The men remained silent. Even the admiral didn't have any comments to add. The prints were of every room in the chief's home, especially the living room where she had found the body.

Her eyes zeroed in on the pool of blood, then traveled outward. She leaned closer and squinted at the print. There was something under a chair near the desk.

Tapping the print, she asked, "What is that? This print doesn't show a good view of what that is."

"Oh, you mean this?" Issik pulled a small, vacuum sealed evidence sack from a pocket. "They didn't even notice it. I tagged it and sacked it, but I haven't connected my work interface yet. So this is off the Sub for the time being."

"Yes, that. Not surprised they ignored it," she replied, taking the bag and examining the evidence. "It's a token for a club. Club La'caille. Only thing I know about it is that no one under the rank of captain is allowed in. Dad never went, so I don't have any information on it."

"Military have their own… clubs," Mc'narrd explained. "They aren't child-friendly, either. Your father preferred going places he could take you."

"My boss supplies alchemists for both clubs, so let's decompose any superiority complexes," Malik interjected.

Issik lifted a brow but didn't say anything. Violetta knew he was sharp and was probably starting to suspect they had comms.

Violetta handed the token to Malik. "What do you know about the club?"

"You are correct about no one under the rank of captain. It's a fairly exclusive club." Malik studied the chip. "Military are allowed entry but rarely show. Most of the time there are more staff than patrons, but the theory is that the patrons like it that way, with more people to tend to their wants. The tokens aren't personalized, though. So this one could belong to any regular member."

"Why aren't they personalized?" Issik asked.

"It's to keep activities within the clubs private. No subnet records of how often any particular member shows up, what kind of services or consumables are requested, used and wasted. That's all written on hard copy and memorized by the staff. They take pride in memorizing each individual member by the second time they frequent the establishment."

"Chief Me'addn would not have allowed just anyone into his home," Violetta said. "I don't know if Ziph would have known the chief well enough to be invited into his home."

"No, but the captain would definitely be welcomed. Not sure about Cancio, though. The captain and he go out for drinks often enough, but Cancio wouldn't be able to get into the club," Issik added, sitting on a stool beside Violetta. He reached in front of her and tapped a print of Chief Me'addn's office. "There's a holo of Chief Me'addn, the captain, and Cancio on a shelf in his office. If they're not friends, they at least know each other."

"I wonder if they didn't bring Ziph into the fold to be the enforcer?" Violetta mused. "It still leaves the question of if he was on the take with them, or just turning a blind eye. Also, if he was murdered, the question still remains: why? Was he ready to turn on them to save himself? Or was he willing to stop ignoring them and admit something was happening?"

"All of those are possibilities. Without knowing who did it, there's no way of knowing the real reason behind his murder." Issik gestured towards the holo. "There are more complaints with the name Ziph Rc'dollph attached to them than anyone else in the department. A fact the captain would know. Having him as an 'enforcer' makes the most sense."

"Why aren't you considering all of the captains?" Malik interjected. "This little conspiracy stinks of a larger scale and crew than you seem to give it credit for. Why are you fixated on your captain and not all of them, even on this side of the river?"

"It would have to be someone intimately aware of homicide," Violetta began. She tapped the photo of the living room. "Someone had to know what could be found at a homicide scene, such as this one. If there had been anything obvious, someone would have found it. Possibly exonerating me. Possibly pointing to the weapon they're trying to perfect. The methods used to collect fingerprints and DNA sync automatically with multiple servers. Removing that information wouldn't be nearly as easy as removing vidclips from bodycams."

Issik nodded. "Homicide is handled from 'our side' of the river. We're located in the main office. The one on the other side of the Nimkelu River is a branch. Separate, but still under the same chief of police."

Mc'narrd's voice cut in. "Malik does have a point. That token could belong to Me'addn or the captain. Did it have fingerprints on it?"

"Any fingerprints on that thing, Issik?" Malik asked.

Issik shook his head. "It hasn't been delivered into evidence, so it hasn't been checked yet."

"We will handle that," Mc'narrd stated firmly. "Don't need the department to fark things up in an effort to further frame Detective Cq'linns."

"We have a contact who can handle it," Violetta stated, sharing a look with Malik. "Don't worry. There won't be questions about the integrity of the results."

"More secrets?" Issik sighed and shook his head. "One day we're going to have a long talk about all of this."

"You have your secrets, I have mine. Like the fact you've been on Morelli's payroll." She gave him a sly smile. "Besides, it should be rather obvious if you really thought about it and connected the dots."

"Maybe I don't want to," Issik retorted, nudging her playfully.

She chuckled before turning to Malik. "Is there a way you could go to the club, Malik? Maybe ask around about the chief and these tokens? If there is someone else involved, they might have a clue as to who it would be."

"I can do that if Issik agrees to stay and watch you here."

Issik nodded his agreement.

Malik snorted. "I'll drop this off on the way to the club. Regardless of whose prints may be on it, you're going to need more evidence than just that token."

"I'll arrange a pickup," Mc'narrd stated. "We'll discuss it while you head to the club."

"Wear a bodycam," Issik said. He tipped his head to the side. "Do you have one here?"

"We'll include that, as well as a link to that interface," Mc'narrd assured them. "No need for your guardian there to question things too much."

Malik nodded. "Violetta will fill you in on the one we'll be using."

"Good. It should be easy enough to sync up here," Issik stated.

Malik narrowed his eyes at him. Issik rolled his eyes; a very human behavior Violetta would never have expected from her native partner.

"We'd like to be able to see everything and listen in." Issik paused, before adding in a sour tone, "Or at least *I* would like to be able to listen in. I suspect that wouldn't be an issue for your lady."

"I don't have a lady." Malik stared directly at Issik. "I might have a partner."

Violetta's eyes widened. Her pulse raced and she felt warmth flooding her entire body. She tried to control her reaction, but knew she was failing. And on top of it all, the biosuit was sending the information to the military. If anyone had questions, they were now being answered.

All someone needed to do was check the readings.

"Issik can be a part of this little party. For now." Violetta could hear Mc'narrd's smile in his voice. Which made everything all that more confusing to her. "After this is finished, we will need to discuss renewing your clearance, bures'o Addelia. It will make our lives a lot easier. Probably yours, as well."

Malik glanced at Violetta who raised her brows slightly before dropping them. Their own, personal version of a shrug.

The smile was impossible to hide as she answered Malik's unspoken question.

"Partner sounds... perfect."

Chapter Fifteen

As Malik and Admiral Mc'narrd discussed the drop off of the token while Malik drove to the club, Violetta tuned out the discussion. It wasn't one she could participate in, nor did she need to be a part of it.

Issik mixed himself a drink, ignoring the interface and giving her space.

"You mentioned the krishii earlier. Is Monroe seriously considering bringing them out to find me?" Violetta asked, hating having to ask the question, but needing the answer. "Would the DA actually agree to it?"

Instead of replying, Issik tapped his ear. The signal between them to turn off anything live or that would feed the subnet in any way. Violetta took a few moments to turn off the tablet. When he narrowed his eyes at her, she rolled her own.

"Record Private Channel, Violetta Cq'linns, daughter of Vrehn Cq'linns. Code P'awsks Linaa."

There was a chirp in her ear signaling the code had worked. It had been the code she and her father had used when they hadn't wanted anyone else to hear their conversations over the military comms they wore during her childhood. She hadn't expected it to still be active. She'd only said it to ensure Issik would continue with whatever he wanted to talk about.

"I haven't heard that code used for a long time," Mc'narrd said in her comm. "It's still available to you. I'll be the only one able to hear what's said or view the recording." There was a pause before his voice turned sly. "I added Addelia to the channel. I didn't think you would object."

He's just determined to see how well I can ignore him, Violetta thought, keeping her expression neutral. He knew she wouldn't mind, also. Damn him.

"Good enough. I suppose." Issik eyed her warily. "I didn't want anyone else to hear this, until you decide how to handle it. The department got orders to increase funding and resources on the hunt for you. They're ready to call out the dragons if you aren't apprehended by daylight."

"They'd actually put the krishii on my scent?"

Issik nodded. His expression was dour and his eyes did not waver from hers. "You might want to see if your military chums have anything they've hidden away to defeat or fool them."

The krishii were indigenous beings that the Earthers had immediately labeled "dragons" after creatures of myth from their past. The visiting humans said that the race, which resembled Komodo monitors from their planet, were also called dragons. Although komodo dragons did not have wings, could not understand other languages with *or* without translation, and never sat on their hind legs and tail. The krishii did all those things, and had multi-hued scales that helped with camouflage.

While they had been identified by natives whose gift was to communicate intelligently with other races ("the krishii" were what the beings called themselves), the nickname of dragons had caught on world-wide. Even the krishii, who had more than moderate intelligence, enjoyed being called such.

The greatest problem with krishii was how their minds worked.

They could track literally any being anywhere on the planet, and had shown little limitation to that skill off-world. However, they did not consider themselves pets or domestic workers. Snobbish, prone to volatile tempers, and easily offended, along with a clear sense of superiority to any bipedal beings who could not fly? That described them better than anything.

Worst of all, their instincts were powerful. The natural urge when finding intended prey, or the target they are helping the "lesser beings" to find, was to make a meal out of said being. More than a fourth of the criminals or missing persons the dragons were sent to find ended up mauled, consumed, or at least injured. Along with the so-called handler who went along.

"Great. Since obviously I'm not going to be apprehended by morning, we're going to have them to deal with, too," Violetta grumbled. "Have there been any who have managed to evade, or escape, the krishii?"

"Two," Issik replied. "One was a military serviceman who had been doing military work, unbeknownst to anyone else at the time. The other was a criminal who we suspect escaped offworld."

That was not reassuring.

"Does anyone else in the department suspect I have military 'chums', as you put it?"

"Most at the department figure there are people in the military who care about you, because of your dad." He met her eyes and held them as he finished making his drink. "The general belief is the military were at your apartment because it was your father's first and they're protecting his property. Which makes sense, if there's classified data in his office."

"Yes," was all Violetta said at his raised brows. "What's being said about the tip?"

He frowned, but didn't push for more of an answer. "The question of the day is how you 'escaped' the military.

Did you manage it before getting to the base? Did some of your dad's pals help you escape? Or is there another faction at play?" He shook his head. "To make it even more interesting is the fact no answers are coming from the military. They keep saying it's a local affair and they aren't involved. Monroe, I might add, is thoroughly pissed about the fact you 'slipped through his fingers.' He's been saying some rather rude things about our esteemed military who can decide whatever they want."

"That's their choice," Violetta replied with a human-like shrug. "The military has always been able to follow the laws regarding local versus national instances as loosely or strictly as they desire."

"Right," Issik said dryly. "News also came down about some deaths in the building you were escorted out of. Rumors claim it was the Moyii Tsaa."

"What do you think happened?"

Issik studied her. "I suspect you somehow ended up in their hands. For some reason, the military decided they had committed a grievous act that called for their deaths. Perhaps having you as a... captive? Hostage? Or perhaps they were sent by those involved in your frame-up and were waiting for Cancio to arrive?"

"All plausible theories," Violetta replied evenly. Though she wondered how she was able to remain so calm when Issik may have just answered why Monroe was there so quickly. "Though I do not have any facts or knowledge behind why the military chose the actions they did."

"Smooth, detective," Mc'narrd said in her ear. "If I hadn't been in the room when you made the report, I'd believe everything you just said."

She didn't react to the praise. Instead, she asked, "Did they search Me'addn's place for prints?"

"They left the big stuff at the office," Issik replied, sitting across from her at the bar, drink in hand. "I figured to go and use my Gift after everyone had left. Wanted to come and warn you about the elevation in your pursuit, first."

"Thanks for that. I appreciate it." Violetta paused, then lowered her voice. "Feel free to not answer this question, but do you object to my having a relationship with Malik? You have to know we have a past."

Who didn't know Malik and she had a past?

It seemed to be common knowledge with every faction in the city, from the military to every organization and syndicate. Admittedly, there was no lack of evidence showing she and Malik were friends throughout their childhood and teenage years. The news vidclips even showed Malik beside her during her father's memorial service, funeral, and the days surrounding the trial of her father's murderer.

"I don't like his boss." At her raised brows and incredulous expression, he shrugged. "Just because I work for Morelli, doesn't mean I have to like him. I do like Malik's sense of humor and style, though. As long as he makes you happy and doesn't make you choose between him and your job, I won't maim him or lecture you."

"That's fair… I think," Violetta said.

Mc'narrd's snort of laughter reminded her he could hear everything, and was still listening to their conversation.

"Not gonna happen, Vi," Malik finally said over the comms. His voice was low and reassuring. "The token has been delivered to the admiral's man. The cam is going live in the count of five. Might want to change frequencies."

"Time to turn things back on," Violetta stated. "End private recording. Comms on."

Another chirp sounded in her ear, signaling the change. She counted down silently, and when she hit zero, she turned on the interface. The screen flashed once before showing the view from a bodycam.

Malik's voice came from the interface, loud and clear. "I'll be at the club in less than five minutes."

Issik tossed back half of his drink. "Here's hoping he can get some useful information without causing any trouble."

"I have no doubts he can get the information we need," Violetta reassured him. "Some talents don't fade, and Malik has always had a glib tongue."

"Is that what you call it?" Malik murmured.

"Oh, I could call it many other things, but that applies to your ability to talk your way into, and out of, nearly any situation. I'll bet it's part of how you acquired your current position with Don Morelli."

"It's more about my understanding of why they do what they do. Being quick on negotiation and democratic discussion gave me a position within the syndicate. The rest was earned through work," Malik informed her. "Now hush so I can work."

Violetta laughed. Issik merely shook his head.

Malik's bodycam showed the front door of the club. He opened it and entered the establishment. A podium stood directly in front of the door, behind which they could see part of the main room. There was a 'calm night sky' atmosphere to the room, enhanced by multi-colored holo-lights that displayed nearby moons. Soothing music could be heard. Violetta made a few adjustments on the interface, until they heard the sound of crashing waves and running water beneath the music.

Issik pulled back and gave Violetta a curious expression. "The hox?"

"I've got nothing," Violetta said. She changed the interface back until the other sounds were hidden again. "Looks like a quaint place."

"If you go for that type of thing," Issik remarked.

"What a pansy-ass club," Mc'narrd said.

Is this how it is with everyone in the military? she wondered. *Or am I just special?*

"Get Captain Ae'staa to take you to one of our clubs. You can bring the boyfriend, if he wants to join you. If Addelia had remained in the military, he would already have one of our tokens." The tone said it was a suggestion, though Violetta wondered if it was actually an order.

Malik cleared his throat. Violetta chuckled, but otherwise remained silent as Malik approached the podium and the maître d' of the establishment.

The maître d' was just under two meters tall, a pure blood native with dark skin and long hair atop a deep green suit and light green shirt. His gold eyes sparkled when he looked at Malik. A mouthful of even, shining teeth grinned.

"Hello, handsome," the maître d' said in greeting. "I know I haven't seen you here before, which is a shame. Are you here to join one of our regulars, or—" the gold eyes took their time moving down Malik's body, finally returning to Malik's face, "—are you here to set up preparations for someone? Going to be the fabulous host for a party?"

"I think he's in love," Issik observed.

"He's in something, all right," Mc'narrd chimed in, despite the fact Issik couldn't hear him. "Looks like you might be in trouble, Violetta."

Over the comms, Malik cleared his throat. It came through the interface clearly. All three listening in on the video feed chuckled. Which caused Violetta to be even more amused by the current situation.

"I'm here on behalf of the late Chief of Police's family," Malik declared, putting enough brevity in his voice to sound like an Earther mortician. "He spoke highly of this place, and I thought I should give his last regards to the staff."

"Oh, that's so dear of you!" the maître d' said, his demeanor losing a good bit of joviality. "The chief was such a lovely being, always personable to all the staff. He made us feel more like family than anyone. Did you know he never used the private rooms? His preference was to stay in our lobby, greet whomever was working or coming in. Meals, drinks, conversations, he wanted it all out here where nothing could be hidden."

"Chief Me'addn was a bastion of courtesy and service," Malik agreed somberly. "Whoever takes the Chief's office won't be able to replace him. Only succeed him."

"Agreed," the maître d' said, his face frowning. His gold eyes glittered with unshed tears. "I apologize, I get too familiar with our clientele. I never worked with him, only knew him from time here at the club."

Malik's camera moved forward, his left hand coming into screen before squeezing the unhappy staff member's right shoulder.

"There's no shame or need for apology," Malik said.

"Oh, my. He's getting cozy, isn't he?" Issik asked. "Looks like you're losing him, Cq'linns."

"At least he's easy on the eyes. Sleek black hair, lithe body. Also has a safer job," Mc'narrd added in the comms.

"But does he have a better ass?" Violetta asked. "Sure, it's a safe job, but does he look as good from the back as the front?"

"He looks like he does squats on a regular basis," Mc'narrd replied thoughtfully. "The question is if Malik likes them tight or just up-tight."

Malik snorted a single laugh, before covering his slip with a few well-executed coughs.

Issik started laughing at Violetta's dumbstruck expression while the conversation resumed. Never in her entire life would she have expected such a response from a three-star admiral.

"Me'addn would appreciate how close you feel toward him. I can see why he spoke so well of this place," Malik said, allowing a little warmth into his voice. "I hope the other patrons appreciate you and the rest of the staff. It's a comfortable, calming place you've made here."

"Oh no, not all patrons seem to appreciate it as much as the Chief did. The DA, for example. Rarely comes here. Keeps to himself, unless he's meeting someone. Always in a private room. If the man knows how to socialize, I've never seen it."

"What about the captains? Any of them avoid talking to the Chief, or the DA?" Malik asked, leaning forward slightly.

"Oh, all of the captains acknowledge their superiors here. They seem to understand that the DA doesn't make social chat or even casual work chat. The Chief was like the grandparent who was happy to see everyone, no matter how difficult a day they'd had."

"So much for any connection to our dirty captain," Issik grumbled.

"I'm curious..." Malik's bodycam lost visual of the maître d's face. He had leaned in that close. "I know you are amazing when it comes to recognizing your patrons by sight. What do you do if someone loses their token?"

"After the first few visits, the tokens are truly just a formality. Most of the patrons are, understandably, very strict on what they perceive as rules, so most request a replacement token." There was no mistaking the smile in the maître d' voice. "The Chief hasn't needed to show me or any member of staff his token since the first year we opened."

"Thank you," Malik said, and dropped his voice into a conspiratorial tone. "Tell me, who's the worst? I know there have to be a couple of patrons that you just dread seeing come through that door."

"Oooohhhh, my flower, you know it!" The maître d' sounded delighted. "Mostly the newer captains who seem to think we run a brothel, buffet, and sleep-over hotel so they can be as debaucherous as the people they have arrested! Of course, I think they get that from our worst patrons. Those would be Captains Monroe and Baramore. They bring in whomever they want, no matter what rank, stink up the place, leave a mess."

Malik chuckled. "Why, pretty bloom, are you an anti-Earther?"

"Uh oh, Cq'linns, your boy is putting on the charm," Mc'narrd interjected over the comm. "They're going to run off together and you'll never see him again. Time to cut him loose and spare yourself the heartbreak."

"You two are just jealous that he can play this fellow like an instrument." Violetta argued, momentarily forgetting Issik couldn't hear Mc'narrd. "He's doing fine, particularly since he has us in his ear."

Issik, Violetta noticed, kept his eyes on the interface even as he hummed. "Do I need to see about placing protection on Addelia's wanna-be-suitor? And it's a little confusing, trying to keep track while I don't hear what else is being said to you."

"Such a narrow mind you have, Ha'kksworth," the admiral said, drawing out his words in obvious enjoyment of Issik being unable to hear him. "Detective Cq'linns is very skilled with weapons. You should consider placing bets on a Duel. Just make certain his 'flower' is incapacitated and can't be his Champion."

"Very funny," she muttered, though the smile didn't leave her face, despite their teasing.

Issik looked at her, clear annoyance on his face.

"No, no, I have met several lovely Earthers, even if they don't compare to your looks," the maître d' said.

Violetta, Issik and the admiral could still only see the man's immaculate suit and shirt in the bodycam feed. Malik was still leaning close to him, ignoring the teasing.

"But you remember all the anti-Earthers' rhetoric about the poor habits and hygiene of humans? Flower, there is a reason it rings true. Some of them are *just like that*. The bad habits seem to accompany a general sense of entitlement and lack of empathy when they don't have anyone watching over them."

"So, they are all manners and proper behavior until the public and bosses aren't looking?" Malik suggested.

"Yes! So much that!"

The bodycam moved and the entire top half of the maître d' was visible again, along with the top of his podium.

"Stop!" Issik suddenly exclaimed. "Don't move, Malik. Stay right there."

The camera shook slightly, but did not significantly move.

"Sorry," Malik apologized, "I'm drinking in your scent and getting a bit heady. I need to stay clear headed."

The maître d' giggled. "Oh, must you?"

"Sadly, I am working. Perhaps I will be able to get a ranking officer to bring me back? As long as it's not Monroe or the other one, of course. Maybe I should try to make friends with our DA."

"Don't misunderstand," the maître d' rejoined and the suit shifted slightly closer. "The DA is friendly to staff, even though he comes only a few times a year. Not like the Head of Council, who is worse than the Earther captains. The other council members are gracious and even flirty, but the Head? She is, as the Earthers say, a hateful bitch. Thinks she's better than everyone. She and Monroe ought to be close friends, since they have similar attitudes, but no. They avoid each other, looking across the club like a Duel is about to start. Or, if I'm being truthful, like krishii ready to fight for who is going to rule a pack."

Issik pointed towards the interface screen without touching it. "Can we get a capture of this?"

In response, Violetta leaned forward and tapped the interface screen twice in a specific sequence. Malik, she noticed as she made a capture of the screen, was trying to wrap up the conversation with the maître d'.

"Unfortunately, I need to get back to my clients. Perhaps I will see you again soon."

The maître d' produced a data chip and token from… somewhere. Violetta couldn't see where his hands vanished before returning.

"Here's my information, and a complimentary pass to come for an evening as my guest."

Malik's hand came into view as he took the items. "Very nice. See you soon, bloom."

The video screen caught the broad smile and wink of the maître d' before the view spun and started back towards the club's entrance.

"It appears we may have something," Violetta said aloud. Partly for Malik's attention and partly for Mc'narrd. "Going off the live video feed for now."

"Acknowledged," Mc'narrd said.

From the single word and curt tone, Violetta suspected he was busy with something at the command center. Probably discussing Malik's return to the safe house.

Dismissing whatever was distracting Mc'narrd, Violetta turned to what she'd captured on the interface's screen. Using her finger, she tapped the interface controls until the still capture she'd taken filled the entire nine inches of the interface's screen.

Issik reached over and zoomed in on the ledger he'd seen on the maître d's podium. Once he'd rotated the image one hundred eighty degrees, he sat back and pointed at the image.

"Tell me what you see," he invited.

Names, dates, requests, departure time were listed for the past four days. Violetta quickly realized what Issik had spotted.

"The night of the Chief's death, he was at the club. So was Monroe," she said. "Monroe arrived five minutes after the Chief and left at the same time."

"Precisely," Issik replied.

"Can you track their vehicles from the club?" Violetta asked.

"You know I can. I'll have answers tomorrow." Issik stood, patted her shoulder, and left.

She blinked a few times, surprised that he'd leave before Malik returned. Shaking her head, she turned back to the interface and its contents.

"Did you catch all that, admiral?" she asked in the empty room.

"Not quite," Mc'narrd replied. "I've been monitoring your boyfriend and making sure he isn't being followed."

"That's fine. I can tell both of you when he returns."

"Remind me not to play poker with you or Addelia." Mc'narrd's joke brought a grin to her face. His voice grew serious as he added, "Good job. The three of you make a good team."

"Thank you, sir," Malik and Violetta said as one.

"I'll let Issik know you said that, next time we see each other," Violetta teased.

"As long as you don't use my name, do that," Mc'narrd replied in a serious tone. "I'll be sure there's a commendation in his file after your name is cleared."

Chapter Sixteen

There was nothing ruder to be woken up by than alarms going off and a voice shouting "Get out, get out!" in your ear.

Violetta grabbed clothes and hurriedly pulled them on over the military biosuit. Shoving her feet into her boots, she holstered the weapon Malik gave her, as well as the one from the military. She ran from the room to find Malik already in the living room. He tossed her hooded trench coat to her, which she pulled on without a thought.

"They've sent the krishii, and they're closing in on the safe house," Malik said without preamble.

"What's the plan?"

"We 'get out.' Come on, there's back stairs and some of the don's soldiers will try to hold off the dragons," Malik replied. He shoved the interface into a small pack, which he shouldered easily. "Let's go."

Violetta gave a nod and followed Malik from the room to the same hallway where her room was located. He led her into the library and pulled a wall light towards him. The sconce-shaped light shifted, and a door slid open.

There were no lights in the hallway, though a light mist flowed from the corridor. Violetta gave Malik a curious look, but followed him without a word. This was why she was thankful for Malik being her bodyguard. Anyone else she would have questioned. The constant uncertainty would have been there. The constant alertness.

With Malik, though, she knew she could trust him. There was a connection between them that went further than physical attraction. He was as solid and constant as any healer she knew. Part of why those beings became healers:

their psyches were constant and unwavering. Their personalities were too set in their ways. The healers were the solid rocks that kept people grounded, safe, and healthy. They were dependable.

Trustworthy to an extreme.

So she followed him down the narrow staircase, ignoring the door that closed behind them, and hoping there weren't any krishii near whatever door he was leading them to.

The voice in their ears was silent. Violetta wasn't certain if that was a good or bad thing. A play-by-play on where the krishii and their handlers were and what they were doing would have been nice.

After four flights of stairs, she realized they were going farther down than she'd originally expected. The air was growing cooler, and the area darker. She noticed the sounds of their steps were more closed-in, and she was thankful for not being claustrophobic.

Finally, Malik reached a door, which he opened with a metal key. Though the click should have been quiet, it filled the area around them, causing her to cringe. The door opened without a sound, and Malik went through first, holding the door open for her. On the other side was a small room with a door on each side. Against one wall were stone shelves, filled with supplies.

"I know a place where we can find temporary refuge and assistance." Malik's eyes remained fixed on the door behind Violetta. "Have you been in touch with Admiral Mc'narrd?"

"Yes, sir. It's been arranged," the woman on the comms said. "If you can reach the river, your person will meet you there."

Violetta raised a single brow. "I hope you have a plan for going several blocks over to the river without being seen. Or scented."

Malik grinned. "You didn't ask what that was we walked through."

"My guess? Something to hide our scent, at least temporarily."

"Good girl," he replied. She gave him a sour expression, which made him chuckle. "Fine, you can smack my butt later. Morelli is putting another play into action, but it will take some time."

"Delightful. What do we do once we reach the river?"

"You both are to head across the river. The base on your side is crawling with the local police service and krishii," Mc'narrd said over the comms. "Once on the other side, you're to make your way to the docks. The harbormaster will give you aid and shelter."

Violetta and Malik nodded to each other. It made sense.

The harbormaster was a career military position that lasted the entire lifetime of the person who obtained the title. Jozelyn Fr'osst had been harbormaster for at least a decade, and her job was to ensure the safety and security of the military ships, decoys, and target vessels on Crom's Drop Lake. There was a Harbor Patrol that reported to her, but was part of the police service. It was a curious dynamic, but one that worked well.

Harbormaster Commander Fr'osst kept the lake, which fed out into Echge Sea, and docks safe. She also had a floating home in the center of the lake. It wasn't a boat, but rather a small island-like home that remained fixed in the center of the lake. No one knew how the home, given to every harbormaster, remained in that one place, but it did. Not surprising, the position of harbormaster had been held by the Fr'osst family for several generations.

"You're avoiding my questions," Violetta stated, narrowing her eyes at Malik.

"That's really not threatening," Malik replied. "This is part of the oldest section of the city. Do you remember the Tunnels your dad mentioned when we were little?"

Violetta blinked in stunned silence. She opened her mouth, then shut it before nodding.

Malik's eyes twinkled. "Yeah, they're real, and this is part of that system. Wanna see?"

"Yes!" she shouted, then cringed at the sound. "Sorry. Just excited."

"Really? Would never have guessed," Mc'narrd teased. "Get going. The longer you stay there, the more likely you are to be caught."

"Yes, Dad," Violetta teased, giving Malik a wink. Better to hold onto humor than give into the growing concern knotting her stomach.

Malik crossed to a door on the left of the stone room. With the same metal key, he opened the door. Violetta gave him a smile and stepped past him into the dark tunnel. He followed behind her. As he locked the door, she ran her hand along the wall. The packed dirt was smooth and cool to the touch.

One of her favorite tales as a child was about the district she grew up in, and how once upon a time her people had been warriors. Warriors who used tunnels to keep the women, children, and elderly safe while battles were fought. Though not all the women stayed in the tunnels; only the mothers of young children and those too young or too old to fight. Many women fought beside their men during those ancient days. Both genders were vicious, though they held to a code of honor.

Then the tunnels were used by those smuggling illicit products. Since the tunnels were ten meters in diameter, there was enough room to pilot smaller vehicles through them. K'laisians had long since stopped using giant lizards for mounts for the most part. There were a few areas on K'lais where you could ride them. Especially the jungles of their world where the only other option was walking.

Other tunnels were sealed, the rooms used for storage. Some creative beings had turned the rooms into places to make unique foods and other products. Most had been long-forgotten or destroyed with the passing of time.

She followed Malik through the tunnel, marveling at the obvious age and wondering who had passed before them, and why.

The tunnel was long, curving this way and that. Violetta had an above-average sense of direction, thanks to her unusual childhood. She knew the city better than most. It wasn't difficult for her to keep up with where they were in comparison to the roads above them.

Though she knew most beings would become lost quickly in the tunnels. Her father had spoken of it several times during their childhood. She'd always thought it was a tale to keep her and Malik from searching for the tunnels as children.

If all the tunnels were built to be confusing, she suspected that their ancestors had cultivated their sense of direction.

"How many of these are still used?" she finally asked, thankful for the trench coat. The tunnels were damp and cool.

"In this district?" Mc'narrd asked. "There are twenty currently being used. Including the one you are currently traversing."

"You know all of them?" Malik asked.

The admiral chuckled. "We have extensive maps of all the tunnels ever used. It comes in useful when young children decide to go exploring the fabled tunnels and become lost."

"Or for other reasons that will remain unspoken because we don't have the clearance?" Violetta added in a sly tone.

"That, also," Mc'narrd admitted. "You are about to enter an area where comms don't work. Too much interference from the heavy ores in the soil around that section of the tunnels. Will check in when you are past it."

The last sentence was muddled by static. A few seconds of white noise followed before complete silence. Violetta looked at Malik, wanting to see how comfortable he was with this development. He shrugged.

"Alone at last? Come on, we have a good bit of distance to cover," he said.

"At least we can now talk without worrying about it being listened in on or recorded," she commented. At his raised brow she shrugged. "You can't tell me you don't have a lot of questions about what's happened."

"That's fair," he admitted. "Though is now really a good time to ask them?"

Violetta shook her head. "There isn't anything pressing enough to cause me to question our military. It can wait until we have privacy that doesn't include possible danger and a need for expediency."

"Always reasonable." Malik glanced at her from the corner of his eyes. "More lessons from Vrehn?"

"Dad always said a commander couldn't concern him or herself with their feelings until after the threat ended," Violetta stated. She shook her head. "I've been doing it, but they keep popping up when things calm down. I don't know how Dad did it every time he stepped onto his battlecruiser and commanded his crew."

"It's something commanders are easily capable of," Malik admitted. "It's part of the testing and evaluations. To be able to turn that part of themselves off, or if you prefer, to shove those emotions down. Regardless of the verbiage, it all means the same: they don't allow their emotions to show, though they do have them."

"Your instructions are showing," Violetta said, trying to lighten the mood.

"The fact you're able to do it just shows you may have been able to follow in your father's footsteps." Malik gave a slight smile. "And that's how it is with commanders, also. Once the situation passes, and the concern is gone, they have to deal with their feelings. Their conscience. The consequences of their decisions. Not just anyone can become a commander."

"Thanks." When Malik paused in his steps to look at her, she met his gaze. "For telling me that. Thank you."

"You're welcome."

Without another word, he turned and continued down the tunnel. A comfortable silence settled over them. Five minutes passed as they traversed the tunnel before a crossroads of four tunnels intersected with their path, opening into a large chamber. As the pair stepped out of the tunnel they'd been traveling and started for the tunnel just ahead of them, a voice rang out.

"Where do you think you're going? You have to pay the toll, first."

"Ah, shat," Malik whispered. "Wonder who is laying claim here, now."

Before Violetta could ask him what he meant, eight beings poured in from the tunnels to their left and right. The clothing worn by these people were mismatched and unclean. Violetta recognized some of the articles as being Earth fashions. The weapons that each carried were also a jumble of native and Earth styles.

For every three Ka'rr knives, there was one club that she remembered being called 'baseball bats' by Earthers. She was more concerned about the knives. The twenty centimeters of edged metal were infamous for leaving tiny fragments of the blade inside wounds. The apparent leader held a large sidearm that was one of the old-Earth weapons that fired lead projectiles via chemical explosion.

He pointed the wide barrel of this sidearm between Violetta and Malik.

Every one of these beings was of mixed heritage. Mostly Earther, but at least one had a parent that was a native of Centauri. The blueish hue of her skin, along with white hair, was unmistakable.

"When did the Polaris Opposis push out the Morelli Family?" Malik asked in a casual tone.

Violetta suspected he had to really force it, from the tension in his body.

"Hox, the Morelli goons got shoved out yesterday by the Anti-Earthers," the leader said, sweeping the curtain of long black hair out of his face. "Which was a joke, because we took out the Anti-Earthers an hour ago! We let them do all the difficult work, then jumped them when they were sure they had the claim."

A new voice cut in from the tunnel Violetta and Malik had been trying to get to.

"You strangled the single guard we left, while we gathered a proper group to hold The Cross, halfer. Taking down a single, tired being is just the kind of thing you P.O.'s would brag about."

Thirteen natives walked out of the north tunnel. Each one had brilliant silver hair and radiant silver eyes. They wore old gray military biosuits, probably the second generation, Violetta guessed, as she noticed the old pinstripe designs on the cuffs.

The male who emerged from the tunnel first had the old pattern designating the rank of commander on his wrist cuffs. His hair was in a ponytail that trailed over his shoulder and down to his narrow waist. The bottom of the tail was tied with a metal cord, and a triangular blade was almost hidden by the hair.

The twelve other beings fanned out around the leader, six on each side of him. Each was armed with a sword and some manner of sidearm. Those weapons consisted of early versions of the military-issue or police-issue pistols. When the military upgraded their weaponry on K'lais, the outdated gear was made available to the police with specific modifications.

The outdated police gear was available in limited quantities to citizens. The rest were marked for recycling or liquidation. The belief of many in the police service was that the gangs, individual criminals, or the Morelli syndicate managed to get most of the marked weapons, and sell them on the black market. Perhaps all three groups, maybe an unknown player as well.

All the information ran through Violetta's mind as she looked over the current situation. The data that kept coming to the foreground of her mind was that these early models only had lethal settings.

No one planned on disabling their adversaries.

"All lethal settings," she whispered to Malik, hoping he would understand the reference.

"Thanks for the warning," he whispered back.

"Is this how you recruit new members?" the native leader said. There was no lack of mockery in his voice. "Any halfer that walks through the Crossroads is given the choice of paying a ferry or joining your pathetic group?"

"We fight for a cause, just like you," the P.O. leader retorted, pointing the barrel of his firearm at the native. "Ours just happens to be for justice. Yours is holding onto the past and stupid notions of superiority."

The natives laughed.

"You remind me of the Earthers in their history displays. Shouldn't you be wearing dyed animal hides and playing a primitive instrument?" the native leader taunted. "You think having that kind of simplistic, self-serving arrogance is justice? Or progress?"

Malik brushed Violetta's hand with his. She glanced back and saw Malik moving at a slow pace backwards toward the tunnel they'd come through.

What the hox, she thought, *maybe they'll argue long enough for us to get out of here.*

"You act like we had a choice to be born! Like we'd choose this dull planet to live on! Where we get discarded and left to scrape an existence for the lowest level of necessities!" The P.O. leader yelled. "All because we don't look like this place's usual varieties: Dull and Dark, but Dull."

One of the natives made a sound similar to a snarl. She stepped forward, whipping one arm out ahead of her torso. Blue energy poured from her palm and flew against the

P.O. leader. He writhed before collapsing to one knee. Violetta was impressed that he hadn't cried out in pain.

"Hi'rrn! That was uncalled for," the native leader scolded. "But it does highlight a point to our argument. *We* have Gifts. *We* were born to it. Most of you can't, or can barely use your Gift. Because you don't belong here."

Violetta estimated they were maybe five meters from being able to run for the tunnel. *Just a bit longer…*

The Centauri girl stepped forward, rage in her expression and taunt body.

"I'll show you who can use a Gift!" she declared, just before clamping her hands to her throat.

The scream that came from her open mouth was louder than an explosion. The air moved in visible ripples wherever she faced. The noise reached fever pitch in less than a second, causing all the natives, Malik, and Violetta to clamp their hands over their ears.

The sonic attack had already taken effect, as everyone's equilibrium was scrambled, making all the afflicted fall down, still trying to dampen the noise and pain beating at their ears.

Violetta noticed, somewhere in the haze of deafness and vertigo, that the woman's comrades were not affected. They were scrambling after the natives, taking weapons and shackling the fallen foes.

Luck didn't favor Violetta or Malik. Both were shackled, forced up onto an old cargo HAV and dropped next to the equally helpless native gang. The older vehicle was equipped with a long seat in the cab to accommodate the driver and one passenger. Behind it was a four meter by two meter platform for hauling just about anything one could fit on it. Laid carelessly side by side, the platform was filled with captives.

The leader and a different female, this one with black, spiked hair, got into the cab. The woman started up the engine while the remaining P.O. members hopped onto the platform, or sat upon a captive or two. The vehicle went into the left tunnel entrance and drove for a distance.

Violetta fought the pounding headache and disorientation to try and acquire some measure of direction and the situation. She was facing Malik, whose eyes were mere slits. The dour expression on his face gave her the impression he was struggling as well. They were almost nose-to-nose, and the ride shifted the natives on either side of them to press into their bodies from time to time.

It didn't feel longer than five minutes to her before they came out of the tunnel and into a large cavern. It had once been a military location, perhaps an underground hangar, as she saw decades-old bunkers, security booths, equipment sheds, a cafeteria, and a garage marked with "District 42/50".

The vehicle parking was broken up into gardens, tents, and fire pits. Dozens of people were walking around, having discussions, working, even chasing after small children. Most wore mismatched clothing in some state of disrepair, but a few were clothed in old military biosuits. The biosuits, while faded, still seemed to be intact.

Several people ran up to the transport. Violetta braced herself for an ugly reception.

As an officer, she had been on duty during riots in the less accommodated sections of District 42. One thing that incensed groups of people into violence was a daily struggle for basic necessities, and the opportunity to improve one's station above that. These people were making due with even less, and here she and Malik were, stacked with people that probably disliked their very existence.

"Who are these people, Er'ick? They're mixed, as we are!" some female voice demanded.

"They were at the wrong place at the wrong time. Se'en had to cry at the Anti-Earthers here, they got caught in it. Didn't want to leave them lying helpless at the Crossroads, in case the 'righteous' had backup coming along."

Er'ick must have been the leader of the group that brought Violetta and Malik, she reasoned to herself, since the voice was the same.

"How high did she cry this time?" a new female voice asked.

Er'ick came into Violetta's sight. He pushed back his black hair and plucked something from his pointed ear. The device was a bit larger than the comm devices nestled into her and Malik's ears. Er'ick held the device in his palm, as he presented it to the women whom he'd spoken to.

"She went past ten decibels," he explained. "But your plugs cut out the sound before she went past two. Not a single fighter on our side fell or got vertigo. Fantastic work, Gi'lnn."

The taller of the women smiled and took the device. After a nod to her comrades, she walked out of Violetta's sight.

"Quite a cozy little band they have here," Malik whispered.

Violetta started a little, surprised by him speaking, and her renewed ability to hear. She looked at him and nodded the tiniest bit.

"Looks like we have some early risers," an enthusiastic male voice said.

The accent sounded distinctly Earth-based. Hands grabbed at Malik's shoulders just before he was pulled out of sight. Seconds later, Violetta felt strong hands on her shoulder and arm as she, too, was lifted to a standing position.

An Earth male was holding her up, smiling at her. He had blue eyes, reddish hair and facial whiskers. He wore one of the old biosuits and managed to look comfortable in it.

"Do you believe you can stand on your own?" he asked.

Violetta took a moment to check her body for sensation and weakness. Feeling nothing but some sore spots and a headache, she nodded. The headache was already fading. The human released his hold, but remained close until she stood on her own and took a few successful steps of her own.

"Apologies for the abduction. Your fellow natives in this little coven of ours can be a mite aggressive," the human said in a cheerful, courteous tone. "Even when they're saving you from possible death by small-minded members of the same planet."

"Perhaps we should buy some sound dampeners from your fellow Earthers the next time we have to travel through the tunnels," Malik suggested.

The human looked at him and smiled wider. "Our 'ear plugs' wouldn't be enough to spare you or anyone else from this planet," he advised. "Simply because our ears developed on a planet around a different kind of sun. Well, that, and we are pretty deaf compared to most races."

The human laughed, apparently pleased with his own critique.

Malik smiled back. "Always a pleasure to meet an Earther without a fatal case of 'head-in-ass-syndrome.' What brought you here?"

"Got stranded here about four of your years ago," the human replied. "Was sleeping off a long night of drinking the local brews and spending quality time with indigenous personnel. Woke half a day late to leave with my old space mates, discovered that all was not magic for non-citizens and citizens alike. Started gathering beings that had no recourse or aid from your otherwise considerate and helpful government, and began building a community."

He gestured to the area and people around them.

"It's not perfect, and we have enemies, but at least no one goes hungry or cold here."

Violetta asked, "How are there beings, at least part native, who are provided nothing? Did no one Serve?"

"Aside from the children and myself, every single person who's lived in our tiny community spent at least their required year in the military," the human rejoined. "But for medical or political reasons, often both, they were erased or lost in the subnets and databases. You must have been fortunate; never having to confront such animosity from your home planet or the people who are supposed to serve the people."

"It's because everyone here comes from mixed heritage," Malik explained. "And they could be forgotten or pushed aside instead of treated like citizens."

"Maybe I read you wrong, sir. Seems you have a good grasp on what your fellow citizens actually dealt with," the human said.

He gestured at the Anti-Earther natives being placed on the ground. Although many of the people moving them had expressions of disgust or ill-will, none of the captives were being mistreated or handled in a rough manner.

"You may have dealt with some of their kind, but it's unlikely you had to plan against them trying to kill or burn everything you know on a daily basis."

Malik glanced at Violetta, who felt herself bristling. He gestured with a slight lift of his brows. They had both dealt with bullies who disliked their bi-species heritage. Malik more so than herself. But this was not a situation in which to drag out such experiences. These people were being civil, and she and Malik had other places to be.

"I'm sorry that we came along and attracted the attention of everyone," she said, shoving the irritation aside. "But we have no quarrel with you. My companion and I need to get back to the surface, near the river."

Malik stepped forward and slipped a credit chip into the human's hand.

"Use this to provide better supplies for your people, here. We will be on our way," Malik said.

The human glanced at the chip before slipping it into one of the biosuit pockets.

"That's a decent gesture, and one that might garner a less benevolent response from some here," he remarked.

"I wasn't about to offer it to the leader of the group who brought us here," Malik responded.

"No, he's a bit too... opportunistic from the bad experiences in his life," the human agreed.

"Are we going to cause difficulty by leaving?" Violetta asked, although she was ready to fight her way through this place, shackles or not.

"No, I think myself and the other leaders can manage his temper. Won't be the first time," the human said.

"Buy him something pretty," Malik suggested.

The human laughed hard. He hadn't fully stopped when he withdrew a key from a pocket and unlocked their shackles.

"I just may do that," he admitted.

"Welcoming them to your flock, Earther?" the voice of the native leader of the Anti-Earthers rang out. "Going to break out the homemade ale and year old rations to have a party?"

"That's *Mister* Earther to you, Vv'llad. Or Fred if you buy me dinner, first," the human retorted, not reciprocating the hateful tone. Instead, matching the sarcasm perfectly.

"Fred?" Violetta had to ask.

He smiled and shrugged. "That's me. A boring Earthling with a boring Earthling name. Or human, if you prefer our people's term for us."

"We prefer to call you trash! Or just deceased!" one of the Anti-Earthers shouted.

"It's very tempting to hustle you two into a safe building and let Se'en give them another taste of her 'magic'. Ah well," Fred the human said. "They're awake, so they can walk themselves to the stockade." At their puzzled expressions, he chuckled. "Oh, that's what I call the detainment pods. Sorry, just can't get all the Earth out of my language."

Others among the shackled had begun to shout insults and threats. Fred led Violetta and Malik a few paces further away so they could hear each other speak.

"No need to apologize," Malik offered. "Nor should you lose all of your home's influences. Your people are much more eloquent at swearing, after all."

Fred laughed again, and Violetta noted how genuine the smile was. His eyes twinkled as he did so, and his body released positive energy. Little wonder to her that many of these people looked to Fred as a leader of sorts. He was what most of the natives had hoped Earthers, or any other visiting species, would be like. Open, not reeking of fear or lies. Personable without being unintelligent.

"Yeah, that sounds about right. Humans, or Earthlings, or Earthers: Greedy, horny, dishonest, but damn if they can't swear better than anyone else!" Fred joked.

"You did invent pizza and sushi," added Malik.

"True, but the Centaurians on Alpha Centauri's second planet perfected it," Fred said with some regret in his voice.

"What do you intend to do with the A.E. group you've captured?" Violetta asked, changing the topic.

"They get placed in detainment pods, fed and given water, we tend to any medical issues if they act civilly about the offered help. Trade them back to A.E. for whatever will benefit us best."

"Open passage, supplies, their prisoners from your group?" Malik suggested.

Fred frowned. It made his ears and cheeks droop, while deep lines creased his brow.

"They've only ever taken one prisoner alive, and I doubt even this elite hunter group we have caught would be traded for five minutes of talk with that unfortunate individual."

"Why do you call the prisoner 'unfortunate'? What earned that title?" Violetta asked.

"They torture him on a regular basis," Fred explained sadly. "They send vidclips of such to remind our merry band of what our resistance costs, or how bad it could be. He doesn't even have any information that would be useful, strategically or otherwise. We didn't have this base when he was taken, and we have more than doubled the number of members since. They just… like torturing him."

"Why?" Malik and Violetta asked together.

"He's a native, not a drop of 'alien' in his bloodstream. But he was the reason I missed my ship. We had spent the whole night together, fell asleep in each other's arms," Fred said with some whimsy. "I was too happy to hear the wake-up alarm. Or the backup alarm. When we woke, I didn't care that I was stranded."

"The Anti-Earthers care about that?" Violetta asked.

"They are beings who live to feed their hate," Malik said. "So others who hate as strongly are attracted to them. It ceases to be about whatever excuse they used in the beginning to act out, and becomes a group that lash out at anything they are uncomfortable with."

"Frighteningly enough, there's less of it all here than on Earth. As a world society, we evolved enough to where such individual choices didn't attract the ire of politicians or corporate sponsors. But there are always beings who, as Malik said, live for their hate. Maybe they're fewer in number, or less public about it, but you can always count on them existing," Fred observed.

"I've had to break up gatherings of such groups," Violetta admitted. "But they never showed the open hostility I saw today."

"Then you're lucky," Malik and Fred said in chorus.

"Earther!" the native leader of the A.O group yelled. His voice echoed off of the cavern ceiling. When Fred, Malik, and Violetta turned to face him, he continued. "What did you do to my soldier? Beat him while he was passed out? He isn't regaining consciousness!"

"Damn, you elves don't seriously think the old 'sick or dying prisoner' routine still works, do you?" Fred muttered.

Violetta cocked an eyebrow. "Elves?"

Fred smiled and his eyes crinkled with the expression. "It's a very old Earth legend. Elves were like humans, just… better. Smarter, faster, lived for centuries, very wise, practitioners of magic, that kind of stuff. Appeared perfect with no blemishes. You people look very much like how they were depicted. You call us Earthers, although we are no more the only species on our planet than you are, here. Anyways, Earthers means humans, elves means K'laisians. I don't like the term 'Halfers,' by the way. Reminds me too much of the stupid bias my people can't seem to ever rid ourselves of."

"Earther!" the voice boomed again. "Answer for your group! Or did your sick pet have the only active tongue?"

Malik winced. Violetta noticed and looked at him, but he nodded towards Fred.

The skin of Fred's face had become red and deeply lined. Usually, it meant a human was blushing; the skin along her own cheekbones would often turn pink when she blushed. Even while the rest of her skin would darken, which was the typical 'blush' for a K'laisian.

There was a moment of concern which doubled when she recognized that Fred was well aware that he and his beloved were being mocked. Violetta realized anger was rising within him.

The camp seemed too still and quiet.

"What kind of K'laisian acts like a wounded pusslug, crawling around and looking for places to vomit his useless seed?" snapped Malik, louder and sharper than the leader had managed. "Mayhap your comrade decided to accept death instead of working under you!"

Fred managed a giggle, then a full laugh. Other members of the camp joined in.

"Such wit," drolled the A.E. leader. "Obviously from a Halfer who at least comprehends the better race's sense of humor and sense of the Duel. Perhaps we should give you all a lesson? You must all want to be a Master of Ceremonies! Let the Duel commence!"

Malik charged past Violetta and Fred.

"Arm yourselves!" Malik roared to everyone and no one in particular.

"Infernom!" someone around the detainment area yelled.

The voice was terrified and angry; a warning call to the camp.

Scarlett flames licked the air at the detainment area's entrance. Screams of pain followed soon after. Camp members scattered in all directions, which allowed Violetta to see three beings, covered in fire, walking hand-in-hand. The two on each end pointed with their open hands, sending streams of flame across the camp.

She heard Fred scream in defiance as he ran towards the scene. He sidetracked to a bunker entrance, and ducked inside.

Malik had reached the detainment area, where he tackled a man and child who burned while they ran aimlessly in pain and despair. Once they all struck the ground, Malik began rolling the pair to extinguish the flames.

Violetta had started to run towards the three burning natives without thought. At the moment her mind began to wonder what other Gifts the A.E. members might possess, she and the rest of the camp quickly discovered them.

The one identified earlier as Hi'rrn hurled bolts of blue energy in what appeared to be an indiscriminate manner. Buildings, vehicles, storage crates, beings of any age were struck. The leader was gesturing to the remaining members of his group.

He used hand signals that Violetta recognized as those used by paramilitary and was instructing them where to attack. The A.O. leader had one of Er'ick's group, those who Fred was part of, by the throat with his other hand. The halfer male twitched like a helpless bug caught in a web. His features appeared to melt, even as his body sagged further and further.

Violetta made her choice and headed for Hi'rrn.

As she neared the bunker, Fred ran out, holding a large red cylinder with some manner of hose attached to the top. He hurled it at the trio that had continued to burn everything around them. The object struck the center person, whose arms instinctively broke from the other two and clutched at the cylinder that struck her chest.

The instant the contact between the three broke, their flames began to extinguish. Details became visible of each person. The three females bore no resemblance to each other, aside from being the same height. The cylinder made a sharp screeching sound. The women on either side began to intertwine their arms with the one still holding the cylinder. She dropped the object to grasp the other two women, which made the flames leap higher.

The screech coming from the cylinder grew louder. White foam leapt out as the cylinder ruptured. The foam engulfed the women and any surface a meter from them.

They fell as one to the ground, covered by it just as completely as flames had covered them moments before.

"Engage! Engage!" Er'ick yelled from somewhere past Violetta.

Malik had moved on to extinguish other members of the camp. Violetta ran on, centered on Hi'rrn, who continued to hurl destructive bolts of energy from her hands in all directions.

Shots from K'laisian rifles rang out. Out of the corner of her vision, Violetta saw the A.E. leader struck by several rounds.

Hi'rrn noticed Violetta coming at her. She threw several bolts just as Violetta cast her energy shield.

The bolts struck the shield and reflected back towards Hi'rrn. Hi'rrn tried to dodge, but she was struck multiple times in the face and torso. She sagged and her knees buckled, but she did not fall until Violetta used all her momentum to punch Hi'rrn across the jaw.

Once the native woman collapsed, Violetta turned her attention to her surroundings.

The hangar was a scene of wreckage and damage. Corpses and injured littered the grounds, but the fighting was over. Malik worked with Fred to put out the last of the flames. Fred put a hand on Malik's shoulder and spoke a few words. He then headed towards Violetta, who met him halfway.

"Go, get to where you need to be. We can handle this," Fred insisted.

Violetta opened her mouth to object, but spoke no words. Malik strode towards them, his expression grim and set. She recognized his body language. There would be no point in an argument: Malik had already tried.

They needed to go. Too much time had already been lost. Hopefully Mc'narrd wasn't sending out a unit to search for them yet.

Nodding, Violetta shook the man's hand, in a customary human fashion. Fred spotted someone and waved them over. A female with silver and red hair came over. She might have passed for a native if she changed her hair color, except her rounded ears and ocean blue eyes were distinctly human.

"Fay," Fred addressed her. "Make sure our guests get to where they need to go."

The woman nodded and gestured for Violetta and Malik to follow.

Instead of heading for the large tunnel they came through to get to the camp, Fay led them behind the parked vehicles at the opposite end. At the rock wall, Fay touched three places on the wall surface. A doorway revealed itself and slid open without more than a soft click to prove its existence.

"Emergency escape route," Malik guessed.

"Very good." Fay shot him a smile. "Not just a pretty face and sultry voice."

Before Violetta could ask what she meant by that, Fay stepped into the dark, narrow hallway. Malik followed close behind her, leaving Violetta to bring up the rear.

The doorway clicked shut behind them, making the passage completely dark for an instant. Soft blue lights illuminated from the floor once a couple seconds had passed. Fay smiled at them and gestured for them to follow her.

"Are you part native?" Violetta asked, not meaning to vocalize the question her mind was hung up on.

"Far as we know, I'm human. Earther, born and raised," Fay answered. "Although it's come into question often. I have traits that would suggest someone in my family genealogy was K'laisian. So far, no hard evidence has proven either way."

"Are your people able to use universal translators?"

The typical translators were similar to the earbud comms the military used. Since the translators became small enough to tuck into an ear, over a century earlier, they had become available to any who wanted one. Even before then, translators were free to the residents of K'lais.

"Some of those at the camp use them. I've always been a fast learner. Knew how to speak Standard when I arrived here. Learned K'laisian within sixty moon cycles. I still have the earbud, though," Fay replied. "Hated having the thing in my ear, and I hate relying on technology for anything."

"Were you part of Fred's merc group?"

"No, no." Fay seemed to find the question amusing, since she smiled and her voice had twinges of laughter. "I came here a year after Fred. Part of a diplomatic convoy. This place feels more like home than Earth ever did, so I stayed. Despite the kind of reception I got from most on the surface, I helped Fred put the camp together. Along with organizing most of the mixed groups into a single entity."

"How does that even work?" Violetta asked.

"Despite feeling to the contrary, every one of the groups had one thing in common: a need to expand numbers and be able to survive. Instead of recruitment, we offered a shared goal," Fay explained. "Support for one another, all working for recognition and acceptance by the governing body. The gang mentality down here already existed. We adopted it to survive. Don't really have any interest in taking turf, but if you don't look like you're making an attempt? They come to take yours just because you haven't fought them off before."

"And that's every gang," Malik interjected. "Despite the reality of resources and that no one owns K'laisian property."

"Yep, that's the kick in the nuts, no doubt," Fay said.

Although the phrase meant nothing to Violetta, Malik grunted an acknowledgement.

Fay slowed her step and held up one hand. When she spoke, her voice was a controlled whisper.

"They're above us. Try to not disturb them."

Violetta and Malik looked up, searching for the source of concern.

Directly above them, at least forty creatures moved sluggishly or not at all. Shiny carapaces glittered in the dim light and each had eight legs longer than a biped's fingers. The faint blue light glinted off of some heads, which highlighted the quadruple eyes. There wasn't enough illumination to discern any colors or patterns to the small, oval heads or bodies.

A muffled shriek made Malik and Violetta start. They turned and saw Fay pressed against the wall, her feet moving as if she wanted to pass through the stone itself. One of the creatures had dropped right in front of Fay. Violetta could see the bright red of each leg, the solid black of the segregated body parts, and the fangs below the four eyes. It was a fairly young specimen at about twelve centimeters in length.

"Goddamned mother fucking spiders!" Fay hissed. She appeared terrified.

"What? The rachna?" Violetta asked, keeping her voice extra calm.

"Yes, the damn rachna! You call them rachna, but they are *spiders!* And... and... and..." Fay began to stutter.

The rachna on the floor quivered. Violetta saw flashes of bright light blue just as the carapace split open and the rachna went airborne, headed straight for Fay.

Malik came from nowhere and punched the rachna out of the air. It hit the wall with a loud splat.

"And they fly. Yes, flying gorram mother farking spiders. We have them. It's in the newest round of welcoming brochures for K'lais, since some Earthers are particularly bothered by them," Malik said, sounding like a salesperson in a vidclip. He'd obviously heard the phrase used multiple times to be able to quote it so easily.

The swarm at the ceiling chittered and buzzed. Fay covered her mouth with her hands to keep another shriek from rattling the tunnel walls.

"No, they do not like loud noises or to have their slumber disturbed," Malik continued. "Perhaps we can make our own way from here? So you may return to camp?"

With her hand still covering her mouth, Fay nodded quickly.

"Do we just follow this tunnel to the surface?" Violetta asked, keeping her tone calm and soft. She wasn't as bothered as Fay, but she'd never been a fan of the rachna, either. Especially when around a swarm of the unhappy creatures.

Fay nodded again.

"Most pleasing. We shall carry on from here. Pleasure to make your acquaintance, Fay. Please assure Fred and the others that we will keep you all a secret. I know how much you want to avoid being noticed by the military or police," Malik added, giving her a slight bow.

Fay's eyes darted from the dead rachna on the floor, up to the ceiling, to Malik, and finally settled on Violetta.

"We will both keep your secret," Violetta assured her.

Fay nodded, before she looked back to the ceiling and stared. Her mouth was still covered.

"Remember: if they are sleepy, they have eaten recently," Malik offered. "They won't swarm you, repeatedly bite you until their venom liquifies your innards, and empty your corpse via their straw-like proboscis."

Malik gave a sly wink to Violetta and moved past Fay. Violetta patted Fay on the shoulder as she also moved past the terrified human. Glancing over her shoulder, Violetta watched the woman move slowly back the way they'd come.

Turning back around, she exchanged grins with Malik as they continued down the tunnel. Ten minutes later, they were back into range of the comms while they traversed the last few meters of the tunnel leading to the surface.

"About farking time," Mc'narrd growled. "I do not want to know what took you two so long to get back into signal range."

"Since you don't wish to know, we will cheerfully not inform you," Violetta replied.

"Get to the checkpoint," Mc'narrd snapped.

"Yes, sir," she said in a demur tone.

There was a round of muttered grumbling, but nothing else from the admiral.

Malik and she exchanged smiles and continued their trek. Mc'narrd could think whatever he wanted. It was doubtful he'd figure out the true reason they took so long arriving back in range of signals.

Several more tunnels later, another door loomed ahead of them. Malik produced the key and unlocked it. This time, he went through first, before gesturing for her to follow. He locked the door behind them, and they started climbing a narrow staircase.

"This brings us out near the river, doesn't it?" Violetta whispered.

"Affirmative," Mc'narrd said. "Good deduction, detective."

The door at the top of the stairs opened into the basement of a building that Violetta didn't recognize. Malik led her up a narrow metal staircase and out a side door. It was then she realized the basement belonged to a homeless shelter. The outside of the building was plain with no unique features. It reminded her of a box with windows, if the box had a sharply-angled corner.

They didn't enter the shelter, instead going into a building marked 'Supplies'.

That building, Violetta did recognize.

In the poorer sections of the city, on each side of the Nimkelu River, the military had two buildings for their overflow of food and other products. The overflow was provided to the homeless and those who needed assistance, free of charge. They were run by semi-retired military personnel and civilians were not allowed entrance.

Malik entered a code into a keypad and the door opened. It obviously wasn't the first time he had been in one of the buildings, since he seemed to know exactly where he was going. It was the first time Violetta had been inside one, though.

She followed Malik, not turning her head to stare at the shelves of supplies. The setup of the main room reminded her of a sort of grocery store. The room wasn't large, though, because the counter was maybe one hundred fifty meters into the store.

What was surprising was the woman standing behind the counter.

A native with silver hair, blazing silver eyes, and the palest skin Violetta had ever witnessed, aside from the admiral, she also had startling similarities to Malik. The shape of her eyes and jaw, the same poker-face Malik used. It took everything Violetta had to not stop and stare at the woman wearing a uniform with the stripes of a major.

"I knew one day this would happen," the woman said, her brilliant eyes not leaving Malik's face.

"I'd be in this much trouble?" Malik asked, stopping in front of the counter.

The woman shook her head. "Oh, I'm certain someone in the family has won the betting pool for that already. I was referring to you and her." She bowed to Violetta. "A pleasure to finally meet you."

Violetta returned the bow. "We appreciate your assistance."

"Major Rosora Me'riil is my aunt," Malik explained to Violetta. "I do not know what she meant by her comment about us, though."

Major Me'riil laughed. "He has been pining for you since before you went into the academy. Please, put the dear out of his misery and keep in touch. He's been such a grump, as the humans say, at the family gatherings these past years."

There was a suspicious sound of a liquid being spewed, followed by Mc'narrd coughing, as though he had choked on something.

"That woman and her sense of timing," he managed to say between gasps.

There was a definite smile on Major Me'riil's face, as well as laughter in her eyes at the comment. Violetta guessed she was part of the comm's channel, at least for the moment.

"Aunt, please. We don't have a lot of time."

"Obviously, since they've turned the krishii loose on your lady. Don't worry, they aren't allowed inside military compounds without prior authorization. That includes this building and the docks out back," Me'riil said. The smile was still on her face, but her tone was otherwise serious. "You'll need some assistance, though. I work closely with one of Don Morelli's men who watches over the homeless along the river. We have someone coming who will be able to help get you both to the harbormaster."

"Thank you, Aunt." Malik gave her a slight bow.

"Just make certain you come out of this in one piece," Me'riil chided. She turned to Violetta. "Don't be a stranger. Either in this boy's life or with our family." She paused, her features softening. "You may be your father's daughter, but you look so much like your mother."

Violetta's jaw dropped. "You… you knew my parents? My mother?"

"I did. Maybe you can talk Malik into bringing you over for a visit. I can tell you stories about your parents and we can toast their memories."

"I… I would like that," Violetta said quietly, glancing at Malik.

He shook his head in what Violetta suspected was resignation. "When this is over, we will arrange it."

"Good." Me'riil looked behind them. "And here comes your escort."

Malik and Violetta turned around as the door opened. Violetta glanced above the door and discovered an interface that showed the outside of the building. That explained how Me'riil knew who was entering the building, Violetta realized.

A woman with brilliant copper hair, braided away from her face in typical K'laisian fashion, strode into the supply building. Her bronze eyes and sharper features indicated she was a fellow Halfer. Thick, curly hair covered her ears. Several stray tendrils fell around her face, adding to her attractiveness.

Unusual for anyone of mixed heritage to have such a variety of hair color and type. Rare, but not impossible. It just meant the human genes had somehow been stronger than the K'laisian genetics.

"Major," the newcomer said, her tone brisk. She paused in her steps as she took in Violetta and Malik's features, understanding dawning on her face. "This explains everything. I was wondering if you weren't why I was being summoned when I saw the krishii flying."

"Thank you for coming and giving assistance, Lieutenant." Me'riil turned to Malik and Violetta. "This is Second Lieutenant Verilda Flanagan. She will be your escort."

"I'm no longer in the military, Major," Verilda objected.

Me'riil gave the other woman a sad smile. "Perhaps not, but you're going to need to pretend you are for this excursion."

Verilda sighed, her shoulders drooping. "Damn. I was hoping to never wear one of those jumpsuits again."

"It will only be for a short while, dear. Once you get these two troublemakers to the Harbormaster, you can return the suit and pretend it never happened."

"Not likely," Verilda muttered. She squared her shoulders, then snapped a salute. "In service, we prosper, Bures'a Me'riil."

"Be safe, be well." Me'riil returned the salute with the same gravity. "Your boat is out back at the docks, ready to go across the river. An unmarked military HAV will be waiting for you there."

"I have one question," Violetta interjected. When the others looked at her, she smiled apologetically. "How are we supposed to get to the harbor without the krishii scenting us?"

"Oh, that. She didn't tell you?" Verilda asked, nodding towards the major. Violetta and Malik shook their heads. "I have the ability to cover scents. As long as you two can remain calm and not have your scents or pheromones spike, I can keep you hidden as long as I'm awake. I started doing it the moment I saw you both in here."

Chapter Seventeen

Despite the entire escapade through the tunnels, Violetta and Malik still wore their hooded trench coats. They pulled their hoods up, so their features were not their own. The military nanites were far superior than those Malik had used earlier.

Verilda wore the standard dark purple and black camouflage field suit and her hair was pulled up into a tight bun. She did not wear a trench coat, hooded or otherwise. She slid into the driver's seat as Malik and Violetta climbed into the back of the HAV.

"Will these pass a Seer?" Violetta asked as she settled against the backseat.

"Depends on the Seer, though I doubt we'll encounter one who could," Verilda said. "The police don't typically employ ones that powerful."

"To further clarify, those who could see through those nanites would not be out on the streets searching for you," Mc'narrd explained over the comms. "It would take a powerful Gift and those are typically either members of the police service, the larger hospitals, or financial institutions. No need to worry, detective."

There were plenty of other things to worry about, so Violetta turned her attention to the three hundred sixty degree view offered by the HAV. It afforded a staggering spectacle of the city.

Violetta hadn't had the opportunity to see this much in far too long. When driving a police HAV, she remained focused on her destinations, or the activity around her. The last time she'd been able to just look at the city, from either side of the river, had been when she was young and her father took her in a military HAV to see what the city looked like from above.

She'd loved it.

Now, Violetta could appreciate the view, even if it wasn't from far above the city. They were just high enough to see roofs of home dwellings and some businesses. Cefnteg Avenue ran parallel beside Nimkelu River on 'her' side of the city. Past the Dra'as Avenue Bridge, she could see all of Service Park.

Even though details were just specks from their current position, Violetta could easily spot the Fallen Memorial Fountain. It was in the center of the park, and even at a great distance, the colored gels made the water jets look like flowing streams of candy. The 42nd District Police Service building, where she worked and had spent most of her adult life, was unmistakable with its blue-gray exterior and unadorned architecture.

To the other side, she recognized locations such as Aertas Plaza. The 42nd District Police Service Extension sat in the center, among the tall dark green everwood trees. The trees obscured the upper two floors of the fire department, but she could still see the large, all-terrain water HAVs with their distinct red bodies and white lights as they pulled out to answer a call.

As they came closer to Saerkan Avenue, Violetta noticed that Malik was trying to see something. She nudged him. He smiled and pointed, drawing her attention to what had him so determined to see. Between the buildings, on the side of the river they currently traveled, the farmers market was visible in bits and pieces.

The bits and pieces she could see revealed there was a celebration happening. Tiny dots, which were unquestionably citizens attending the market, raced around while short range holographic explosions filled the sky above them.

"Must be the harvest festival," Malik suggested, his eyes twinkling.

"Pity we can't go there, instead. I could use the simple joy of celebrating prosperity right now," Violetta mused, her eyes riveted in the direction of the farmers market.

Still smiling, Violetta looked at the front of the vehicle. Verilda smoothly piloted the HAV along the thermal pockets and wind gusts. She did not appear comfortable in the HAV, though.

"Are you well?" Violetta asked as she watched the other woman.

Verilda drew a breath and let it out slowly. A calming technique everyone used. After ten seconds, not that Violetta was counting, the lieutenant spoke. "I am not comfortable with enclosed spaces. Part of my PTSD."

"I'm not asking for details, bures'a," Violetta reassured her. "My apologies for the distress this is causing you."

"Thank you. However, talking helps me not focus on my discomfort. The event is why I chose to be homeless, and will likely be so until my death."

"I am helplessly curious about that," Violetta admitted. "Most of our fellow mixed beings end up homeless for a good portion of their lives, along with the first generations of Earthers who came here to make new lives. Why would a former decorated soldier be so? Our society provides for all, as long as there is service to the people."

Verilda nodded. Violetta could see the smile from where she sat, though it wasn't a warm one.

"Do you understand why we have homeless beings at all?"

The question made Violetta pause to consider what she actually knew.

Before she could answer, Malik joined the conversation. "We know that most beings born of alternate DNA have medical issues, usually for life. Some have speculated that is why it's so rare that we have fully-developed Gifts or none at all. The DNA from alien races cannot fully flourish on our planet, at least in the short term. Perhaps enough mutations will occur in a century so that children will not require so much medical assistance to even survive birth and the first years."

"All three of us were fortunate," Verilda admitted. "We survived being born, and none of us probably spent more than a couple of months in the hospital nurseries while our bodies were being trained to accept the planet we were born on. So many of the mixed that live are unable to serve the way natives do. Since our society works on the theology of the greater the service, the greater the reward? There was never a reason to plan for anything other than a small contingency to insure those who were wounded or otherwise unable to contribute full-time."

"All are cared for, all serve as they can," Malik said, quoting from the planet's Declared Agenda.

The Agenda had been written and agreed upon centuries ago, but it was still the driving force. It was where the world's motto originated. The words every citizen of their planet quoted: In service, we prosper.

"Except the influx of the humans and other aliens changed the scope of the contingency," Verilda continued. "So our planet, our cities, now have at least ten percent of a populace that falls into a category that was only planned for less than five percent."

"I am starting to understand," Violetta said. She didn't like what she was hearing, either. "But how does that pertain to you?"

Verilda replied, "I cannot abide being in rooms smaller than twenty meters by forty meters by five meters. Crowds do not trigger my anxieties, so even a crowded gym or cafeteria is tolerable for a little while. When the weather is bad, I will join the others and sleep in those rooms. Otherwise, I am more comfortable being outside."

"The shelters provide meals, basic amenities, and a daily list of jobs available," Violetta stated, realizing what the woman was pointing out to her. "So you have no need of a permanent residence."

"Precisely," Verilda said. "While I do work enough to qualify for very pleasant accommodations, I don't want them. Many of the Earthers who came here, hoping for new lives, feel the same way. They want to exist comfortably, away from the trappings of their own society. That doesn't require lavish living quarters or excessive material possessions."

"Why hasn't the contingency been changed to accommodate the much larger numbers of people?" Violetta asked.

"Because the councils want to believe all other aspects of our society are working," Malik said, his tone bitter. "So they argue about what can be done, and very little else."

"That's the issue," Verilda continued. "Much of it doesn't work as efficiently as it once did. The councils are busy making sure the system that worked for ages is kept intact, while being unsure of how to change what needs to be changed."

Violetta let that sink in. She felt she had nothing to bring to this conversation. Once her current situation was concluded, and her name cleared, she would need to discuss it all with her grandparents. Perhaps they could bring light to the subject.

"That is why I work for the don," Malik explained. "We fill in the holes that the system ignores. Homeless people eat well and wear decent clothing in this city, and have access to entertainment, education, job training, and more. Because we are in the business of doing so." Malik's eyes met Violetta's and she was struck with an odd sense of pride at his choices of how best to serve their world. "Yes, the argument can be made that all is funded by unsavory means, but we work for the people we protect and provide for."

"Being able to have front seats for most of the Duels is a nice bonus," Verilda added.

"Unsavory, perhaps, in some people's opinions," Mc'narrd allowed, finally adding to the conversation. "But not illegal."

"I may need a week to process everything I've learned since the Chief's murder," Violetta grumbled.

She slid her hand to Malik, who twined his fingers in hers. They shared a smile as she squeezed his hand. A very human behavior, but one they'd always shared. A promise to talk later, even if it hadn't been what humans meant by the action. A fact that had amused them immensely during their youth.

"You can't start now, sorry. We've got a traffic stop up ahead," Verilda advised, tipping her head forward.

Violetta leaned forward slightly to see the traffic stop Verilda mentioned. Ahead of their vehicle were several Police Service HAVs with their lights flashing. Officers in uniform stood across the road, speaking to every driver that approached them, regardless of which side of the road the approaching HAV happened to be on.

What looked like black blocks glittering with emerald lights were set along the road on both sides that led to and from the Nimkelu River Bridge.

"Dampeners," Violetta said, recognizing the blocks. Malik looked at her questioningly. "They're standard use for traffic stops. Designed to slow any oncoming traffic to no more than eight kilometers per hour. They're very effective in preventing anyone from speeding away from a stop."

"We used them in the military, also, to keep people from speeding through areas," Verilda added. "Remember: keep calm."

"I'd feel a lot better if they didn't have several krishii flying above us," Malik muttered. Though he didn't shift his head, his gaze went to the sky above them.

"Agreed," Violetta murmured, nodding as a shadow fell over the HAV.

A large krishii spiraled down, landing a few dozen feet away from the police HAVs. One of the handlers moved forward, nearing it.

It was the first time Violetta had seen a krishii in person. They had been released several times during her life, but every other time she'd been kept at home or at the military base when they'd flown.

Nearly three meters in length, with a girth to match, the krishii's leathery, bat-like wings were easily twice its size. Its scales shimmered in the sunlight, shifting from emerald green to turquoise, to shades of gold. Brilliant gold eyes stared at the car.

The krishii was close enough that Violetta could tell they had round pupils, not a cat-eye shape.

She leaned back in the seat and shared a small smile with Malik. Drawing a deep breath, she let it out slowly and shoved the fear and worry far down. If her father did it while commanding a battlecruiser in the bleak vacuum that was space, she could do it planetside.

The krishii stomped his front feet in agitation, swinging his head back and forth in reply to something its handler was saying. It snapped its jaws, long, sharp teeth flashing as it did so.

"Impressive, detective," Mc'narrd commented. "Your suit is showing you as being perfectly calm. Despite the multiple krishii at your locale. Malik's is showing the same. Keep it up and you'll be fine."

Neither Malik nor Violetta replied. Instead, they turned their attention ahead, their faces expressionless, as Verilda slowed their HAV to a stop.

When the window slid open, she turned to the native officer approaching them. "Good day, officer."

The woman nodded, her silver hair swaying with the motion. Her eyes zeroed in on Verilda's uniform. "Good day to you, Second Lieutenant. May I see your identification, please?"

"Of course." Verilda removed it from the console and held it out. "I'm surprised to see a stop on this side of the river."

The officer wrinkled her nose. "I don't even know why we need to be out here. It isn't as though the fugitive would come to this side of the river. The military base is over there. Her friends are over there. What would interest her on this side? Farms? The warehouses?"

Verilda chuckled. "Maybe they think she's going to go for a swim in the lake."

"Hah! Wouldn't that be something? Harbormaster Fr'osst would enjoy plucking her out of those waters." The officer handed back the identification, then paused. She nodded toward Violetta and Malik. "What about them?"

"I'm taking them to the docks for some testing," Verilda replied smoothly. "Do you need their identification, also?"

"I-" the woman began, before another officer gave a shout.

Verilda looked past the officer, who had turned towards the shout. Another officer, wearing two stripes to the woman's one, jogged over to them.

"That's a military HAV, Officer Pl'ncco. Didn't they train you to not stop those or otherwise impede their progress?" the new officer said. His gold eyes marked him as a native, though his dark hair and hat hid his ears. The stripes marked him as a sergeant. "Sorry for the hold-up, madam."

"It's no trouble, Sergeant," Verilda replied, pleasantly. "We're ahead of schedule, so it will be fine."

The sergeant nodded, despite the frown on his face. Violetta didn't change her demeanor, though she was starting to get a bad feeling in the pit of her stomach. Something was wrong. She hoped it wasn't the nanites malfunctioning with their disguises.

With a nod, Verilda put the HAV into gear and drove forward. She closed the window and gave a loud sigh of relief. The moment the HAV exited the zone of the dampeners, she sped up to just barely within the speed limit.

"I don't think it went as smoothly as you expected," Malik stated, glancing over his shoulder and out the back window at the flashing lights of an approaching marked police service HAV.

"Let's see what they want," Verilda said. "Can they use portable dampeners, Violetta?"

Violetta shook her head. "No. They take too long to program and set up."

"Good to know they haven't gotten as good as the military." Verilda moved the HAV to the side of the road. "Make sure you're both buckled in. Just in case."

"I'm really not liking how this is going," Malik grumbled.

"She can't be worse than Dad," Violetta offered. "Remember the camping trip to the Ae'railin Mountains?"

Malik groaned. "Please, don't remind me of that trip. I swear your father drove fast up that winding road just to see who would scream first."

"No, that was our bet," Violetta murmured as an officer approached their HAV.

"Sorry to interrupt your drive," the officer said as she stopped at the driver's side window. "It seems we had a reason to detain you, after all."

Malik and Violetta remained motionless in the back. Motionless, except for Malik slowly withdrawing a small pistol from an ankle holster.

"Is that the truth?" Verilda said in a voice much calmer than Violetta felt she could have mustered. The woman even managed to sound amused.

"Indeed so," the officer answered. She bent slightly at the knees and peered in. Her helmet's lantern shone into the cabin, revealing all three occupants. Malik was covertly aiming his hold-out pistol, in the hopes of a clean shot. Violetta braced herself, determined to turn whatever happened next into a chance for further escape.

The officer reached up into her helmet and yanked. A single cable came free and dangled against her collarbone. The single beam of light from the helmet extinguished.

"One of the krishii broke loose and tried to chase your vehicle," the officer said in a lowered voice. "The handler prevented him from going further. I volunteered to scout ahead and attempt to detain you long enough for them to arrive. Whatever direction you need to go? Head away from it, abandon this vehicle and take another."

"Thanks, cousin," Verilda said. "We will make it look convincing."

"You'd better. And you owe me the best dinner of my life."

As Violetta was about to speak, Verilda slammed the vehicle door into the officer, dropped a small cylinder next to her now-prone cousin, then sped off. The door closed automatically in response to the vehicle moving.

"Malik, can you hack a vehicle?" Verilda said, not looking back at the unconscious form in the road.

"They haven't made a model yet that could thwart me," he replied.

Violetta stared at him. Verilda hit the accelerator even harder.

"Was that a volt grenade you dropped next to that officer?" Violetta asked, wondering when Malik had learned to hack HAVs.

"One of the second generation grenades, yes. It's already been discharged," Verilda explained. "It completes the story my cousin will have to give. That she got hit by the door and stunned by the grenade. So the camera and comm in her helmet went off. The little shit will probably demand sushi for compensation. Loves that Earther food."

The car lurched as she made a hard turn onto Tz'wwor Street.

"Do you normally carry old volt grenades?" asked Malik.

Verilda made another hard turn down an alleyway, heading north.

"Actually, I do," she told Malik. "The older ones don't retain prints or other DNA, and you can toss them instead of having to launch them via rifles. Got at least two under each seat. That way no one gets the drop on me or can take control away from me."

"The plaza you're heading towards has two HAVs and six officers on foot," Mc'narrd said through the comms. He sounded exceedingly calm, considering their situation. "Ea'ndar Street already has a blockade going up."

"There's a blockade on Ea'ndar Street, and multiple officers plus HAVs at the plaza up ahead!" Violetta repeated, since their driver didn't have a comm earpiece.

"Of course, can't make any of this easy," Verilda muttered.

The vehicle banked right into the only other alleyway that connected before the plaza. Verilda slowed to go right again, taking an alley that led back to Tz'wwor Street. She pushed hard on the accelerator, her right hand holding down the lift control at the same time. The vehicle rose higher and higher as the speed increased.

Malik exchanged an uneasy look with Violetta. The alley was only seventy or so meters, and they had already sped through half that distance. The vehicle was just below the roof of the buildings. The signature blue and amber strobes of police vehicles were visible at the end of the alley, which meant Verilda's cousin had been found.

"Stop acting like nervous children," Verilda scolded.

Five meters before the end of the alley, she cut off the engine. The low whine made by the engine ceased. The vehicle started to lose speed, but only a little. Violetta realized that with the engine off, the repulsors would not displace the air beneath the vehicle, and there would be no glowing light either.

Then they were flying over Tz'wwor Street, four meters over the police HAVs, both of which were on the ground. Violetta saw three officers standing at different positions to cordon off and guard the area, and another tending to the fallen cousin.

Only a meter of height had been lost when they finished crossing Tz'wwor and flew into the alley opposite of the one they had left.

The paved alley road was coming closer, as speed and height rapidly decreased. Verilda kept checking her back and side camera displays, showing no concern over the possibility of crashing.

With less than two meters distance between the ground and vehicle, Verilda started the engine. It responded immediately, repulsors firing, pushing air towards the alley's surface.

The vehicle bounced violently once, twice, and then settled at the standard operating height of ten centimeters above the surface. Verilda had kept the vehicle from impacting against the walls or crashing against the ground. She piloted forward, the ride smoothing out as they moved down the alley.

Violetta and Malik hadn't been quite as fortunate as the vehicle.

The torso restraints held, but the inertia from the fall and subsequent bounces slammed them against the straps, the ceiling and each other. Violetta felt bruises trying to form and the progress of the nanites in trying to repair the damage to her body. The latter was a curious sensation, and not pleasant.

"Are you well?" Malik asked.

"Bruises, nothing else. Not used to feeling the nanites do their work."

Malik smiled. "Just be glad you aren't severely injured."

Before she could ask him why, the HAV came to a stop.

"Okay, we have to find another ride." Verilda announced.

The door lifts engaged, bringing in the stench of burning sulfur and something else that Violetta couldn't identify. Her unencumbered view included the parking plaza for this section of the industrial neighborhood.

All three beings exited the vehicle.

"Incoming!" Mc'narrd bellowed through the comms.

The world became a blur of pain to Violetta. She was flying without a HAV or similar vehicle, a crushing weight smothering her.

She hit the ground and the weight was no longer on her. Something huge, with the beating of wind around it surrounded her. Violetta opened her eyes, knowing what would be there.

One of the krishii. The beast had flown into her, dragged her down, and now loomed over her. Hues of red and purple colored the scales, highlighted by streaks of light blue. Wings that were at least two meters each were unfurled. The head was long, its muzzle opening wide enough to swallow Violetta from her elbows up to her head, and it was coming closer. Her body wouldn't respond. She felt blood spilling from her side.

Something flew into the massive maw, right past the teeth and tongue. A second flash of gray followed after the first. Hands grabbed Violetta under her arms and dragged her backwards. She felt sensations in her body again. As either Verilda or Malik continued to pull her back, Violetta pulled the two pistols she was carrying and opened fire on the krishii. She pelted the beast's left wing and head with so many disabling rounds it went rigid and collapsed, its massive body convulsing on the ground.

"Ease down, detective!" Verilda cried.

Violetta kept her weapons pointed at the krishii, even though it was limp on the ground.

A white film covered the beast's eyes. She knew that meant a state of shallow unconsciousness, but her arms refused to lower her sole means of defense.

"I guess we know how to take down a krishii, now," Malik said.

She saw his hands come into view and gently grasp her wrists. Violetta relaxed, and let him take the pistols.

"How badly are you hurt?" he asked.

"I'm bleeding from somewhere." Violetta tried to sit up. Pain shot through her right side. "I may have some broken ribs, as well."

Without another word, Malik and Verilda eased Violetta into a standing position.

"Can you walk?"

She took a few steps forward. The pain was no worse, and her legs felt intact. She nodded to Malik and Verilda.

"You need to get a HAV and get out now." Mc'narrd didn't sound thrilled in the least. He muttered an order laced with profanity at what Violetta suspected was a subordinate. "The local police are on their way there. That krishii was the one who tried to follow you earlier. The handler isn't happy that it 'got away'."

Violetta frowned. Malik had stopped beside an empty HAV that was a newer model. He had a pocket interface in one hand and was furiously tapping on it. The doors opened and he slid into the passenger seat. Verilda helped her into the backseat.

She missed everything Malik was doing in the front, because searing pain shot up her side. A startled gasp escaped her lips. She clenched her fists, squeezed her eyes shut, and focused on her breathing. After several shallow, quick breaths, she was finally able to ease the pain just as the HAV started.

"Hope whoever this belongs to knows how to get blood out of their interior," Violetta muttered.

Malik turned around in the seat as Verilda eased her way from the parking garage. "Let me see."

Violetta turned slightly in the backseat, ignoring the pain of the movement. She looked down to find the nanites weaving a net above a deep gash in her side. "Looks like the nanites have begun the healing process."

"That's going to take a while," Malik said slowly. "If you didn't have the suit, you'd be needing stitches and a wrap for your ribs. Not to mention antibiotics to prevent infection. As it is, the nanites are going to have to work on your ribs and that gash. I don't know what they can do about infection, though."

"The suit will take care of that, also," Mc'narrd said in a dismissive tone. "Go right on Melituar Avenue, then take Orchard Road to the docks. So far that route is clear."

Malik relayed the information to Verilda, who nodded and accelerated. Several police HAVs sped into the parking garage they had just left, but none followed them.

All of them breathed a heavy sigh of relief at that fact. Verilda followed the route Mc'narrd gave them, encountering no traffic. Violetta checked her side as the HAV turned beside the docks. The bleeding had slowed, though it hadn't stopped completely. She suspected it would continue seeping for a while longer. To her surprise, there were nanites also removing the blood from the biosuit.

Mc'narrd remained silent, though she suspected he wasn't far from the comms. She knew her father would have been in the command center during an operation like this, and she suspected he hadn't been unique in that.

The HAV slowed to a stop near the main berth for ships. A large military cruiser was in one of the berths and the harbormaster, Commander Fr'osst, was standing on the deck of the cruiser.

The woman wore a standard military jumpsuit, except hers was dark blue and black. Her stripes and name were sewn onto it in white, making them stand-out against the dark fabric. Her coal black hair was pulled back into a braided ponytail. Despite the fact she worked on the water, her bronze skin was smooth and not weather-roughened. Brilliant gold eyes seemed to take in everything at once, not allowing even the tiniest detail to escape her.

As Violetta cautiously scooted from the HAV, a figure moved from the sides of the industrial buildings. She stiffened as she recognized the being striding towards them, a sneer on his face. His silver hair shone in the light, matching his gleaming eyes. Malik moved around to her side, blocking Ziph Rc'dollph's view of her injury. Verilda moved to her other side, a step behind them.

The long coat Ziph always wore billowed around him as he approached them, revealing the dark clothes he favored. His sidearm was visible at his waist, his hand hovering near it.

"I knew you'd be here." Ziph spat the words out, as though they were distasteful. "Your daddy's too well loved for the military to not help you."

"So... what? You're here to arrest me?" Violetta asked, ignoring the pain in her side.

Ziph lifted his chin. "You're not getting away this time."

"You want me? Fine. I Challenge you," she replied, not keeping her anger from her voice. If she were lucky, it would buy them time to get onto the military cruiser and to the harbormaster's home.

"You can't Challenge me," Ziph said with a snort. "You're a wanted felon."

"A Challenge has been issued; it cannot be ignored," the harbormaster cut in. "Those are the rules. Those are our laws. Wanted felon or not. You can forfeit the Challenge and yield, in which case she can leave without you stopping her."

"She's not leaving here," Ziph snarled.

"Then you accept," Malik stated.

Ziph growled. "Yes, damn it, I accept."

"Very well. We can do it here," Malik replied, a sly smile on his face.

Violetta didn't trust that smile. She opened her mouth to object—

"You can *not*, I repeat, can *not* do the Duel, Violetta," Mc'narrd shouted in her ear. "You have multiple broken ribs and a four inch laceration on your right side. *You* cannot do it." He paused. "Name Malik as your Champion."

Clenching her jaw, she made a negative sound under her breath.

"Name Malik your Champion. That's an order, Violetta," Mc'narrd shot back.

"I name Malik as my Champion," Violetta said without hesitation, before cursing herself silently. Mc'narrd had sounded far too much like her father, and it had been instinct to do as ordered.

"You better not get hurt," she added under her breath to Malik.

"What weapons do we use?" Ziph demanded, glowering at them.

"I have swords!" the harbormaster called.

Harbormaster Fr'osst sounded a bit eager to Violetta. She glanced at Verilda who suddenly appeared excited and thrilled at what was happening. Malik was nodding and also seemed far too eager at the idea of a Duel.

What the fark was going on?

"Swords," Malik replied. He turned to the harbormaster who was moving around on the deck. "Will you also record this?"

"Oh, most assuredly," Fr'osst called back. Within moments she had a large interface propped on its stand, pointing towards the docks. "It's recording," she declared, before walking to the back of her boat.

Fr'osst returned, and with two sheathed swords approximately ninety centimeters long in hand, jumped onto the boardwalk. Crossing to Malik, she handed one to him before taking the other to Ziph. After bowing to both, she returned to the plank and boarded her cruiser.

Violetta leaned against the stolen HAV with Verilda close beside her. The pain in her side was growing and she could feel the nanites working. It was a strange sensation she did not enjoy.

In an effort to ignore the odd sensations and discomfort, she turned her attention to what was happening in front of her.

As Malik said the date and time, she couldn't help but wonder what she was missing. Ziph obviously recognized Malik, though she didn't think they'd ever met. Verilda and Commander Fr'osst were watching with excitement on their faces.

Were Duels really this exciting? Did people actually find them entertaining? Or was there something else going on here? She'd participated in plenty during her days at the academy, but it was expected to have an audience for those. This was considerably different and she'd be hoxed if she understood it.

"I am Malik Addelia, Champion for Violetta Cq'linns, sergeant detective of homicide of K'lais' 42nd District. Detective Cq'linns initiated this Challenge. The Challenged is Detective Ziph Rc'dollph, also a sergeant of homicide of K'lais' 42nd District. Do you accept the Challenge, Sergeant Detective Rc'dollph?"

"I accept it," Ziph said, his tone formal. He met Violetta's eyes. "You're going to regret this. I'll cut through your pretty boyfriend and then I'm coming for you."

"Oh, he's going to regret that," Verilda murmured. Violetta looked at her sharply. Verilda grinned. "Malik isn't going to let anyone come near you."

"Unless it's him," Mc'narrd stated.

Violetta did not smile at the comment. She didn't even respond to it.

"Last chance. Yield and confess, or your life ends today," Malik stated.

The coldness in his voice was unexpected and caused Violetta to shiver. It was not a shiver of pleasure, either.

"We will see who dies today." Fury distorted Ziph's face, turning the otherwise pleasant features into harsh, twisted lines.

Malik slid the sword from its sheath, his fingers wrapping around the hilt. He tossed the sheath behind him, as though he'd done it before multiple times.

Violetta watched as he slid his feet shoulder-width apart, his knees slightly bent. Malik's familiarity with the sword was surprising. They'd Dueled plenty during their high school years, but she'd always been his better. But she'd been taught from the moment she could hold a blade.

Watching him, she realized he'd improved considerably since they graduated.

She shouldn't have been surprised. In a world where Dueling was a part of their daily lives, you didn't just sail through life without learning how to use a variety of weaponry. Though she knew most preferred swords, there was a wide variety of weapons a being could choose.

Sidearms were never allowed for Duels.

She wondered what else he'd become skilled at. For the first time, she wondered just how much he'd changed since the last time she'd spoken to him.

"Let the Duel commence!" Malik said the words with a smooth and confident voice.

Ziph yanked his sword free and tossed the sheath to the side. "Let's see what you've got. I know all that stuff from the vidclips are fake."

Wait, what? What stuff from what vidclips?

Violetta was growing more confused by the moment. She didn't dare say anything aloud and distract Malik from the Duel. Even if he did seem eerily calm.

"Oooooooo! He's going to be surprised," the harbormaster said with childlike glee. Standing on the deck of her ship, she had removed a civilian pocket interface and was holding it before her.

Violetta supposed Fr'osst wanted her own vidclip of the occasion. She didn't personally own a pocket interface. She didn't have much of a social life, and was satisfied with using her home interface for personal communications. At work, subspace comms and police frequency interfaces were part of the standard equipment.

Further thoughts were interrupted by the Duel beginning.

Ziph lunged forward, his arm outstretched in an attempt to thrust the sword into Malik's torso. Using the flat side of the blade, Malik swatted his opponent's sword away. He pivoted to his right and flicked his wrist. His sword slid away from Ziph's only to strike it back towards its master.

To avoid a nasty laceration across his face, Ziph had to move back and away from his own blade. His face contorted into an angry expression.

Malik stood before him, weapon raised.

One vicious swing after another brought Ziph's sword close to Malik. Each was parried with ease and minimal movement. Ziph began to sweat.

"I thought this was a challenge, not a learning experience for you," Malik said, loud enough for the harbormaster to hear.

She laughed, as did Verilda. Even Mc'narrd chuckled.

"There's nothing you can teach me. I don't care to perform for public adoration," Ziph said.

"Really?"

Malik stepped forward, fluid strides moving into two short swings of the sword. A thrust moved him past Ziph's guard. Ziph grunted in pain.

Silver blood slid down Ziph's sword arm from the elbow to mid-bicep. His clothing flapped around the slice. Violetta's eyes zeroed in on the injured arm.

Malik had already spun around, his sword held before him.

"How about humility? Respect for others' abilities and accomplishments?" Malik asked. "Little chance of educating those concepts to you, perhaps."

Ziph snarled and took a long, sloppy swing at Malik's neck. Blood droplets fell to the ground as he did. Malik blocked the swing, and rotated his arm. The swords made two circular motions together. He pushed with his body at the end of the second motion, forcing Ziph back.

In addition to having to regain his footing, Ziph almost lost grip of his sword.

Malik continued to talk.

"To me you seem the type who takes what he wants because he thinks he deserves it. No drive to do the work yourself, so you ignore how much others have done and take it for your own. Such a pathetic attitude for someone who's in the service of helping and protecting others."

Violetta wasn't certain if Malik was trying to distract Ziph or make him so angry he would do something rash. He obviously wasn't a stranger with a sword, but she didn't know what he was attempting to do with Ziph. At least she was no longer concerned that Mc'narrd had made the order simply to save her skin.

Ziph used his free hand to wipe blood from the cut and flick it to the ground. Malik appeared at ease. He tossed the sword from one hand to the other without effort, rotating the weapon in quick circles around him.

"Showing off as usual," Ziph rejoined. "You think you have me figured out? Let's see!"

When Ziph charged, Malik held his ground, holding his sword with both hands. He swung up with considerable force, meeting the downward slash of Ziph's sword. The weapons clanged when they met. Little ground was gained by either being.

The swords shook as the opponents pushed against each other, trying to gain an advantage. Ziph's free hand punched Malik just under the armpit. Malik grunted, his muscles contracting in response to the impact. The punch made his position and leverage wane. Ziph took advantage of it, and punched Malik near his right eye.

Forced to step away, Malik pivoted right, freeing his sword from the clash. Ziph's blood was on his face, but Malik made no effort to wipe it away.

"So little confidence in your sword skill? Well, it *is* warranted," Malik said.

As Ziph opened his mouth to reply, Malik came at him, quick and smooth.

Three times Malik jabbed, forcing Ziph to block and move back. By the third jab, Ziph was unsteady on his feet. His block of the sword tip coming for his throat was clumsy and almost failed. Malik pushed the swords away from Ziph. He used the momentum to slam his elbow across the bridge of Ziph's nose. Blood flowed immediately from both nostrils.

Malik slid back to give room for movement. He was out of arm's reach when Ziph brought his free hand up towards Malik's face.

Brilliant light poured out of the still-bloody palm. Malik had no idea Ziph's Gift was light manipulation, nor that the man was fully prepared to cheat in a Duel.

Disoriented and blind, Malik stumbled drunkenly. He blinked rapidly trying to gain sight, and held the sword in a defensive position in front of his chest and neck.

"Cheat! Filthy cheat! You have no honor!" Fr'osst bellowed. The water between her boat and the shore amplified her voice. Ziph snapped his head around to glare at the harbormaster.

"Magic is never used in Duels!" Verilda yelled at Ziph. "Forfeit and show you have some honor left!"

"Once I've killed him, you're next," Ziph declared. "All of you! Won't be a problem to create a believable tale for the reports, either."

He glanced back at Malik, who was taking small steps in a half circle but appeared otherwise unchanged. Ziph looked back at the women and smiled.

"I don't care to wait. He can die last," Ziph declared.

He went after Violetta and Verilda with a fast, lumbering walk.

Violetta tried to remember if she had any weapons on her. The nanites were working on her wounds, causing more pain than the injuries they were attempting to heal. The pain brought confusion, something she wasn't accustomed to.

She looked to Malik and found hope.

Malik was watching Ziph.

He was still blinking rapidly, but his eyes followed Ziph. Malik pivoted his body. The movement wasn't as fluid as it had been, but it was steady. He swung the sword back, even with his shoulder before pitching his arm forward.

A heartbeat later, the top six inches of Malik's sword came out midway through Ziph's right leg. The kneecap was whole but dislocated, resting in its new unnatural position against the steel tip.

Ziph screeched in pain and collapsed in a bleeding heap. The rest of the blade, along with the hilt, stuck out from behind where the knee had been. The sword he'd been using fell from his hand and came to a rest two meters away.

Another scream tore through the air, loud enough to echo against the water. Ziph had attempted to pull the sword free using the hilt, then the grip, but did not have enough leverage. He'd succeeded in making the wound larger by moving the blade up, where it cut further into tendon and muscle. He shrieked, the words he tried to say drowned in tears, mucus, and blood.

With a cautious, determined stride, Malik walked over to the sword that Ziph had dropped. He picked it up backwards. He spun the weapon in a figure-eight pattern before snapping his wrist, making the sword turn in the air. Malik caught the grip right side up, then looked at Ziph.

"You turned your vidcam off before you came here?" Malik demanded, standing in front of his opponent. "Who knows where you are?"

Ziph mumbled something that sounded close to "Go fark yourself".

Malik pushed the tip of Ziph's sword just under the surviving knee.

"You have an intact knee. And fingers. To say nothing of your hip bone, and oh so many ribs to fracture, one at a time."

Ziph looked at Malik's smiling face and cold eyes.

"You won't." Ziph managed to say.

"Because we are recording?" Malik replied. "That is the best part. All can witness you cheating, attempting to attack witnesses, and your subsequent defeat. Even the laws will be against you, to say nothing of the public and those in the police departments that aren't moonlighting as a criminal."

Ziph kept silent. Tears and mucus ran down his face, but he made no attempt to clean himself.

"Do something good with your life, before it's over," Malik suggested.

"Why did someone kill the Chief?" Violetta asked, struggling to ignore the pain. "Was it you or the captain who did it?"

Ziph smiled, pushed his body up and settled on the remaining knee. Malik kept the sword pointed at Ziph's heart.

"Answer her," Malik demanded.

With a speed not seen before, Ziph lashed his arm out and grabbed Malik's sword at the guard. He jerked the sword forward even as he jumped to meet the blade.

The sword passed between his ribs, through his heart, and exited out his back.

As the light dimmed in his eyes, Ziph looked over Malik's shoulder at Violetta.

The malicious smile stayed on his face as he died.

Chapter Eighteen

There was silence. Violetta, Malik, and Verilda stared at the corpse, unaware that Harbormaster Fr'osst had left her boat and was coming up beside them. "Check his arm," Violetta demanded. When the others turned to face her, she gestured towards the arm Malik had cut. "Check his arm. There's something on it."

Malik slid the sword out of Ziph's corpse, then used the tip to move the fabric away from the dead man's arm.

In pale blue ink, stark against Ziph's dark skin, was a symbol. The lines were simple. A single eight centimeter line parallel with his arm was intersected by another line about two and a half centimeters from the top. The sides of the intersecting line curved upwards until they paused a half centimeter above the line, half a centimeter apart.

The brand of Moyii Tsaa members.

This just kept getting better and better, Violetta thought grimly.

"I think the Earthers have a perfect phrase for such a development," Fr'osst said.

"What is the phrase?" Violetta asked.

"'Well, shit.'"

"Fitting," Malik replied, "Since we are deep in figurative excrement and this corpse is a literal pile of it."

Verilda snorted, then giggled. That broke the tension, as Fr'osst and Violetta joined in. Malik smirked while he pulled a handheld interface out of a pocket.

"What are we supposed to do about this?" Violetta asked. If she breathed shallowly, talking wasn't as difficult as she'd expected. Thank the Stars for a high pain threshold. "The other officers in my department likely don't know he was dirty. They'll be after me, more determined than ever. Not to mention the Moyii Tsaa." Her face twisted into a grimace. "Despite the fact the Challenge, and subsequent Duel, was legal."

"They will not find anything," Malik declared, and then spoke into the interface in his hand. "I require cleaning services. East port side of the lake. A personal vehicle or possibly a police HAV will be in the area, traceable to the deceased. His name? Officer Ziph Rc'dollph, formerly of the 42nd District Police Service. Immediate incineration and recycling. HAV returned to the precinct."

Malik turned off the pocket interface and returned it to his pocket. He looked at the trio standing together.

"We need to get out of here."

Five minutes later, Verilda was on her way to the other side of the river in a modest civilian HAV, while Violetta and Malik sat aboard Fr'osst's ship. Fr'osst piloted the military water cruiser back to her home in the center of Crom's Drop Lake.

The cruiser wasn't small, by anyone's imagination. Violetta and Malik sat inside the cabin, where the ride was smoothest. Violetta suspected it was also so Commander Fr'osst could keep an eye on her and her injuries.

To take her attention away from the growing pain from the nanites working overtime, and the fact her broken ribs hurt when she breathed normally, Violetta turned to the most current event.

"What was that all about? What are the vidclips Ziph was talking about? And how were you able to just start a Duel there on the boardwalk?" Violetta asked between pained breaths.

"You really shouldn't be talking," Fr'osst chided. She looked at Violetta in amazement. "You really don't know?"

"Know what?" Violetta demanded. "Take pity on this poor broken woman and please clue me in!"

"I am Master of Ceremonies for the Duel Arenas of this city," Malik explained, crouching on the floor beside her. "The Morelli syndicate runs all the arenas. They rent the spaces, broadcast the Duels, own the vendors… all of it. That is the primary source of income for the Morelli syndicate here." He paused before adding gently, "I am the public face of that business."

Violetta stared at him for several long moments. Other odd events in the past few hours suddenly made sense. The teasing from the A.E. gang leader, Malik's confidence in the Duel, so many little clues she'd been unable to put together.

In a small voice, she asked, "Why didn't you tell me? What about the consulting and protection work? Was… was that a lie?"

"I assumed you knew," Malik said, trying to reassure her. "My face is on display all over the city, on any subnet page displaying events, costs, or the arenas in general. I may be what the Earthers call a 'celebrity', even though I don't know all that entails. I'm a Person of Popular Interest."

Violetta understood that term. POPIs ranged the gambit from entertainers to musicians to pretty much anyone that managed to catch the public's ever-fleeting eye. They received special attention and service from the private sector. The special treatment did not extend to the military, though. She also had to admit that she spent little to no time at all on news, or anything social, outside of what her job involved. She needed to get a life.

"When you asked me what I had been doing, my belief was that you meant besides the obvious. I do consulting and protection. A few times a year I am asked to be a Champion for arguing parties at the arenas."

"He's ever so good!" Fr'osst said over her shoulder. "I love watching him Duel, especially with swords. That farking rectum named Ziph? He never had a chance. The smartest thing he did was come after you instead of continuing to fight Malik."

"Nothing Malik has said to you is a lie," Mc'narrd added.

Violetta could tell Mc'narrd was talking only to her because Malik's demeanor didn't change.

"In case it has to be said: I was not joking about having Malik renew his clearance once this is over. Society may not approve of your relationship with him, but for what it's worth? You have the military's blessing." He paused, before adding quietly, "As well as my personal blessing. Your father would be thrilled, if he were still alive."

Violetta ducked her head, realizing that Mc'narrd's words meant more to her than she would have ever expected. Perhaps it was because he reminded her so much of the father she'd lost. Once she had her emotions under control, at least outwardly, she looked back up at Malik.

"I honestly didn't know. I've never been interested in the Duels at the arenas. In fact, I've never been to one of them," she replied, refusing to look at Malik. "I don't watch the vidclips of the arenas. Everything done there is sanctioned, legal, and not part of anything homicide has to deal with. When I'm home, I read. If I'm at the gym, I listen to music."

Mc'narrd snorted. "The word 'sheltered' does not even begin to cover your life since graduating from the Police Academy. 'Hermit' may be a better word. You don't even pay attention to anything that doesn't involve the safety of you, the city, or its residents."

Malik coughed and Violetta suspected it was to hide a laugh, if the amusement in his eyes was anything to go by. "I guess I'll have to change that."

Fr'osst turned to look at them, a knowing smile on her face. "I suspect if anyone can get her to visit one of the arenas, it will be you. How skilled are you with a blade, detective?"

"My father taught me," Violetta said slowly, uncertain of why Fr'osst had asked. "I haven't had to Duel anyone since the academy, and this was the first time I've Challenged anyone for at least as long."

"I seem to remember you Challenging people frequently during our school days," Malik interjected. "There wasn't a time you didn't Challenge bullies throughout our school years. I'll bet you did the same at the academy."

"That's different," Violetta said dismissively. "I made a reputation for myself at the academy and my nickname is known department-wide. Most of the people I deal with are dead or willing to help. It's not like I'm walking a beat arresting people on a frequent basis."

"Okay, that makes sense. Even if you are avoiding the question," Malik teased. "Naughty, naughty, detective."

"Fine. I'm skilled. I know how to use a sword and I have a pair at home," Violetta grumbled, finally looking at him. "Why?"

"Oh, I was just thinking that if you weren't very skilled, I'd wager that your fellow would be willing to give private lessons," Fr'osst replied as she piloted the cruiser.

"That would be one way to get her to go out of her home," Mc'narrd joked. "It might even make Captain

Ae'staa's unit's job a little more interesting. Until now, they've had an easy time with you."

Violetta started to laugh, then winced. "Oh, that hurt. That hurt. Don't make me laugh again."

Fr'osst jerked around to study Violetta for a few moments. "No, broken ribs don't lend well to laughter." Turning back around, she added, "You should know better, Admiral Mc'narrd."

Malik and Violetta shared smiles and a nod. Violetta knew military personnel constantly wore comm-links, just as the police service did the same.

It didn't take a genius to figure out Mc'narrd had added her to the frequency they were using. Considering the harbormaster had to have a high security clearance, dealing with the security of the lake and subsequent docks, Fr'osst was probably already aware of Mc'narrd's non-death long before now.

"Sorry, detective," Mc'narrd said, not sounding the least bit contrite. "You three should be nearing Commander Fr'osst's home. I want you, Violetta, to do everything the commander says. Starting with going to the bunk of her choosing and staying put until you're fully healed. We don't need a punctured lung on top of those broken and bruised ribs, young lady."

"Now you sound like my father did when I became ill," Violetta muttered. She grimaced as another wave of pain shot through her.

"I'll make certain she doesn't misbehave," Malik stated, his eyes never leaving hers.

Fr'osst snorted. "Now that I know what works for the lady, I'll make certain she stays in bed, Admiral. It will take at least thirty-six hours for the nanites to heal those broken ribs. Forty-eight would be better. And that's if they continue to work the way they are."

"We'll discuss it later, Commander," Mc'narrd said.

"Yes, sir." Fr'osst turned to her passengers as there was a gentle bump as the cruiser stopped. "Welcome to my humble abode, lady and gentleman. You will be my guests for the next day or two, at least. So please, be welcome."

With Malik's help, Violetta stood and stared out the window at the house that floated on the water, as though it were a tiny island in the middle of the lake. Her eyes widened at the two-story building, complete with a wrap-around deck and dock. A couple smaller, non-military boats were tied to berths, and Violetta could just barely discern fishing equipment in one boat.

"Look over there," Malik suggested, pointing to the bottom of the building's roof.

She followed the direction he indicated, and had to blink a few times to be certain her vision was interpreting what she saw correctly. A pack of eight gigri hung on the roof, upside down. Their fur of muted colors blended with the lake's waters and the sky. The larger pair, presumably the parents, yawned wide displaying a mouthful of sharp teeth just before opening their eyes. They appeared to be looking right at her.

"You have a family of gigri?" Violetta asked Fr'osst.

A ridiculous question, since she was staring straight at them. They, in turn, were returning the stare with open curiosity.

"More like they have us!" Fr'osst laughed. "That's the fifth generation of the family that lives here. Their ancestors nested when the place was being built. So they technically occupied the house before the first harbormaster. They return every day, and welcome each new harbormaster when the old one retires. They or their future relatives will be here long after me and mine."

"Aren't they supposed to be friendly?" Malik asked. He hadn't taken his eyes off the furry creatures, either.

"If you are here long enough, they will fly down and perch on your arm or shoulder, expecting acknowledgement and the good manners to stroke them affectionately. Hold your positions, I have to finish up."

Once Fr'osst locked down the cruiser, she and Malik assisted Violetta from the cabin and onto the dock.

The moment Fr'osst's feet touched the wooden planks, a young voice shouted "Momma!"

A warm smile spread across Fr'osst's face, even as Mc'narrd muttered, "Uh oh."

The source of the voice was a young boy with shoulder-length hair the same shade as the commander. He raced from the deck to his mother, who moved ahead of Malik and Violetta, and caught him in her arms. She swung him up and around as he squealed with glee.

As she put him down, she turned to her guests.

"Violetta and Malik, this is Alekel, my youngest," Fr'osst said.

Her son gave a short bow, the grin still on his face. "Nice to meet you!" He turned to his mother. "Are they staying?"

"Go get the swords off the cruiser, Alekel," another male voice said. "We need to get the lady to a bed. She's been injured."

The young boy peered closer at Violetta, his head tilted to the side. With a nod, he carefully stepped by Violetta and Malik before boarding the cruiser.

"I'm Atos," the man said, giving a slight bow.

Unlike most natives, his black hair remained free from constraint, and fell forward with the movement. He didn't wear military clothing. Instead, he wore a loose tunic, pants, and boots. All of which appeared resistant to the dampness of living on the lake.

A smile formed as he continued to speak. "I'm Jozelyn's mate. I'll show you to your room." He paused and gave Violetta a thoughtful look. "I've been told you have broken ribs. You'll want to be sitting until they are repaired."

Malik gave a nod. "Thank you."

"Where's the girl-child?" Fr'osst asked.

Atos chuckled. "Preparing the room for the detective."

"Mom, why is there blood on the swords? Did you have a Duel?" Alekel asked, appearing behind Malik and Violetta.

Fr'osst sighed and exchanged exasperated looks with her husband. "I'll explain later, dear. Can you clean them for me?"

Alekel stared at the swords in his hands and nodded. "Sure. Will you tell me about it while I clean them?"

"Yes, sweetie," Fr'osst replied. She turned to Malik. "How do you feel about being quizzed endlessly?"

Chapter Nineteen

The room given to Violetta was void of all but the basic decor.

A painting of a sunset over the lake graced one wall and a vase filled with artificial flowers sat on a dresser beside the bed. She suspected it was their infirmary from the lack of personal mementos and the faint scent of antiseptics, mint, citrus, and sage.

The bed was raised so her back was not quite completely upright and she found it surprisingly comfortable. That did not stop the pain, though.

Had it just been her broken and bruised ribs, she could have remained stationary and probably been able to handle it. The nanites, though, made that impossible as they worked to heal the ribs and laceration. She leaned against the pillow, her jaw clenched, her hands in fists. Her breathing was shallow and it was all she could do to not cry.

Now that everything had calmed and she was able to relax, her body was telling her how much it hurt. It was amazing how being concerned about one's survival made said being able to shove pain away so easily.

A hand slid over hers and she opened her eyes to find Malik sitting beside her on a small stool.

"Hey," he said softly, concern filling his every feature. "Anything I… that is, we can do?"

"Some pain meds would be amazing. If not that, then just knock me out?" Violetta asked. "I'm sure you could find something to club me with."

"Those suits may be life savers, often in very literal ways, but as the humans say: they hurt like a bitch when healing,"

Fr'osst said from the doorway. She moved further into the room. She spoke as though she'd been through it multiple times herself. "We keep a well-stocked medical cabinet out here. Sometimes we have to fish the soldiers out of the lake and babysit them until they can be reclaimed by the military. They usually have some nasty injuries."

Mc'narrd snorted. "You do know I can hear you, Commander."

Fr'osst grinned as she touched a panel in the wall. It slid open to reveal a recess with an interface. She pressed her hand against it. Another door slid open, revealing shelves of medical supplies.

"I can give you pain medication, though I'm not entirely certain how well it will work with someone of mixed heritage."

"Hold up, Commander," Mc'narrd said. "I'll check with Zh'oros and get back to you." There was a brief pause. "Sorry, detective, but I'd rather not chance you receiving no relief, or worse, a bad reaction."

"Understood, Admiral." She gave Malik a pained smile. "Somehow I get the feeling I came out on the worse end of that fight."

"Just wait until that krishii has to pass those stun grenades," Malik replied, returning the smile. "I also suspect it will have ulcers from that electrical shock to its system."

Mc'narrd burst out laughing. "Is that what you did? Damn, son. No wonder it's so angry. That krishii has been doing nothing but growling and snapping at anything that nears it since it woke up. Probably has a headache, too." There was another round of laughter, except this time it was loud humming. "Sorry, detective, but it sounds like the krishii actually came out the worse on that one."

"Oh, please don't make me laugh. Please," Violetta gasped as she laughed. "Oh, Stars, that hurts."

"Sorry," Mc'narrd and Malik said together, which only made Violetta laugh more.

Tears fell from her eyes as she squeezed them shut and pressed back into the pillow. "I'm going to remember this."

A hand brushed the tears from her cheeks. She opened her eyes to find Malik looking at her.

"You can Challenge me later." There was laughter in his voice, and a smile on his face. But his eyes were full of worry and concern.

Fr'osst cleared her throat. "Challenge each other anywhere but here, please."

"That Challenge will probably last their lifetimes," Mc'narrd muttered.

"It certainly lasted her parents' lifetime," Fr'osst replied.

Violetta found herself staring into Malik's face. Her heart jumped at the tender expression he wore. Ignoring the pain, she drew a deep breath and let it out slowly. The pain it induced was certainly distracting. Lifting a hand, she brushed it along his jaw. He caught it and kissed her palm.

"Behave. Both of you," Fr'osst scolded lightly. "She's never going to heal if you two keep doing that."

Malik kissed her wrist at her pulse point before resting it on her chest, his fingers interlaced with hers. It helped to distract her from the pain for a few moments, at least.

"I'm surprised the suits don't have pain medications built into them," Malik said, changing the subject. Though he didn't move away from her.

"It was tried," Mc'narrd admitted. "But the suits were not able to administer the medications correctly. They either gave too much or too little, which made it pointless to continue."

"Commander?" Violetta asked when the silence grew. "You knew my parents?"

"Oh, yes," Fr'osst replied, leaning against the wall. "Though I'm not sure now is a good time to start telling stories about them."

"It would help distract me from the pain. At least until I'm able to have some medications."

Fr'osst sighed and moved to an empty chair in the room. She settled into it. "I don't know if you've been told this, but you resemble your mother a great deal. You have her face, her eye shape, her hair color. Your father often spoke about how much you were like him but looked like your mother. He wasn't wrong. You have his attitude, though the stubbornness comes from both."

"How did you know them?" Malik asked, curious. He'd turned to face the harbormaster, even if his fingers were still entwined with Violetta's.

"Kali was in charge of the armory. Her skill at handling and servicing any weapon was uncanny, especially for a human. Your father may have been renowned for his work off-planet, but Kali was equally known at the base." Fr'osst chuckled. "She also made a name for herself off-base."

"What do you mean?" Violetta managed to ask. She tried to ignore the growing pain in her right side, but the repair of broken bones felt worse than the bruising and laceration combined.

"Your mother embraced our culture," Mc'narrd said, amusement in his voice. "She learned everything there was to know, and once she discovered Duels were allowed, she memorized every rule there was about them."

"She also was a fast learner with a sword," Fr'osst added. "Though her favorite weapon was a flail morning star. The woman mastered that weapon and could take just about anyone down with it."

Violetta smiled. "Dad kept it in his office on a shelf. Right beside her other prized possessions."

"Kali was deadly, even before she settled on our planet," Mc'narrd said. "One of many things she and Alyssa had in common. Except Kali got into more bar-room brawls than anyone else. It's actually how she met your father."

"Dad only ever said he met Mom at a bar," Violetta said slowly. "There's more to the story than that?"

Fr'osst and Mc'narrd burst out laughing. The humming filled the room and earbuds.

When they calmed, a few moments later, they both said, "Oh, yes."

"Your mother's mercenary unit had stopped on the planet for a layover," Fr'osst began, still humming lightly. "Mercs aren't loved by most natives, but as long as they're peaceful and stick to themselves, they usually travel through without trouble."

"That is, until your mother's group and father's squad happened," Mc'narrd corrected. "Now we keep tabs on all the mercenaries who travel through the Districts. It's safer for everyone."

"Safer how?" Malik asked, his attention on Fr'osst. Apparently, he wasn't aware of the story, either.

"We're getting to that," Fr'osst assured him. Her gaze shifted to Violetta. "Your mother's unit was at one of the bars near the river. It's changed names a few times since then. I think it's called 'Bishops' now. Unless it's changed names yet again. Regardless, your father happened to also be there with a group of his men, back from an off-planet mission. They were still antsy and hoping to have a relaxing time at the bar."

"Depends on what you mean by 'relaxing'," Mc'narrd grumbled. "I still think they were itching for a fight."

"What happened?" Violetta asked. She had a few suspicions on where the story was going, but wanted to hear it from them.

"Someone said something to either your father's crew or the humans," Fr'osst said. "The stories never did match. A few even said it was over a game of darts. Who knows? The fact of the matter is, a brawl started between the merc unit and your father's group. Everyone else in the bar either high-tailed it out or joined in. Most, I might add, joined in."

"Yourself included, Commander," Mc'narrd stated. Fr'osst had a smirk on her face. Nor did she deny it. "Everyone but your father and mother were in heaps on the floor, the bar, the tables, and through the windows. Your parents began fighting each other, minus weapons. When they had each other in a hold, your father decided to ask your mother for a drink at another bar. She, for whatever reason, agreed. The pair left, and behaved at the next bar."

"When your mother's unit was ready to depart, after being detained long enough to make full restitution for the damage done at the bar, your mom decided to stay," Fr'osst concluded. "Her desire to be a mercenary had been replaced with a more intimate desire."

"Dad never mentioned anything like that about Mom," Violetta murmured. She grimaced as another wave of pain hit her.

"Are you well, Violetta?" Mc'narrd asked.

"Not really, no. I'm in a great deal of pain. Why?"

"Your blood pressure is elevated," he answered. "How is your breathing?"

"Painful, but I don't think I've punctured a lung. Yet." She grimaced again. "I think it's mostly from the nanites doing their job."

"Good." There was a pause while he talked to someone. "According to Zh'oros, your records show you should be okay using any of the usual recommended pain medications."

Fr'osst rose from her chair and retrieved a bottle from the cabinet. She tossed it to Malik before leaving the room. Within moments, she returned with a tall glass of water.

"Give her one for now. If she needs more, we can give another, but let's start with a standard dose." Fr'osst handed Violetta the glass. "Just be glad you had the suit. You don't want to know what you'd be dealing with if you hadn't been wearing it."

"I have an idea," Violetta replied, accepting the glass. She swallowed the pill before chasing it down with water. "Thank you."

"Make sure someone stays with her," Mc'narrd advised. "If she's anything like her parents, she'll be trying to do everything on her own before those ribs are fully healed."

"I'm not that bad," she muttered.

Malik snorted. "Remember when you broke your ankle? I think your dad threatened to permanently attach the crutches to you."

Violetta opened her mouth, then shut it. "I thought you would've forgotten about that."

"Nope. Or when you sprained your wrist, and your father simply wrapped you up. If I remember correctly, he wrapped it against your chest. You couldn't move your arm, let alone use your hand."

"Shut up," she snapped, though she refused to look up from the bed covers.

Mc'narrd snorted. "She may actually Challenge you when she's on her feet again, Addelia. Either that or jump you."

"Maybe we should start a betting pool?" Fr'osst asked, her eyes dancing with laughter.

"I hate you all," Violetta said, though her lips were starting to twitch into a semblance of a smile.

"Aww. Reminds me of when your parents were still alive," Fr'osst stated, not bothered in the least. "I got that from your mother frequently."

"Oh, she never threatened to Challenge you?" Mc'narrd asked Fr'osst. "I think I got that a few dozen times. She never actually Challenged me, though she did Challenge quite a few of the recruits. Eventually had to forbid Challenges to and from the Armorer. I did allow them to fight it out in the gym, though. Still had a lot landing in the infirmary the first few years she handled the armory."

"Nah. We went out to dinner too many times for that," Fr'osst replied in a decidedly smug tone. "I was one of the few who she trusted to have her back when anything went belly-up."

"Your dad never mentioned any of this?" Malik asked Violetta.

She shook her head. "He never mentioned anything about Duels or any Challenges he or Mom were issued or received."

"Vrehn wasn't Challenged as much after his first couple excursions out into space. After he married your mother, he had even fewer," Mc'narrd explained. "He was skilled at anything he touched. Sword, every blade known to a being, sidearms of every type. None of it made a difference to him. Even hand-to-hand the man was frighteningly efficient. He didn't take Duels lightly, either. It helped him on his off-planet missions, and simply made him even more proficient and frightening to those here on K'lais."

"Kali hated when he Dueled. As much as he hated when she did it, but she did enjoy watching him move." Fr'osst smiled and leaned against the wall again. "They were well suited for each other. Either could talk their way out of almost any situation, yet could tear a place up if pushed. It's not surprising, to me, that you're so much like them. What is surprising is how much you've avoided the Dueling arenas."

"Not really," Mc'narrd cut in. "Vrehn didn't approve of the arenas, even if the logic was sound. He believed it would encourage more Duels among K'laisians. Even if there were laws in place regarding the process, he didn't like it. He also didn't want to encourage Duels, for fear Violetta would be as eager for them as her mother." He paused before adding dryly, "Especially considering her penchant for Challenging any bully in the schools she attended."

A look of dawning crossed Fr'osst face. "Oh. Yeah, that would make sense. The fewer Duels she engaged in, the safer she'd remain."

"Well, she has me now," Malik declared. He lifted his chin in defiance. "I'll gladly be her Champion any time."

"Excuse me?" Violetta snapped as she glowered at him. "I can handle my own Duels, thank you."

"Doesn't this sound familiar?" Fr'osst asked in a sotto tone.

Mc'narrd chuckled. "Doesn't it? Why don't you two spar later? You can use the gym at the base. A better method of settling the argument, in my opinion."

"Fine," Violetta stated, settling against her pillow.

Malik grinned and nodded. He tilted his head to the side. "You're looking tired."

"A little. The pain is less." She wrinkled her nose at him. "Shouldn't you wash up?"

"Good. Means the meds are actually working," he replied. "I'll wash up if you promise to stay put and try to sleep."

"I'll stay here with her. The shower is through that door." Fr'osst nodded towards a door to their right. "It's a small bathroom, but it's fully stocked."

Malik looked at Violetta, but didn't move. She rolled her eyes and nodded. He brushed a hand over her cheek. "I'll be back shortly. You better be asleep."

Violetta stuck her tongue out at him. He laughed and vanished into the bathroom.

"Sleep, Violetta. The sooner you sleep, the faster you'll heal," the admiral said in a tone that sounded strangely soothing. Violetta decided it had to be the pain medication. "You're safe."

She didn't know if he was speaking directly to her or if the others could hear also, but her eyes were growing far too heavy to question him. Or object. With a sigh, she let her eyes close and sleep overtake her. The pain had become a mild annoyance that was gradually fading.

It had been a long time since someone had to tell her to sleep and that she was safe. It wasn't unwelcome, even if it was strange.

Chapter Twenty

Violetta awoke to the odd sensation that something heavy was on her feet and the feeling someone was watching her. She felt groggy and her head was in a fog. The pain was returning, but hadn't hit the same level it had been before the medications had knocked her out.

Looking around the room, she found a young girl in her early teens reading from an interface. Just as Violetta was about to greet her, the young girl looked up, a pleasant smile on her face.

"How are you feeling?" she asked, tucking a strand of wayward dark hair behind her ear. "I'm Avesa, Commander Fr'osst's daughter."

"I'm not entirely certain just yet," Violetta replied honestly. "Nice to meet you, Avesa."

She shifted in the bed, only to discover something beside her. She reached over and picked up a soft, fluffy, brown and black teddy bear. A type of toy from Earth that had caught on quickly on K'lais. Violetta stared quizzically at the stuffed bear.

"My little brother insisted on tucking 'Mister Teddy' beside you while you were sleeping. He said that you were away from home and hurt, and Teddy would help you feel better." Avesa rolled her eyes. "It was easier to let him than to argue with him over it. I think every being who has come here injured has had Teddy shoved at them."

"That was very sweet of him," Violetta said, setting the teddy bear beside her.

The blankets had been tucked around her, hiding the injury. She looked towards her feet to find three small furred shapes piled on top of each other. The pile of furry creatures were also on her ankles.

Avesa grinned. "Would you like something to drink?"

"That would be lovely."

Crossing the room to a dresser, Avesa poured some juice into a tall glass. Condensation suddenly formed on the glass, an indication that the girl was using her Gift to chill it.

Avesa held out the glass. "Do you like drekka berry lemonade?"

"I love it," Violetta said, wondering if Malik had mentioned it to someone. She took a long drink. "Delicious."

Avesa took back the glass and set it on the dresser near her. "Are you in much pain?"

"Not at the moment," Violetta replied.

"Oh, good. Mom said she would be done in an hour or so, but to let her know if you needed any pain medications before she got here." Avesa returned to her chair and plopped into it. "Dad said to let you know Bures'o Addelia is sleeping."

"Thank you," Violetta said. "Are those lutrae pups?"

"Yeah," Avesa replied. "When I was about Alekel's age, Mom found a pup that had washed up onto our deck after a storm. We cared for it and it decided to stay. The pup found a mate, brought it here, and they've had several clutches since living here." She hopped up, scooped a pup up into her hands, and deposited it into Violetta's lap. "They're pretty friendly."

Gently, Violetta stroked the soft, silky fur of the lutrae pup. It wiggled around until its head was in the palm of her hand. She rubbed its head and the pup purred and rolled over. Stretching its legs out, it revealed the flaps of loose skin used for gliding. Long claws sprang from its paws before retracting. Long, slender, and agile, the pup was cute and seemingly cuddly.

Violetta knew it was deceptive. Though she was no expert on the creatures, everyone knew lutrae were the only natural enemies of the krishii.

Adult lutrae could zip up a tree, bounce from branch to branch without rustling the leaves, then spring out, legs extended and glide through the air. In pairs, sometimes even packs, they would strafe a flying krishii with their razor-like claws, tearing its wings into tatters. Once the beast was on the ground, the lutrae would pounce, their claws digging into their prey's leathery hides with frightening ease. Because of how the krishii were made, they couldn't snap around and pluck the lutrae from their bodies.

For such a small creature that ate shellfish, small amphibians, and vegetation, the lutrae were stealthy and deadly to anything that threatened their families.

"Can I ask you a question?" Avesa said after a few moments of silence. Violetta nodded, though didn't stop stroking the soft purring lutrae. She was rewarded with an eager grin. "How did you meet Bures'o Addelia? He's the Master of Ceremonies for the arenas, but he doesn't show up at all the Duels. Even when he does, he usually stays in his own private box. Yet, you know him! Mom said you're close friends with him, too."

Great. A fan, Violetta thought, wishing she could hide in her pillow. But, she couldn't ignore the girl's excitement and didn't want to disappoint her by refusing to answer the question.

"We went to school together," Violetta began. She shifted in the bed, which caused her side to ache more. The other two lutrae pups popped their heads up, looking at Violetta. "I didn't really meet him until second grade."

"When she punched me in the face."

Violetta started. She hadn't noticed Malik in the doorway until he spoke, and the doorway was beside Avesa.

"Why did you punch him in the face?" Avesa asked, looking between Malik and Violetta. "Did he Challenge you?"

Malik laughed. "No, actually she punched me because I punched another student who was harassing her."

"I told him that I could defend myself and his help wasn't needed." Violetta grinned. "All three of us were sent to the superintendent's office."

"What happened?"

"While the superintendent was calling our parents, the bully started harassing me again. Malik held the bully while I pummeled him." Violetta watched Malik as he crossed the room and sat on the stool beside her. He reached over and scratched the pup under its chin. "Our parents weren't happy that we got into trouble, but they were angrier with the bully than us."

"So, how did you become friends? Because he helped you beat up a bully?" Avesa asked, looking between them.

Malik's grin grew. "More or less. After that, we had each other's back. Anytime I would try to goad someone into Challenging me, she'd jump in front and demand they fight her, instead. We would argue over who got to Duel. Sometimes we'd end up Dueling. Sometimes the other person would walk away because they didn't want to ultimately end up being Challenged to two Duels." At Avesa's confused expression, he added, "Violetta and I would both issue Challenges. Sometimes we'd be nice and issue them a day apart."

"It was fun," Violetta admitted. "By the time we were in high school, we were practically inseparable, despite the school's best efforts. By our junior year, we had every class together and the school was bully-free."

Avesa stared at them in wide-eyed wonder. "That's just awesome. My parents would have my head if I did anything like that."

"Our parents weren't exactly thrilled." Violetta shared an amused look with Malik. "They gave up trying to stop us by our freshman year of high school, though."

"My sisters still love the fact you punched me," Malik grumbled.

"Oh, then they're going to love me even more when they find out what I did recently," Violetta teased. Malik groaned. At Avesa's expression, she smiled. "I used him to escape from a bad situation. I'm not sure your parents would appreciate me telling you what happened, though."

"She threw me into the police who were trying to catch her," Malik admitted, to the girl's instant delight.

"That's so awesome!" Avesa exclaimed. "I can't wait to tell my classmates I got to meet you both!"

"Avesa!" someone called from the floor above.

Avesa sighed and stood. "Guess that's my cue. If you need anything, please let me know!"

With a final smile, she bounced from the room, full of giddiness. Once she was gone, the lutrae pups stood. They stretched out their entire length before standing and chirping at each other. The one Violetta and Malik had been rubbing stretched languidly and stood. All of them hopped from the bed and trotted out of the room.

The amusement from watching the pups faded as Malik turned to Violetta. His face grew solemn as he asked, "How's the pain?"

Violetta shifted slightly. "Manageable. I don't want to take anything unless I absolutely have to."

"Hungry?" he asked. The pleading look she gave him had him laughing. "Come on, then. You should be able to handle dinner with the family. Though I suspect they'll be sending their kids to bed soon."

"Oh? I slept that long?"

He nodded as he took her hands and gently helped her stand. She inhaled sharply as she came nose-to-nose with him. Desire burned in his eyes and she knew he saw the same in hers. It wasn't the time or the place. Not to mention she was still healing.

"Do you two need a chaperone all the time?" Mc'narrd asked, breaking the moment. "Your pulse is racing. If I didn't know what was happening, I would wonder if you had an arrhythmia and would be calling for a Healer."

"Now that's just mean," Violetta grumbled, though she couldn't pull her eyes away from Malik.

"He's just jealous," Malik joked, taking a step back. "Let's go join the harbormaster and her mate before they come looking for us."

Mc'narrd snorted, but otherwise remained silent.

Giggling, Violetta slid her hand into his and squeezed. He kissed her knuckles and led her to the dining area. The kids weren't there, for which Violetta was actually thankful for. She didn't want to have to do a lot of talking, and kids could be very talkative.

"Did you sleep well?" Fr'osst asked, placing a dish on the table. "Please, sit and enjoy."

"Yes, thank you. This looks delicious," Violetta said, as Malik pulled a chair out for her. She eased into it. The nanites were still working, but breathing was easier and the pain wasn't as horrible.

"According to the reports from the admiral, your ribs have been repaired," Atos said. "They'll feel bruised for a while yet, but you're responding better than expected." He handed her a plate and smiled. "My clearance is equal to Jozelyn's level. It was required for me to live here due to the military personnel that come through."

"What about the children?" Malik asked.

Atos heaped some of the steamed vegetables onto Violetta's plate. "The children have clearance, also. Just as Violetta required clearance to go to the base as a child."

"That explains a bit." Malik retrieved a plate of his own and began filling it with food. "We appreciate your assistance."

"It's a pleasure," Fr'osst said, joining them at the table. She had a cup of jakka in hand.

"How well did you know my father?" Violetta asked, taking a bite from her plate.

Atos laughed. "He was older than us, which meant we got to watch all the fun and wish we could be as amazing as him."

"Did he ever tell you how he was promoted to commander? How he received missions for off-world planets?" Fr'osst asked.

Violetta shook her head. Swallowing her mouthful of food, she said, "No. He never told me and it isn't mentioned anywhere that I could find."

"There's a reason for that," Atos said, sitting back in his chair. Laughter shone in his gold eyes. "It was before he and Mc'narrd really made it known to other races, our world isn't one anyone wanted to attempt to conquer. There was an armada nearing orbit, preparing to attack."

"Our military had experimental ships they were working on," Fr'osst said, taking over as her mate took a drink from his glass. "The ships hadn't been cleared for use in space, but that didn't stop your father. Vrehn knew the mechanics and often drank with them. Despite being part of the military guard, he helped to figure out the designs. He was certain the ships would work, but the pilots hadn't been cleared for flight by the admiralty."

"The planetside commanders were busy strategizing the best attack method," Atos continued. "So, Vrehn slipped into the bay and fired one of those ships up. Before anyone could stop him, supposedly, he piloted it out and into space." He smirked. "My cousin was there that day. Recorded the whole thing."

"I *was* there," Fr'osst said, nudging her mate. "My mother had been called in and she had taken me with her. I'd already decided I would take over here as harbormaster, so I was excited to go to the base during an invasion. Little did I know I'd get to see history in the making."

"Wait. Dad stole a ship? How did he not get a court martial?"

"Better question: what happened after he stole the ship?" Malik asked, equally enthralled with the tale.

Atos and Jozelyn hummed loudly.

"After your dad took off, he began firing on the would-be invaders. Every shot he made hit an enemy fighter. For someone who had supposedly never flown before, he was doing a damned good job. Once the pilots saw what was going on, they jumped into the other ships and took off to join him," Jozelyn answered, leaning forward against the table. "While the commanders were trying to create an attack plan, Vrehn was commanding the pilots while attacking the enemy. He was a master strategist when it came to battles. They pushed the armada back."

"The rest of the military ships swooped in and crushed them. Sent the Zira running," Atos added.

"It was decided," Jozelyn cut in, "That there were only two choices: court martial or give him command. Vrehn Cq'linns made it known he had zero remorse and didn't give a fark what his superior officers thought. The general consensus was it would be better to send him off-planet and let him be a problem for other races. Turns out, his straight-forward attitude served us better there than it ever had on K'lais."

"Our world lost a great man when he was murdered," Mc'narrd added over the comms. There was honest remorse and sadness to the words. "He didn't back down from anything the universes placed in front of him. Alien races learned to respect him or have their asses kicked."

"He loved your mother," Fr'osst said gently. "She was his world. Then when you were born and she died? He vowed he would do everything in his power to keep you safe. To protect you."

Atos grunted. "Ask the admiral what he promised your father." Violetta stared at Atos. His eyes narrowed slightly. "He doesn't take a personal interest in everything that happens planetside, and he's certainly not the only three-star admiral. He and Vrehn were close friends, not just comrades in arms. Whatever he's told you? It isn't everything. It's not a lie, but it won't be the entire truth."

"Atos." Jozelyn's voice was filled with warning. "You don't know what you're saying."

She reached up and flicked the bottom of his ear. Violetta suspected it was a reminder to the comm he probably wore.

"Doesn't matter if the admiral's listening, Joz." Atos smirked. "And, yes, I do know what I'm saying. I knew

Vrehn before he retired. I served under him for a brief time, remember? He had a powerful presence. What a lot of people called reckless? It wasn't recklessness. Vrehn never did anything without a reason or purpose. Probably one of the most insightful beings I ever knew. There are some in the military, high up, who he made promise him something towards his daughter. Don't know what the promise was, but one was made."

"Does it matter, though?" Violetta asked after playing with the food on her plate. Her mind was on the file her father kept on his console. A console kept off all subnets that required her DNA to access. She looked up and met Atos's gaze. "If what you say is true, and I honestly don't know, does it really matter? The admiral is assisting for his own reasons. Everyone does everything for their own reasons, even me."

Fr'osst nodded slowly. "You have a point. What was done in the past doesn't always matter in the present. If it means you have unexpected allies, then it shouldn't matter how it came to be."

Despite her words, Violetta knew Atos was right. She couldn't help but wonder what her father could have made the admiral promise. To watch over her? That didn't make a lot of sense. She was also a bit afraid to know if there had really been a promise, and what that promise had been.

Maybe it didn't matter, after all. She felt Malik nudge her foot with his and she looked at him. He lifted a brow and she shrugged her shoulders slightly.

"When you're older, I'll tell you about the promise," Mc'narrd finally said. "Atos is correct. One was made years ago. Long before Vrehn's death. How he became aware of it, I don't know. Unless Vrehn had him make the same promise."

"Did Vrehn make you promise anything?" Malik asked outright, taking a bite from his plate.

Atos smiled, but remained silent.

Fr'osst stared at her husband. "You sly old dog. You did!"

"Thought as much. Seems Vrehn was thorough," Mc'narrd said thoughtfully.

The sound of a loud air horn stopped anyone from saying anything else. Everyone at the table looked at each other. The horn sounded again. Jozelyn stood slowly.

"You two stay here," she said to Malik and Violetta. Turning to her husband, she added, "You have your interface?" He nodded and pulled out a pocket interface. "Good. Please bring the cameras up so they can listen in and watch."

Without another word, the harbormaster strode from the room, leaving her jakka coffee behind. By the time she was outside on their deck leading to the docks, Atos had loaded the camera and sound to the cameras.

It showed her walking towards a police HAV. The brilliant lights flashed and there were fog lights on the front of it. None of it hindered Commander Fr'osst as she neared the gently swaying dock.

"Harbormaster Fr'osst," a voice called out. The lights dimmed and a tall figure silhouetted against the darkness could be seen. "Forgive our interruption of your night."

"What brings you here, officer?" Fr'osst called back. She didn't move from the threshold of the deck. "I haven't received any distress calls to signal your need to be out here."

"Did not expect that comment," Violetta murmured.

"She doesn't like her family time interrupted needlessly," Atos informed them. "They have no business here, and they know it."

"There has been news of the death of Sergeant Rc'dollph, a detective of the 42nd District Police Service. The fugitive Violetta Cq'linns Challenged him and Malik Addelia was her Champion. The krishii lost her scent near the docks. We were wishing to know if you've seen anything," the officer replied. "The krishii refuse to leave the perimeter of the lake."

"I'd be surprised if they left the docks," Atos intoned. "With packs of lutrae around the lake, and their scent strong over the water, the dragons aren't going to chance encountering their enemies."

Violetta gave Malik a sharp look. He tipped his head from side to side before straightening it. "That makes sense about the krishii. Not so much about the rest, though."

"Duels and the results have to be reported within twenty-four hours," Malik explained. "It's required by law. They obviously haven't seen the vidclip, or they'd be asking about Verilda, also."

"I have neither seen nor heard about any civilian traffic on the lake tonight that doesn't have proper authority to be out," Harbormaster Commander Fr'osst intoned.

The officer remained silent for several moments.

"Want to bet he's trying to figure out how to ask about the military?" Atos asked, a sly grin on his face.

When the officer didn't say anything, Fr'osst asked, "Is there anything else, officer? Because you're wasting my time, something the military does not take lightly."

"And there she's done it," Mc'narrd said smugly.

"Have a good night, Bures'a Fr'osst," the officer shouted. He sounded a bit frantic to Violetta.

The lights returned to full and the HAV pulled away slowly before accelerating once it was a safe distance from the dock. It wasn't until the lights had faded into the distance that Jozelyn returned to the table and her jakka.

Atos turned off the interface, sliding it back into his pocket. "They won't be back."

"Not if I have any say in the matter," the admiral muttered. The line went quiet.

"They shouldn't have been out here, regardless." Jozelyn took a sip of her jakka. "If anything happens on the lake, I handle it. If it involves civilians, I contact the police service. Not the other way around. I suspect someone is going to receive a demerit or two for that foolishness."

"Are you certain they won't return?" Malik asked, finishing the last of his plate. He glanced at Violetta, before nudging her shoulder gently. "You need to eat more."

"They won't be back," Mc'narrd and Jozelyn said together.

"One: I told them I'd neither seen nor heard anything in the civilian sector. If they return, I have the authority to arrest them for impeding my duties. Two: they should not have come to me asking anything about anyone. Someone is determined to find you, Violetta. Hopefully not at the expense of angering the military."

"I've contacted those who need to know," Mc'narrd added. "The fact they interrupted Commander Fr'osst's duties for a local police matter, would never go over well with the military. Even on a normal day for a normal situation. As far as the police service is aware, the military has not become involved with the search for Violetta." He allowed his words to die before adding, "No one will come near Jozelyn and Atos' home again tonight. If they do, they will be arrested and face military prosecution."

Leaning over, Atos kissed his mate's ear tip. "Come, my dear. Let's let these two finish their meal." He turned to Malik and Violetta. "Once you finish, feel free to enjoy the comforts of our deck. At this time of night, you should be able to view the aquatic life easily. It's something everyone should enjoy at least once in their lifetime."

With that, Atos stood and led his mate from the kitchen, leaving Malik and Violetta alone.

"Finish eating and we can go for a walk outside," Malik instructed. Violetta glowered at him, but shoved a fork full of food into her mouth, anyway. "If you need anything for pain, let me know. Jozelyn gave me some pain medication for you. But you need to eat something or it's going to take the nanites longer to repair you."

"I'm eating! I'm eating!" she exclaimed, before taking a sip of her drink. "This is more than I think I've eaten all week, to be honest."

Malik leaned over and kissed her cheek. "I know."

Chapter Twenty One

Crom's Drop Lake was easily the size of the district they lived in. There was nothing but water as far as the eye could see. The sound of gentle waves splashing against the floating house was peaceful and calming. Bioluminescent fish swam near the deck where Malik and Violetta stood, sometimes leaping out of the water, creating small splashes against the surface. Every so often the sleek body of a lutrae would zip by in search of food or simply play in the water near their home.

Malik and Violetta stood near the rail of the deck, watching the fish and lutrae in silence for several minutes.

"Admiral? Could we have some privacy?" Violetta finally asked quietly.

"Comm silence, you mean?" Mc'narrd asked in return.

"Yes, sir. We'd like to talk without having anyone listening in to the conversation," she replied.

"Very well. You're safe enough there and you're still wearing the suits. I'll give you three hours for your 'talk', detective," Mc'narrd said. "Make the conversation count."

With that, there was absolute silence from the comms. Violetta looked a bit stunned.

"You didn't expect that?" Malik asked as he studied her.

She shook her head. "I hoped he would give us an hour at the most. He's being generous."

"Maybe he likes you. What did you want to talk about?"

"You. Me. Us. Everything." She stepped to the railing. Crossing her arms over the edge, she leaned against it gently. When it didn't cause pain, she settled her weight against it and her arms.

"Okay," Malik said, caution in his voice as he joined her at the railing. "Where to start?"

"There is so much," Violetta replied with a heavy sigh. "I'm not even sure I remember all the questions I had when we started just a few days ago."

"We'll have time to go over all the topics later. You must know where you want to start," Malik insisted.

"Okay. That's fair. How about… with us, I guess?" Violetta didn't look at Malik as she spoke, for fear he'd see her inner turmoil. "It's been five years since we last saw each other. Here we are, thrown together because of this mess. How do we know what we're feeling is true? And not just because of the current situation?"

"Because it never changed, at least in my mind?" he suggested, leaning his side against the railing. There was a tenseness to him that belied his real feelings.

"That's why I avoided anything social. Why I was such a hermit. It kept away any chance of being Matched. I couldn't grasp the idea of anyone else. When I thought about it, I only saw your face."

Violetta turned her head to look at him. With only him there, and no one listening to the comms, she didn't mind admitting the truth. In fact the complete silence in her ear meant it had been turned off completely.

"I've never stopped loving you. No one else has ever made me feel safe and wanted. I've never had such a strong connection with anyone else. When I saw you again? I couldn't believe the gift I had been given. The hope of a second chance I didn't deserve."

Malik cocked an eyebrow before replying, "Should I take that seriously, or blame the pain medication? Because you deserve plenty."

Warmth crept along Violetta's cheeks as she lowered her eyes to the water. "Probably the pain medication, though I *was* the one who pushed you away. The one who didn't stay in touch after our night together."

"You had a lot to work through. I thought I added to that, which was the last intent I'd ever have."

A finger trailed around the curve of her ear, to the tip, then along the outer edge. She shivered in pleasure and looked up at him, even as he continued to trail the finger along her cheek, until it stopped in the middle of her chin.

"You weren't the only one afraid they would cause problems being a Halfer. I was afraid courting you would cause you even more problems. Despite my family's insistence that it wouldn't matter."

"So, we were both idiots?" she asked, a smile pulling at her lips. "I've confessed my feelings for you. What about you?"

"Loved you since I first saw you," he said, curling his finger under her chin. "It hasn't changed a bit."

Violetta felt as though she were floating on a cloud as she pushed back against the railing and turned to face Malik. He drew her into his arms, pulling her close before his lips descended upon hers.

Closing her eyes, she wilted against him as they kissed. One hand slid around his waist as the other dove into the hair at the nape of his neck. Her body felt as though it were on fire, and she couldn't be close enough to him.

The kiss began to deepen when the comms came back online and Mc'narrd's voice interrupted them.

"Sorry to interrupt," the admiral said. This time he actually sounded apologetic. "But we have police inbound to your location. I know you're both still wearing your biosuits. They aren't built for intimate occasions, so the fact that we are receiving your body stats means you're still clothed."

"Not built for intimate occasions," Malik grumbled. "Talk about a design flaw."

"We're on the deck, admiral," Violetta managed to say, her mind still on the kiss and the fact Malik still loved her. "Though going below deck doesn't sound like a bad idea."

"I hope you are more cognizant of the current situation, Malik," Mc'narrd drawled.

He definitely sounded like her father when he did that, Violetta noted with amusement.

"Her ribs are not up for anything that strenuous, nor is the harbormaster's abode the place for such dalliances."

"You're right, Mc'narrd," Malik replied, still looking at Violetta. His arm tightened slightly around her. "We can wait until we're elsewhere. The next safe house, perhaps."

"Get off the bloody deck now!" Mc'narrd bellowed.

Malik and Violetta winced. The comms didn't dampen sounds, so it was equal to him yelling into their ears.

"Why are they returning?" Violetta finally asked. "I thought you said they wouldn't come back."

"Good question." Mc'narrd practically growled the words. She wasn't certain if he was angry at them or the incoming police service. Or both. "I have a squadron heading to meet them there. Though Fr'osst will have to keep them at bay long enough for them to arrive. For now, get inside and keep out of sight."

The moment they stepped inside, Atos met them. The seriousness in his eyes didn't hamper the grin on his face.

"Come with me. There's a safer place for you to stay, in case things become dicey topside."

Malik and Violetta glanced at each other before nodding. They followed Atos into a lift that took them down. The silence grew as they descended into the belly of the floating island home. When the doors to the lift opened, Violetta gasped.

The room they stepped into was almost completely windows. Small sections of each wall held interfaces, showing camera angles of the entire abode. Everywhere else there were floor-to-ceiling windows that revealed the underwater life of the lake.

There were short counters a few feet from the windows with conforming chairs near them. There were also a few human rocking chairs and a plush bags children loved to flop in.

Violetta crossed to one of the windows just as a large thorkish swam by them. The turtle-like creature was as large as Violetta. The bioluminescent shell glittered in the soft glow of the lights around the outside of the ship-like home. Thorkish, Violetta knew, had retractable claws and preyed on fish, small mammals, and water birds. The larger the thorkish, the older the creature. They were considered a delicacy, and there was a limit on how many could be harvested per lake on the planet.

As with most creatures, multiple parts of the thorkish were used. The shells were turned into jewelry, the hides used for various items. Even the bones were used in handcrafted products.

Violetta watched as the thorkish snapped at a fish that swam in front of it, catching it in its mouth. With only a couple bites, the fish was swallowed and the thorkish swam away, in search of more food. In its place swam a lutrae with what looked like some sort of frog in its mouth. It was swimming towards the surface, probably to board the dock and eat its catch in relative peace.

"The kids love this room," Atos said as he crossed to one of the interfaces. "To be honest, they aren't the only ones."

"It's peaceful here," Malik said in a hushed tone. He crossed to the interface nearest Violetta. "And serene."

"And the safest place there," Mc'narrd added. "The room is reinforced. The lift doesn't work for anyone but those who live there and those of certain active military clearance levels."

Atos touched the interface. It sprang to life as he began keying in commands. The rest of the interfaces in the room changed to show the exterior of the main floor of the home.

One window, directly opposite the door, shifted until it revealed Commander Fr'osst as she stood on the bow of her home, hands clasped behind her in the standard parade-rest stance.

The windows had also been designed to be an interface. It was ingenious, in Violetta's opinion. She moved back until she could see the screen better. Malik stood beside her, their shoulders touching.

Gone was the pleasant, friendly demeanor Violetta associated with Jozelyn. In its place was a formidable expression that promised hox and damnation to any who dared to cross her path. Violetta was familiar with the expression, having seen it often on her father when he was ready to tear someone a few new orifices.

"We should know soon what is going on," Atos said, nodding to the interface. "Jozelyn is going to enjoy this thoroughly, I'm sure." At their confused expressions, he grinned boyishly. "The life of a harbormaster isn't as exciting as you may think. Her 'fun' comes from plucking the military from the water and watching Duels at the arenas on her off-time."

"And *he* knows I can hear him, also," Mc'narrd grumbled.

Two pin-points of light grew larger as a boat neared the floating island home. It was a marked police boat. Unlike the earlier HAV, it did not have fog lights. Nor did it have a cabin, like the larger police boats.

"That boat is usually used on the Nimkelu River," Violetta stated, recognizing the boat. "It's typically employed for short-distance duties."

The boat turned around and pulled up, so its bow met the bow of the harbormaster's home. They ignored the berths, choosing to pull it just feet from the main entrance.

Violetta likened it to someone pulling up to a person's front door, so they would have less distance to walk. Rude and unwelcomed, these two officers were already pushing their luck with their arrogance.

Atos smirked as he touched the screen. Lights flooded the home's wrap-around deck and dock. Every one of the lights was pointed towards the police boat. The pilot and passenger of the boat jerked their heads to the side, covering their eyes for a few moments.

"What do you want?" Jozelyn called out. She hadn't moved from her position and Violetta realized she was armed this time.

"We've come for the fugitives you're harboring," the pilot answered. "The 42nd District Police Service received vidclip evidence that you retrieved the fugitive Violetta Cq'linns and Malik Addelia, who is suspected of aiding her."

"You are on military property," Fr'osst replied, not moving. "Take a step onto my dock, and I will arrest you and hold you until the military arrives to collect your sorry asses."

"Ma'am, you're lucky we aren't putting shackles on you first," the second cop said. "Your cooperation would go far towards receiving lesser charges."

Atos's skittering humm filled the room. The K'laisian equivalent of snickering from a human.

"I don't think so. In fact, I know you won't be shackling anybody here," Commander Fr'osst countered. "This is *my* jurisdiction. I answer to our military command, which your commanding officer also answers to. To whom *you* answer, also."

"We have a warrant-" the second cop began.

"Which I can tear up, piss on the pieces, and laugh at, right in front of you," Jozelyn interjected. "Because unless and until you are accompanied by the military guard with clearance to see sensitive data, who would have a military warrant, you have nothing. My jurisdiction. My job. My home. And you've just worn out your welcome. Best if you push off and be on your way."

"We have vidclip evidence that a wanted criminal was on the east dock, and that you were present," the first cop continued, his voice getting louder and more insistent. "There is a warrant for her apprehension and any who aid her."

"Which you have yet to present," Fr'osst countered, her tone growing colder. "If I called it in, which I could do, some or all of your claim to be here on official business would fall apart. Last chance, children. Get. Off. My. Lake."

"You are impeding officers in the line of duty," the second cop declared.

He put one foot on the deck, while his partner began to withdraw a volt baton from his belt.

In the lower hold, Atos hummed loudly. "This is going to be amusing."

As the second cop was bringing his other foot to the deck, Jozelyn sprang forward. Using only her right thumb, she struck the closest cop in the middle of his chest and once against his neck below the ear. She pushed gently against his forehead, toppling him backward into the boat where he landed as an unconscious heap.

The remaining man stood still, in wide-eyed wonder. The volt baton remained in his hand but held at his side. He looked up at Jozelyn.

"I've got another thumb just for you," she declared. "If you take one more step towards this dock."

He hesitated and glanced between her and his partner laid out at the front of the boat. He dropped the baton and unholstered his service pistol. He brought the pistol up, sighting Fr'osst down the barrel, just as an energy bolt struck him in the head. He fell faster than his partner had dropped.

"About time you got here!" Jozelyn yelled at the lake.

A military HAV lowered silently beside the docked police boat. Five military servicemen in the standard purple and black camo suits could be seen. Two more HAVs lowered beside the first. None made a sound as they settled onto the lake. A total of thirteen men and women poured from the HAVs. A rifle was settled against the shoulder of one of the men who approached Fr'osst.

"Figured you'd want to have some fun before we stepped in, Commander," the man said cheerfully. "Good to see you again, Jozelyn."

"How's the family, Tarev?" Fr'osst asked, as the pair gripped shoulders. "Any leads on who sent these idiots out here?"

"Not yet," Tarev replied. He turned to his unit. "Cuff these two and confiscate their boat. The 42nd District Police Service can make a formal request for its return after we charge their officers."

Several of his unit jumped into the boat. Two began restraining the two unconscious officers. From the flopping of the bodies, Violetta suspected they weren't being gentle about it, either. Two others began searching the boat and moving items around until there was an empty space away from anything that could be used as a weapon.

"We'll be keeping patrol to head off any others that might think they can harass you," Tarev said. His white teeth flashed as he grinned. "We're due for some night maneuvers, anyway. Maybe we'll get lucky and find some more fish to catch."

"Good," Atos stated, nodding at the interface. "Maybe we can sleep without any more interruptions. Tarev and his squadron won't let anything through their perimeter. Not even a paddleboat."

He touched the interface again. The window shifted back to being a window again as the cameras returned to their prior positions. Once done, he turned the interface off and faced the pair. "I'll leave you two here for a while. The lift will go up without one of us with you. Don't make me regret this."

Without another word he entered the lift and vanished from sight, leaving them alone once more.

"About that radio silence, Admiral? Do we still get that?" Malik asked, wrapping his arms around Violetta once more. "Or was it nixed due to a pair of crooked cops?"

"No, you two still get your time," Mc'narrd replied. "If those suits go silent, I'll send Jozelyn and her mate down there without warning."

"We'll behave," Violetta murmured, snuggling into Malik's arms. "At the very least we'll keep our clothes on."

Mc'narrd's chuckle cut off as the comms went dead once again.

Malik turned Violetta around until she was facing him. His lips found hers and they kissed again. By the time the kiss ended, both were breathless and Violetta could tell her lips were swollen. She rested her head against his shoulder as he kissed the tip of her ear.

"You know this may not work?" he asked gently. When she stiffened, he kissed her temple. "Not because of anything on our part, Vi, but because of those around us."

Violetta felt as though her heart had dropped through the floor and was on its way to the bottom of the lake. "I don't care. I lost you once. I refuse to let it happen again."

"What about your job? Your dreams? Your desire to go up through the ranks until you're at the top?"

"Promotions are based on years of service, ethics, and performance. As long as I put in the years, don't receive any demerits, and pass the tests, I can continue rising through the ranks," she replied stubbornly.

"The Council is who places the Chief of Police, though," he argued. "And what about when you're questioned about my connection with Don Morelli?"

"What about your connection with the Don?" Violetta tried pushing away from him, but his arms tightened around her. Since she didn't want to test how healed her ribs were, she didn't fight but so hard. "Your record is shockingly clean, Malik. I don't know what you've done, but that's what matters to the police service. If they want more? They'll have to go through the proper channels to get clearance."

"I'd swear you were telling the truth, except I know for a fact you know more than that." Malik narrowed his eyes. "When did you become so adept at lying?"

"I've always had that talent. I never bothered using it with you until now. But am I wrong?"

"No, though I can't say I'm happy about how easily you can lie." He sighed, but didn't give up. Instead, he continued pressing. "Have you forgotten how our society thinks? How most of the Halfers mate with natives? Or don't have children? I know you, Vi. You've always wanted children. You've always wanted a family."

"What I want, what you want, holds no threat to our society. That should be far more important than anything our society currently expects we should do," Violetta said, trying to push away from him again. This time, she managed to be able to push back far enough to look in his eyes. No further. "One of the highest admirals in our military approves of us, Malik. You've seen how we're treated by those with some of the highest security clearance our world offers. If anyone cared about 'keeping the blood pure' it would be our military."

"Fine. What about any child we might have? Have there even been any other children by Halfers? I haven't heard of any. There has to be a reason for that, Violetta."

"Why would the public know about it, even if there have been?" she countered. "I. Do. Not. Care. I love you, Malik. I'm not turning my back on us because of what narrow-minded bigots think or because of idiots who don't think I won't do my job simply because we're together."

"Oh, so you'd arrest me?"

"Yeah. I'd arrest you if you did something to warrant it. So don't make me!"

"Tu sei l'unico per me," Malik said, pulling her against him.

Violetta melted against him, wrapping her arms tightly around him. Tears formed in her eyes and she squeezed them shut.

You're the only one for me.

He had said those words that night five years ago. She hadn't truly realized he meant it then. But she knew he meant it now.

"You are my life. My everything," she whispered in their native language. Words spoken for centuries from one mate to another. "No matter what comes, I will not leave. Not again."

"You'd just arrest me," Malik teased, brightening the mood. She laughed even as he kissed her nose. "That's my lady. Just so we are clear, I am not planning on leaving your side. We will have to be cautious and wary."

"I suppose you moving in with me wouldn't be a good idea once my name is cleared," she said with a sigh.

"Well, not right away." He grinned. "Maybe in a year or so, once people figure out we're not trying to use each other."

"Oh, no. I plan on using you. Just not in the way most people will be thinking."

Chapter Twenty Two

The following morning, Malik and Violetta joined the rest of the Fr'osst family for a late brunch. Both children were sitting at the table, arguing over the fruit and cheeses and what paired together the best. Malik handed Violetta a plate and she filled it with poached eggs, fried protein, fruits, and cheeses.

"Would you like some jakka?" Jozelyn asked.

"Please," Violetta replied, looking up at the woman.

Atos handed her a mug of jakka. "How are you feeling?"

"Better. The side only aches if I rub it."

"Finish up, you two," Jozelyn said to the children. "You have classwork."

Avesa made a face. "It's not fair. Schools are closed, but we still have to do work."

All of the adults exchanged amused expressions.

"I forgot the schools would be closed when the krishii were called out," Malik said thoughtfully.

"Did you ever have to do classwork if school was closed?" Avesa asked.

Violetta nodded. "Even when I missed school due to illness or injury."

"Ugh. Yeah. Same with us," the young woman replied, grabbing a handful of berries. "Come on, Alekel. I'll help you with your work." She turned to her mother. "Can we do it in the fish tank?"

"Sure. Just don't take all day to do it. Say farewell to Malik and Violetta. Their ride will be here shortly," Fr'osst said.

The two children rose and bowed deeply to them before bidding them a safe journey. Malik and Violetta replied in kind and watched as they left the room.

"You must be very proud of them," Violetta said, dropping some honey cubes into her jakka.

"Usually. Though they have their moments," Atos joked. "The supply drop will be here within the hour. It will take you to the base. The manhunt for you hasn't been called off, but once you get to the base, you'll be safe."

"The cruiser coming to pick you up is a military cargo HAV," Fr'osst explained. "The admiral is very insistent you get to the base as soon as possible."

"Do you think they'll call off the hunt?" Malik asked, as he delved into his plate of food.

Atos shook his head. "Nah. They're too determined to find her. Someone high in the command chain is behind all this."

Violetta didn't look up. She remained intent upon the food in front of her.

"Why do you say that?" Malik asked.

"We've all been part of a larger organization. I'm a marine biologist, but I spent plenty of time in the military and around it. The scientific community has its own rankings and political maneuverings. You were set up from the start, detective. We all know that. Someone had to command those fools to come out here." Atos paused and drained his mug. "Keep your wits about you and keep that sidearm in reach until this is completely over."

"You're going to make her paranoid of everyone around her," Jozelyn chided her husband.

"Are you saying I'm wrong?" Atos asked, his eyes settling on his wife.

Jozelyn sighed and looked away from her mate. "No. I can't say you're wrong."

"My father ingrained a hefty dose of paranoia in me," Violetta rejoined. "So an intelligent reminder is welcome. It will keep me from growing complacent."

"Do you have any thoughts about who might be running this?" Malik asked before taking another bite of his food.

"It has to be higher up than sergeants and lieutenants," Jozelyn said. "Perhaps there is a corporate sponsor? Are there any businesses, domestic or alien, that would stand to benefit from her being out of the police service?"

"Not to lower your importance, detective, but should we presume that she's the primary target?" Atos asked. "What if she's a target of opportunity?"

"A distraction, you mean," Violetta said.

"She had evidence against members of her own precinct, and was taking such to the chief," Malik argued. "Are you thinking the chief was guilty, also?"

"It's possible. Perhaps he was considering turning on the others? To save his tail, cut a deal, or even to act as though he were innocent?" Atos shrugged. "Granted, there is motivation to stop her specifically. To make sure the evidence is not received by those who can and will prosecute police servicemen who abuse their responsibilities and authority."

He paused long enough to refill his mug and return to the table.

"But, if someone has devised a way to convincingly frame an officer so that her own comrades-in-arms are hunting her? Bringing out the krishii to find her? These are extreme measures. Such planning and unquestioned use of resources takes time, effort, and preparation. Why would they go to all that trouble just to silence Detective

Cq'linns? It would have been easier to kill her before she got to the chief, make it look like any number of violent crimes this city witnesses on a regular basis."

Silence greeted his observation.

Violetta couldn't argue his words. From the grim expression on Malik's face, he was thinking similarly.

Atos cleared his throat. "I apologize. I have a tendency to say everything on my mind before I can shut my mouth."

"No, it's not that," Violetta assured Atos. "What you've suggested makes far too much sense."

"Unfortunately, we cannot reveal more details," Malik said. "What is troubling is that even with the information we now have, your theory holds strong. The means by which Vi has been framed were undoubtedly costly and required a great deal of time to test and implement. Who knows if anyone else has been framed by this method? Held accountable for actions they truly did not do?"

"That last pair of questions may never be answered," Fr'osst mused. "Even when the guilty are brought to answer for the crimes."

Violetta smiled at the harbormaster.

"You said *when*, not *if*, they are."

"That is correct, detective. I have every confidence you will succeed."

A chime sounded and Jozelyn pulled out a pocket interface. "Your ride is approaching. Come on and I'll introduce you."

Fifteen minutes later, Violetta and Malik were sitting in a small cabin below the deck of the supply cruiser. The only piece of furniture in the cabin was a padded bench half the length of the vessel. Sitting on it, the only noise was the soft hum of the engine and the splashing of waves against the hull.

"This is rather cozy, isn't it?" Malik asked, pulling Violetta to him.

She went willingly. "It is rather pleasant." After a few moments of silence, she asked, "Can I ask a silly question?"

"You haven't already?" he returned.

"Fair enough," she admitted. "Do you still enjoy going to concerts and the theater? Or the solstice celebrations?"

"I do. Though usually I can't enjoy them because they're part of my job."

"That's a shame." She paused. "I've only been going when Issik made me."

"Didn't you used to go to them all the time?"

She shrugged. "Yes, but after Dad died, and you weren't there, they lost their appeal."

"There is a concert next week," Malik stated. "Would you go with me?"

"We'll have to make sure your clearance has been renewed by then," Mc'narrd chimed in.

"You can get it done that quickly?" Violetta nudged Malik, then added, "Why is it so important he has his security clearance renewed to be around me?"

"Because your clearance was not low or even mid-grade. Since Malik is obviously courting you, and I doubt even we could keep you two apart, it's easier to simply renew his security clearance and deal with the difference in levels later. It's standard for those who are mates, due to the knowledge the mate, or potential mate, may view."

Mc'narrd laughed. "You truly did not know, did you? No one ever informed you that your father had a high security clearance, did they? That the data on his console was so sensitive."

"Not in the least," Violetta grumbled. "Anything else I should know that no one bothered to tell me?"

Mc'narrd laughed again. "I'm certain there will be more. As for the security clearance, it can be done within seventy-two hours, if we had to. We just prefer to have longer. Remember, detective, we aren't starting with a new recruit. Malik's clearance expired only a couple years ago. We've kept a watch on him and he hasn't done anything to cause us concern or worry. His renewal should go fairly smoothly and quickly."

"In other words, you have an extensive file on me," Malik stated, not sounding worried. "That's fine. I haven't done anything that would jeopardize my clearance."

"I know," Mc'narrd replied. "We'll set up a time for you to come in for everything required. Before your date next week."

"Would you be interested in going to one of the arenas?" Malik asked, turning the conversation back to them.

"I wouldn't object," Violetta said. She wasn't certain how well she would enjoy the Duels, but she wanted to see what he did as Master of Ceremonies. "I may not be a fan, but that won't stop me from watching you."

"She'll be your biggest fan," Mc'narrd said drolly.

"I am going to be so glad when I can give this comm back to you," Malik retorted. "Maybe then we can have a normal conversation."

"We will discuss that, also."

"I'm starting to think that he wants to keep close tabs on us," Violetta joked.

"It does seem so," Malik replied. "We will have to remember to send a gift basket during the next solstice celebration."

That got a bark of laughter from Mc'narrd.

They chuckled and began talking of the concerts and theatrical productions they had seen within the last several years. Mc'narrd, thankfully, remained silent as they talked. After some time, Violetta didn't know how long, a knock from above signaled they had arrived.

A marked military truck awaited them near the docks. Within minutes, Violetta and Malik, wearing their hooded trench coats, were on their way to the base surrounded by a military squadron. The trip was fast, silent, and uneventful. The moment the truck parked and the back opened, Violetta and Malik were escorted into the base itself.

Once they were inside, they removed their hoods and Violetta looked around. Her eyes rose to the sea glass windows, a smile curving her lips.

A private dashed from a set of doors and skidded to a stop in front of them. He bowed low before speaking. "If you follow me, I will escort you."

He didn't wait for a reply, instead turning and walking away briskly.

"Good thing my ribs are healed," Violetta murmured to Malik.

He nodded, but remained silent. His eyes darted around, taking in everything they passed.

Finally, after going through several doorways and corridors, the private touched an interface. The door slid open and he stepped to the side, gesturing for Violetta and Malik to enter.

"If you need anything, just use the interface," he said, bowing yet again.

Malik and Violetta gave a nod and entered the room. Issik waited for them there, a glass of water in his hand.

"Took them long enough to extract you. I've been here since breakfast." Issik held up his glass. "The jakka is worse here than at the station house. I almost tried that Earther coffee. Would have, if you didn't show in the next five minutes."

"Why are you here?" Violetta asked, debating if she should embrace him or not. "Did you hear about the pair of officers who grievously forgot the military is a higher authority than the police service?"

"Not by the gossip at any of the stations," Issik said. "The only reason I know anything is because I frequent the right jakka bar. The rookie who had to write the reports on them was complaining to a pretty server."

"What was the gossip?" Violetta asked.

"The krishii lost your scent at the lake. One is still angry about it. Then a corpse report comes attached to a Duel assessment over one Sergeant Ziph Rc'dollph, who was Challenged by public enemy number one, also known as you. Vidclip file is also attached, and everything is green and clean about the Duel and his demise. Few shed tears over his loss. But, somehow, some way, two officers who trained under Ziph and Captain Monroe find themselves the keys to one of the few police boats and go out on the lake to harass the harbormaster. The rest is pure entertainment as far as I am concerned."

"That was rather amusing to watch," Violetta admitted. "But why are you here? I'm glad to see you, don't get me wrong. But isn't it risky for you? Everyone and their child must suspect I'm receiving assistance from the military by now."

"This stuff isn't all over the news sources or even the gossip sites on the subnet, Violetta," Issik said. "Only police know and most only know a little. Your image is on the 'wanted for questioning' ads everywhere, yes, but that's as far as the information stream runs for this city. As for why am I here?"

He fished around in a jacket pocket, pulled out a tiny evidence sack, and dropped it in front of her. Inside was a single shackle key. Police issued, with a serial number. White powder highlighted the partial thumb and forefinger prints.

"It's our captain's. Found it stuck between the cushion and seat frame of the chair facing the Chief's last living location," Issik explained.

"The results from the prints on the token returned, as well," Mc'narrd added over the comms. "They also match Captain Monroe."

"So, everything points to the captain. I wish I could say I was surprised, but I'm not." Violetta's eyes did not leave the bag. "Did you ever receive the report from Nualith? Weren't the results due today? Or was it yesterday? Stars, I can't keep up anymore."

"You?" Issik asked, his tone incredulous. "The person who has always known exactly what day it was? Could probably tell you what rotation of the moon we were in?" He rounded on Malik, his eyes glinting and furious. "What the fark have you been doing, Addelia? I knew you two were close. That she's been pining over you since she joined the service. But by the stars and seas, if you've done anything to jeopardize her…"

A low whistle came over the comms followed by Mc'narrd's voice. "Do we need to send in spec ops? Didn't realize Issik was such a self-appointed guardian." There was a pause, then a thoughtfully said, "Or did someone else send him to watch over you?"

"I don't need more to worry about." Violetta all but growled under her breath.

Mc'narrd answered with a deep, loud humming.

"Nothing she hasn't asked me to do," Malik retorted. Before Issik could make a counter argument, he answered Violetta's question. "Nualith contacted the military the moment the test results were finished. While you were resting, Mc'narrd informed me of the results. Your sidearm came back clean. Tests revealed it hadn't been used since the last time you were on the range. Qualifying is what those reports declared. Over three months ago."

"Thank you," Violetta said, ignoring Issik's growing irritation.

"How do you plan on handling this, Ha'kksworth?" Malik asked.

"It will take time to get everything together," Violetta interjected. She met Issik's glower. "I'll have to make out a report, complete with copies of the vidclips of the dirty officers and proof of the weapon they used to frame me. We will also need a copy of Nualith's report."

"You'll be safe on the base," Issik grumbled, tucking the sack back into his pocket. "Contact me when you're ready to go to… who do you plan on taking this to? The DA? Governor? Or are you planning on just going to the Military Overseer?"

"The DA," Violetta said without hesitation. "It should go to the DA. So we can follow the typical chain of command. No need to make people hate me more than they already do because of the military's involvement with this."

The district attorney typically made the reports that were sent to the military oversight committee for the police service, regardless of the district. She was determined to do everything by the book and follow the typical steps for presenting a case. Otherwise, it may appear she was using her father's name and influence to get what she wanted.

"Let me know when you want me to go with you," Issik declared. His glower didn't diminish as he glanced back at Malik. "There's one other thing you need to know about."

"What?" Violetta asked, not liking his tone.

"The new Chief of Police is Endn Ta'natha."

"Oh, fark," Violetta breathed. She stared at Issik in disbelief. "You have to be joking."

Issik shook his head slowly. "I wouldn't joke about anything like that, Violetta."

"Who is Ta'natha?" Malik asked, stepping closer to Violetta.

"He was a captain. I don't remember which department, though. Narcotics, maybe?" Issik nodded and Violetta continued. "He's part of the sector that believes anyone of mixed heritage should mate with only fellow natives. To remove the 'impurities' of the Earthers and 'return strength to the native bloodline'."

"He doesn't care how a job is done, as long as it gets results," Issik added, not hiding his disgust. "And if you're someone of mixed heritage? He does everything he can, while keeping it just barely legal, to make you miserable."

"Remember what we talked about, Vi?" Malik asked, his voice gentle. "Are you sure?"

"My performance speaks for itself," she replied stubbornly. "I've weathered worse storms. I'll get through this."

"You could always Challenge him," Issik stated, half jokingly. "Just be ready when you return. Especially if you and your friend there decide to make your feelings for each other known."

"I have to get back first," Violetta replied.

"If a large portion of the police service will need to be replaced, where do those officers come from?" Malik asked suddenly. "We know of a captain, lieutenant, and a now-dead sergeant that belonged to homicide. They will require replacement. From the vidclips on that data chip, there weren't a small number of dirty cops."

Issik gave him a thoughtful look. "If something disastrous happens, something that takes out a large number of officers, replacements come from the military while the academy makes an appeal to the public. They sometimes make their recruitment deals better to draw more people into the service."

"So, the very people who are currently assisting her will enter the very place where she currently works," Malik said.

"Basically, yes," Issik replied, nodding. "She should have more allies on her side after the investigations and cleanup is done."

"That will help, certainly," Violetta admitted. "Thank you. I'll be in touch. Or, someone will be in touch when I have everything gathered to take to the DA."

Issik nodded, grasped her shoulder, then left. He shot a final glower at Malik.

Violetta turned to Malik. "You're still stuck with me. If you haven't changed your mind," she said. "We will just need to be even more cautious now."

"Not gonna happen, Vi," Malik reassured her. He slid his hand into hers and drew her closer to him. "We'll have to go slow, that's all."

The door slid open again and the private stood in the threshold once more. His eyes shifted between the two, and a smirk flashed across his face. "If you will follow me, please?"

This time he did wait for them to follow, taking them further into the depths of the base. She and Malik remained silent as they walked beside each other, their fingers still entwined.

As they turned a corner, the private slowed his pace. A male native with silver hair and eyes stood at the end of the hallway beside a frosted glass door.

"Thank you, private," the man said. "I am Loros Wc'kinns, liaison for the K'lais military. There are… guests who wish to speak with you."

Violetta looked at Malik then back to the liaison. She had no idea who he could be talking about.

"Okay?" she said, when it seemed he was waiting for an answer.

The liaison opened the door, entering first. Violetta and Malik followed him into the eerily silent room. When the liaison stepped to the side, Violetta faltered in her steps.

Four humans in flight suits stood next to the table that all but filled the room. Violetta recognized each person, but it was the patch on the shoulders that had her standing in stunned silence.

The patch was in the shape of a teardrop with a sharp point at the bottom. The hood of a cobra-like snake vanished into the curving sides of the tear drop. The top jaw of the snake's mouth had sharp teeth jutting down. The snake's body curled around, forming the bottom jaw. Violetta would have recognized it anywhere.

These four humans, two men and two women, were members of the Serpent's Fangs mercenary unit.

Her mother's mercenary unit.

"Violetta?" Malik asked quietly. He placed a hand on her shoulder. "You know them?"

She could only nod. Her mouth refused to open or form words. The mercs were the last people she would have expected to ever meet at the military base.

"Allow me to introduce Victoria Delacruz," Loros said. "Commander of the mercenary unit called the Serpent's Fangs."

"Thank you. We can handle everything from here," Victoria said to Loros.

Victoria was a tall, solidly built woman with honey blonde hair that was starting to silver, and classically beautiful features. She met Loros's gaze with hard, steel gray eyes.

Loros bowed low before leaving without another word.

"Damn, Tori," one of the men said. "Did you have to be so harsh to the guy?"

Victoria elbowed him in the side. "Keep it up and you'll be cleaning the toilets."

"Again," the other woman quipped. Her curly red hair swayed as she turned towards Victoria. Laughter brightened her vivid emerald green eyes. "I'm starting to think he enjoys it."

"I believe we're ignoring our young friends. Violetta knows us, but her companion does not," the other man said. His blue eyes sparkled with laughter. "I'm Raymond

Schwartz. The other joker there is Nathaniel McLeod. Stella Araceli is the fiery redhead with a temper to match."

"They…" Violetta trailed off, trying to figure out the right words. She paused, drew a breath, and let it out slowly. "They're my mother's mercenary unit. Or rather, she was a member of their unit."

"You seem surprised," Malik stated, not looking away from the group of humans.

"That's because I am! They aren't usually around unless it's during Poaching Season. For the longest time, I only knew they were Mom's friends."

Victoria shrugged. "Didn't think it was important. We wanted you to know us as individuals, not as mercs. Eventually, we knew you'd figure it out, and you did."

"What are you doing here?" Violetta asked. "You're usually not around this time of the year."

"Your grandparents contacted us when the shit hit the fan," Stella replied. "They hired us to come help."

"Yeah, we made a beeline for K'lais the moment we got the message," Raymond added. "Took longer than we wanted, though. By the time we got here, your military pals had jumped in." He ran a hand through his curly black hair, his piercing blue eyes flicking from Violetta to Malik. "Didn't expect to have the military intercept us. Let alone invite us to the base."

"Neither did her grandparents," Nathaniel added. He leaned against the wall, arms folded across his chest. The tallest of the group at just over six-feet, he was wide-shouldered and muscled. He wore his light brown hair shorn close to his scalp and dark eyes hid whatever he was thinking. "They knew you'd gone into hiding, but nothing else. Couldn't even get answers from their old military pals.

We figured Morelli was helping. Never expected your dad's pals to be helping out. Or keeping it close to their chests."

"You were hired by Violetta's grandparents to come and help her," Malik asked skeptically. All of the mercenaries nodded. "Why?"

Victoria laughed. The smile made her appear far more approachable and younger. "They wanted her to come out on top. Since they couldn't do anything publicly, without causing problems for them or her, they did the next best thing: they hired mercenaries who could do whatever was needed."

"We mercs get a little more leeway than most," Stella chimed in, her eyes twinkling with mischief. "And we don't mind Dueling."

"They aren't lying," Mc'narrd said over the comms. "Your grandparents claim they contacted the Fangs to inform them of what was occurring, and offered to pay for their travel to the planet. As well as reimburse them for any missed work, since they were certain the Fangs would want to assist Kali's only daughter."

"But… what can you do now that the military has stepped in?" Violetta asked. "How long will you stay?"

"Oh, we're staying until this is over. Maybe stick around a while to refuel and restock the ship," Stella said cheerfully. "We volunteered to shadow you and be your bodyguards or escort, but the military shot it down. Said they could handle it without our 'interference'. We plan on seeing how many bars we can drink dry since we're still getting paid, even if we aren't allowed to help you."

"Ah, fark," Mc'narrd said with a groan. "I'll have to arrange at least two squadrons to follow them around, now."

"Who's the friend?" Victoria asked, turning her attention to Malik.

Nathaniel pushed away from the wall. "He's not a native. Not a full-blood one, anyway. Pure bloods have silver or gold eyes."

"Wait. Vrehn often talked about a boy close in age to Violetta." Raymond studied Malik. "Mixed heritage like her. Said they were besties. Always encouraging each other."

"No, no, that's not right," Stella interrupted, a brilliant grin revealing white teeth. "Vrehn said the boy would try to talk her out of doing dumb shit and she'd do it anyway. Always gave the poor kid hell for it." She snorted. "As though anyone could talk Kali out of doing anything. It always ended up in encouraging her to do it that much more. Seems like the apple didn't fall far from that tree."

"Malik," Victoria said suddenly. "You're Malik. About time you two got together." She gave him a once-over before nodding. "I think Kali would approve."

"Thanks," Malik grumbled. "Nice to know you approve."

"If we didn't, we'd have to kill you," Raymond retorted.

Violetta couldn't tell if he was serious or not. Mc'narrd, however, gave a bark of laughter.

Raymond grinned. "Good to meet you. Glad she's finally got someone on the planet to watch her back again." His eyes swept over Malik. "Explains why she never mentioned you sooner, too."

"In all seriousness, though," Victoria interrupted, her voice turning grim. The other three straightened, responding to her tone. "We've been updated on everything that's happened. Nothing your military is doing makes sense. Haven't you wondered why they've taken such a keen interest in you?"

"They've explained it," Malik said. "Unlike many worlds, our military doesn't have malicious intentions towards its people."

All four mercenaries rolled their eyes and wore equally disgusted expressions.

"Malicious or not, it's not typical for them to take such a keen interest in one person. Why would someone who is probably the highest-ranking admiral in this world's military take a personal interest in one police officer?" Nathaniel lifted his chin, meeting Malik's gaze evenly. "Her father may have been one for the history books, but he wasn't the only one. Don't see your military taking an interest in the kids of those people."

"Look, we're not saying that your military has fiendish designs," Stella interjected, as she placed her hands on the table and leaned forward. Considering she was five-foot nothing, it shouldn't have been intimidating, yet it was. Violetta attributed it to her grim expression and the hardness in her eyes. "All we're saying is that it isn't normal. There's an ulterior motive at play. Whether it's because you're Vrehn's daughter, they owe your father and this is how they're repaying it, or it's something else? No one but they know."

"We're going to be on planet until your name is cleared," Raymond said. "Our plans are to stick around for a few days after it's over. We hoped you'd have a drink with us and catch up." His gaze slid to Malik. "You can come, too."

Chuckling, Violetta crossed the room. "I would enjoy that."

Victoria pulled her into a tight hug. The others moved closer, waiting their turn. Once hugs were exchanged, Victoria draped an arm around Violetta's shoulder. "What about it, Malik? Want to join us for a drink before we head back out?"

Shaking his head, Malik crossed to the group. He held a hand out for a more traditional human handshake. Victoria took it and shook his hand with what Violetta knew would be a firm grip.

"I think I'd enjoy that," he said, smiling.

Chapter Twenty Three

Violetta and Malik chatted with the Fangs for several hours. They laughed and teased each other and welcomed Malik into their 'family'. Once the mercs bid their farewells, for the time being at least, the liaison Loros returned.

"I won't be able to join you until later," Mc'narrd said over the comms. "For now, you can enjoy the amenities of the base, within reason."

"Does that mean I can't steal a ship for a quick ride around the moon?" Violetta asked, feigning disappointment.

Mc'narrd snorted. Loros chuckled.

"I guess that's a negative," Malik replied. "Pity. Could have been fun."

"Perhaps we can offer other forms of entertainment?" Loros offered. "There is the gym, as well as an indoor pool. We also have a rec room with other forms of enjoyment."

A sly smile curled Violetta's lips. "A gym you say? Does the gym still offer sparring equipment?"

"Of course," Loros replied.

"You're certain you're up for sparring, Vi?" Malik asked, nodding to her side.

She raised a single brow. "Unless you're planning on wrestling or hand-to-hand sparring, I think I will be okay."

"The wrestling I have in mind wouldn't be on a mat in a gym," Malik replied, a gleam in his eyes that had her pulse racing. And a lot of memories returning.

Loros coughed. "Indeed. If you two will follow me, I'll take you to the gym. I presume you both are familiar with the base and can find your way around once I deposit you at the gym?"

"Yes," they said together.

"Very well. If you require assistance, please let me know. There are interfaces available in the gym, or you can request me over your comms."

They made non-committal sounds, but otherwise remained silent as Loros led them to the gym. Once they neared the doors, he bowed and returned the way they had come. The doors slid open soundlessly and Malik gestured for Violetta to enter before him.

The gym was easily nine hundred meters squared and had two levels above ground. Violetta was vaguely familiar with the gym, having visited it on rare occasions.

The main area of the first level above ground was used for physical activities; boxing, sparring, and the like. Around the main area were rooms dedicated to sports that required enclosed areas, as well as activities that did better in small groups. Including battle simulators. The second floor was exercise equipment, as well as a small indoor track. There was a small open area in the middle of the upper floor, centered directly above the mats, allowing those above to look down and watch the sparring below, provided no one was running around the track.

A third level was below ground and used as a shooting range. That level was divided in half. One half was used for rifles and sidearms. The other half was used for more ancient-styles, such as bows, and weaponry that could be thrown. The indoor pool and saunas were to the far left, in an adjacent building.

Malik and Violetta headed for the cabinets against the far wall, passing a couple dozen military personnel in field suits. Two mats covered the floor in front of the cabinets.

She suspected the equipment was in the cabinets, and was proven correct when Malik opened the one in the corner.

Multiple practice swords of various sizes, styles, and lengths hung in rows. Violetta reached for one and removed it from its designated spot. She hefted it before backing away.

Moving away from Malik, she swung it a few times to test the weapon's weight. It felt comfortable in her grip and was perfectly balanced. She held it out, peering down the length of the blade, checking to ensure it was straight. The edges, though keen, were not sharp enough to cut.

When she looked up, she saw Malik doing the same. She nodded and he closed the cabinet. Shrugging out of the coat, she dropped it beside the cabinet. Malik did the same.

They moved into the center of the mat nearest them and saluted each other. So far, no one was paying them close attention. They were just two more visitors to the gym. They still wore casual clothing, which garnered a few curious looks from those on the first floor. Not that Violetta was concerned.

"Standard rules? Fight until one of us yields?" Malik asked, holding the sword beside him.

"To the victor, the spoils," Violetta said with a nod. She gave him a wicked grin. "We can decide on what the spoils will be later."

Angling the blade towards him, Malik's smile was pure mischief as he tapped his blade against hers. He flipped his down and she tapped hers against his. An old tradition between the pair ever since they'd begun sparring, then Dueling together. Something they'd always done, no matter what.

A promise and a vow of honor and friendship.

Violetta was delighted he'd remembered, and even happier that he was continuing it.

Malik nodded and they saluted again before adopting their preferred fighting stances. He stood poised, knees slightly bent, but otherwise not different from his usual stance. Violetta smiled and mirrored him.

They stood, staring at each other, waiting for the other to make the first move. When Malik didn't move towards her, she frowned and took the initiative. Stepping forward, she brought her sword down in a slashing motion. Malik brought his up, meeting hers. Their weapons clanged and she grinned. Malik, however, wore a solemn expression.

She turned the blade, pushing back and sliding hers off in a swooping circular motion. When she brought it back up, he met it easily. Pushing away, she took a step back. He was still holding back. It was going to be a very boring, unexciting, and painfully joyless fight if he didn't at least try to fight back.

A plan began forming as she brought her blade up, towards his throat. He blocked it, again, pushing back before sweeping his weapon down towards her stomach. She blocked the swing, but she could tell he was worrying too much about hurting her.

Making a huffing sound, she swung the sword up. He met it easily. She pushed against his blade, pivoting with him. As they moved, she turned, sweeping her blade down and around. Her blade slapped against his hip as she slid behind him on light feet.

"That doesn't count as a hit," Malik snapped. His eyes narrowed as he turned to face her.

"No, but it was fun," Violetta quipped, saluting him with her sword. "Don't like it? Do something about it."

It was the right thing to say, for Malik's eyes flared to life with fire and challenge. His fingers tightened around the hilt and he slid into a more defensive posture. Violetta smirked as he lowered his chin and went at her.

She parried his first three thrusts with a few steps and a couple small movements of her sword. Apparently it was a warm-up, for his strikes sped up. Malik had gone on the offensive, and now she was on the defensive. As he brought his sword around and down, she was a little too slow to completely block his attack. His sword tapped her on the side, and he gave her a wicked grin.

"That was a proper hit," he teased.

"So it was," she replied, sliding back a few steps to place room between them.

It was then she noticed they had garnered a crowd. Moving until they were in their starting positions, if not on the opposite sides, she tipped her head towards those watching them. Malik followed her eyes and chuckled.

"Guess they finally figured it out," he murmured.

Her eyes darted above them and she nodded. "They're watching above us, too."

"Indeed," he said, darting in once again.

She was quick-pressed to block the onslaught of strikes, but she did. If not with ease then with efficiency. It had been a few years since she'd had to use a sword against someone as skilled as him, but not all knowledge had departed her.

Malik brought his sword in, and she blocked it, pushing it to the side. It left her right side open, but he didn't take advantage of it. She hopped back, glowering at him, before moving in again. He met her blade, the swords clanging between them. He pushed her back, sliding her sword around until he was able to maneuver his beneath hers.

With a sharp movement up, he knocked her sword from her hand. It skittered across the mat.

There was a collective sound of awe from their audience, and Violetta's eyes burned.

Before Malik could bring his sword around, she moved in close to him. Drawing her arm back, she punched him in the face. Just as she had in second grade, after he had punched the bully. This time she punched him with more force, and her whole weight by swinging with her hips.

Just as her father had later taught her.

As he stumbled back, Violetta snatched the sword from him. With a twist of her wrist, she settled the blade at his throat. Applause and cheering erupted, filling the gym with a near-deafening roar.

"What the farking hox, Malik?" She lowered the sword, furious. "You gave up an advantage! You, of all people, should know better!"

"I didn't want to reinjure your ribs." He rubbed his face. "How would that be fair?"

"I want a rematch. You owe me a rematch."

"Fine. But not until after you're cleared by a Healer." Malik picked up the sword Violetta had lost. "You really *haven't* changed much. No wonder you haven't been Challenged in the last five years."

"Oh, I was in the academy. A few times at the station. They just weren't as good as you. And I *did* say I was skilled. The admiral even said I was skilled." She offered him his sword, which he took with a short bow. "We just didn't say how skilled. I doubt the admiral would've said that if he didn't know my skill level."

"You are aware you've just defeated the Master of Ceremonies in a sparring match. In front of witnesses,"

Malik stated. He didn't sound concerned, only amused. "I am not certain I will ever live this down."

"We can always return here for our next match," Violetta stated formally, bowing to him. "Perhaps we can even give warning, so you can have plenty of witnesses for it, Bures'o Addelia."

"Are you certain you want that many people witnessing your defeat?" Malik shot back as he returned the swords to the cabinet. "It could be rather embarrassing."

"That depends on if you plan to actually give a worthy fight the next time," Violetta returned.

"If you two have finished, I can meet you now," Mc'narrd's voice cut in. "If an audience is what you desire, I can arrange it. In fact, I may sell tickets."

Violetta and Malik laughed as they collected their coats. They turned to find their audience had dispersed, though it was impossible to not notice many were standing in small groups, talking. As they crossed the gym floor, several called out congratulations to Violetta, or teased Malik.

For perhaps one of the few times in her life, Violetta felt extremely self-conscious. She brushed a strand of hair behind her ears, a smile plastered on her face. Malik, on the other hand, replied with easy remarks, comfortable with the attention he received.

He leaned closer to her. "This is just a taste of what it will be like when your name becomes associated with mine. It will start when the civilians begin to notice you, and then more so when they see you with me."

Violetta waited until they had left the gym and were alone in the hallways before replying. "How do you do it? How did you even become accustomed to the attention?"

"The only way you would get accustomed to it is if you're foolish enough to start enjoying it or expecting it," he explained. "So the best way I've discovered is to accept it, remembering that it won't last. I try to be gracious, even thankful for how I'm received by beings I don't know. There are, of course, many occurrences when the attention is poorly timed and unwanted. You have to expect it, plan for it, and appreciate it when you are away from it."

"How long did it take you?" she asked, slipping her hand into his and squeezing it.

Malik gave her a troubled expression, and the smirk he gave was apologetic. "I'm still working on it."

"Will you hate me if I say that makes me feel better?"

"Not at all. You're the only being I've told that to."

"I wouldn't have guessed. You don't show it. In fact, you seem comfortable with the attention." Violetta paused. "Did the admiral tell us where we're supposed to meet him?

"He didn't tell me, so I'm presuming no," Malik said.

"Meet me in the room where you spoke with Issik," Mc'narrd said over the comms.

"That answers that question," Violetta muttered.

Picking up their pace, they made their way to the designated room. They let go of each other's hands as they neared the door, which opened ahead of them. Inside stood Mc'narrd, wearing the same clothing as the first time they'd met. A helmet sat on the table.

"I presume you still have the data chips," he stated without preamble. Violetta nodded. "Good. Please use the interface here to make the needed copies of the data on the replicating weapon, as well as the evidence you have against the 42nd District's police officers."

Crossing the room, she settled into a chair. When she removed the poker chips from her boot, Mc'narrd chuckled. She glanced at him, but he didn't say anything.

Beside the interface were black chips with a silver diamond in the center. She picked it up, and turned it in her hand before looking at Mc'narrd with a confused expression.

"Those have a larger storage capacity than any commercial chip," Mc'narrd explained. "You won't have any trouble copying everything onto a single one. Don't worry, though. They can be read on any standard interface."

"One for you and one for the district attorney?" Malik asked, taking a seat opposite Violetta.

"Exactly." Mc'narrd turned around and his fingers flew over the interface in the room. The comms in their ears went silent. When he faced them again, he crossed his arms over his chest. "Now that you're both here, and the lines are dead for the next thirty minutes, I can share some information with you."

"Let me guess," Malik interrupted. "It has to do with how the police service knew we were in a military vehicle, and then later with the harbormaster."

Mc'narrd nodded, approval shining in his eyes. "Don Morelli has a mole in his organization. That information didn't come from any of my people. Just to be safe, I've begun investigations to confirm it. You will need to inform Morelli in person."

Leaning back in the chair, Malik studied Mc'narrd. Violetta watched him from the corner of her eyes as she began copying the data from the first chip with the evidence to the military-provided chips.

"It will be resolved." Malik's eyes never left Mc'narrd and his expression became emotionless before he continued. "You were rather quiet when the mercs were talking about you. Is there any truth to what they said?"

"I don't deny any of their theories. They all are intelligent and know how the military works on several worlds. Including K'lais."

Violetta snorted. His statement sounded like one of the nebulous answers her father would give when he didn't want to admit she had part of a theory correct, but not all of it. He often refused to tell what she had figured out when he used statements like that one.

Military speak. It was a way of life, even if she didn't like it.

"Something you would like to say, detective?" Mc'narrd asked, turning his attention back to her.

"Do you seriously plan on putting a guard on the Fangs?" Violetta asked, changing the topic deliberately.

"No. Of all the mercenaries that come to our planet, they are one of the groups least likely to cause a lot of trouble," Mc'narrd replied, amusement showing. "In fact, they are one of the groups frequently hired by us. For mercenaries, they have a strong opposition against poachers. They also enjoy hunting said poachers in ways that do not harm the flora or fauna of our planet. When Stella said they have more leeway than most, she was accurate. They are one of the few merc units granted permission to use lethal force in extreme situations without repercussions."

There were few who didn't know that mercenaries were hired to curtail poaching from other races. K'lais was brimming with unique flora and fauna. Many other races had discovered a market for it, and they had taken to poaching whatever they could find.

It was difficult for the military to do it all, for K'lais had more wilderness than cities. The preservation of the natural resources were important to all who lived upon the world. When approached with being hired to hunt poachers, many mercenaries accepted the task, often with glee.

Not all mercenary groups liked the world or the natives who could 'do magic.' Those that didn't mind the world, the natives, or the laws enjoyed the prospect of a fairly easy task and money in their coffers. After a decade or two, the alien races stopped poaching as they realized they had become the prey. Despite the fact that poaching had\mostly stopped, K'lais still hired mercenaries during the peak seasons.

"Good to know," Violetta said as she removed the first chip from the interface. She held it out to Mc'narrd. "Your chip, sir."

Mc'narrd accepted it graciously. "Thank you, Violetta."

She gave him a tight smile before returning to her task of copying the data onto the second poker chip. "Will you keep the originals safe for me? I'd rather not take them."

Mc'narrd nodded. "Give me a few moments to acquire an evidence sack. Once you're finished, you can seal them up."

The sacks, once sealed, would show if they were opened and resealed. It was a method to prevent tampering.

After Mc'narrd stepped from the room, Malik tipped his head to the side and studied her. "You suspect something?"

"Aside from wondering why Mc'narrd didn't have an assistant fetch the sack instead of him getting it? No, but I can't stop thinking about what Atos said, about it being someone in a position of power." She shook her head and watched as the files copied to the black and silver chip. "I guess Dad's lessons are ingrained too much for me to ignore his words."

"Plan for the unexpected. You dad loved to say that," Malik said, amusement ringing in his voice. "The captain isn't someone of low power. You went through the vidclips. There were none higher than the captains."

"Either way, I want the originals safe. Can you think of anyone safer than Admiral Mc'narrd?"

"No. No, I can't," Malik replied. "What do you think is going on with all of this?"

He gestured around the room. Violetta suspected he was referring to the military assistance and the admiral's keen interest.

"I-" she began, then stopped. Frowning, she removed the comm from her ear and gestured for his comm. He removed it and dropped it into her hand. She cupped them together in her hand. "That should give sufficient feedback for a few moments, if the comms have been turned back on. As for what I think? I think I need to take a closer look at my father's interface."

"Think you'll find anything there?"

She shrugged. "I don't know, but it's the only place I can think of that isn't connected to a subnet. It also has his personal files and journals on it. Complete dossiers on Mom, me, you… everyone he knew, I think. If he made a note of any promises, they'll be there."

"Let me know what you find."

"Of course." She grinned. "You know, once you get your clearance renewed, you'll be able to go into his office."

"That should be interesting," he said thoughtfully. "I've wondered many times what kind of keepsakes your father collected. What he deemed important, what he had to keep secret."

"Once you have your clearance, visit me," Violetta implored. "You can see Dad's office and we can search his files together."

"You can be at ease, Vi. I will visit you within the hour of regaining my clearance." He brushed his fingers along her cheek. "Better hope it's not in the middle of the night."

"True. If it's in the middle of the night, I may not be dressed when I let you in."

"Fortunately, I'm good at improvising in unexpected situations."

"Do you two ever stop?" Mc'narrd's voice bellowed from the doorway. He stormed into the room, glaring at both of them.

"No," they said in chorus.

"This is what I get for coming in from the dark," Mc'narrd complained. "You know damned well that holding comms close together produces feedback loud enough to drown out anything else."

He snatched one set of comms out of her hand and tossed it at Malik, who caught it with one hand.

"If I hear any more feedback from your sets, I'm separating you like children on the activity field!"

"Yes, sir," Violetta grumbled, though the grin didn't fade from her face. "May I have the report for the fingerprints found on the token, sir?"

"It's already on the chip," he replied, still fuming. "I downloaded the reports and a holographic duplicate of the token on both chips before you arrived." He held out an evidence sack. "As promised."

"Thank you, sir," Violetta said, taking the bag. "What about the report from Bures'a Nualith, sir?"

"It's on the chip, also." The words were barely more than a growl.

Violetta did not look at him as she removed the last chip from the interface and dropped both into the sack before sealing it shut.

"Thank you, sir," she repeated demurely. "We appreciate your assistance, sir."

"Enough with that 'sir' crap," Mc'narrd snapped. His silver eyes were hard and glinted as he fumed. "I know what you're doing."

"Is it working?" Malik asked, slyly. Mc'narrd glowered at him. "Certainly looks like it to me."

"Do not make me throw you into our detention cells," Mc'narrd growled.

"Yes, sir," Malik replied with a smug smile.

"I have never been so thankful for a pair of beings choosing a career somewhere other than with our military," Mc'narrd groaned.

"Delighted to be the oddities," Violetta replied, bowing her head.

"I've noticed," Mc'narrd replied dryly.

Chapter Twenty Four

There was nothing to do but wait until the next morning.

Violetta had everything she needed to prove her innocence and clear her name on a poker chip. Issik would arrive the next morning to go with her to the district attorney's office with the captain's key. Then it would be over. She would be able to return to her job. To be with Malik. She would still owe Don Morelli for his assistance, but that was a small price to pay for what she had gained.

Unfortunately, sleep would not come for her or Malik. So instead of sitting in the separate quarters they had been given, they went in search of the bar. Talking over drinks and snack food was more appealing than watching minutes tick by on an interface.

The on-base bar was a haven for those in the military. Both career military and those who were only spending the required year. Though not large, compared to the bars within the city, it wasn't a hole-in-the-wall, either. Booths lined the walls with tables scattered about in the center. A bar stretched across the back wall with shelves filled with empty glasses and bottles of various liquors. Stools were bolted to the floor, a standard for any bar.

Neither Malik nor Violetta expected to find the Fangs already in the bar with a large pitcher of an amber beverage and half-empty tankards for each mercenary. Nathaniel and Stella threw darts, their boisterous banter loud enough to carry over the din. Victoria and Raymond sat at their table, watching and needling their friends.

Choosing a booth a couple tables away from the mercenaries, Malik used the interface at the booth to order their drinks. Violetta scanned the place to see who else was frequenting the libation and game center.

She mentally noted a group of six soldiers, playing cards and drinking. Multiple empty glasses sat on their octagon shaped table, at least one glass with some colored beverage in front of each person. A captain from the off-world corps told stories at the end of the bar to a lady who could have been a friend or an employee. Violetta hadn't seen anything resembling a uniform code on the servers or libation makers, so she couldn't be sure. The soldiers looked back towards her and Malik, their expressions less than thrilled.

A pair of tired but happy sergeants walked in and went immediately to the bar. The head maker greeted the pair, already filling two glass chalices with what Violetta suspected was a honey ale which she placed in front of them as they sat down.

Nathaniel must have scored high on his throw. He roared with enthusiasm, which was echoed by Victoria and Raymond. Stella rolled her eyes and finished her drink. She walked to the dart board and began removing the darts.

Some of the soldiers playing cards glanced over at the mercs, sour expressions on their faces.

"Something interesting, Vi?" Malik asked.

She kept her voice low as she said, "I think those soldiers at the table are going to be trouble."

"You never shut down the police training, do you?"

"It's more Dad's training than anything else. The Academy training just made it, well, worse."

Malik laughed. "At least you admit that! You've changed that much since school."

"Not so much," she argued, "but hopefully I've improved in some ways."

"Hopefully we both have."

A male server came over and placed a hovertray next to their table.

"Good morning or evening, whichever you want it to be," he said with a cheerful disposition. "A tuckroot ale for each of you, jakka chaser for the lady."

He placed the drinks on the table before fetching the large bowl, which was placed in the center between Violetta and Malik.

"One large appetizer of grilled moratoes and Earther radishes," the server explained before wishing them enjoyment of the refreshments and departing.

"Isn't it amusing how the most common food of our planet pairs so well with a tuber from another world?" Malik said as he picked up one of the hollowed out moratoes and filled it with thin slices of the red and white vegetable.

"Considering how bland moratoes can be for half of the year, I'd call it a blessing," Violetta quipped. She helped herself to the food, piling the radish high on her morato.

Malik nodded, choosing not to comment through a mouthful of food.

Violetta took a bite from her appetizer and groaned in pleasure.

"I think we got lucky," Malik said once he'd swallowed. "These taste fresh. Maybe the Fangs brought a supply run as well?"

"Actually, we grow them on our ship!" Stella exclaimed as she walked over to them, "The demand for radishes, Brussels sprouts, and poblano peppers here never slows down. We built a hydroponic garden in an unused storage room to have fresh food no matter how long we are out in the void. It's a nice little side business whenever we make port at K'lais. Glad you two get to enjoy the spoils."

"They are so much better fresh. Most of the time they are rehydrated," Violetta said.

"Either of you fans of poblano peppers?" Stella asked.

"I am. Vi says they don't have enough flavor," Malik replied.

"Before we head to the big black space, I'll make sure you get to try a real pepper." Stella nodded to where Victoria, Raymond, and Nathaniel sat. "Feel free to join us, if you get bored being in this corner."

"Perhaps you can show us how to properly play that game," suggested Violetta.

"If I stop getting schooled by Nathaniel, I'll be happy to!"

Stella gave them a brilliant smile before returning to her comrades. Malik and Violetta sat in comfortable silence, enjoying the food and drinks.

For a few precious minutes, the noisy bar was peaceful in the way such establishments can be. With everyone having a good time going about their activities and enjoying their food and conversations. Even the waitstaff maneuvering between the tables all seemed to be in a great mood.

And then, perhaps inevitably, someone had to fark it all up.

"Why are you here?"

This question was yelled from the table of card playing soldiers. One of them had stood up, and now she weaved her way towards the table where Violetta and Malik sat. Two of the male soldiers from the card game had also stood, but they hadn't left their table just yet.

Violetta noticed the hard gleam in Malik's eyes before he extinguished it and turned to the approaching soldier.

He spoke in a clear, pleasant tone. "Which being are you referring to?"

The inebriated soldier pointed directly at Malik. "You, fancy man. What reason do you have to sit at a table where hard working soldiers try to forget what they've had to deal with?"

Malik kept his pleasant expression and tone. "Was this table reserved for someone? It wasn't marked as such and our server didn't ask us to relocate."

"No, I mean anywhere in this place. Why do you think you can be here? Don't you have a fancy party to host somewhere? Or go get praised and given stuff for smiling and talking on the subnet?"

Violetta felt her blood begin to boil.

"Fortunately, I don't have any Arena business today," Malik replied. "I get to avoid the fake smiles and enthusiasm for vidcams and just enjoy doing service. Right now, I'm enjoying the company of a comrade, just as you and your group are."

"It's bad enough these get allowed through the door." The soldier gestured towards the mercs. "But after the kind of day we've had, I don't understand why we have to watch you get treated special. Neither you or your..."

The soldier trailed off as she got a good look at Violetta. The bloodshot eyes widened, and Violetta knew this was going to go downhill fast.

"We got Sir Fake Fighter and who does he bring along? But the most famous criminal of the week!" the woman bellowed to her comrades. The two standing males started toward Violetta and Malik. The others got up from the table.

"Hey," the captain at the end of the bar called out. "Stand down! They could only be on base if it was cleared by someone high up, which means you don't have the clearance to know why. Shom, I don't know why they're here, or the mercs, but they aren't bothering anyone."

"Lay off, captain," one of the sergeants said. "This crew had the roughest time today, and they don't need someone giving them orders right now."

"Oh, that explains everything! This must be the group who had to clean the latrine trenches after yesterday's fish buffet!" Violetta smiled sweetly at the soldier standing near her. "Did you get the pipes extra shiny, sweetie? Feeling bold and entitled?"

Malik groaned. "Oh for fark's sake, Violence!"

The woman took a swing at Violetta.

Everything became crazy after that.

When questioned later, the mixer behind the bar testified that the soldier was very drunk and swung slowly. That must have been how Violetta came out from behind the table and tackled her to the ground before the blow had a chance to land.

He claimed to not know how the table ended up overturned on the floor, or if the mercs started on the drunken soldier's comrades first, or if they were defending themselves.

He was fairly certain that the captain went to intervene and was tripped by one of the sergeants.

There was no question that the captain punched both sergeants out cold. The mixer saw that very clearly.

The servers who did not hide in the kitchen until military guards arrived corroborated the mixer's visual account of Violetta picking up the soldier that she had tackled off the ground. The manner in which she used the barely conscious soldier as a battering ram against her drunken comrades was also verified.

Nathaniel was quite cooperative, some might say enthusiastic, in giving a literal blow-by-blow account of how he and his fellow mercs stepped in to protect Violetta.

They had, after all, been hired to protect her.

Malik claimed to not know whose blood was covering his knuckles and most of his biosuit. Only that it wasn't his.

Admiral Mc'narrd took the time to drink most of a bottle of bourbon given to him by members of the merc guild before seeing to the mess.

In an interesting coincidence, later that same night, a vidcapture of Malik, Violetta, the mercs, and the mixer, all bruised, bloody and smiling fiendishly, went up on the wall of the bar.

Chapter Twenty Five

"I am confident that most details will not be remembered of this incident," Mc'narrd stated. "However, there is enough evidence and testimony for me to have an account, and who is going to be reprimanded."

Violetta kept her features expressionless. She, in fact, remembered every detail. One thing that she did not know or understand from the battle was the term *mother fuckers*. She did distinctly hear Raymond declare "It's on, motherfuckers!" before pummeling one of the soldiers. She presumed it was meant to be offensive, and reminded herself to ask the mercs about it later. Especially since it was the second time she'd heard the phrase used.

Another thing that wasn't on the vidclip that had been played for them? The captain shaking hands with Malik and leaving with the lady he'd been chatting with.

Malik headed to the bar to assist the mixer, who was having some difficulty getting free of the thrown sergeant. Unless she was mistaken, the mixer also had a broken nose. Malik and the mixer emerged from behind the bar, dragging the unconscious sergeant.

"Could I get a stillgraph with all of you?" the mixer asked.

The pleasant male server who had tended to Malik and Violetta was happy to operate the mixer's pocket interface. The military police arrived right after the moment had been captured for posterity and bragging rights.

"Am I boring you, Cq'linns?" Mc'narrd snapped, pulling Violetta's attention back to the situation at hand.

"No. Just trying to remember everything," she replied, not untruthfully.

The admiral narrowed his eyes at her. Fury still burned in his eyes. "Indeed. Perhaps you will explain why you thought it would be a good idea to make such an incendiary comment to an inebriated soldier who was obviously looking to start trouble?"

"No, sir," Violetta said, meeting his eyes.

Mc'narrd opened his mouth to say something, then snapped it shut. He stared at her for several long moments. Finally, he said, "You are too much like your parents."

"You say that like it's a bad thing," she commented.

There was no mistaking the fact Mc'narrd wanted to say something more, but was debating if he should or not. He turned abruptly, shaking his head in what may have been defeat. "What of you, Addelia?"

Malik shrugged. "I don't know why she said it. We went there to have a drink and maybe some good food."

"I don't want to ever even hear you placed a toe inside that bar," Mc'narrd ordered. "That goes for you, too, Cq'linns. There is no refuting the evidence showing that the soldier started the fight. She is being reprimanded, will have to pay for damages caused by all of you, and have to perform community service. With luck, she may keep from being demoted."

Violetta was very tempted to ask if the soldier would be cleaning all the public latrines in the parks, but somehow resisted the urge. She suspected it would not go over well with Mc'narrd and may end with her and Malik being in even more trouble.

"What of the Serpent's Fangs?" Malik asked.

Mc'narrd sighed. "They didn't join the fray until after it began. I cannot, unfortunately, fault them for doing their job of protecting Violetta. They've been requested to not visit the bar, also. Since neither of you will be going there, they shouldn't have a reason to return."

"Is there anything else, sir?" Violetta asked, wanting to retreat as soon as possible.

"Yes," he replied, crossing his arms over his chest. "Do you have any other plans for the night? Or can I expect you to return to your appointed quarters and remain there until morning?"

"Well, if you'd allowed us the same quarters, we wouldn't have gone to the bar to begin with," Violetta said mischievously.

When Mc'narrd drew in a deep breath, Malik interjected, "We will return to our quarters." He chuckled. "You should have known she would say something like that, sir."

"Go," Mc'narrd snapped. "As long as you don't remove those biosuits or start another brawl, I don't care what you do. Stay clothed and out of trouble. Issik will be here in the morning at 0900 sharp. Do not be late, detective."

"Thank you, sir," Violetta said cheerfully before turning to Malik. "Shall we?"

"Yes, I think we shall," he replied.

Together, they departed the office and headed for their quarters.

"That went better than expected," Malik said as they traversed the hallways.

"Agreed. Have you noticed he's sounding more and more like a frustrated parent? I wonder why that is?"

Malik laughed. "Probably because you aren't under his immediate command."

"I'd have been court martialed by now, if I'd gone into the military instead of the police academy. It's still possible, since he's technically my superior." She glanced at Malik. "Do you ever regret not becoming a healer?"

"Do you ever regret not going into the military?"

"Sometimes. I think I'm the first in our family line that isn't career military."

"I've met far too many people who need healing that I wouldn't want to treat." He shrugged. "I've used what I learned, but I don't regret not finishing the training."

They walked in silence for a while as Violetta thought over his words.

"You wouldn't have been here to help me if you'd finished your training," she finally said.

"No, I wouldn't," he agreed. He nudged her with his shoulder. "Fun, wasn't it?"

"Yeah, it was," she said, grinning. "We should do it again sometime."

"I swear, if it's not one extreme, it's the other," Mc'narrd snapped.

"I'm sorry, sir. Would you like to join us next time?" Violetta asked, winking at Malik.

"To have a drink, yes. To partake in a barroom brawl, no."

"A few drinks together could be fun," Malik said thoughtfully. "We'll even try to behave."

"I'll believe that when I see it," Mc'narrd groused. "I see you both are at your quarters. Have a good night, you two."

"Good night, Admiral," Malik and Violetta said together before entering Malik's appointed quarters.

There they remained, talking and laughing about their childhood until sleep overtook them.

The following morning, Violetta met Issik in an office. Unlike most offices Violetta had seen on the base, this one was austere and plain. A painting of the world and a map of the 42nd District were the only things on the wall. A desk, chair, and interface were the only furniture to be seen in the room. Nothing marked it as to who used it.

Not surprising since Mc'narrd was supposed to be dead and, according to him, this was the office he used.

In fact, it wasn't even Mc'narrd who stood before her and Issik.

Admiral By'kett leaned against the desk in a formal uniform facing them. The uniform consisted of a dark teal tunic with two wide stripes around the cuffs of the sleeves and equally dark teal pants. Two starbursts were positioned above the two stripes. He wore the military crest on his left shoulder and the command emblem on his right. Black boots completed the uniform. Dark hair was pulled back into a simple ponytail. The tips of his ears peeked through his hair. His brilliant gold eyes studied Violetta and Issik.

"You will be given a military escort to the district attorney's office. A squadron will enter with you, but remain in the outer office while you speak with the DA."

"What of the krishii, sir?" Issik asked. "The manhunt hasn't ended, and the precinct is actively searching for her on this side."

"The military has ordered all krishii to be brought back in. The governor has agreed that if they haven't found her by now, they will not be able to do so at all. By now, they are growing too dangerous for even their handlers." A smile slid across his otherwise stern face. "We do not need them attacking civilians simply because someone walked in front of them."

"That explains a lot," Issik muttered. "The captain was rather unhappy this morning. He must have just received word about it."

"Indeed. The squadron will remain with you both until they receive clearance from the base. If anything should happen, they will be there for assistance. They have the authorization to make any required on-the-spot decisions."

Violetta understood that to mean they were aware of who they were escorting and probably even a basic understanding of the circumstances. No one would be allowed to interrupt their journey, and if needed, they would ensure her safe return to the base.

Not to the jail or a detention center.

"Do you have everything you need, Detective Cq'linns?" By'kett asked. Violetta nodded. "Good. Do either of you have any questions?"

"No, sir," Violetta and Issik said as one.

"Very well. Make sure you wear the hood the entire time. No need to incite the krishii more than they will be if they scent you." Violetta gave him a confused look. By'kett chuckled. "The nanites of the trench coat have since been programmed to remove your scent. You were not close enough, nor did we have a… large enough blood sample to do so earlier. If there's nothing else, let's get you two to the HAV and your escort."

Violetta hated not being able to say anything about the injury, since she wasn't certain Issik was aware of what had happened. She'd have to remember to ask Mc'narrd or a healer about it later.

When they remained silent, By'kett gave a nod. He pushed away from the desk and led Violetta and Issik to the main entrance. Outside was a squadron of thirteen soldiers wearing the standard jumpsuits waiting in small groups around three HAVs. The moment they noticed the admiral, they saluted him. Two approached at a minute gesture from the admiral.

"Admiral," one said, snapping a second salute. "The HAVs are prepped and ready."

"Very good, Ap'errson," By'kett replied. "Violetta. Issik. This is Commander Ap'errson. He will be your driver. Major Johnson will also join you in your HAV. The rest will be in their own HAVs."

Violetta nodded to the commander, who returned the gesture. She pulled the hood up and felt the familiar sensation of the nanites changing her appearance. Ap'errson studied her for a moment before giving a second nod.

He turned to the squadron and called out to them. "Start 'em up!"

Those under his command, a collection of men and women, human and native, headed for the HAVs. Ap'errson led Violetta and Issik to the one they would be using, which happened to be the middle HAV. The four doors slid up, and everyone took their appointed seats.

The convoy followed the main street to the Government Center, where the district attorney's office was located. All government business took place in that entire block of buildings. It was also where the Council members and most government officials lived. It was believed that living close to where they worked made it easier to serve.

The main building was on the corner of Caelshos Street and Dra'as Avenue, and spanned half of the west side of

Caelshos Street. The convoy had no problems stopping directly in front of the government building, effectively blocking traffic.

As Violetta and Issik departed the HAV on the west side of the street, they heard the familiar growls and snarls of a krishii. Nearby, a group of handlers struggled to force one into a cage. Even with it contained, the squad members formed a protective ring around Violetta and Issik.

The krishii snapped at all of them, trying to break through their line in an effort to get to Violetta. The handlers didn't stop to look to see what or who was behind them. They were too intent upon their task.

"I'm getting the feeling that is the one you pissed off," Issik murmured to Violetta.

"It does look like it," she whispered back, noticing burn marks on the creature's face.

"Let's get you two inside," Ap'errson said, his voice low. "The sooner you're out of its range, the better."

Violetta and Issik nodded and followed him into the building.

The interior of the government building was lavish. A large crafted waterfall rose to meet the ceiling, allowing water to cascade down with a gentle sound. Lush greenery surrounded the waterfall, giving it a natural appearance, even if it was in the middle of a building.

To each side of the foyer were desks with assistant droids, moving from side to side helping anyone who approached. Lifts could be seen just behind the enormous waterfall. Small tables and chairs were scattered around strategically, offering visitors a place to sit. Several were occupied by people using handheld interfaces.

Citizens and civil servants filled the foyer. Most stopped to look at the military group entering the center.

Conversations paused and a hush settled over the foyer. Violetta felt incredibly self-conscious as they moved further into the building. Slowly, whispered conversations began again, and she could hear some of the comments.

What are they doing here? Why are they in the building? Who were the ones not in uniform? Someone commented that maybe the one in normal clothes had something to do with Violetta.

The soldiers didn't pause as the group walked past the waterfall and to the lifts. All of them ignored the questions spoken and comments being made. When they reached the lifts, half the squadron went with the detectives. The other half used the adjoining one.

"That was fun," Violetta grumbled. "Definitely glad for the escort, now."

"You're welcome," Admiral Mc'narrd said over her comm.

Violetta didn't bother with a reply. The lift's doors slid open once they reached the fourth floor. They followed the commander as he traversed the hallways to the district attorney's corner office.

Several soldiers stopped outside the DA's doors, while the rest moved into the attorney's outer office.

A secretary sat behind a tall desk. A pretty human woman with honey gold hair and pale blue eyes, she didn't look up from the interface screen when they entered.

Violetta took a moment to glance around the office.

The office was a large room with sparse furnishings. A plaque sat in front of the interface screen with the attorney's name on it. A vase with real, cut flowers sat near the wall below a portrait of the world from space. Two chairs with a table between them were positioned across from the secretary's desk. The door to the DA was behind her desk and was closed.

"May I help-" she began, before looking up and stopping mid-sentence. "Oh. Uh, how may I help you, Commander?"

"District Attorney Lc'sonn is expecting Detective Issik Ha'kksworth and his companion," Commander Ap'errson replied politely.

"A moment, please," the secretary said politely. She tapped the interface. "Attorney Lc'sonn, Commander Ap'errson is here with a Detective Ha'kksworth and a companion." She paused before turning to the Commander. "They may go in."

The door slid open and Issik and Violetta entered the DA's corner office. The DA sat behind a large desk, typing on a desktop keyboard connected to the interface screen.

Unlike most offices Violetta had been in, this one had thick carpeting, walls that appeared to be dark wood panels, and there was a bookshelf filled with small models of ships, miniature weapons, and stillgraphs of him with friends. Violetta noticed there was even one with the former Chief of Police.

Once the door closed behind them, Violetta pushed the hood of her coat down, revealing her true identity. That caught the DA's attention. He turned to her and Issik.

"I'm not here to turn myself in, sir," Violetta stated before he could say anything. "I'm here to clear my name."

"That's very admirable of you, detective. You'll have to have solid evidence for me to clear your name of all wrongdoings," Lc'sonn replied. "Please, state your case."

"I have evidence that leads us, Detective Ha'kksworth and myself, to believe that Captain Monroe is the one guilty of killing Chief Me'addn. A key with his serial number was found by Detective Ha'kksworth at the Chief's home. A token for an officer's club was also found at the chief's home, the prints on the token were revealed to belong to Captain Monroe, also."

"Who found that evidence, detective?" Lc'sonn asked.

"I did, sir," Issik said, speaking up.

"Who ran the prints on the token?"

Violetta smiled slightly. "The military, sir."

Something flashed through the DA's eyes, but Violetta couldn't tell what it was before it was gone. Briefly, she wondered if she should request that Commander Ap'errson be in the room with them. Her gut was telling her something was off and she didn't like the feeling.

"Do they also have the key?" he asked.

"No, sir. I still have it," Issik replied. "It was placed into an evidence sack and has remained sealed."

"Good. That's good. Do you have it with you?" When Issik nodded, he continued. "Perfect. What about you, Cq'linns? Do you have evidence to back up what you're saying?"

"Yes, sir. I do. I also have evidence showing that there is a widespread problem involving a large number of the officers at the precinct."

Lc'sonn's eyes narrowed. "Very good. Do you also have the evidence with you?"

"I do."

"Good. Good. Please give me a moment." He turned to the interface and began typing. "Allow me to make notes of everything you've just told me."

Violetta and Issik nodded.

"You have a very lovely view," Violetta said, turning her attention to his window. Something looked familiar, and it took her only a few moments to figure out what was familiar about it. "Is that Chief Me'addn's former apartment across from your office?"

"Yes, it is," Lc'sonn replied, glancing at her.

"There should have been vidclip footage from that night. Did you check it?" she asked suddenly.

"No, the cameras around my office were down for maintenance that evening," Lc'sonn replied, "There is no footage from when Me'addn died."

"Hox," Violetta said. "The captain must have learned about that and decided that was the perfect time to start this whole mess."

"You're certain he was the one in charge?" Lc'sonn asked, opening a drawer of his desk.

"We have no evidence suggesting he answered to anyone but himself," Issik replied.

"Good. That's very good," Lc'sonn said.

Violetta looked out the window again to the former abode of the Chief.

"Who could have told Monroe when the cameras were going to be down?" she asked.

"He could have learned it by checking with the security detail for the building," Lc'sonn suggested. "But there's little reason to bother them now. Monroe and his crew will be prosecuted, and Chief Me'addn's memory will go on throughout the Department."

"Interesting coincidence that the maintenance happened the very same night that I was to talk to Me'addn," Violetta said, tearing her eyes away from the apartment. "If I had gone the day before or after, there would be footage showing who actually killed the chief."

"A coincidence?" Issik repeated, giving Violetta his complete attention. "You don't-" he broke off, not completing the sentence as he turned back to Lc'sonn.

Issik knew she didn't believe in coincidences. Neither of them did. That belief had helped them with multiple cases, and now Issik was starting to appear concerned. Violetta kept her expression neutral, despite the fact she was now very worried.

"Maybe we should question the security. It wouldn't do to leave any questions unanswered," Issik suggested, and Violetta recognized the tone. It was the same he used when he suspected they were in a bad situation.

"Especially if you have to prosecute multiple officers. We wouldn't want to miss anyone, would we?" Violetta added.

"No, no, that wouldn't do at all," Lc'sonn agreed. "We can't have anyone wondering if there was someone missed, possibly the one in charge."

In the split second it took Violetta to recognize what the DA was pointing at her partner, he'd fired. The shot hit Issik full in the chest. He fell to the floor.

Violetta went for a sidearm that was no longer on her hip. Lc'sonn had the clone gun pointed at her even as she remembered she wasn't armed with anything but her wit.

"I gave you an out. All you had to do was be pacified with the story and not question further." Lc'sonn sounded scornful, as though Violetta and Issik were children caught playing with toys that weren't theirs.

"What's your story going to be? That Issik and I came here to kill you, and you managed to outshoot both of us?"

"That's a silly tale," Lc'sonn said. "Sadly, you refused to wear a weapon and the military confiscated your service sidearm. Which means Issik, despite his years of service, will die a traitor. You will be his victim and I will have shot him to protect myself."

Lc'sonn glanced briefly at the interface on his desk, tapped at the screen twice before focusing fully on Violetta again.

"Unfortunately, I hadn't changed the settings once I duplicated his weapon, so he's only incapacitated. A full shot to the heart can be messy, but he gets to live his last moments asleep and peaceful. However…" Lc'sonn continued. "I've just corrected that problem. Your death will be swift and, I am told, relatively painless. Your partner gets the same, after you've been dispatched."

"*Stall him*," Mc'narrd's voice hissed in her ears. She took a moment to be grateful that everything was being recorded. Even if she didn't make it out of this alive, Lc'sonn would be prosecuted to the full extent of the planet's laws. Which meant an inevitable death.

"Tell me why, at least?" she blurted. "Since it's just you and me, now."

Lc'sonn barked a laugh. "Thinking your partner will recover in time to save you, or hear my confession?"

"Guess that's rather predictable, huh?" Violetta raised her hands, palms out, to show she was unarmed.

"You've never taken a fully charged incapacitating round, have you?" Lc'sonn guessed. "Issik won't be coming around any time soon. I will have more than enough time to finish you both. Although it is a shame."

"Let your conscience be your guide?" Violetta suggested. "Knock me out, leave town with whatever spoils you've accumulated and live in splendor on another planet?"

Lc'sonn laughed again. "No wonder Monroe wanted to frame you. You are simply clueless about everything! Your father must have taught you nothing. He was insightful enough to survive extraplanetary travel and war, and he settled back *here*. Do you think any planet would be better to live on, if he decided to finish his days on this planet, in this city?"

"Then you set up Captain Monroe. Was that before or after I evaded the police department, and even the krishii?"

"Unlike your dear captain, I think ahead instead of just focusing on the money. I had plans and backup plans to frame him before you were even part of the equation."

Violetta didn't have a reply to that.

"I'm quite happy being the alpha predator in this city, and learning why the Earthers used to covet wealth and material possessions so strongly. But, you're wasting my valuable time, so it's time to end you." Lc'sonn raised the clone gun to properly aim at her chest.

Glass shattered beside Lc'sonn, followed by the whine of a discharging weapon. Violetta's eyes squeezed shut in reflex.

She felt nothing. Nothing at all.

When her body remained upright, and there was no pain, she understood she actually had not felt a single thing. She had not been shot. Opening her eyes, she looked at Lc'sonn, who had collapsed onto the desk, and was sliding to the floor. Silver blood and gore was splattered on his desk. The right side of his head looked like an exploded volcano, with silver lava trailing down from the gaping hole. The clone gun fell from his lifeless fingers.

"Cq'linns! Cq'linns!" Mc'narrd yelled through the comm. "Do you read? *Violetta!*"

"I'm fine, sir," she said after a moment, her voice quavering. "Remind me to buy a drink for your sniper. Although she or he could have taken the shot before I soiled the biosuit."

"My... snipers... are not in position yet." Mc'narrd spoke his words with care. As though he were trying to calm a startled animal. "Hence my high level of concern for your well being after we heard a shot fired."

Dragging her eyes away from Lc'sonn bloody corpse, Violetta followed the suspected trajectory of the fired charge that killed the now-former DA. There was a hole in the window of the apartment that belonged to Chief Me'addn.

"That... wasn't you?" Violetta repeated, taking a step back, only to bump into someone's chest.

She jerked around to find Commander Ap'errson standing directly behind her. He didn't seem bothered by the fact she stepped on his toes. Several other members of his squadron entered the room and spread out.

"Issik will need medical aid," Violetta said, even as one of the soldiers knelt down to give him a quick examination. "He took a full disabling charge to the chest."

"We'll take care of him, detective," Ap'errson said soothingly. "Are you well?"

"I'm fine," she said, drawing a shaky breath. "I'm unharmed. Physically, anyway."

"Let's get you out of here," Commander Ap'errson said, cautiously placing a hand on her shoulder and left arm.

He led her from the room, where two of the soldiers were keeping the secretary from entering the room. They were also positioned so she couldn't see the grisly scene of her now-dead boss.

"Orders, sir?" one of the soldiers asked.

"Remain here until further notice. No one enters or leaves without the proper clearance. Command will give you further updates," Ap'errson replied.

"She will need to be debriefed. Governor Av'inss will want to speak to her," Admiral Mc'narrd said. "I'll alert Av'inss and give her a brief summary of what's happened."

"What about Issik?" Violetta asked, looking back towards the room. "And who… that is, if it wasn't your person who did what… they did, then who did do it?"

Though Violetta suspected the secretary knew what had just happened, she wasn't going to be the one to say anything about Lc'sonn being shot. Someone else could break the news to her.

"We have emergency services on their way for your partner," the admiral reassured her. "I'm still investigating who took that shot. When I find out who it was, I'll let you know."

Malik's voice came over the comm. "If you think about it, Vi, I'll bet you'll figure it out."

Hearing Malik calmed her nerves more than anyone else had so far. Violetta pressed her lips together as she considered his words. She wasn't going to say who she suspected. If one of the Serpent's Fangs had taken that shot, the military could figure it out on their own. After all, the only thing she saw was a silhouette of a person moving after the shot had been taken. There was no way she could make a definite identification.

Besides, whichever one it was, they'd just saved her and Issik's lives. Ratting on them would be a poor thank you.

She didn't say anything as Commander Ap'errson and Major Johnson escorted her from the DA's office and back to the lifts. Three other soldiers followed behind them.

Once again, they took the lifts up, this time to the top floor of the government building. There were several meeting rooms, but only one office on the top floor. Violetta had been to various parts of the government building, but this was the first time she'd been to the top floor. One of the soldiers behind them moved to the front, leading the way into the governor's outer office.

The outer officer for the governor felt like a museum to Violetta, in both appearance and atmosphere. Spacious, with a wide desk for the secretary, there were shelves filled with holograms of planets and maps. A flag for the districts, the military, and for the police department were positioned in the three corners opposite the entrance.

The secretary, a native man wearing a light tan tunic, stood abruptly, his gold eyes widening at Violetta and her armed escort. After a moment, he composed himself.

"Governor Av'inss is expecting you." He tapped a key on his interface, and the door to his right slid open.

Much to Violetta's surprise, Ap'errson and his soldiers entered the governor's office with her. They remained near the door, but didn't leave. Nor did the governor request to be left alone with her. For which Violetta was thankful. After what had just happened, having the military at her back gave her a sense of safety that she shouldn't have needed.

Violetta took a moment to observe her surroundings. Unlike the DA's office, the governor's office was large, spacious, and austere. The carpet was thick and lush, with the emblem of K'lais in the center of the floor.

Violetta found it amusing that the ke'snwa, the national bird used on their planet's emblem, reminded her of the Earth bird called a swan. If the swan had spikes along its neck, instead of feathers, and the features of the wings were as sharp as a finely-edged sword. The head and neck of one sat on each side of a three-pointed shield, heads pointed inward and the wings unfurled, overlaying the sides of a larger shield. Behind the birds and shield were elegant swirls and the ancient designs used on the first shields of K'lais.

Pulling her eyes away from the emblem, she took note of the elegant chairs positioned around a large desk. A stark reminder this wasn't just anyone's office.

The woman behind the desk stood as they entered. Violetta couldn't help but admire the dark brown tunic she wore. The silver embroidery around the cuffs and neckline matched her eyes and the sinspar pendant that graced her neck, sparkled against her pale skin. She wore her silver hair up in a braided chignon that Violetta could only wish she could emulate.

Governor Av'inss was, without a doubt, a beautiful woman, despite the grim expression on her face. Violetta wondered if many of the people she commanded during her career in the military had underestimated her due to her beauty. She strongly suspected many definitely admired the woman, at least from afar.

"So, you are Violetta Cq'linns, the woman the police service has spent several days and a great amount of resources trying to locate," Av'inss said without preamble. The woman's silver eyes swept over Violetta, who felt as though she had been completely assessed in that single look. "I would be surprised at your skill of avoiding capture and talent at garnering allies, if you were anyone other than Vrehn Cq'linns' daughter."

"Thank you?" Violetta said, uncertain if it was a compliment.

"Yes, that was a compliment. You're welcome." A smile softened her features. It only enhanced her beauty. She gestured towards the chairs in front of her desk. "Please, have a seat so we can discuss the events leading up to you being here in my office."

"Thank you," Violetta repeated. She settled into the chair opposite the governor, surprised at the softness of the chair's padding. "Where would you like me to start?"

"Start with the evidence. I understand you still have the chip. May I have it?"

Reaching into an inner pocket of the coat she wore, Violetta retrieved the black and silver chip. She held it out to the governor. "I discovered the folder of vidclips when I had to use Lieutenant Cancio's interface. I do not know if I was set up to find it or if it was accidental, but I found a folder with deleted vidclip footage. I saved the vidclips once I realized what it revealed. I later used my father's interface to make a copy. I was going to give it to Chief Me'addn the night he was murdered."

"Tell me about the case you were presenting to the former DA." Av'inss loaded the chip into her interface and began examining the files.

"With Detective Ha'kksworth's assistance, we were able to discover items pointing to Captain Monroe at the crime scene. Issik, that is Detective Ha'kksworth, discovered a token to a local club: Club La'caille. With assistance from the military, the prints on the token came back as belonging to Captain Monroe. Detective Ha'kksworth also found a key that belonged to the captain. It had both the captain's serial number and prints on it. The vidclips I found included footage of the captain, as well."

Av'inss took a moment to shift her gaze from the interface to Violetta. "It appears as though you made a solid case against your captain."

"Yes, ma'am," Violetta replied. "Though it has since been discovered District Attorney Lc'sonn planted those items in Me'addn's home to frame the captain."

"We will question Captain Monroe about his involvement with the chief's murder, as well as Lc'sonn's involvement during Monroe's interrogation," Av'inss stated. She turned back to Violetta. "Tell me about Detective Ziph Rc'dollph."

"He first appeared in the investigation as the being who shot a human scientist and the developer of the replicating weapon that District Attorney Lc'sonn used to shoot Detective Ha'kksworth."

Violetta settled in the chair, hoping she appeared calmer than she felt. She was still on edge from the event that had just transpired and uncertain of what the governor's response was going to be.

"You're doing fine, Violetta," Mc'narrd's voice said over the comms. "I assure you, you are safe there with Governor Av'inss."

That helped, she admitted to herself. That definitely helped.

"Ziph Rc'dollph appeared on the lake's docks. He stated he knew I would be going to the lake, because the harbormaster is military. He claimed he deduced that the military would be assisting me. I Challenged him to a Duel, hoping to use it as a way to escape. I was unaware that Malik, Bures'o Addelia, that is, also happens to be Master of Ceremonies for the Dueling Arenas."

"You were unaware that your high school classmate, whom you were very close to up until you entered the police academy, is the Master of Ceremonies?"

Violetta shrugged. "I have never been interested in going to the arenas, nor have I been Challenged since my academy days and my first year with the police service. Those Challenges were always handled at the academy or police service's gym. I do not spend my free time watching or reading anything not related to my job or developing my skills. Or for pure entertainment. And until I was accused, I hadn't been in contact with Malik."

Amusement flashed through the governor's silver eyes and a smile teased at her lips. "How did he become involved with your situation?"

"He was the only one I could think of who could possibly help me," Violetta replied. "I knew his father once worked for Don Morelli, so I contacted Malik in the hopes that he would know how to help. Malik's parents had always been kind to me, so I hoped if Malik was unable to help, then his father could assist me by using his contacts."

"How did you acquire his personal information?"

Violetta smiled. "He hadn't changed our method of contacting each other."

"If I didn't know better, I'd swear you were telling the truth," Mc'narrd said in admiration. "Even the suit isn't showing anything to indicate a lie." He paused, then added, "Remind me to never play poker with you."

"Did you receive assistance with Don Morelli?" the governor asked, seemingly satisfied with her answers. "Who else assisted you?"

"Don Morelli assisted with providing a safe house. I believe he also assisted with providing HAVs, but I don't know that for certain. Issik, my partner for the past several years, aided with the investigation. I do not know who contacted Issik or who helped him locate me at the safe house. Nor do I know how he managed to get there without being followed."

Violetta sighed and shifted in the chair. "The military began assisting after I contacted Captain Ae'staa when I needed to search my father's interface. I also received assistance from Nualith Ln'ann, who ran tests on my sidearm to prove that it had not been fired during the time I was accused of using it. Those reports are also on the chip. The civilian, Matt Gomez, assisted by providing the proof that he created the replicating weapon for Captain Monroe using funds from the Officers' Memorial Fund."

"Do you know who shot District Attorney Lc'sonn?"

"No," Violetta said, and it wasn't a lie. She honestly did not know who shot him. Suspicions were not fact. "I thought one of the military snipers had moved into place and shot him. It wasn't until later that I was informed it was not a military sniper."

"What do you plan on doing now?"

"Once it's known that I'm innocent of all charges, I plan on returning to my job."

"In service, we prosper." The governor finally turned to face Violetta. Av'inss leaned back in the chair to study her. "What can we do to repay you for your service to the city? You uncovered a vast corruption in the police service. Regardless of the grave danger to yourself, you completed your duty. You surpassed great odds and ignored your own freedom being in peril. For that, you deserve a reward."

"My reward is my name being cleared so that I may return to my job in homicide," Violetta insisted. She had no need for a reward, being able to continue her job on her own merits, was all that she desired. "Honestly, Bures'a Av'inss, that is all I desire."

"If that is your wish, then it shall be made so. I will ensure that your name is cleared completely and unequivocally so you can return to your job, with the field promotion of lieutenant. I have no doubt you will finish the proper paperwork to finalize that promotion."

Violetta stared at the governor in stunned silence. Being promoted to lieutenant shouldn't have come for a couple more years, at the earliest. Yet, here it was, being handed to her for a job she felt was her duty to perform.

"You've earned it, Violetta," Mc'narrd said softly. Violetta could have sworn there was pride and admiration in his voice. "Congratulations, Lieutenant Cq'linns."

"If there is anything else that I can assist you with, don't hesitate to contact me," Governor Av'inss stated. "You honor your father and mother with your work. I'm certain they would be proud of the being you've become."

"Thank you, Bures'a," Violetta finally managed to say. When the governor stood, she did as well.

The governor walked from behind her desk and grasped Violetta's left shoulder in a firm grip. Violetta returned the gesture.

"It has been an honor to meet you, Lieutenant Cq'linns," Av'inss said, dropping her arm.

"The honor is mine," Violetta replied, releasing the governor.

Chapter Twenty Six

Once they had exited Governor Av'inss office, Violetta stopped in the hallway. Her escort paused beside her.

"Come back to the base, Cq'linns," Mc'narrd said. "It will take some time to clear everything up. I'm certain you could use a drink, as well."

"I thought you said we weren't allowed in the bar?" she asked, as she began walking again. "And I think I'm going to want multiple drinks. Multiple drinks of large quantities."

Loud humming filled the comm. "Good point. You can have a drink with me in my office. I'll make sure your boyfriend is here, also. He's been a bit antsy since the DA was shot. I think he's wanting to ensure you're in one piece for himself."

"Why don't you just show him the readouts from the 'suit?" she asked, ignoring the comment about Malik being her boyfriend.

"I did."

Oh. Well. That was something else, then. She couldn't stop the giddy grin that appeared on her face. Or the extra bounce in her step.

"Then I guess I'll have to come back to the base so he can see I'm alive and well for himself."

"Indeed." Mc'narrd grumbled something unintelligible before saying, "The krishii have been contained. All have been accounted for, which means life just got easier for you."

"Meaning?"

"Meaning come back to the base, and I'll take you and your boyfriend out for a drink."

Commander Ap'errson coughed. Violetta suspected it was to hide a laugh. Once they were inside the lift, he asked, "Will you need us to act as escort, sir?"

"No, not this time, Commander," Mc'narrd replied. "Her appointed bodyguards, I'm certain, will do just fine in that regard."

"Then I take it you've figured out who killed Lc'sonn?" Violetta asked, keeping her gaze on the doors as the lift went to the ground floor.

Mc'narrd snorted. "I'll answer that question later."

A short time later, Violetta was sitting at a bar with Malik and Admiral Mc'narrd. Mc'narrd was wearing colored contacts that turned his silver eyes bronze. Since some people of mixed heritage shaved their heads bald, the only other oddity was his lack of brows.

He wore street clothes instead of anything marking him as military. Though Violetta could see the peek of the biosuit every so often. The clothing and contacts changed his entire appearance. Even though he still moved and held himself as a soldier, the tunic and loose pants gave him a more approachable appearance. Unusual, yes, but definitely more approachable.

On the opposite side of the bar were the Serpent's Fangs. All of whom were being what Violetta was discovering to be their typical loud, boisterous selves. It was so strange seeing them now and trying to compare them with the calm, indulging beings she'd known when she was younger. Even in the past couple years, she hadn't been witness to their loud, boisterous selves.

They lifted their glasses in salute to the three of them before draining the glasses of their contents.

Of course, she'd also never met them out at a bar. They'd always worn street clothes and taken her out to restaurants. Or into the wilderness to shoot their weapons.

She liked the fact they no longer had to hide their true selves from her. Hopefully this would become a more common event in their lives.

The bar they were in was one of the seedier establishments and according to Mc'narrd, also happened to be where Violetta's parents had first met.

"Which one was it?" Violetta asked, once their drinks and food had been delivered to their table. "And how's Issik?"

"Victoria, actually," Mc'narrd replied, taking a pull from his mug of hard cider. "The woman is an expert shot. Taught your mother. Neither the windows or the distance were a problem for her. As for Issik, he should be released tomorrow morning. They're keeping him for observation, to ensure no complications develop from the replicating weapon that was used."

"Good. I know he's going to hate that, but I'm glad he'll be okay." Violetta took a drink from her glass before continuing. "She was in Me'addn's apartment. I'm guessing she broke in?"

"Yes. The Fangs suspected the DA once they found out what was going on. Apparently, they've had some dealings with him, and knew other groups he worked with, none of which are very reputable. They said he was 'a snake' and couldn't be trusted. When they found out where you were going, the other three created a diversion so she could break in and set up her rifle."

Malik gave a low whistle. "Remind me not to get on her bad side."

"But you didn't arrest or deport them," Violetta stated. "Despite the fact she killed the DA in, well, cold blood."

Mc'narrd chuckled. "They were doing what they were hired to do: protect you at all cost. Considering they were able to get in and set up before anyone else, I can't punish them. Not when they were able to take that shot before Lc'sonn killed you." He gave a very human shrug of his shoulders. "We were on our way to do exactly what she did. So no one will object to her actions."

"You're talking about us," Victoria said as she approached the table. "My ears are burning. Hope you're saying nice things about me."

"We were discussing that shot you made," Malik spoke up. "We're fortunate you were there to be of service."

Victoria grinned. "Always wanted a reason to take that fucker out. He made my skin crawl every time we had to deal with him." She gave a short bow, her eyes twinkling as she spoke again. "In service, we prosper. We completed our contract, provided a valuable service, and prospered in the end. In our opinion, we came out on the better end of the deal. Money in our coffers, able to catch up with Kali's daughter, and meet her beau. Not to mention managed to do something your own people were unable to accomplish."

That was not how the motto of K'lais was meant to be used, but Violetta couldn't argue the logic behind their reasoning. Her entire outlook on many things had been shifted greatly, and now she understood what Lc'sonn had meant a little better.

Maybe, just maybe, it would help in future homicide investigations. Or even life in general.

"Let us know if you decide to have a human wedding or native celebration," Stella said, appearing beside their table. "We'll make sure to be there, if you give us enough warning."

"And if she doesn't, her grandparents will," Nathaniel added, towering above the women. He winked at Violetta. "We still have to give them a debriefing now that the contract has been completed."

"If and when it happens, I'll be certain to make sure you all have enough time to come," Violetta promised. "Along with all the details."

"Good. Now we can go finish our drinks," Nathaniel said cheerfully. He draped his arms around Victoria and Stella's shoulders. "Let's go before Raymond drinks it all."

The trio watched the mercs return to their table.

"They aren't bad people," Mc'narrd said, as though he were trying to reassure himself.

"When do you want the 'suits back?" Malik asked.

"Actually, the military would like for you both to keep them, especially you, Violetta," Mc'narrd said. "You would be doing us a service and the 'suits would be beneficial to your job. Yours, as well, Malik."

"How so?" Malik asked, suspicion showing in his features.

"Those biosuits are actually experimental. Most of the suits we've developed only work for natives. For those of mixed heritage and the humans, the biosuits only provide basic information and perform the most rudimentary of functions. Like the one you wore when you entered the military. They're capable of life-saving techniques, but not to the same extent as the 'suits used by full natives. The fact that these suits have worked so well for you and Violetta gives us hope. Hope that we can continue to improve upon the design until they're equal to the ones our native military servicemen and women wear. The longer you wear them, the more data we can collect."

"That's why Commander Fr'osst said I was responding better than expected," Violetta said, the pieces falling into place. "How many people know about the 'suits?"

Mc'narrd took another pull of his cider before answering. "Only those involved with the project are aware. Commander Fr'osst was informed due to your injuries. She needed to know, in case a Healer was required or you needed a faster evac."

"What about our comms? When would you like them returned?" Violetta asked.

"We would also like you to keep your comm, Violetta. It can be synced with the local police service, so you wouldn't need to replace the one you lost. Since it'll be an added frequency, it won't even affect the military side of communications. Should you ever need emergency assistance, you can just speak the proper code, and you'll be linked up with the command center. Complete with top emergency priority. That code hasn't changed since your father was in the service." Mc'narrd turned to Malik. "If you desire, you can keep yours, also. You've been instrumental in this operation, also. She can tell you the code."

"Only if I don't have to wear it constantly," Malik said, before taking a pull from his glass.

"No, you won't need to wear it constantly." Mc'narrd's eyes twinkled with amusement. "I won't even demand you wear the 'suits constantly, anymore."

"Oh, good," Violetta quipped. "That means we won't have to worry about breaking that rule and you storming whoever's home we happen to be in when it happens."

"Does that mean you both will be keeping the 'suits and comms?" Mc'narrd asked, looking between the pair. They nodded. He breathed a sigh of what Violetta suspected was relief. "Thank you."

"What's going to happen with the department? How widespread was the corruption, or do you know?"

"It went across the departments," Mc'narrd replied, leaning forward. "At least a fourth of the precinct was involved. From officers who patrolled the streets to the captains. We're also going to have to go back over arrest records and open any case touched by any of the corrupted officers. Every single healer involved with all those cases, especially homicide cases, will be evaluated and dealt with as necessary. Especially the ones involved with the Fw'ntees murder. It won't be a small task and will take a lot of time."

"What about Gomez?" Malik asked, lifting a fry in the air before him. "And you'll want to contact Nualith Ln'ann. She's the one who checked Violetta's gun. She's been working on a countermeasure to the replicator, without even knowing there was one currently in existence."

He popped the fry into his mouth after speaking. Giving a slight nod, he grabbed a breaded and fried jalapeño popper and took a tentative bite before popping the rest in his mouth.

"There's still one in someone's possession, also," Violetta chimed in.

She lifted her glass to her lips and downed a third of the extra large tankard of hard cider. If she was going to drink, she had decided to go with something that could be refilled easily. And the stars knew she'd earned it.

"We know, and we're searching for it. As for Gomez? Our Healers are already caring for him. They began the moment Violetta was being escorted to the DA." He shook his head. "Damn. We should have seen that one coming. Should've had someone set up before you and your partner ever went into his office. Let alone allow you to enter completely alone."

"You didn't know. Why would you have suspected the DA?" Violetta asked. "Nothing pointed to him."

"Not at a glance, but considering the money and resources used just to make the clone gun, and setting you up?" Mc'narrd shook his head. "That should have been a clear signal that someone with more power and influence than a police captain was in charge. It isn't as though I haven't seen such corruption and betrayal before now. I am usually suspicious of everyone."

"Going back to the widespread corruption in my department," Violetta said after a few moments of silence. "If a fourth of the precinct was involved, where will the replacements come from? I know there aren't that many in the current class at the Academy. Nor would they have the experience to be placed in higher ranking positions."

"The request has been placed for volunteers in the military to take those positions," Mc'narrd answered. He grabbed a fry, studied it, then took a small bite before nodding and popping the entire thing in his mouth. After he swallowed, he continued. "Monroe's replacement, for example, is Sergeant Major Daes Os'shye. Once the paperwork is finalized, he'll use the title of captain and take over the department, simply to keep things running smoothly. But he'll be above the other current captains.

We, the military, are offering special packages and options to those who volunteer to move to the police service in this district."

"How many have already stepped up?" Malik asked, genuinely curious.

"More than I would have expected," Mc'narrd replied. "Some have asked if they could return to their military positions after a certain time period. There are several officers who would be promoted to the appropriate positions within the next five to ten years. So there are also negotiations going on within the military."

"Hopefully there won't be an extended period where the precinct is understaffed." Malik grabbed another popper, chewed and swallowed, before continuing. "In the meantime, I will inform Don Morelli that extra protection will be needed in the neighborhoods."

"That might be for the best," Mc'narrd admitted.

"Am I going to have more work to do as a result?" Violetta glanced at Malik.

"The era when the syndicate 'shook down' people to pay for protection is done," Malik replied. "Morelli owns the real estate. Renters and those who buy homes on his property have a tax, same as the government does for property. The civilians pay for the private security when they pay their rent and property tax."

"Speaking of the don," Violetta said, lowering her voice. "I need to arrange a meeting with him, now that my name has been cleared."

"Should I be concerned?" Mc'narrd did not sound the least bit worried.

He reminded her of her father yet again. She wasn't certain if she appreciated it or hated it. For now, she settled on appreciating the memories Mc'narrd brought back.

"No," Violetta began, then stopped herself. "At least, I don't believe so. Don Morelli gave the impression that he's fair. I'll owe him… something, but he said he wouldn't make me do something unnatural to me. I suspect he won't make me compromise my honor."

"Doubtful," Malik admitted. "If he wants something done, he finds people who are likely to do it if they had a reason to."

"Hire a killer to kill someone, hire a personality to be in front of the vidmachines," Mc'narrd suggested.

"In the extremes, yes," Malik replied. "I was referring more to hiring a constructor if you want something built, or a silk clerk if you want something sewn a certain way."

"Good to know my initial impression of him was accurate," Violetta took another pull of her drink. "Will you arrange it?"

Malik nodded. "I'll let you know when he wants to see you."

"Thank you. There are a few things that still puzzles me about all this." Violetta grabbed a fry and studied it before glancing at Malik from the corner of her eyes. "How were you who he sent? Was it because of our past? Not that I'm complaining. I'm thankful it was you."

"Actually, I was with him when he received the call saying you were going to see him. That you would be needing help." Malik met her eyes and held them. "I volunteered before he had the chance to say anyone else's name."

She all but melted in the booth. Mc'narrd laughed, even as Malik slid his hand into hers.

To distract herself from the growing desire to jump Malik there in the bar, she instead turned to the other question that had been plaguing her.

Dragging her attention away from Malik, she asked Mc'narrd, "What tipped Monroe and Cancio off? Was it because I didn't delete the recycle folder on Cancio's interface, like I normally do with mine? Or did they send me to use his interface to begin with in the hopes I'd find the files?"

"You didn't delete the folder or command history," Mc'narrd said. "But I would bet a night's worth of drinking that the late D.A. had a plan to get you involved sooner or later."

"I still don't understand the 'why' of that, and I probably never will," Violetta confessed.

"After we'd established you and Issik were safe, I had my staff healers look over Lc'sonn's mental history. He had a very strong hatred for anyone who went off-planet, since he didn't qualify. Your father, his accomplishments? Lc'sonn likely thought those should have been his marks in history. You, as his only offspring, had to pay. Because he obsessed over things that could never be."

That was an explanation she could understand. Jealousy wasn't an emotion only humans and other races felt and acted on. She rubbed her elbow subconsciously. So much jealousy, hatred, and greed, only to become a corpse in the end.

"I've been meaning to ask you," Malik interjected, sliding his hand up her arm. "How did you get that injury on your elbow? You had it when we met at the safehouse, and it's healed. But I've been wondering about it since then."

"Oh, fark," she muttered. "That was where the tracking device the police service uses to keep up with their officers was located. It's why they weren't able to find me so easily. 'Betty' at that diner removed it before I met with Don Morelli."

"Our soldiers get them, also." Mc'narrd gave a dismissive shrug. "Though we at least inform our soldiers of it. The chips are removed whenever the soldiers leave the service for civilian life. We can handle getting you a replacement back at the base."

"Are they still putting them in the elbow?" Malik asked. Violetta and Mc'narrd nodded. He grimaced. "At least having a Healer remove it had to be better than having it dug out. How did she do it, anyway?"

"With a farking pocket knife," Violetta grumbled. She shrugged. "At least I'll know what's going on when it's replaced."

Malik lifted his glass and held it towards the center of the booth. "To the future."

"The future!" Mc'narrd and Violetta chimed. The three of them clinked their glasses together before they all took long pulls.

Stella sidled up to their table, a handful of darts in hand. "You still want to learn?"

Violetta looked up, grinned, and nodded. Grabbing a fry, she popped it into her mouth as she followed Stella.

Raymond, Nathaniel, and Victoria were at their table, enjoying a variety of K'laisian appetizers. Violetta found it amusing how those who visited enjoyed native foods, while those who lived on the planet preferred foods brought from other worlds.

Standing about two meters from the dart board, Stella handed Violetta one of the darts.

"Hold it like this," she said, curling her fingers around the dart's shaft. "Think of it as a paintbrush."

"Or stylus pen!" Raymond called. "Y'all have those, right?"

Violetta made a face, but copied how Stella was holding her dart.

"Now, hold it up and aim for the board," Stella instructed. "The goal is to get it into the center-most area."

The mercenary pulled her arm back before snapping it forward, letting the dart go in one fluid motion. It landed near the dead center of the circular board.

Giving Stella an uncertain look, Violetta copied her movement. The dart wobbled through the air, landing near the edge.

"Good start," Stella said encouragingly. She handed Violetta another dart. "Here, try again."

A dozen dart-throws later, Violetta figured out the mechanics of the game. It was a game of physics, not unlike learning to throw knives. Something she was very adept at doing.

"Why don't you try, Malik?" Violetta called as she threw another dart into the center circle. She held a dart out to him.

Standing slowly, Malik crossed to Violetta, and took the dart. "How do you know I haven't played it before?"

"I don't, which makes it that much more exciting," she replied.

"Don't let her goad you!" Mc'narrd called.

"Whose side are you on?" Stella shot back.

"Someone's got to take Malik's side," Mc'narrd returned.

Malik glanced towards the board then back at Violetta. With a smirk firmly in place, he threw the dart. It landed dead center, next to hers.

"Game on."

"Loser takes the winner out to dinner," Violetta declared.

"Winner picks the place," Malik countered.

A collection of "ooohs" sounded from the mercenaries.

"You sure about that, Violetta?" Mc'narrd called.

"Don't see a problem with it. Since I'm going to win," she replied.

"Hope you can afford his tastes!" Mc'narrd shot back.

"No need to worry about that," a stranger's voice said.

Violetta and Malik turned to the newcomer. A slender native with dark hair slicked back approached them with the darts in his right hand. His gold eyes swept over Malik before dismissing him. Behind him stood several others holding tankards of a frothy beverage.

The mercenaries stilled. Each one stopped what they were doing and saying.

"I'll be your Champion," he stated, puffing his chest out.

Violetta could smell the cheap beer on his breath. "Thanks for the offer, but it isn't needed."

The stranger's face darkened. "What? I'm not good enough? Only interested in the Master of Ceremonies being your Champion? Would've thought you'd rather have a pure blood."

"Actually, there were extenuating circumstances, or I wouldn't have needed his help. As it is, this game is between us and you're intruding."

"I can show you a better time," he said suggestively, brushing a finger over the tip of her ear.

A sly smile curled her lips, even as she grabbed the stranger's hand. "You know, I think you can."

Without another word, she jerked his wrist backward and away. As he yelped in pain, his buddies moved forward.

There was a roar of excitement from the mercenaries even before the first punch landed.

"I think I may just start calling you 'Violence', as well," Mc'narrd's voice carried over the noise of the bar.

Some things would never change.

End.

We hope that you enjoyed this title and look forward to many more to come. Please, leave us a review! Reviews matter to all of our authors.

Take a look at some of our other award-winning series at https://threeravenspublishing.com/series-universes/

Visit us at https://www.threeravenspublishing.com and sign up for our newsletter for the latest and greatest news on upcoming titles and events.

Other series and titles you might enjoy.

JOINT TASK FORCE 13
AVAILABLE ON
AMAZON
HOLDING THE LINE
BETWEEN HEAVEN AND HELL
13

B.E.N.T.
BIOLOGIC   ENHANCED   NASCENT   TALENT

STARFLIGHT

IT CAME FROM THE
TRAILER PARK

You can also keep up to date with our latest release announcements on <u>Scifi.radio</u> and get some of the best fandom programing on the planet.

Scifi for your Wifi

And don't forget to check out our other Sponsors and Affiliates

A southern Appalachian jewel for craft beer lovers, Buck Bald Brewing offers something for everyone.

To discover more visit us at buckbaldbrewing.com

Revolution X is a testament to the power of collaboration, blending four unique styles into a cohesive, revolutionary sound. When these four individuals unite, the result is nothing short of musical Revolution!

Would you like to learn how to write and market your own titles? The following affiliates links might be helpful.

Don't forget to check out the latest edition of Car Warriors: Autoduel Chronicle fiction series.
https://threeravenspublishing.com/car-warriors-autoduel-chronicles/

…or the latest in the *Car Wars* game series

http://www.sjgames.com/car-wars/

Or the other amazing titles from
Steve Jackson Games

http://www.sjgames.com

Comprised of active or retired servicemen and civilian volunteers, Shepherd's Men enthusiastically raises awareness and funds for the SHARE Military Initiative (SHARE) at Shepherd Center in Atlanta, GA.

This nationally renowned program focuses on assessment and treatment for American military veterans who have sustained mild to moderate Traumatic Brain Injury (TBI) and Post-Traumatic Stress Disorder (PTSD) during post-9/11 service.

Find out more at: https://www.shepherdsmen.com/